Praise for *Our Memory*

'Proves that the best science fiction can be not only socially
relevant and thought-provoking, but entertaining ... a brilliantly
reimagined near-future Africa ... he interweaves ecological and
political intrigue with Senegalese folk myths to tell the ultimately
uplifting story of a continent sadly neglected in SF'
Eric Brown, *GUARDIAN*

'Uncannily in tune with the time it was written ... at once
dreamlike and harrowingly believable, this is not a comforting
read. It is, however, a gripping and frightening one'
SFX

'A multi-layered narrative that builds momentum and depth
and inexorably draws the reader in ... there is a dignity to
this book, a quiet power and charm that breathes life into its
pages ... this is a book of prophetic realism, determined
optimism and magical storytelling that sets it apart'
SFCROWSNEST

'Timely and intelligent ... blends magic realism and action
to poetic and thrilling ends ... it's packed full of fun, danger,
stolen moments and hypocrisy – much like the modern world'
SCiFiNOW

'As speculative fiction it is completely on the money ... an
important commentary on present-day headlines and a
prescient warning of what we can expect if our ways do
not change ... highly readable ... Chait is a very good
writer, juggling several emotionally powerful concepts
with the timeless magic of aural storytelling'
STARBURST

Praise for *Lament for the Fallen*

'Refreshingly different . . . exhilarating . . . a compulsively readable, life-affirming tale told in direct, lambent prose, and Chait does a masterful job of juxtaposing a traditional African setting with a convincing depiction of a far-future alien society'
GUARDIAN

'Lyrical prose and imaginative world-building . . . the book is gripping, powerful and frequently impressive . . . an ambitious and intelligent work that marks out Chait as a writer worthy of further attention'
SFX

'Out of this world engrossing. You don't have to understand the science to believe in it . . . superb world building . . . aided by enchanting fables and philosophies weaved into the narrative, *Lament for the Fallen* is an often poetic, occasionally disturbing, and always enthralling tale that has all the thematic ingredients to make it one of the best sci-fi books of 2016'
CULTUREFLY

'Richly drawn . . . a smart, ideas-driven novel . . . a promising and ambitious debut'
SCiFiNOW

'Highly readable . . . Chait should be applauded for managing that all important trick of getting you to keep turning that page until there aren't any left . . . smart, ideas-led science fiction with a literary fiction bent'
STARBURST

OUR
MEMORY
LIKE
DUST

GAVIN CHAIT

BLACK SWAN

TRANSWORLD PUBLISHERS
61–63 Uxbridge Road, London W5 5SA
www.penguin.co.uk

Transworld is part of the Penguin Random House group of companies
whose addresses can be found at global.penguinrandomhouse.com

Penguin
Random House
UK

First published in Great Britain in 2017 by Doubleday
an imprint of Transworld Publishers
Black Swan edition published 2018

A CIP catalogue record for this book
is available from the British Library.

ISBN 9781784161323

Typeset in 10.56/14.19pt Adobe Caslon by Jouve (UK), Milton Keynes.
Printed and bound in Great Britain by Clays Ltd, Bungay, Suffolk.

Penguin Random House is committed to a sustainable future
for our business, our readers and our planet. This book is made
from Forest Stewardship Council® certified paper.

MIX
Paper from
responsible sources
FSC® C018179

1 3 5 7 9 10 8 6 4 2

For those we forget.
For those we remember.
For the wings and tail.
But most, for her.

Amongst those of the Ghimbala of West Africa, the river genii *are neither angels nor demons but – like them – have the capacity for good and evil. The priests of the genii, known as the* gaw, *sing their songs and lead their ceremonies, inviting the genii to enter their bodies so that they may speak with these spirits and learn what is hidden or ask that they intercede in complex matters. This is dangerous, for the genii have great power and can overwhelm those who lack the will to master them. Get too close and they may change the narrative of the world in unpredictable and destructive ways.*

For stories are not only told, they listen and gather the memory of those with whom they are shared. Names, places and experiences may reappear but be utterly transformed, creating new stories carrying an essence of what it means to be these characters, while telling of lives and paths which may differ entirely.

This is the story that Goŋ, the greatest of the gaw, told me many years ago, and now I tell it to you.

I

WHEN THE GODS MISSPELL WRATH

There is an arc of fire burning across Africa, its flames now scorching the beaches of Europe. Will we recognize the suffering and hope in the journey of these refugees? Or will we raise a wall of steel and drown their faith in the waters of the Mediterranean?

Dr Ettien Enkido, Special Rapporteur to Federation of European States, March 2055, closing remarks at emergency spring summit

Of course I ordered the boats destroyed, and of course it isn't a solution. But we cannot allow a marauding swarm of illegal migrants to break into our country unchecked. We need time to prepare. There are over six million people trying to get across, and this is only the beginning. We need time.

Glenn Thibault, Minister for State Security for England and Wales, December 2057, in answer to a heckler at a community forum

The genii are not testing our faith or punishing us for some historical wrong. It is worse. It is as if they have absent-mindedly forgotten their role in our lives and − in writing the future − have misspelled wrath and enjoy observing the chaos this brings.

Sidiki Cissoko, parliamentary candidate for Parti Démocratique Sénégalais, campaign speech, 2064

1

Sticky, chalk-like dust coats the naked man as he lies curled tightly on the cave floor. There is no light, no sound, merely continuous heat from the rock sweating all around him, and the distant plink of water dripping from the calcified ceiling.

With each drop he imagines waves rippling across the unendurable blackness and rasping against his skin: relentless sensations haunting his sanity.

He crawls towards where he knows the bars of the cell to be, finding the bucket of water and drinking sparingly. There is no regularity to when his captors replace it. No way of knowing how long it must last or how much time is passing.

He had howled and wept the first few days here, demanding they listen, offering any ransom. They kept food from him until he became silent. He tried calming himself, but his fear is crippling, stalking him, restless in the desolating dark.

Relieving himself in the soil bucket he returns to the rear of the cave where he can feel the smoothness of the wall against his back.

Something warm and furry brushes against his legs and he flinches, pulling his knees in and holding his ankles. His keening mewl rattles along hidden passages, echoing, haunting and feral.

Something grunts in answer in the darkness. An outline, squat and with rounded shoulders glowing like dust in a shaft of light.

The prisoner no longer trusts his mind and holds up a hand to ward off the growing brightness, doubt and terror clouding his senses. His arm is a silhouette without feature against the gathering shape.

The beast takes form, a burst of olive-grey fur surrounding a long snout, the canines curved and hugely terrifying. The baboon's eyes are brown, warm and filled with curiosity.

Even in his mental anguish, the naked man notices that – though the baboon appears as brightly as if standing beneath the desert sun – he can see nothing else. No light escapes to cast aside the blankness of his prison. His throat is raw with his shrill wailing, and he cringes back against the stone.

The baboon grips a two-headed metal stave in one hand. He advances on the naked man, who cowers and presses further into the wall, gesturing with his other as if stirring a pool of water, searching in the rivers of memory that coalesce on this place here in the heart of the ancient watercourses of the genii carved through the bony chitin of the earth.

A fragmentary image of a man with strange blue eyes, and the naked man moans in tepid outrage. The baboon presses at the moment, like a wound, and follows the liquid thread towards a thin, silvery track like a river in the vastness of the Sahara.

The dust trail of the vehicle ahead lingered in the air, and it was easy to follow behind. The five seekers – two men, two women and a small child of indeterminate gender – clustered in the vehicle with him believed that he would take them to Nouadhibou, and he intended to, but first there would be a reckoning.

They travelled for hours, always roughly northwards, with the clatter and smash of stones on the undercarriage the only sound, and the sun was beginning its descent when the dust source ahead began to near. There was nowhere to hide amidst the rocky desolation of the hamada, and he simply ordered the vehicle to park alongside the stationary Haval.

Its occupant had been sitting inside waiting. Now he stood and walked towards them, surprise and unmistakable anguish on his face.

'What are you doing here, Oktar?' he asked, his strange blue eyes bright, even compared to the clarity of the sky.

'I might ask you the same thing,' said Oktar Samboa, triumph in his thin smile.

'You shouldn't be here. You'll get us all killed,' said the man, glancing into the vehicle where the seekers were equally confused and uncertain.

'They know where the planes are,' said Samboa, nodding at the seekers. 'They stumbled on them the first time they tried crossing the desert. Now we'll see how much your information is worth to Ansar Dine.'

A shimmer, and twelve jihadis set aside their invisibility cloaks. They had walked unnoticed over the nearby dunes. They were black-clad and inscrutable inside their turbans and djellabas. By their bodies and posture, though, they appeared to be young, and they held their weapons nervously.

They began shouting, pushed the blue-eyed man aside and dragged the seekers from the vehicle. The child screamed in terror; the women were sobbing.

Clearly, they were demanding to know who all these people were. Why was he not alone as agreed?

Blue-eyes sought those of Samboa and, even here as the prisoner sees this once more, he struggles to understand the expression on his face. Of grief and loss.

Samboa trembles and shakes, his body prone upon the cave floor, the moment swirling before the gleaming eyes of the baboon. He had felt so certain the jihadis would listen to the seekers and then depart, leaving the blue-eyed man with nothing. Instead he cannot tell who is more panicked: the seekers or the jihadis.

The blue-eyed man began to speak quickly and firmly; he stepped between one jihadi and the tallest of the seeker men. Smiling, he grasped the man by the arm, as if they were old friends, speaking all the while.

'What are you saying?' Samboa shouted, willing himself forward as the blue-eyed man's rims translated loudly.

The jihadis were more insistent, shoving again at the blue-eyed man, pushing one of the women to the ground.

The blue-eyed man put up his hands, continuing to smile warmly.

Samboa was close enough to hear him speaking under the translation. To hear him say, 'This is Oktar Samboa, a colleague, and these are our guides. You would not expect us to find our way here without the support of the Senegalese military?' A statement that condemned them all.

Gasping. A moment frozen as the jihadis reacted.

The shooting did not stop, even after one of the seekers managed to climb inside the Haval, hammering on the controls until the vehicle lurched and drove south, back along the track. His legs jammed between the seats and his torso hanging limply out where it dragged in the dust.

'What did you do?' shouted Samboa as the jihadis grabbed him, tore his rims from his face and shoved him to the ground. 'Simon!' screaming his name. The blue-eyed man looked down at him in sadness before he too was thrown to the dust.

The baboon places his hand close to the face of the naked man, stifling his scream, digging deeper, following the path into the lives of others, seeing shapes flying over the desert, pressing at the horizon and casting shadows against the sky.

2

'Can you see anything yet?' asked João, peering over his co-pilot's shoulder.

They were flying low over the desert, the moon painting a blue line on the crests of the shadowy bruise of the erg almost brushing the fuselage below. The A380 was an ancient carcass salvaged for this one flight. At forty years old, it was still younger than any in the convoy flying behind them.

Vitor, his eyes hidden behind the disposable visor incongruously wrapped around his temples, flicked his eyes instinctively out to the horizon. For a moment, it was almost as if the face of a beast, with a burst of fur surrounding a long snout, stared at him from the dark sky.

He shook his head, glancing down at the flat console stapled over the cockpit controls. A clutch of wires snaked from it and into the control panel, rewiring the obsolete systems into its more modern computer.

For the last hour, their concentration on navigation had given way to a strident fear. They were almost out of fuel.

'Either that transponder has a really short range, or we missed it,' said Vitor despondently.

João opened a bag of chocolate biscuits from the pile behind his seat and chewed on one. If they missed the landing zone, they would have to ditch the planes well beyond any chance of rescue.

'Two days' work and retire forever,' said Vitor bitterly, repeating the pitch which had led them there.

The Caracas Cartel had been shedding its pilots as it transitioned to entirely autonomous drones. Offered the choice between flying model planes at amusement parks or a one-time suicidal freight delivery, there had been more than sufficient volunteers from amongst those laid off.

Five Airbus A380s, average age forty-five, had been acquired. Their seats and fittings had been torn out and their control systems patched. Ten pilots were needed to fly the planes, masked and damped to prevent remote observation or interference, to a specific region in the Sahara, wait for a transponder signal to locate a temporary runway, and land them there. The pilots were then to be smuggled to Dakar and flown back to Brazil on a commercial flight.

Their pay from this one job would be sufficient to allow them to enjoy a wealthy retirement.

The catch was that they would be carrying five hundred tons of weapons and one hundred and fifty tons of synthetic heroin destined for Europe. A convoy of planes worth $75 billion would be hunted by both law enforcement and any of the other criminal syndicates. And the planes would be landing in the middle of the world's most violent and hostile failed state, deep within an aggressively policed no-fly zone, to be met by its most violent and hostile occupants: the jihadis of Ansar Dine.

'You worry too much,' said João. 'We've done this hundreds of times. Remember when we ditched an entire convoy in the Atacama when that Yanqui corvette caught us offshore?'

Vitor stifled momentary nausea. They were not inside those planes when they crashed but had been safely piloting them from a distant control room. What had the man said?

'You will be flying blind, without anything but the most basic navigation, low and at speed to avoid pursuit, and no one can help you until you land where you're supposed to.' The words delivered in a quiet staccato by the stranger in the Panama hat who had arrived the day before they were due to leave.

'Be sure, they will be listening,' he had told them, his face obscured in the twilight of the room, and his strange blue eyes hidden beneath the white of his brim.

'Who?'

His smile had been wicked. 'Everyone.'

In the darkness, each plane followed the lights of the one before and hoped that their leader knew where he was going.

At a specific time, and for a specific duration, a small short-range transponder was supposed to be turned on to guide them to the landing site. That time had passed and, almost two hours later, they had not yet heard it. In ten minutes, their agreed landing window would end, the transponder was due to be switched off, and they would be lost.

João reattached his visor, and the augmented-reality display flickered. He could see Vitor holding his virtual controls. He nodded, and authority was handed back to him. Vitor busied himself searching through the aether for the transponder signal.

As time ran down, they unconsciously began preparing for the inevitable. There was no way to let the other pilots know what they were about to do and, without a prepared runway, these vast planes would be difficult to land.

'How far do you want to fly? It looks like we have about thirty minutes of fuel left,' said Vitor.

João shook his head. 'We're getting further away from the transponder zone, and we've already risked too much. I'd rather land and hope they find us than be shot down by drones.'

'And that box?'

Vitor had happened to observe as their bosses arrived to inspect the final cargo load. Saw them usher the man in the Panama hat up the ramp for a brief secretive visit into the hold. He was carrying a small square case when he arrived, and he left without it. Vitor hunted amongst the bales of heroin and crates of small arms. He could not find it.

'It's still better than being shot down by drones,' said João.

'OK, the others will have realized we're lost by now,' said Vitor, his hands numb with fear.

'Brace yourself,' said João, grinning, a chocolate biscuit clenched between his lips.

Landing went about as well as could be hoped given the uncertain terrain. João pancaked into the sand and skated over the tops of the erg before their aeroplane shoved its nose into the ground, coming to an obliterating stop. Two of the other A380s managed to land in parallel in a similarly shattering way.

The last two collided as they landed.

An overly high, unfortunately cambered peak flung the one into a rolling tumble and into the path of the other. They crumpled together. Their surplus fuel expanded and exploded, casting a sudden red glaze over the fury of the last few minutes.

There were survivors. João, Gabriela and Carlos stood blinking under the stars as fine white powder settled on them, like a surreal desert snowstorm.

They built a small cabin in the wreckage. They had a party that lasted two days, until Gabriela overdosed. A day later, João and Carlos ran out of water.

Within a week, the steady blast of the harmattan covered everything and buried the planes, and their cargo, in the desert.

In the sky, a face blurred within a burst of fur narrows his close-set eyes and grunts. There is so much more to know. He turns his gaze forward in time and further into the deep desert.

3

'Duruji, what does he say?' asked the youngest of the men, his invisibility cloak worn out and only partially covering his black djellaba.

Wind rattled where the men were huddled together inside the wreck of an ancient aircraft, its nose still buried in the sand of the erg. Its hull had been torn open, either after its original crash or from decades of tortured wear by the motion of the desert.

Two men were out on watch on the crest of the surrounding dune, their Igla-AD14s, the flat-nosed anti-drone radio-frequency guns Ansar Dine had made their symbol, pointed at the sky.

Duruji sighed. Another disappointing journey had gained nothing of value. At least this crumpled bit of scrap was actually an aeroplane. He stared at the ugly broken hulk, the metal rusted and perforated like lace. A black shadow against the night sky.

The desert is a graveyard. Each new war adding another scattering of lost craft, their crew bleached offerings to the encroaching sands. Finding Abdallah Ag Ghaly's missing cargo was an impossible task, but their equipment had to be replaced. Their invisibility cloaks were in tatters, their weapons needed repair, and ammunition was in short supply. Movement above ground would soon be impossible. They had to find where those aeroplanes crashed before their ability to control the region became even more restricted.

On this excursion, they had spent almost a month traversing the erg fields, using the limited access they had to the maps on the connect to try *to find anything of use. Ansar Dine troops had been criss-crossing the desert for the better part of a year.*

Duruji would prefer not to be out here, but Ag Ghaly insisted.

They were long past recriminations for the loss of the cargo. Duruji and his men had waited in the desert, switching on the transponder at the agreed time. He had obeyed Ag Ghaly's instructions, staying well after the duration of safety when it became clear that the aeroplanes were not going to arrive.

There had been a mistake. They were at the landing site a day late. The aeroplanes already crashed and the cargo lost. Someone needed to be held accountable.

The Cartel were unsympathetic. They had been paid. They provided instructions. If Ansar Dine were careless with their dates, it was certainly not their problem. However, losing the pilots was unfortunate and would need to be added to the cost of future deliveries. Would Ansar Dine be interested in another shipment?

Jihadis tortured the man who had taken the details for the aeroplane arrival from the Cartel emissary. They raped his children before him. He died without revealing how he had got it wrong. Perhaps he did not know.

Duruji believed the confusion over the date was deliberate, that the Cartel lied.

'They were greedy, Janab,' he had said to Ag Ghaly. 'We should never have put so much money into a single deal. We should never have paid in advance. Should we ever find those aeroplanes, we will discover there is nothing in them.'

Ag Ghaly had slapped him then, screaming incoherently, beating him even as Duruji cowered, and still continued to punish him by sending him out repeatedly into the desert to search.

Once a week, at a random time, their radio was unshielded and a brief burst of encrypted messages was broadcast on the connect. They stayed online for less than a second to minimize the chance that their position would be given away. Sometimes they would receive messages back with new instructions and new coordinates to visit.

Today, Duruji had received a message from Ag Ghaly himself. He had read it, but he had not yet shared it with the others. Each hoped that perhaps their missing cargo had been found and they could return.

The men sat in darkness, for light and heat risked attracting observers. The desert belonged to Ansar Dine, but the sky belonged to those who hunted them.

They had eaten the tasteless food bars that each carried, drunk a little water, and now they rested, preparing for the next long slog.

The young man, his face clammy, asked once more, 'Duruji? What does he say? Can we go home?'

'The boy is afraid of the surface,' said one of the men, chuckling. 'He sees demons walking on the sands.'

Each of the men suffered from a lingering agoraphobia from being above ground, exposed to the satellites and drones which searched the desert. Each hid it as best he could, except for this young man.

It was his first time on the surface.

'I saw it. It is following me,' said the young man, fighting to keep his terror from his voice. 'A baboon. It pointed at me.'

'Khalil thinks he saw Gaw Goŋ,' and a mutter of dusty laughter amongst the others. 'That old woman's tale, told to scare disobedient children.'

'He says he saw a painted dog walking with the baboon,' laughed another. 'He lives the stories of Gaw Goŋ and Painted-dog's child.'

'They are real,' the young man's voice trembling and defensive. 'My grandmother told me that, up here on the erg, during the day the horizon shimmers and the dark shapes we see are the demons trying to get in. Our world and theirs are closest in the desert. Gaw Goŋ judges us. He is judging me. Please, Duruji, can we go home?'

Despite his youth and palpable fear, Khalil was enormous, a hulking giant chosen from amongst the children of the families closest to

Ag Ghaly to join Ansar Dine's elite troops, those sent out into the desert to exercise his power.

He was too young to be out so early in his training, but any sympathy would get them all killed. The men offered him none: as much as they each received on their first tour on the surface.

'No,' said Duruji. 'We go west, Khalil. Our Janab orders us west.'

'Another wreck, like this one,' said one of the men.

Duruji shook his head. 'He says he has captured a man who knows where the aeroplanes are. He travels to interrogate him.'

'Without us to guard him?' asked one of the men, his voice horrified and incredulous. 'He never leaves the sanctuary.'

'We are almost three weeks from him. He says it is too important to wait. We must get there when we can,' said Duruji.

Khalil was shivering, staring up at the face in the sky only he could see.

The men walked all day, sleeping briefly in the evening, and began walking long before the sun rose. It was too risky to drive, too exposed. Only during the worst of the harmattan dust storms would they attempt to use vehicles on the surface.

Two weeks previously, they had climbed over a rise and surprised a group of people out on the reg. They were seekers, attempting to cross without paying their tax to Ansar Dine. They had been unarmed and exhausted. They fell to the ground, quailing and begging not to be slaughtered. Money had been offered but too late to assuage the punishment due to those who dare travel without permission.

Some of Duruji's men had wanted to rape the women.

'We have no time,' Duruji had said. 'Do not waste bullets. We need them to last.'

They had shot the men and used their knives on the rest. The women had fought fiercely to protect their children, but they were all weakened by their journey. They were little trouble to the jihadis.

They massacred them, leaving their bodies to dry in the sun.

Duruji had noticed a look of anguish on Khalil's face at his order. He had approached the young man, wiping his bloodied knife on a shawl taken from one of the women. Behind him, the men were looting the bodies, keeping anything that looked useful.

'Do not worry, Khalil, there are more than enough seekers crossing. When we return, we will have more time to take slaves back with us. You will have your fill.'

'Do you see?' Khalil had said, pointing towards strange shapes in the shimmering mirage that lingered on the horizon. That was the first day he had seen the baboon Gaw Goŋ pointing at him, his two-headed sombé in his hand.

Khalil could no longer sleep, and in his nightmares he heard a howling roar as of a wildcat tearing at its prey. He felt something stalking him, encroaching on him, as if preparing to cross from the world of the gaw into his own. Duruji, determined to lead his men where ordered, could spare him little sympathy.

'It is only the harmattan,' said one of the men, as close as he could come to reassuring the traumatized youth. 'It takes time to get used to the sounds and visions of the surface. We have all made that journey.'

'We will rest for three hours,' said Duruji. 'From here, we will journey to the ouahe outside Timoudi. Your water must last until we get there.'

He turned to the young man. 'It will be months before we are home, Khalil. Make your peace with the desert.'

Khalil trembled, his eyes locked on the horizon where the air shimmered and shadows pressed as of genii trying to reach him, the voice of the baboon, Gaw Goŋ, scratching at his ears.

Another path beckons and Gaw Goŋ, his eyes two dark points in the sky, follows across the desert to where others are gathering.

4

Amadou cherished this time of day, when the sun set behind the guelb *and turned the jumble of rocks sloping down from the rough-hewn outcrop into gleaming bronze. Its shadow stretched across the barren hamada – the hard, rocky plateau stretching far into the Sahara – towards the vast field of solar collectors, and he could feel the warmth of the rock face on his back and legs.*

It had been an exhausting start, and his skin was sticky with dust. He leaned back in his chair, scrutinizing his men as they completed their chores and prepared their evening meal.

Rich peanut-butter steam rose from the mafé *stew simmering in the pot, its black sides steeped in coals. Dark shapes gathered at the fireside, assembled themselves into men, and sighed gratefully as they sat down. A pot of coffee was passed from man to man. Amadou smiled and waved his empty mug, motioning for a refill.*

'The genii are with us,' he said, gesturing towards where dark eyes in a burst of fur looked down on them from the sky.

'It is Gaw Goŋ,' said one of the men, gratitude in his voice. 'Perhaps he will ask the genii for a good season?'

Amadou smiled and nodded. He could smell the hivernage *coming: the brief rainy season that would cool daytime temperatures down into the mid-thirties. It was still far too hot this early in May – he tapped the tracker on his wrist and grunted as he saw it had reached 43°C at noon – but if he waited too long the roads would be choked with other* farmers heading out of the coastal city of Saint-Louis and from villages along the Senegal River Valley.

This way was cheaper. It had taken three hours to drive the one hundred and fifty kilometres from Saint-Louis, over the river crossing at Rosso, and to the turn-off at the tiny village of Mbalal.

Dodou had arrived with his convoy of old rental trucks just before midnight. It was coolest to travel at this time, and Amadou had hired Dodou's cheaper unrefrigerated vehicles for his goat herd.

He had spoken softly with Dodou while watching his men as they loaded the tools, food supplies and spares they would need, then the goats, docile and heavily pregnant, before cramming themselves into the remaining space and sleeping as best they were able.

The two old men had smiled and held hands. Their skins loose, clinging like the surface of dried dates over bone-lean bodies hardened by the passing of the sun. Their friendship measured in the accumulation of years and the experience of hardy survival.

'I will see you at the turn of the season,' Dodou had said. The other had nodded and swung up into the lead truck. 'Good luck with those milkers,' Dodou had called, and cackled.

Amadou had ignored him, fastening his turban across his face, his eyes shining in the dark cabin.

The trucks had engaged, electric motors silent in the sleeping streets, and wound their way through the endlessly sprawling city. Shattered glass outside an immigrant shop, stones and blood on the road from one of the mercifully dwindling fights between old residents and new arrivals. Lamp posts dense with election posters promising change, and every yard an assembly of awkwardly leaning temporary shelters filled with seekers.

He was ten when his father had decided they could no longer risk their herd to the dry season. They had lost the majority of their pregnant does and all their ewes to the heat that year.

Villages to the north of them had emptied. Towns like Mederdra and

Beir Tores given back to the desert. Hundreds of thousands had migrated: a hostile, frightened mass of different nationalities and tribes, antagonized by their differences of language and culture, united in their pursuit of refuge and opportunity. Some to the river valleys of West Africa, some to Europe.

Then had come the wall of steel built across the waters of the Mediterranean; the civil wars triggered by the unending drought had cast millions more from their homes, their harsh journey tempering them into the tenuous nation of seekers, and Ansar Dine had taken what was left and made an empire of it.

The border had migrated north of Nouakchott following Mauritania's collapse. Senegal had no wish for the destitution of that land, but they had required a buffer between the valley and the violence of Ansar Dine jihadis. Long columns of dust shadowed soldiers moving back and forth from the border.

'We are Senegalese now,' Amadou's father had said. 'Let us seek a living amongst our new people.'

He had walked his family and their herd south, along the Senegal River to Saint-Louis. They had been lucky, arriving before the surge of fleeing farmers plunged goat prices to mere centimes, and had been able to sell most of their herd. He had bought land outside the city where they had built a shelter for their remaining goats and a one-roomed house for themselves. He had hired a drilling rig and returned to their farm, striking the aquifer fifty-five metres beneath the surface.

Amadou had helped his father as they set up a small solar-powered pump and laid out drip irrigation pipes. Each year, during the cooler rainy season, he and his younger brothers would join his father to extend the range of the pipes. They had planted a row of palm trees, interspersed with tamarisk bushes and swallowworts, enclosing two acres around the guelb.

Slowly, they had claimed life back from the desert.

This was not land for the soft-of-hand. The guelb sloped up to stark shards of rock face, like the jagged teeth of some ancient desert beast, its skull buried in the hamada, and the scorched scales of its skin scattered across the earth. The ground was burned, and the surviving trees were blackened and bent. The horizon loomed, pressing in, searching for weakness.

Those years had been difficult. Amadou had seen famine sweep away familiar faces and leave barren land which used to support sheep and goats. He would not wish this life for his children and was grateful that they worked in the city and would not need to depend on the herd.

He had given himself another five years before he sold up and retired. Until a year ago. The year he met the man with the strange blue eyes.

First had come the surveyors with their maps. They had shown him the extent of his farm and had given him the formal title. Amadou had grown uneasy, concerned that this was a prelude to men with guns coming to take his land away. They had assured him it was not so, but that he was to get a new neighbour and that man had insisted he would only buy land with clear ownership.

A few days later, just as his does had begun to birth, an electric helicopter had flown from the direction of Dakar and landed on the hamada. Amadou had been standing nearby, on the far end of the farm, the calls of his men, whooping through the dust as they counted and digitally tagged each new kid, rising from the plain. He had been holding a console, watching the numbers change as each kid was sexed and added to the herd tally.

A toubab – *a white man* – *in tailored trousers and shirt had left the helicopter, placed a white hat on his head, looked around and walked towards him. He had stopped at the farm's invisible border and waited patiently until Amadou looked up.*

'Azul, ma idjani?' *the man had asked, speaking in Zenaga.*

'Azul. Ijak alxer da iknam,' *Amadou had said, pulling back his* turban, his head tilted and eyes squinting in surprise at hearing a language few still spoke. He had stared up at the man standing so much taller than himself. His hair was greying where visible beneath his hat, but his body was strong and young-looking, like one of those laamb wrestlers. Amadou had met few toubab and could not read much from his face.

'You have a fine herd,' the man had told him, continuing in French.

Amadou had nodded, acknowledging the respect shown to him. He had looked back at the helicopter and out on to the hamada. 'What will you do here? You cannot farm,' he had said.

'We will harvest light,' the man had said. 'You will be the first person to see it happen.'

Amadou had squeezed his eyes to disguise his confusion. Sable de Lumière. He tried to imagine buckets of light.

The blue-eyed man had grinned at him. 'I'm building a solar generator. There will be some noise at the beginning. I wanted to apologize for any nuisance and introduce myself should you need anything from me.'

Amadou had thought quickly. Every household bolted matt solar panels to their roofs, each providing only sufficient power to run their lights and heat water or, with care, one or two small machines. Even in Saint-Louis, electricity was only available for a few hours a day. Here on the farm, there was none at all.

'To whom will you sell your electricity?' he had asked.

'We will build a transmission line to Europe and sell it there.'

'Why? They have and we do not.'

'They have more money,' the man had said. 'Once we have enough capacity, we will sell here too. We will build at least seventy of these farms all across the Sahara.'

'And the Big Men, will they not take it from you?' nodding his head in the direction of the government in Dakar.

The blue-eyed man had smiled, his eyes narrowing. 'It would be no different than if they took your farm. Stealing my property will leave them with nothing but sand.'

Amadou had stared at the dust and activity: a sudden vision of his farm and what he might be able to do with bigger water pumps and refrigeration. 'Would you sell electricity to a neighbour?'

The blue-eyed man had looked at him and grinned. 'For a friend,' he had said, and put out his hand.

'I am Amadou,' and grasped the hand firmly with his.

'I am Simon.'

And so it had been agreed, but he had not been sure it would happen until five months ago. A small substation had been built at the edge of his property and a line run to the collection of barns and sheds at the base of the guelb and on up to the living quarters on the shady slope.

Amadou had rushed back to Saint-Louis, asking his children to invest in buying electric pumps, refrigerators and tanks. He had traded five hundred of his Red Sokotos for one hundred Black Bedouin milkers.

At his age, to take such risks with his wealth – but he had felt a prickle of excitement. Rosso was only half an hour away, and there was a ready market for fresh milk in the river town. Perhaps, with permanent electricity, he could even farm throughout the year, increase the scale of his irrigation and raise sheep again.

Amadou had not seen Simon at the Sable de Lumière offices today, although he had seen some of the engineers walking amongst the solar collectors.

He remembered when they started. An enormous container flew in from the sea, supported by four heavy drones, and touched down gently on the hamada. He and his men had gathered near it, astonished at its size. It was almost thirty metres long and as high as a four-storey building.

Drones flew in equipment and piles of material, and then the container had opened at one end and out rolled a massive vehicle. Amadou had not even realized the block was a machine and that it was operating.

Simon was happy to answer his questions, explaining that the container was a printer and would produce mobile factories that themselves would print the solar collectors. When it was finished there, the container would be flown to the next farm.

As each machine had emerged, it was flown out on to the hamada and began work. After twelve days, the container had produced ten machines and was flown away, leaving behind only a small set of offices and a transmission station. This first farm was filled with engineers who were studying the efficiency and resilience of the collectors exposed to the persistent sand-blast of the harmattan winds. What they learned was used to improve the designs of the printing machines while they operated.

Amadou had joined Simon walking alongside the first machine. It was slightly larger than a bus, a waist-high gap underneath, and featureless except for a series of hoppers on its roof and narrow traction wheels at its sides.

They had watched as it prepared the ground, scraping up sand and rock from the space beneath itself, and could feel the heat from the furnace where that material was converted for use in the printer. It moved at walking speed, pausing periodically to open and embed a single solar collector in the earth.

Drones flew out to the distant machines, topping them up with some of the rare minerals and metals they needed. Otherwise, the farm was almost silent.

Amadou had watched the rows of collectors grow in number. If he listened carefully, he could even hear them. Somewhere between a purr and a growl as they tracked the sun.

Every eight hours the farm sang. He could think of no other way to describe it. He understood that each panel must clean itself, oscillating at high frequency to throw off the thin coating of dust accumulating from the continual harmattan. Groups of panels oscillated in a flowing sequence so that the noise was not unbearable. A technical process became, to him and his men, as if the entire surface of the farm began to ripple and sing.

There was a call of delight from lower down the slope from one of his men, and a man in a delicately embroidered ochre-brown boubou and matching kufi skull-cap stepped into the firelight.

'Azul, ma idjani?' said the man, and chuckled, his voice the delight of small pebbles being tumbled in a fast-flowing stream.

'Azul, Griot. You are here early,' said Amadou, standing and happily embracing the younger man. 'Sit, please, the stew will be ready soon.'

'How could I miss the start of your new herd? I hear your Black Bedouin are extremely fine.'

Amadou drummed his fingers on his knee. 'I feel like a young boy, Griot,' he said. 'My whole life has been spent surviving the heat, watching as the sand burns and forces us from our land.

'It is almost too much to believe that I can revive my farm. But I have hope. With that blue-eyed man's help, I have hope,' he smiled. The griot reached across and squeezed his hand, holding it.

'Nit ku amul jom, amul dara,' he said.

Amadou nodded. 'My father used to say that. "The person who lacks honour, lacks everything." And this man has great honour. I know this Sablière is meant for the toubab across the sea. I hope that he will see what I can do and will also sell our people some of this electricity. It will change everything for us.'

The griot smiled gently, guarding his thoughts. 'Sablière?' he asked.

'Yes,' laughed Amadou. 'It is the name I hear the engineers calling the solar farm. The Sandpit. It is appropriate, yes?' He laughed again. 'Please, Griot, it is good to have you. Will you sing for us? One of the songs of our fathers?'

The griot reached behind himself and, pulling his koubour *towards him, began to pluck at the strings.*

His music rose up into the clarity of the night sky, lifting with the smoke, sprays of sparks and tears of flame.

The men began to sing, their voices blending with the distant calling of night birds and the gentle shifting of leaves in the breeze. They sang of home, of their wives and children far away, of their hope for the season, and of the rains still to come.

Later in the evening, after stories had been told and laughter shared, Amadou and the griot were the last two left by the fading embers.

'You say you have not seen Simon today?' asked the griot.

'No. I went looking for him to give him my thanks, but the engineers said that he had gone out into the desert a few days ago. They are expecting him back either this evening or tomorrow. You have business with him?'

'I have heard troubling news about Ansar Dine. I was hoping to warn him, but I fear I am too late.'

'Why would the jihadis have interest in this man? Their war is to the east.'

The griot did not respond, staring far to the north where the brighter line of the dusty road ran alongside the solar collectors.

'It is best you not know, my friend,' he said. 'Whatever happens, stay here on your farm. Please, for your safety,' pointing to a column of dust growing nearer on the road, glowing in the moonlight.

They watched as an off-road vehicle dragged itself out of the desert, something hanging off the back, tearing at the hamada. It shuddered to a halt outside the engineering quarters. A light went on inside and, even from this distance, they could see bullet holes and blood in the glass and a crumpled shape in the cabin.

The griot rose to his feet and started down the hillside. 'Stay here, Amadou. I fear he is lost.'

Amadou watched as he went, his eyes obsidian in the darkness.

5

'What are you doing to me?' asks Samboa, his voice invisible in the darkness, his mind an already dispersing stream of images and experiences from places he has never been and people he has never met.

The baboon ignores him, his eyes glowing in fascination at the storied threads that touch on this man's journey, the choices and lives which led him to this cave in the bones of the earth and the dust of the harmattan.

This blue-eyed man, where else does he go? How far back? Taking up a new strand, seeing a vast, polished building and a bulky man walking briskly, pausing only a moment before his frustration explodes.

'My name is Farinata Uberti,' said the man, who was neither good-looking, nor charming, or patient. 'Which of you mudak *is here for me?'*

He glared at the chauffeurs all clustered in their shambling distaste behind a low rope barrier, a discomforting vigil for the arrivals in Heathrow Terminal 6.

Dull eyes stared back, their gaze galled by those whose wealth and prestige allowed them to escape the degrading assembly line of semi-humiliating immigration and security checks inherent to modern travel.

Each chauffeur bore a sign revealing a small fracture of their loath-ing for those they waited on: barely legible handwritten names, misspelled typescript, uncomfortably small lettering, wildly inappropriate fonts. A calligraphic rebellion.

Each took a moment to consider the words they clasped, to decrypt them and interpret their meaning. To consider whether they held the name of the man irritably standing before them. Whether he was one of the elite who emerged through the glass sliding doors looking refreshed and invigorated, carrying nothing, their luggage following silently at their heels. Their expressions of merry meditation giving way to pleasant recognition as they deciphered their names and nodded ambiguously to the chauffeur who would ferry them onward.

Their reflection would not be rushed even in the heat of Uberti's impatient fury.

A man whose black coat hung from his bony shoulders like the tattered feathers of some neglected museum exhibit expressed an anguished moan. The others shifted uneasily away from him.

The man detached himself from behind the barrier and walked hesitantly towards Uberti.

'I am Phlegyas Quinquapotti,' he said nervously, his skin clammy and pale, stating his name as if fearful he would be forgotten, fearful he would be remembered.

Neither offered a hand in greeting. Uberti scowled and gestured with his head towards the doors.

As they walked, Quinquapotti unfolded his console, scrolling through his list of clients and rapidly gesturing on the surface. He led his charge out of the airport and towards a sleek, translucent black vehicle slowing at the kerb. He placed his hand over the key sensor and the single door quietly swung upwards.

'The limousine will take you to the Savoy,' he said, reading off the words from his mental script, 'but you can ask it to stop anywhere along the way if you wish. If you leave the limousine, though, it will no longer

recognize you. You'll find refreshments for your journey inside. I wish you well on your travels, Mr Uberti.'

Quinquapotti slouched back inside to await the next arriving guest on his list, hoping that his confusion and terror had been covered by overriding one of the reserve limousines, but he knew there would be consequences. Each vehicle was specially prepared to serve the unique needs of each guest. Uberti could scarcely fail to notice that his requirements had not been met.

Uberti swiped at his ear as the limousine left the terminal, already reaching amongst the bottles for the least appalling brand of vodka. Furious that his private label was missing.

'You are back?' he said as soon as his call was connected.

The person on the other end nodded, the movement translated as a downward tug in Uberti's earlobe implant.

'It is done,' said the other person. 'But the jihadis have used the opportunity to attack elsewhere. Libya——'

'You worry too much, Rinier,' said Uberti.

Rinier Pazanov responded in silence.

'I am in London. Those mudak chauffeurs messed up. Let them know.'

A downward tug. Uberti ended the call with a subtle shake of his head, and the limousine was absorbed into the glass and steel of Dry London.

England offered a safe haven for men like Uberti, and a few were pleased to quietly and expensively offer them custom. For most, too many eyes were watching, and services like TheShitList, which identified and tracked the movements of the world's thugs and tyrants, made it easy to organize a financially devastating boycott.

Men like Uberti expected their money to render such moralizing obstacles into a homeopathic reduction. They could express grievance in profound ways.

Quinquapotti's employer offered untraceable service and absolute discretion. Someone had arrived earlier and claimed to be Uberti. Someone took his limousine and drank of his private-label hand-bottled artisan vodka. A small inconvenience but, for men like Uberti, unforgivable. The man who had thought to rupture the serenity of Uberti's journey needed to be found and his transgression explained to him.

As Quinquapotti's shrieks of outrage yielded to the persistent inter-rogation of more brutal men, he tried to remember what the transgressor looked like. All he could remember were the man's eyes.

When he was eight years old, his family had gone to Cornwall for the summer. One morning, on his own, he had crawled through a hedge into a field and stared in wonder at a dense wilderness of cornflowers.

His sense of delight at the pungent opulence of blooms beneath blue skies nestled in that part of the vacation where school is a distant memory, there is nothing but play, and all the opportunity and antici-pation for the future are ahead. All captured in the blue of the petals in his hands.

And he had never felt it again.

The man's eyes were that colour.

He dimly remembered that the man was tanned, dark sandy hair running to grey, tall and lean, and . . . that was as much as he recalled. He had stopped looking. It had hurt too much.

The man had smiled at him, a contradiction of mischief and innocence, but he had not spoken. Quinquapotti had noticed he had no luggage and thought nothing of it.

At the door to the limousine, the man had smiled broadly, clapped him on the shoulder and was gone.

Uberti had arrived forty minutes later and revealed the extent of Quinquapotti's error.

The blue-eyed man's limousine was empty when it arrived at the Savoy, having made one unscheduled stop outside Victoria Station.

The tube drivers were on strike. The union official who could grant them access to security footage was picketing. It may not have helped anyway. The man seemed to have stepped straight from the limousine into a waiting AnoniCar, a service whose paranoia was such that their search was over before they even knew there was anyone to follow.

'Was there nothing else? Nothing happened?' asked one of the brutal men of Quinquapotti, more from duty than hope of learning anything.

'There was a busker,' said Quinquapotti, wishing only to be forgotten.

A few minutes before the blue-eyed man had arrived, a sound, like a bow wave, disturbed the steady, rippling flow of the arrivals hall.

A man in a delicately embroidered ochre-brown boubou and matching kufi skull-cap had walked through the airport. His feet in handmade leather sandals. His every step a drumbeat. He had sung, and children had run laughing and grinning as the tail to his comet.

The man had seated himself against a pillar to the side of the arriving passengers and pulled an obeche-wood mbira from inside his robes. He had held the instrument at his waist between his long, dark fingers and plucked at the tines, filling the hard marble halls of the terminal with warmth. His melody foreign and haunting.

'They spoke,' said Quinquapotti.

There was no trace of the man in the ochre-brown boubou either.

'What did he say?'

Quinquapotti, dazed by violence and fear, hesitated and shook his head. 'He didn't say anything. But I heard the busker – only two words. He said, "They escaped." I don't know what that means.'

By the time they managed to get men to Victoria Station, it was far too late. It was raining, dark and cold. No one had seen the limousine, and any who had had found it unremarkable.

In Heathrow Terminal 6, the prologue of chauffeurs churned. Eyes were met, brows raised, greetings whispered, and wards guided to waiting limousines. Special requests were confirmed, vehicles dispatched, and chauffeurs returned to the huddle.

The search was abandoned and soon forgotten, Quinquapotti most of all.

And in the obliterating darkness of the cave, the baboon continues following the blue-eyed man's tracks left in the dust shed in the journeys of others.

6

Galkin had brought his dogs, long-limbed wolf-like creatures shepherding and hounding the other guests' children across the garden. Yelping and delighted shrieks rose exuberantly into the settling twilight as the evening mist smothered the forest beyond the fence and crept towards the dacha.

It was quiet here in the Novoperedelkino complex. The menace of Moscow receded almost into white noise, and one could put aside the paranoia of the men of force in that city.

His face momentarily silhouetted as he lit a cigarette, Rinier Pazanov leaned back against the outside wall and looked up at the flickering stars, feeling old and very, very lonely. For an instant, he imagined a strange beast-like face looking down at him, and then the moment was gone.

Cigarettes were edgy, their allure at once archaic and dangerous, when he had started smoking as a university student. He had mimicked the siloviki he saw being driven around in their dark limousines, surrounded by blocky men in overly tight suits. Then he had become one, and now, with his body bent and soft, it was another bad habit he wished he could quit.

A little boy – must be Galkin's son – scampered up the stairs on to the wooden deck. 'They're like wolves,' he laughed.

'No, son, those are wolves,' pointing with a glowing end at the bottom of the endless garden where a wolf pack – lean from the winter – were *leaping the fence and, with grey shanks heaving, running for the darkening forest slopes. One of Galkin's dogs clawed at the fence and howled mournfully at the dwindling shadows, impotent to follow.*

A call from inside and the child joined his siblings as they returned to the light and safety of the dacha.

Pazanov sighed deeply, the dank musty smell of wood mulch settling on his shoulders and shrouding him in its scent. He was thinking of Dar es Salaam, the first time he saw the blue-eyed man, and about another little boy.

The Tanzanian government had not been interested in giving Rosneft sole extraction rights to their newly discovered offshore gas fields. Their donors were going through one of their periodic demands for accountability, and the president had been nervous. At least the Chinese were planning to extract the gas, not lock it off the way the Russians intended.

Pazanov had been given an ultimatum.

'If this government will not work with us, get us another one.' Farinata Uberti's voice matter-of-fact, a chief executive making a minor administrative decision. Pazanov had tried to explain that the region might be too fragile and they could lose control entirely.

'Will energy prices rise or fall?' had been the simple response. 'Who cares about these obezyany*?' The bigger man had slapped him hard on the shoulder, his eyes bloodshot and hooded. 'Are you getting too squeamish for this work, Pazanov? All we want is for the oil and gas to stay in the ground. If we have to burn Africa to bedrock to do it, we will. If you will not, I will find someone else.'*

Pazanov had stared back. 'Farinata, you asked my opinion, and you always ask me to think of the worst.'

Uberti had raised his hands, his laughter acrid. 'Of course, Rinier, that is so.' He had walked to the side table and picked up a small box there. 'Go back to Tanzania and do what I ask, yes? Here, a small gift for your wife. Tell her it's from you.' Inside was a deep-blue Tanzanite pendant on a delicate platinum chain. She was wearing it even now, somewhere inside the dacha.

It had been easy to start the war. All it had taken was guns and money, and Ansar Dine's jihad took hold in Dar es Salaam. Pazanov had stayed until the last moment. Until he had been certain the government could not regroup and that the Russian veto at the UN prevented any international help.

The airport had been a long drive from the luxury hotels in the city centre. Even with his own guards to protect him and clear a route, it had taken three hours. Thousands of vehicles and people carrying everything they owned had fled from the city and headed out into the countryside.

He had spotted the expatriate workers, stuck in their expensive cars by the side of the road, begging for safe passage out, being ignored and abandoned. Their opulent estates on the peninsula already in the hands of the jihadis.

His guards had been scornful of the uprising. 'These fighters are a joke,' said one, sitting with him inside the limousine, his skin starkly white against his black fatigues and dark-grey armour. The men called him Belaya, although that was not his name. If he had one, he had not revealed it in all the years he had been with Pazanov.

'They hardly know how to use the guns we gave them. They shoot without thinking. If I was half-asleep and unarmed, I could still fight them off,' he had said.

Even so, they had overwhelmed the Tanzanian soldiers in hours. Troops used to manning checkpoints and extracting bribes from civilians had proven unwilling to take on armed opposition, instead dropping their weapons and fleeing.

Eventually Pazanov could go no further, and they had left the illusive protection of the vehicles. Pazanov had never felt unsafe, only a detached passivity to events he had unleashed.

He had seen a man pulling a cart, a woman pushing behind, and their children sobbing on top. An old woman collapsed, weeping on the pavement, a suitcase torn open by her side. A claustrophobic scrum of people, all shoving and pushing to get out of the city.

As they had neared the airport, they heard automatic gunfire, and the screaming and clamour had become more intense as people tried to get away.

Pazanov's men had grouped closely around him but were still otherwise untroubled. Their agreement had been that this area would not be claimed until their aeroplane had left. There would be a small number of jihadis here to cause panic.

They had turned towards the airport and emerged in a clearing surrounded by shuttered shops, the ground uneven with broken glass and litter. He had spotted a blue-eyed white man within a group of locals a little ahead of them, probably also making his way to the airport.

Jihadis had burst out from between the shops and immediately opened fire. Pazanov's guards had ignored them.

The other white man had not. He had moved with surprising speed, smashing a brick into one jihadi's face and grabbing his AK-47. He had dropped into a half-crouch and deftly fired at each of the now fleeing fighters. He had cast the gun aside and run back to his group, where a woman was sobbing over the body of a young boy, other bodies lying tangled behind them.

The boy had still been alive. Confused, disoriented. The hole in his side jarring against his white cotton T-shirt. His eyes, starting to cloud, had stared at Pazanov.

The blue-eyed man had bent over him, forcing his hand into the wound to stop the bleeding, felt his heart fade and had immediately started resuscitation as the boy's mother screamed.

As Pazanov had been dragged away by his men, he had looked back, straight into the eyes of the other.

The strange blue eyes had held his, judged him, and found him wanting.

'Darling?'

He jumped, his heart pounding, gasping.

'Natalya.' His wife touched his shoulder gently and leaned over him, her eyes filled with concern.

'You were so quiet. I'm sorry, I didn't mean to startle you.'

'No. Thank you. I was . . . It was a year and a half ago.'

'You still have nightmares?' her voice tender.

'Not nightmares. Unpleasant memories.' He smiled at her.

She kissed him softly on the forehead. 'Dinner will be ready soon, and Vyacheslav is telling stories in the living room. You should put in an appearance.'

'Yes, I know. I'm waiting for a call.'

'About Adaro?'

Pazanov nodded, and rested his hand on his shoulder over his wife's. 'Yes. We may have found a way to help the jihadis so they will help us.'

'So, why the nightmares?'

Pazanov sighed.

'You remember when I got back from Tanzania? I told you of that European we passed outside the airport and wondered if he had escaped?'

She nodded. For some reason, it had made an impression on him.

'I never told you, but I recognized him.'

She started, then dragged a chair to sit next to him so she could look directly into his eyes. 'You knew him then? Who was he?'

'I didn't know him then, but I do now. It was Simon Adaro.'

'What? That's—'

'—too much of a coincidence,' he said, completing her words.

'Who else knows?'

'Only me, and now you.'

'Do you think he recognized you?'

'I think this is his revenge. We've spent a year fighting him. We've *bought jihadis, governments. It's chaos out there. He cannot get his power to Europe, and the energy price is still down 5 per cent. It's killing us. If we don't close him off in the next twelve months, we will collapse, and Russia with us.'*

She shook her head. 'Slow down. All you've told me is that a mad Englishman named Simon Adaro is building a solar plant in the Sahara and that this threatens Rosneft. This is the first time we're here at the dacha in eight months because of this man.'

Pazanov bit his bottom lip and looked around him, but this was Novoperedelkino. Only the elite lived there, alongside the ruling class in their dachas in Peredelkino. It was as private and secluded as he could hope for.

'About a year ago, I learned that someone was building new electricity transmission systems in Bologna. They needed to connect to the main grid, and our office in Spain got notice.

'At first I thought it was a joke. How was anyone going to convince any country in Europe to accept a new power plant?

'That was when I first heard of this Simon Adaro. He was promising unlimited power from the desert. "Farms of light," he called them. He told people they wouldn't have to see them. Nobody would, stuck out there where no one lives. Only one transmission line rising from the sea off the Spanish coast into a transformer hub buried in the mountains, and then straight into the network.

'Farinata asked me to investigate and find out how something this big could happen without us knowing.'

'Why is this important? What is it to you?'

He looked at her sadly. 'This is what I do for Rosneft, Natalya. We do not outcompete our rivals. If they will not do as Farinata demands, then I am to stop them, even if that means turning a country to dust.'

She took his hands. They spoke little of his work, about what paid for their lifestyle. She asked him now, 'Do you enjoy this? Is it . . .' her voice trailing.

He smiled, but it did not reach his eyes. 'It is what I know, but truly, it is good to talk. If you would listen?'

'Wait,' she said, 'I think we both need a drink,' and returned with a bottle of vodka and two glasses.

'I'm ready,' her eyes flint, her trust in him complete.

He drank.

'We've kept it very quiet, but we think he will eventually produce about five hundred gigawatts. That's about a fifth what we produce, and will take seven years to complete, but he will start producing a significant part of that within the year. We have not had a rival in Europe in decades. Farinata is under pressure. Rosneft ensures Russian control over the region. If we lose our monopoly, the Europeans might even unite around this Federation. Our president would never forgive such a transgression. Farinata has demanded I put everything into stopping him.

'I went looking for him. His plans were easy to find. I don't think he had even tried to hide them. He must have started immediately after he escaped from Dar es Salaam. Within six months, he was already building the first farm in Senegal.'

'How does he develop such technology inside six months?'

'He has some connection on Mars.'

'Mars? What has Mars to do with this?'

'Sorry,' Pazanov massaged his temples. 'The colony there. They have developed machines to print entire fields of solar collectors. They melt the sand and make these vitreous machines. We think the colony sent him their designs.'

She sat back, shocked, recognizing the implications. 'So, what have you been doing?' she asks.

He refilled both their glasses.

'I have few resources,' his voice bitter. 'The Chinese are still furious about Tanzania. They are threatening to research their own energy alternatives if we start another war, so I am left with a small team. All

we have strength for is to sabotage his operations, but we can't get near his main printer, and you'd have to carpet-bomb these farms to stop them. We sent submersibles to destroy his line printer coming out of the port at Saint-Louis. He tried printing his lines all across Senegal and Mali, looking for a way out. We bribed the jihadis, but he was trying to buy them too.'

'Where does all his money come from? And you think he's spending this much to avenge one small boy?'

'It's more than that. He was in Tanzania to take over their copper mines. He had over two billion dollars invested there. Our actions caused him to lose everything.'

Natalya whistled. 'That is plenty to fight over. But that should bankrupt him?'

'No. He is . . .' Pazanov breathed as if in reverence. 'He is very wealthy.'

'How?'

'So many things. He started TheShitList.'

She gasped, immediately furious. 'That's the bastard who stops me shopping in Paris? How does that . . .' searching for an appropriate word '. . . govnyuk even make money?'

'He started all these technology firms, AnoniCar, GeneWorx, EarBeds, about 2 per cent of the blockchain nodes. We think he's worth maybe a quarter as much as Rosneft. But we carry the Russian state; he carries only himself.'

'But it's all technology. What was he doing in Tanzania? Copper mines don't sound right.'

'No, I know. But the place is a mess now. We can't find any trace of what he was doing there.'

The bottle was half empty, and she replaced the cap.

'Why not just kill him?' Her voice was stark, trembling at crossing some invisible threshold.

Pazanov felt something tear. Even as his work had slowly numbed him to the consequences of his actions he had clung to her innocence of it. He would not have had her enter his world, stifled the thought before it could spread. She was all he had left.

'We tried, but he is like smoke. His people are in London, and we can't operate there, and they never leave. This is the man who started AnoniCar. We can't track his movements.'

'You said you're waiting for a call?'

'Yes, he's getting desperate too. We know he needs to go north, but the Sahara is controlled by these Ansar Dine fanatics. They put out word that they're looking for something in the desert, something they lost.'

'What?'

'We don't know. I'm assuming it's a weapons shipment. Those terrorists are crazy scary. That's fine with us, as long as they don't work with him. We figure that Adaro must have surveyed the desert when he was looking to run transmission across it. If anyone knows where whatever they're looking for is, it'll be him.'

'And you let them know?'

He grinned. 'Yes, and we also know that he was going to meet them. Farinata told me he'd call the moment he hears anything.'

Natalya stood and walked to the top of the stairs, looking out towards the forest. He joined her, held her to his chest and rested his arms across her belly.

'I think the greatest deception we ever pulled on the Europeans was to offer to provide them only with electricity and none of our oil or gas. When hundreds of millions of people can be made to forget how their energy is produced, you know they are completely in your power,' he said.

'And millions more buy eggs and don't even know they come from chickens,' she replied.

'Yes, and now we have to hope that their ignorance will protect us.'

There was a hesitant tap on the door frame behind them. It was one of the servants.

'Sir,' she said. 'I am sorry to intrude. There is a call for you. It is gospodin *Uberti*, he says it is good news.'

7

'You were friends once,' said the grey man in the grey suit. His grey rims deliberately flattened his words and removed any nuance as they translated. The collective known as Ambassador Gong Yuanxing picked at a splinter of wood on the pitted and cracked table between them.

He had not eaten and grimaced with distaste at the rapidly vanishing crepe on the plate of his companion.

'You should have some,' said Tiémoko Diagne, carefully wiping his mouth and fingers with a napkin and then folding it into a point to clean under each nail. 'You would enjoy it.'

The grey man ignored him, his eyes hidden behind the grey lenses of his rims.

They were meeting in a tiny café in the crowded centre of Dakar's business district; the looming buildings produced some shade on the shops below, smothered in the heat. Six misshapen tables squeezed together. The screen door, fly-netting instead of glass, clapped back and forth behind a departing customer. Outside, traffic passed, rattling over the potholes and stones of the battered street.

'I have often wondered what it must be like to be one of you?' asked Tiémoko rhetorically. 'Do you put aside this costume when you go home? Do you have a different name to your wife and children? Do you even have children? Or is it something you must exist within completely?'

The grey man's expression did not change.

'No?' said Tiémoko, having completed his ablutions and dropped the remains of the napkin on to his plate. 'You have no interest in the relationship between myself and Simon. If the Martian colony would license their technology, you would have no need of me at all. If your researchers thought they could recreate it in less than ten years, my price would be lower. This is strictly business. Do not pretend otherwise.'

The grey man raised an eyebrow. 'No,' he said. 'We are not interested in you or the reasons for your –' he paused, savoured the word to come, '– betrayal. We ask so that we may assess whether you can be trusted.' He scratched again at the splinter. 'You have demanded a great deal of money based only on the strength of your position. How are we to believe you?'

Tiémoko pushed his plate into the centre of the table and waved for another cup of coffee. 'With milk,' he said.

The waiter disappeared into the kitchen behind the counter, and an agitated conversation ended as the cook walked briskly through the seating area and out the swing doors.

'It is you who approached me. You would seem to know too well how little a university professor in Dakar is paid.' Tiémoko's face was stern, his eyes unblinking. 'Yes, we were friends. I helped build Achenia. My software, my ideas. I should have been a partner. When I was deported, Simon and Hollis took my share of the company. All this is true. It is you who said that I owe them nothing, and that I owe myself a good retirement.'

'Yet you work for them?'

'Of course I took the job. There are few opportunities to work with this technology anywhere in the world.'

'Why us? Why not Rosneft? I know they have approached you.'

'I have no wish to see the device destroyed. This way I get to continue working with Achenia, and you and Rosneft can fight each other. It will be better for us if Rosneft has a more powerful state to worry about than ours.'

'The People's Republic of China are allies with the Russians. We have no quarrel with Rosneft.'

'Not yet,' grinned Tiémoko.

The grey man let that pass. 'How will you ensure we can take possession of the printer? Especially as your superior is –' chewing on the word '– indisposed.'

The cook returned carrying a small paper bag. Milk was purchased only when required, for there had been no electricity to power their refrigerators that week and it would not last in the heat. She decanted a small amount into a jug and carried it and an old, chipped coffee mug filled almost to the brim to their table.

Tiémoko poured in sugar for so long that the grey man was half expecting a peak to emerge from the surface. He dropped in a splash of milk, stirred and sipped gently.

A tall, blond American man pushed back the swing doors and, glancing briefly at the two who were seated, called out in greeting to the kitchen.

Tiémoko continued unhurriedly sipping at his coffee while the grey man waited patiently. The American placed an order and chatted loudly to the cook through the doorway to the kitchen. He stared at them curiously but did not intrude.

After an uncomfortably long silence, the American left, taking his plastic bag of crepes with him.

Tiémoko responded as if the question had only just been asked. 'Indisposed, yes. What is your view on his capture?'

The grey man considered. 'We have no view. Unless it intrudes in some way on our possession of the printer. Why did he permit himself to be captured by Ansar Dine? And what of the body found in his vehicle?'

Tiémoko sighed. 'He said only that he was looking to bribe them to permit our line printers to pass through their territory. He was supposed to meet them alone. You know the body is still unidentified. I can only assume he came across a group of seekers and attempted to get them to safety.'

'And was taken in the process? It is possible. Will that prevent the handover of the printer?'

'I am afraid that it does. Simon has the encryption keys and has yet to share them with me. Until he does, the underlying software will not be accessible. You may even struggle to gain insight into the hardware since it is heavily shielded.' He shrugged. 'It was designed to withstand concussive damage should Rosneft attempt to bomb it.'

The grey man's eyes narrowed. 'You believe he is the only one who possesses the keys?'

'For this machine? Yes. For Achenia's purposes, it is only required to produce a single design, so no need for anyone else to have access. Press a button and it prints.'

'He must escape from Ag Ghaly?'

'It seems so,' said Tiémoko warily.

'You believe, should he escape, you will be entrusted with these keys?'

Tiémoko shrugged. 'He is not well. Within a year, he will have need to withdraw from his active role. I have managed such codes for him in the past.'

The grey man's eyes widened. 'This is news to us. What is the nature of his illness?'

Tiémoko shrugged once more, offering discretion even for the man he intended to betray.

The grey man was silent. Tiémoko watched him carefully, noticed the delicate nod or shake of the head that revealed the conversation happening via the grey man's implant.

A decision was reached.

'How soon can we have the device?' asked the grey man.

'That will take time. I have no intention of revealing my involve-ment. Your capture of the printer must appear to be random misfortune. We have had three attacks by paramilitary groups – probably from Rosneft – in the last few months. Many such attempts are made, and it is guarded and moved regularly. It may take a year before I can create an opportunity for you.'

'We will pay you only once it is safely in China,' said the grey man.

'A quarter when you accept my terms, a quarter when I pass over the encryption keys, and half when I give you the date and location for your attempt at taking it.'

The grey man scowled. 'I am not sure that will be satisfactory. We will need assurances.'

'There are no assurances. I did not design it. I have no idea how it works. Once you take control of it, I no longer have any leverage. All I have is its location, and all I can change is the level of security protecting it.'

The grey man pushed back his chair and rose. He did not offer his hand. 'I will talk to my superiors, and we will let you know our decision.'

He turned and went out through the swing doors, leaving Tiémoko seated in the tiny café.

Tiémoko laughed and turned to call after the waiter, 'I will have another crepe.'

8

Samboa has been squeezed so long against the saturated sweat of the wall, he can no longer feel where it leans against the flesh of his back.

The baboon appears pleased. The blue-eyed man is explained. Now, what of this husk who pleads and squirms?

The naked man shudders at a glancing moment. 'No.' An exhausted moan yielding before the baboon's continuing swirling search. 'Not her. I don't want to see *her*.'

Capturing it, drawing it out, revealing a dust-swept concrete expanse, people running, surrounded and chased.

'Leave it! Leave it! Keep moving!' shouted Shakiso, grabbing the elderly man under his shoulder and hurling him up the ramp into the freight drone. With a despairing look back at his felt hat being trodden into the dust of the concrete, he was pushed inside.

A child slipped away from his mother and was swiftly returned. Bags were lost and left. There was tension and stilted silence as the freight drone filled.

'There isn't enough time,' said Haroun, his eyes red, blinking with fatigue and terror.

Five French paratroopers stood halfway between the small airport control tower and the crowd pressed around the drone, facing towards the sound of the approaching battle-front.

The crackling static of gunfire and dull thuds from artillery on the far edge of the camp were smothered by a crunching, wrenching explosion on the side of the control tower. Rubble and dust were flung out and towards them.

People crouched, waited and – seeing no further explosions – pushed even more tightly to get into this, the last drone out of Benghazi. Beyond their group, the other drones had closed their doors and begun to take off.

Shakiso thumped Haroun on the arm, encouraging him, and ran to the back of the crowd where Michèle, her husband and father-in-law were struggling with their four babies. She took one small surprised-looking bundle from the old man.

'Merci,' said Michèle, all of them grateful and exhausted.

Shakiso smiled, looking back suddenly as a louder shattering fusillade rattled against the wall on the periphery of the airport.

The camp had been overrun.

Early yesterday morning, Ansar Dine had brought their jihad to Benghazi, having routed the under-equipped remnants of the Libyan army. Seekers fleeing battles elsewhere were once more homeless and running for their lives as international staff began their evacuation.

Paratroopers had pushed their way, amidst panic and shoving mobs, into Shakiso's office. 'We can give you twenty-four hours,' she had been told. That time was almost up. Only staff and their families may escape to Paris on whatever freight drones Shakiso could find on short notice, and only those with legitimate documentation. The nations of Europe were closed to all others.

She had pushed that definition as far as she could. Every drone would leave carrying the limits of its capacity.

'I hope we get away with this,' said Haroun, as Shakiso reached the ramp once more.

Another explosion, shattered concrete. The wall was breached.

A black-clad jihadi emerged through the gap, shouting. The para-troopers crouched and began firing. One turned to Shakiso and shook his head. They had run out of time.

Each of the soldiers toggled their pack and was catapulted upwards to the waiting carrier drone which hovered above them.

'Take him,' said Shakiso urgently, transferring the baby to Haroun.

She ran again to the rear. 'Move! Move!' shouting and pushing the last few up the ramp.

Jihadis were running towards them as the ramp withdrew and the doors began to close.

The drone rose, jerked as a volley of bullets ricocheted across the outside, people gasping and screaming, and lifted rapidly once more.

Shakiso stared down through a window, watching as the jihadis swamped the airport and fired up towards them, safely out of range.

Her hands were trembling, and she wiped her face, smearing dirt and sweat. Haroun was squeezed tightly beside her. He waggled his head from side to side.

'Plenty of time, boss,' he said, and smiled.

She laughed.

'Here, let me take him,' carefully taking the baby back into her arms, the child still staring at her in astonished surprise. She kissed him gently on the forehead, held him close, breathed in his moist baking-bread baby smell, looking through the forest of heads to Michèle. Nodded, we made it.

It would be just under four hours to Paris.

The coast slipped past beneath them, and those able to look out sighed and relayed the news to the others. Tension abated, but many still looked back and forth nervously.

The air conditioning could not cope with so many so close together, and it was hot and dank. Shakiso's team further inside the drone began passing bottles of water through the cabin. People leaned and twisted to get their arms up and drink.

'Will it work?' asked Haroun.

'We need to get through immigration, let the media see us. Hopefully they simply open the doors for us. They'll have to,' she said, hoping that the simple ruse of abandoning their passports would protect all of them.

She looked down through the tiny window. A long grey line of navy ships and netting divided the Mediterranean north from south: a wall of steel to keep out the millions of seekers who had fled war and devastation and hoped to cross.

A woman to her side offered to take the child and, uncramping her arms, she passed him to her. In the heat, standing up, she dozed, leaning against Haroun.

A change of pitch and she awoke.

They were over Paris and beginning their descent towards Orly Airport. Movement, a few moans, of relief and renewed fear.

The drone landed, rattling and uneven. The doors opened and the ramp extended, the air suddenly clean and cool.

Shakiso, last on, was first off, looking around for where the other drones had landed. She wanted them all gathered in a single mob.

'Here we go,' whispered Haroun at her side, gesturing.

Shakiso felt her heart fall. Oktar Samboa, the head of her and Haroun's organization, was striding towards them from the direction of a set of military vehicles, a group of gendarmes close behind him. His thin, angular face was furious.

'Stay together,' shouted Shakiso, the crowd hanging on to each other. She ran to meet him.

'What are you doing? Why are we being met like this?'

'Shut up,' he said to her, his voice filled with suppressed violence. 'You know our funding depends on good relations with the French government. You ignored me. How many of these people are illegals?'

'They're all family,' she said. 'You expect them to leave husbands and wives behind?'

'Only if they have no visas. You know the rules.'

Shakiso turned to see the gendarmes had set upon the crowd, separating individuals, pushing some towards the waiting vehicles and others back up the ramp into the drone. Their rims flickered as they rapidly identified those who had permission to enter the country, and those who did not.

'What are you doing?' she shouted, flinging herself at a gendarme who was attempting to force Michèle's father-in-law back inside, trying to shove herself between them. Two gendarmes grabbed hold of her, lifted her easily. Children were screaming in terror, shouts and sobbing as families were torn apart.

Shakiso leaned back and hurled a fist into the face of the nearest gendarme, dislodging his rims, which twisted and hung from one ear. He smiled, shook her off and kneed her in the ribs. Haroun leaped on to him.

The brawl was over before it had properly begun. Haroun and Shakiso were bundled into the back of an armoured van along with many of the others who had been fighting. Even as she battered at the door, her hands bloody, howling in despair, she saw Michèle sitting on the tarmac, weeping, her babies on the ground beside her, her husband and father-in-law being forced back on to the freight drone. Watched as the drone took off, taking half the people she had brought out back to Benghazi. Behind it, surrounded by gendarmes, other drones were taking off.

'We saved them,' she sobbed. 'They were safe.' Staring with hatred and loathing at Samboa where he stood wrapped in his righteousness watching her, a thin smile on his lips.

'I did what was necessary,' says the naked man. 'She never understands—'

The baboon waves aside his protests, his eyes unforgiving. Where does she go, this young woman with the storm-filled eyes whose hair burns like flame and who stands as if clawing at the earth?

9

'Tuft!' shouted Shakiso as the caracal leaped up off the end of the kayak and on to the protruding rebar.

She turned and stared as Shakiso recovered control of the bouncing craft, her grey eyes cool and unblinking. She sat, yawned and licked her fur. Long ears erect and her characteristic black tufts of hair tailing out from the tips.

Shakiso climbed up and tied the kayak in place, dropped the paddle into the cockpit. She slipped off her spraydeck and deliberately poured water over the cat, who shook her head and glared. Shakiso stuck out her tongue and laughed.

'Entirely your fault for trying to tip me over,' she said. Tuft stood and purred, winding herself around Shakiso's legs.

She hurled the spraydeck into the cockpit and pulled her backpack from the stays at the rear of the kayak.

'Right,' scratching Tuft's head as the cat ran her dry, rasping tongue over her wrist, 'hope you're ready, youngster?'

With a hop, she leaped for the edge of the building above her, planted her feet on to the wall, and propelled herself up on to the roof. Tuft landed silently alongside her and purred.

Shakiso stood and looked around. The New Thames Barrier was almost a kilometre further up, hidden behind the domes of the old fuel storage tanks. She could hear dredgers at work, gradually reclaiming Wet London for the city.

A colourful banner was stretched between two spires stranded at different angles in the water: 'FASCISTS STAY OUT!!!' The words spray-painted by one of the many socialist communes, anarchist collectives or libertarian survivalist groups which squatted in the wreckage of the old city.

Most were harmless and ignored her. Some were fairly militant – more so with the inevitable progression of the reclamation project – and she took care to keep her distance from them. This must have been too close to the works now, and she had seen no one. Perhaps they had moved further down the river.

She opened her backpack and pulled out a folded jacket and two bands. The larger, she slipped over her temples, adjusting it until it felt comfortable. The smaller band went around the protesting Tuft's neck, followed by the jacket, which she slipped over the cat's front legs. Tuft glared at her.

Shakiso grinned. 'So I don't have to get you stitched up again. Stop complaining.'

She stood, checked the seals on her suit, adjusted her own armour and swiped at her earlobe. The augmented display projected from the band showing the route she planned for today. A faint smeared shape in the sky seemed to be a beast-like face. Assuming it was an artefact of the display, she shook her head to clear it, then she dismissed it and opened a broadcast channel.

'Morning, everyone,' she said. 'The sun is just rising over the Wet with a forecast for rain later, and Tuft and I are ready for our run.' Whoops and calls in the background as thousands joined the channel. She laughed in excitement and then muted the sound. No distractions were needed.

'For anyone new to my stream, you can switch between Tuft or myself,' looking down at the caracal, genetically modified for a feral loyalty, who stared wide-eyed up at her. 'She promises to keep her ears and paws out the way, but you know what she's like.'

She did a slow sweep across the skyline where dark purple clouds, a strange animal face fading amidst them, formed gargantuan shapes which pressed on the horizon.

'We're down from the New Thames Barrier. A lot further than usual since the reclamation seems to be going faster than I expected. We're heading for that cooling tower straight ahead, and there's a stack of warehouses, broken machinery, rebar and parts of the old refinery for us to get through.

'The rules are simple. Using any means possible, get there unaided in less than thirty minutes. And, don't get killed.'

She took a few short, deep breaths, and – with a full-body roar – flung herself across the undulating roofs of the warehouses. She vaulted over a low concrete wall between two sections, levering herself over with her left arm. Tuft simply leaped and raced ahead.

With a shout, she accelerated, felt the corrugated roof sagging beneath her, sprang forward, rolled and recovered without slowing.

Tuft flew up the vertical wall ahead of her, scrambled over the last metre and disappeared.

She followed. Left foot, right foot, left hand down, right hand just grabbing the top edge, and her momentum carried her over. Rolled, pushed herself upright and sprinted to build up speed.

There was a gap of about four metres between this warehouse and the roof on to the tangle of pipes at the refinery. The fall between them probably was not sufficient to kill, but the water hid twisted metal and clumps of wood and debris.

Tuft went over with room to spare on the other side. Shakiso leaped, flying horizontally, her arms outstretched.

She landed lightly on her hands, rolled forwards on to her feet and chased into the pipes.

This next part was relatively easy, relying mostly on navigating a way through the tight space, and there were plenty of well-placed hand-holds. There was only one tricky part left, and she made a bit of a spectacle of it.

She had drawn ahead of Tuft, who had gotten slightly lost amongst the pipes, and vaulted through into a clear space, landed and leaped again for a horizontal pipe a few metres ahead.

Her fingers were a little short, and she plummeted, her body already curved and braced to roll. She landed on a metal plate protruding from the water, her metal-gel armour foaming and dispersing the blow. She gasped and took a breath, watched as Tuft flew over her then looked down, panting. She did not wait.

Shakiso grinned and sprang upwards, catching up where Tuft was pacing and contemplating the horrors of the swim.

'Almost there,' as she dived open-armed into the water ten metres below.

There had been an old parking lot between this building and the tower, and the water was at its deepest.

Tuft whined before leaping, paddling frantically to get across.

A pair of grey seals surfaced nearby and swam alongside, staring at them in astonishment before slipping away.

Shakiso waited in the water at the base of the tower alongside the spare kayak she had tied there earlier, and hooked the sixteen-kilogram caracal to her back. The cat sneezed and wiped her face on the back of Shakiso's neck.

'Ah,' she shouted, 'that's nasty.'

A few minutes later, she had climbed the ladder and was sitting at the top, Tuft licking her fur dry.

The sun glimmered over the waters and glowed against the buildings seemingly afloat on the landscape. Dry London rose above it, and she could see tall, glass-clad buildings shining across the horizon. A bank of rain softly advanced from the east. In the near distance, two boats skipped across the surface, a broad red flag crackling from the bow of the leading vessel.

She wiped sweat from her eyes, grinned and breathed deeply.

'That's absolutely spectacular. So, so beautiful. I hope you've loved

this as much as we have. You guys have a fantastic day and join us again next time.'

She swiped at her ear and closed the channel.

'You hungry, youngster?' opening her rucksack, pulling out a water bowl for Tuft and a bottle, pouring half the contents for the thirsty cat. She drank the rest herself, then opened a container and threw a sandwich at the caracal.

'Yip, this is a perfect morning,' scratching Tuft between the ears with her other hand.

Her earlobe vibrated, a whispered 'Frieda Köhler' from the implant, nodding to accept the call. 'Frieda! How's my favourite international tycoon?' grinning, her mouth full as she ate the last of her sandwich.

'Ms Collard, I do wish you wouldn't call me that.'

'Yeah, but your real title is so boring. "Chairman of the Hans Luftig Stiftung" sounds like you should be the villain.'

Shakiso heard the sigh and could imagine Frieda shrugging her shoulders. She grinned broadly.

'Ms Collard, we had an appointment. I take it you are not at home? You're not –' Shakiso stifling laughter as she pictured Frieda's suppressed horror '– doing one of those runs again?'

'Relax, Frieda, we're not running.'

A relieved sigh. 'That's good—'

'We're two hundred metres up at the top of the old Barking Power Station cooling tower. We've finished our run.'

'Ms Collard!' Frieda sighed and recovered herself. 'I'm sorry, Ms Collard. Your hobby frightens me, but I have no place judging you.'

'Don't worry, Frieda,' she said gently. 'I don't even tell my parents what I'm up to. Now, how can I help you on this wet and beautiful morning?'

'Good,' Frieda said, and Shakiso could hear her swiping at a console on her desk. 'Do you remember Oktar Samboa?'

'Yes,' her voice was suddenly icy. 'That asshole still running Climate into the ground?'

'He is still Chief Executive,' Frieda said tactfully. 'We need your help.'

'No, you know I won't go back.'

'You will not have to work with him, but we do need you to take over the organization.'

She leaned back on her elbows, laughing. 'Frieda, I know you fund them, but the Climate board don't usually let donors decide who runs things. How do you figure you'll be forcing him out?'

She heard Frieda hesitate and stand, could visualize her walking around her desk and staring out through the broad windows, across Tiergartenstraße and into the forested park.

'This will only be short-term, and the situation is delicate. The UNHCR camps across the region are emptying, despite millions of seekers passing by and millions of our Deutsche Mark spent on relief. The board wants to know why, and if Oktar has missed something. They're looking for someone who can discreetly come in and fix things. They asked for you directly.'

'"Discreetly?" Huh? First time anyone described me that way. What does Oktar think of this?'

'This is the delicacy. It seems that, over the past six months, Oktar has become obsessed with some industrialist investing in Senegal. They have both gone missing. I'm told that he and this industrialist may have been kidnapped by Ansar Dine.'

Shakiso whistled, drumming her fingers on the edge of the tower. 'Why me? Why now?' she asked.

Frieda's voice softened. 'When you left Climate—'

'It's OK, you can say "stormed out",' said Shakiso brightly.

'When you left,' continued Frieda, 'I advised you to be patient. That the board needed time to accept your ideas, that the right time would come.'

'Nothing else working so you thought you'd try me?'

Frieda shrugged, the gesture translated as a slight downward tremor in Shakiso's ear implant.

'You said "short-term"?'

'You will have at least a one-year contract. Even if Oktar is released earlier, we will ensure he takes a year to recover and receive counselling. After the year, we can look to make your role permanent.'

Shakiso stared thoughtfully down at the rain-blurred waters beneath her, gusts of wind visible as grey welts that pounced and vanished. In the distance, the chase between the police boat and the group of squatters festooned in red banners had devolved into cheerful name-calling which echoed and rippled across the waters as their boats spiralled in ever widening circles, never quite catching each other.

Over a year since she had fled Benghazi and burned her way out of Climate. A year spent running in the Wet, hiding from the memory of fear in the eyes of those sent back. Of Michèle. Too ashamed to find her and see if she was coping.

She shivered and pulled Tuft close.

'I understand your concern,' recognizing the silence, 'but we have little time,' said Frieda.

The two boats disappeared beyond a tumble of eroded buildings, the sound of their motors and shouted insults lingering.

'Frieda, I'm going to need to know more before I'll be comfortable with this.'

'I understand. I can meet you in London tomorrow morning.'

'And I'll want to make my own decisions even if that causes problems for you.'

She could hear Frieda smile. 'Ms Collard, there are over ten million people gathered on the southern Mediterranean coast even now. Our current estimate is almost two hundred million internally displaced. If my newsfeed is to be believed, Europe is traumatized at the thought of all those seekers coming here. I think you will find you will have no *difficulty convincing people to do whatever is necessary to stem the tide.'*

Shakiso stood, her toes over the edge of the tower, staring at the glass city in the distance. The police boat reappeared, alone, and trudged towards Dry London.

'Good. Who's responsible for getting Oktar back? Not me, I hope. I'll tell them to keep him.'

'No, we are contacting the people who work with this industrialist. Another reason for my visit to London. We hope they can help.'

'Who is he?'

'A man called Simon Adaro. He is CEO of a company called Achenia.'

Shakiso shook her head. 'Never heard of him,' shrugged. 'I'll see you in the morning, Frieda, give Gerhard a hug for me.'

Somewhere out amongst submerged buildings, the haunting blast of an air horn grew fainter as the squatters retreated deeper into the shrinking remains of Wet London.

Tuft leaned against her, her legs hanging over the edge. She put her arm around the cat, who rested her head on her shoulder.

And they watched the sun trickling through the rainswept water in silence.

10

Achenia's office canteen on the ground floor was a surprisingly fashionable café called Tyranny. The first 'y' was rusted and hung loose over the lower part of the 'T', making the word look like 'Tranny'. On the walls were pictures of dictators done in transgressive Andy Warhol-style.

'What do you mean you've run out of tea?' bewildered outrage from an elderly man, as his wife kneaded her purse in frustration.

'Tea not popular. Come back next week. Camel is late,' said the barista, her clothes artfully torn, as if beaten by rocks, and her uninterested ambivalence in character with the décor. She was playing with the gimbals around a glass vial filled with a red liquid placed as a centrepiece on the counter, spinning them as the contents remained motionless.

'What do you mean, "the camel is late"?'

There was a cheer and clanking of misshapen tin mugs from a group of students near the window as the elderly couple retreated in confusion.

Shakiso was early and spent the time seeing how many of the portraits she could identify. Tuft was curled up at her feet, under the table.

History's obvious monsters were absent, making it more difficult. She refused to put on her rims and let the connect help her.

'Let's see, Tuft. That's one of the Kims, isn't it? Probably Ju-ae. Ooh –' she grinned as she spotted a recent addition '– that'll be controversial. Oleg Shkrebnev.'

She was distracted by a newsfeed on a wall to the side of the portraits *where a roll of cable was unspooling far out in orbit towards the Earth, its scale revealed where tiny flecks glared from the suits of the engineers as they flung themselves across it. Text scrolling across the feed attempted to explain how the first private-sector space elevator would succeed where others had failed.*

A waiter rushed to the inner door leading into the Achenia lobby and held it wide open as a man in a wheelchair eased his way through the chairs and tables. People – embarrassed or indifferent – made space for him. The chair was an expensive-looking custom print. She noticed how it responded to him, now moving on its own, now assisting as he propelled himself.

As he reached her table, the bottom axle rotated to the top, raising his chair to a height that must have approximated his standing position. He removed a cut-off glove from his right hand, extended his arm, and smiled in obvious pleasure.

'Ms Collard, I'm thrilled to meet you,' he said.

'Mr Agado,' she smiled. His hand was calloused and dry. 'Please, call me Shak.'

'Call me Hollis,' he said. 'Please, sit,' his chair returning to its seated height.

'Oh, and this must be Tuft. She's beautiful,' as the caracal rested her head on his lap for a scratch.

Shakiso raised an eyebrow. 'You know her name?'

Hollis blushed. He was in his late forties, his hair was thinning, his face lean and lined, but the rush of colour made him look boy-like and quite charming.

'I'm sorry, Ms – Shak –' grinning '– I'm a huge fan of yours. I don't get out much.' He gestured at his stomach, straining against his white shirt, his legs strapped to the chair.

'When I was younger, I used to love running in the woods, and watching your feed is one of those vicarious thrills. It's as close as I'm going to get.'

Her turn to blush, and she combed her hair back off her forehead to mask it. 'That's supposed to be anonymous,' she said.

'Frieda told me you have a caracal who goes everywhere with you, and I thought I recognized your voice when we spoke this morning.' He grinned at her discomfort. 'She looks young. One of ours, isn't she? From GeneWorx?' stroking Tuft's head where she appeared to have gone to sleep propped up on his lap.

'Yes, a gift from my dad about a year ago.'

'My husband will be jealous. Me hobnobbing with our favourite beautiful mystery runner.'

'Damn, so the blonde, blue-eyed, damsel-in-distress-thing isn't going to work for me?' she said, laughing, and smiled at him.

'Oh, it might,' he laughed. 'What do you get out of your broadcasts? I always assumed you were a simple renegade?'

'Escape,' she said, lowering her head so he could not see her eyes. 'It helps me avoid thinking about things.'

'And this?' tangentially prying further even as he honoured her privacy.

'It might be time to starting thinking about things again,' she smiled sadly.

A waiter momentarily came between them, depositing two espressos and glasses of water on the table.

'Frieda was quite insistent that I'm supposed to take responsibility for getting your boss back?'

'Not my boss,' said Shakiso, shaking her head, wiping espresso crema from her lips. 'Frieda knows. . .' She sighed. 'Oktar's a loathsome man, but I can't joke about this. No one deserves to be left to those butchers.'

'Well,' said Hollis, looking sympathetic, 'I can assure you, as I told Frieda, we are dealing with it.'

'Going to pay the ransom?'

'They haven't offered, and we wouldn't pay.'

Shakiso was surprised. 'Even for the CEO of Achenia?'

'No,' he paused deliberately, and she had the impression that more could be said, and would not be.

'Fine, so you're up to something. I'm not involved, but I'm not sure what Oktar has to do with it?'

Hollis shrugged. 'To be honest, I hadn't heard of him till Simon was kidnapped. I'm not sure I understand his thinking, but our investments in the Sahara seem to have upset him? He appears to have inserted himself into our battle with Rosneft.'

'Knowing Oktar, you're "evil capitalists out to exploit the suffering of the poor", and he would have been trying to stop you.'

Hollis smiled delicately. 'Ah, the famous contradictions of your industry.'

Shakiso raised her hands, grinning. 'Oh, totally. Oktar's a hypocrite. We're trauma tourists. Oktar gets off on being the saviour of the world, and he's quite convinced any private companies interfering in his business are no worse than terrorists. He knows everything and won't listen to anyone.'

'There have certainly been companies which deserved his mistrust,' Hollis conceded. 'But we are what we say we are. In any event, Oktar didn't seem to intend violence, and Rosneft trying to assassinate Simon every few weeks has been more on our minds.'

Shakiso was unblinking. 'Why do this to yourselves? And this mysterious Simon Adaro?' She looked around the café. 'Building solar plants in the desert seems very remote from all this corporate stuff.'

'Simon enjoys playing around,' he started.

'You lovers?' shocking even herself. 'Sorry, that's rude of me.'

'We were classmates in school,' said Hollis, laughing. 'Adaro, Agado, alphabetized surnames and old-fashioned seating arrangements. I certainly would have wanted to, but he's not, and after. . .' His face was a mixture of sorrow and regret, his eyes focused on the past. 'We are good friends, though. I meant, he likes starting things, the more unusual the better. I like running things. We make a good partnership.

'Simon decided, for reasons of his own, that he wanted to take on Rosneft. Simon's brother is the lead engineer at the Mars colony, and Simon asked if he had anything to help with his problem.'

'All the billionaires are buddies?'

'Something like that,' he smiled. 'You'll find that no one goes to Mars to be wealthy. There are only eighty-three of them, and their lives are dangerous and unpleasant. Hardly the stuff of aspirational dreams. Many of their senior technical folks are old friends. They sent over some designs, and I think you know what Simon has been up to?'

'If you don't mind my asking, what are you supposed to be doing for Climate?' His eyes were curious.

Shakiso laughed, pushing her hair back from her forehead. 'Not at all. A long time ago, Climate ran agricultural adaptation projects. Drought, civil war and Ansar Dine mean there are now almost three hundred seeker camps across Africa. We expanded our role to build the core infrastructure at UNHCR camps, operate their schools and set up their farms. We manage thirty of them in West Africa.

'All of that relies on people actually turning up in the camps. Over the last few months, they've been emptying. We have no idea where the seekers are planning to go, but they're currently heading north and collecting along the southern border of the desert. The fear from our government sponsors is that they may all try to cross the Sahara. And that is before you consider that no one has any idea what to do if the millions of seekers already sitting on the beach in North Africa figure out how to cross the Mediterranean.

'Frieda called me because I've been yelling at her for years that treating camps as temporary accommodation for seekers is a failure, and now they're scared enough to try something else.'

'What will you do differently?'

'I won't know until I get there,' she grinned. 'I was weaned on this stuff, Hollis. I'm an aid brat. My parents dragged me to every major conflict. I've had ringside seats. You're right about my industry's *hypocrisy. We've had a grand time enjoying the poverty porn without achieving anything. I don't know what I'll do, but if Europe won't let the seekers in, then I want to make sure they have a reason to build new lives wherever they end up.'*

'Well, if there is anything we can do, you know where I am.'

She took his right hand in hers and squeezed it. 'Thank you, Hollis, I might need that.'

'Where do you go now?' he asked.

'Senegal,' she said.

'The place of the genii,' he said, smiling.

'What's that?'

'When we first flew our main printer into Saint-Louis, it wouldn't work. The thing is designed to survive a direct missile blast. There was nothing wrong with it, but it sat there like a chunk of stone. We were told it was because we had not introduced ourselves to the genii, or explained our mission, or made any of the appropriate offerings.'

'What did you do?'

'We put the printer in the middle of a local football stadium, invited every drummer we could find and threw a massive festival that you could hear halfway across the country. Suddenly, towards the end of the ceremony, with the printer covered in milk and oil and goodness knows what else, it started working.'

'That's hilarious,' she said, laughing.

'Maybe,' he said, nodding. 'Simon seems to take the genii seriously. Every new farm gets its own ceremony.' He smiled once more. 'How's your French?'

'Terrible. I've got this app that's supposed to help . . .' She was momentarily distracted as a muscular young man in a tight white T-shirt stood and waved to friends as he left. Hollis followed her gaze and grinned.

'Boyfriend-looks,' he said.

'Meaning?' she asked, laughing.

'Well, there are two types of good-looking man. There's the one you want to be, and the one you want to have sex with. That lad's the boy-friend type.'

'Which one's Simon?'

'The man you want to be,' he laughed. 'And I genuinely worry about when you two meet. You're exactly his type. All that youthful athletic sex appeal.'

'Hey,' she said, slapping him on the arm. 'Tell me about you guys. I tried looking you up, but you're cyphers. I can't find pictures of you two. Even this building: lots of offices, a rather discreet private hospital, and you guys only seem to use the top floor.'

'I use the top floor,' he said. 'Simon lives on the Thames, when he's here. Wealth can buy a great deal of anonymity. There are more than enough people wanting to be in the public eye without needing to be entertained by a crippled man struggling out of bed in the morning.'

'Can't it be fixed? I would have thought?'

'It's not a money problem,' he said, sadly. 'The nature of my injury and current medical techniques –' smiling '– I'm told I will probably walk again in the next ten years.'

'How did it happen?' She hesitated, 'If you're comfortable telling me?'

'You would have been a child, I think,' he said, his eyes distant. 'England wasn't a kind place back then. Everything felt like it was in monochrome and about the only thing that gave life colour was that I'd never been so in love.'

It was the year the old Thames Advance Barrier had finally failed, and Wet London had flooded for good. The year England had lost the Ashes for the twelfth year in a row, and the Conservative Party had won their fourth consecutive election on a platform of nationalism and 'traditional' values.

'Traditional, in their case, meant bringing back hanging, and conscription for all school-leaving boys. Our year would be the first *to go into the army, but first we had to be suitably indoctrinated.*

'Once a week, we would march across the Millennium Bridge and up and down on the grass outside the Tate. All the old men would salute us. All the old women would clap. None of these people had ever been to war. I have no idea what they thought they were cheering. It was madness.

'There were a group of us: Simon, Zhi, Tiémoko, Trevor and myself. Scholarship boys, immigrants, minorities. Outsiders amongst the sons of the elite. Trevor and I became lovers, and Simon was the first person we told.' His eyes clouded. *'Do you remember what it was like being a teenager, and being with your closest friends and just – laughing – all the time? That was us.*

'We knew what England was becoming, but it felt so remote. Amongst all these privileged children, we thought we could make fun of it.

'One afternoon, when we were supposed to be marching, it was pouring. We thought the school might flood again. They led all the boys, almost a thousand of us, into the hall. There was a teacher who led the cadets. Mattison. Scrawny, ugly man. Always smelled of gin and cherry pipe tobacco. His clothes seemed to drag on him. The same diarrhoea-green trousers which hung over his knees, like he was carrying lead weights around in his pockets.

'He started ranting at us. About the Poles and the Muslims and the Blacks. How they were all out to get us, the white English, and that it was our duty to defend the realm. I remember him saying, "When you see that foreigner outside your house, they're waiting. When you're not there, they're going to rape your mother, rape your sister and kill your dog." Out of one of his pockets, he dragged this fat steel chain. At the end was a bunch of keys as big as your fist. "See these keys? No kike can steal these keys without me noticing!"'

Hollis looked at his hands, flat on the table, damp. He rubbed them together, like a caress.

'I thought it was funny. Dug Trevor and Simon in the ribs, and we

laughed about it, but then we looked around. Every one of the other boys was sitting there with this look of such frightening intensity. You knew they believed it too.

'That's the scary thing, isn't it? Only once the demagogues reveal themselves do you discover how many of the people around you are similarly possessed with hatred.

'Mattison was there to tell us about a compulsory camp all the form six boys had to go on. We were going to learn how to shoot, and get to play toy soldiers in the countryside. A few weeks later, two big military trucks waited outside the gates for us. Trevor and I ended up in the one, and Simon in the other. We drove out of London to the green belt, on to some farm and then along dirt roads.

'It was raining, and the ground was muddy and slippery. The soldiers organizing things were probably only a year older than us. They decided to race across one of the fields.

'They overrode the controls. I don't think any of them really knew how to drive.'

Hollis coughed, his eyes blurred. Shakiso sat quietly, saying nothing, her jaw clenched.

'Our truck hit a hole, or a rock. No one was ever sure. It flipped. There was only a canvas deck over us. Boys thrown everywhere. A few of us trapped underneath and dragged.

'When I woke up, I couldn't move. I started screaming. A boy whispered in my ear, "Stay still, please, stay still." There were three of them holding me down, one of them with my head so tightly in his hands. Simon had stabilized me and organized these boys to hold me steady. I couldn't see him or anything but the sky raining down on me.

'Trevor was badly hurt. His heart stopped, and Simon was trying to resuscitate him. It took an hour for the paramedics to arrive. A shortage of vehicles. Simon never stopped. The medics had to drag him off. I heard him screaming at them.

'They –' wiping his eyes '– Trevor . . .

'I was in hospital for weeks. Simon was there every day. We had journalists come through, politicians. We never really understood what was happening, dealing with our own grief. Outside, everything was changing.

'Twelve boys died, thirty hospitalized. Four, like me, maimed for life. Hundreds of thousands gathered in the streets outside parliament and near the hospital. I could see their candles all through the night from the hospital window. I remember them singing and how strange it felt to know they were singing for me and the others in wards nearby.

'And it was one of those moments where a small thing catalyzes something hidden and unseen that was probably changing all along. It permitted those who didn't support the bigotry to find each other. You can say what you like about the pettiness of the English, they do love their children. People took a look at the future they were choosing and stepped back from the edge.'

Shakiso had spent most of her childhood outside Europe. 'I never knew what happened. I mean, I know the government fell and the Liberals came in. Ten years later, England joined Germany in the Federation. It seemed like one of those "and then a miracle happened" things, but I never really paid attention in class.'

'I take something from that. Trevor died and the country became a slightly kinder place. I am grateful to be alive. But Simon,' he shook his head, 'I don't think he has ever forgiven.'

11

'If ever an epic saga is written about my life, they'll call this part the Ballad of the Nodder and the Leaner,' thought Shakiso, as she gritted her teeth and tried to imagine somewhere cooler, more spacious, and less a concentrated miasma of humanity.

On her left was the young man she had named the Leaner. He had fallen asleep the moment he sat down and was now moistly ensconced on her shoulder. He was wearing a black vest of abstract vintage and his skin stuck uncomfortably to hers.

On her right was another young man. The Nodder had been kind enough to lean against the wall of the bus, but he was wearing a peak cap clad in very shiny, very heavy stainless steel. His head traced the arc of an ancient typewriter, back and forth, the brim clouting her on the head and neck with every carriage-return.

If she could extricate her arms, she was giving serious consideration to knocking that cap out the open window.

Tuft glared at her miserably. She was crouched inside a cage that must have originally been used to contain a set of incontinent piglets. She had also been muzzled and licked at it in frustration.

'Don't look at me like that,' Shakiso said. 'I tried to get you to stay in London, but you had a hissy fit.'

She had arrived in Dakar the previous evening and promptly got subsumed – despite most vehicles on the road being automated – inside an enormous traffic jam, which everyone had decided to have a huge discussion about, their shouting voices accompanied by the percussion of banging drums and clanging metal.

Several flatbed trucks had pushed through, bedecked in people all howling over amplifiers while surrounded by drummers and singers. Children clung to the sides, hurling sweets and leaflets at anyone nearby. Her taxi had ended up plastered in posters indicating her robust support for every last one of the candidates.

The sleepy looking concierge at the hotel had said, 'It is the elections,' as if that explained everything. She was too tired to do more than nod.

She had a vague recollection that her room may, or may not, have had a sea view. It certainly had a rancid sea smell.

Her wake-up call had been at three a.m., and she was at the long-distance bus station an hour later.

With Tuft on a leash, and her small backpack securely in place, she had barged through the bedlam. She could have arranged for a driver from Ballou, their main seeker camp on the border, to meet her, but she had wanted to get a sense of the country as quickly as possible. She also had no intention of letting the camp know she was on her way. Best she see the place as it was, without them primping it up for the boss.

Each bus was as battered as the last, windowless and treadless, yet each uniquely painted in bright patterns which wove and danced across their corrugated and corroding metal body panels.

Within moments she had been picked up by a grey-bearded man wearing a black kufi skull-cap and a pair of thick plastic spectacles cloudy with dirt and polishing.

'You go to Bakel?'

'Nearby, yes. How full is your bus?'

None of the vehicles would leave until they could no longer cram another paying customer inside. At that time of morning, it should not take long to fill, but she had no wish to end up waiting for hours if she could find one leaving immediately.

'Only three more. Your cat must go on the roof,' he had said. They

71

followed his arm as he had pointed. Three goats were already tied there on top of bursting square blocks of merchandise, standing upright and facing forward. The goats were terrified into silence.

'No way; she goes inside with me.'

The man had made a dismissive waving motion with his hands followed by a clucking noise, and then shouted, 'Yela, yela, bring that,' pointing at a cage. 'You put her in this, you go inside.' Dismissing her with another gesture.

She had squeezed herself into the last remaining seat at the front, propping a seething Tuft on top of a stack of suitcases, while luggage, chickens and the last few passengers had mashed themselves inside. Looking over her shoulder, she had seen a young man in a diving mask, snorkel and shower cap quietly reading. He had noticed her and looked up, staring open-mouthed at the unusual sight of a strawberry-blonde white woman on a bus.

The man in the black kufi skull-cap had returned, pushing a young girl into a space near the sliding door where she sat grinning at Shakiso. She had thumped the red button on the small dashboard. A klaxon had wailed and the last stragglers hurled themselves inside. She had waved at the ambivalent black kufi skull-cap, turned the key to start the bus, and promptly folded herself inside a blanket and went to sleep as the vehicle eased its way out of the rank.

They had turned right on to the street, up on to the kerb, and had come to a cantankerous stop.

Immediately, two men had lifted away a panel at the front of the bus, dropped it on to the pavement with a clatter. Heads had popped out the windows as passengers yelled encouragement or passed comment.

An elderly man, his back bent and his eyes behind thick magnifying lenses, had wobbled out of the building, a boy carrying a wooden seat and a bag of tools alongside him. As others had held lights, he had begun to desolder a panel from the circuitry inside, a gas-operated *micro-soldering iron bunched in one hand, a multimeter pen in the other. He had pulled the panel loose, stared at it in disdain and thrown it into his tool bag, muttering as he sorted through similar panels as burned and scarred as the original.*

Children carrying bags of roasted peanuts had shouted up at passengers who pointed their cards out to indicate their interest. The children called out and a man in a religious thobe had rushed over. He held a cash receiver and passengers had tapped their cards, the children promptly handing them their purchases. The man had rushed off with his cash receiver, back into the taxi rank.

Shakiso had watched in amused horror as, finally satisfied, the old man had begun to solder another circuit panel into the bus. He grabbed a can of something and sprayed it over the circuitry. The bus had jolted and begun to idle. Heads had returned inside as the body panel was tied back in place.

The old man had hobbled off, his chair and tools following behind him, towards another bus which had shuddered to a halt just behind theirs.

Their bus had pulled into the traffic and headed out of the city.

Several hours went by during which they eventually reached the outskirts of the city, and she tried breathing through her ears as she pondered hurling the Nodder out the window along with his cap.

Sunrise added a new torture. She had deliberately chosen the front seat so she could have a full view of the road and landscape. Now the sun was burning straight into her. She squeezed her hands into her bag, stuck under the seat between her legs, and fed her rims up to her face. She slotted polarized sunglass lenses in place. Mercifully, they cut the glare.

Somewhere over the wind-roar coming through the windows she thought she could hear the traumatized bleating of the goats on the roof.

It was still two weeks before the rains were due to arrive, and the long dry was at its peak. Dust hung like a heat haze. The ground glowed unbroken with inedible glass-dry bleached grassland. Bent dusky trees, interspersed with haunting baobabs, were scattered over the grey-red-brown blankness of the plains.

Every twenty minutes or so they passed through villages huddled beneath carefully tended trees, each with its small mosque, each with its own cobbled-together shaded tunnel or arch, under which hundreds of goats stood exhausted, their hips and shoulders angular under gaunt skin. Each cluster of houses tended irrigated plots fed by solar-powered water pumps and a mesh of greying drip-feed pipes running over the surface.

Improbably piled along the tree-cooled roadside within each village were heaps of watermelons attended by tiny old women seated beneath enormous branded umbrellas.

Goods convoys heaving with green beans, carrots, cherry tomatoes and vast trays of salad leaves went scorching past. Some were refrigerated, and Shakiso could only guess at the contents and wonder how much of anything made it to its destination.

'Is this being imported?' she asked the Nodder, now mercifully awake and controlling the steel menace on his head. He stared at her blankly.

'He does not speak English,' said the Leaner, rousing himself and stretching. He looked her up and down. 'You flew in from Europe?' he asked.

She nodded.

'You would have come down over Saint-Louis. Did you look out over the ocean?'

She nodded again, confused.

'Did you see the floating city? All the boats surrounding those big plastic domes under the water?'

Startled recognition. She had seen that and was wondering what they were up to.

The Leaner looked proud. 'They are farming there all year round. It does not get too hot under the waves. My brother grows strawberries for your English cream. I was growing lettuce and tomatoes.'

'Where does the water come from? You can't grow that in salt,' she said.

He scoffed. 'We have those Chinese –' he searched for the English word, shook his head '– you pump seawater in one side and fresh water comes out the other. They are small and you only need one for six domes.'

'Wait, wait, wait,' she said. 'Those are really expensive, and where do you even get electricity from?'

He shrugged. 'Sablière.'

'I don't understand.'

'The solar farm in the desert. Their cable was cut, and now they sell their electricity to us. They put a substation right there on the water for us.'

Shakiso was nodding manically as she remembered. Hollis had told her they tried running a transmission line up the coast. That was before they had discovered Rosneft had a fleet of submersibles waiting for them. Their line would have gone out right next to Saint-Louis. Hollis had not said anything about selling power locally, but it made sense. It was not as if they had much storage capacity, and some income must be better than nothing.

'Where are you going?' she asked the Leaner. 'Are you visiting family?'

He shook his head. 'I am going to Aroundu to set up business. Too much competition in Saint-Louis now, and I get seasick,' he said. 'Where are you going?'

'I'm heading to the seeker camp near Ballou,' she said.

He shrugged, had not heard of it.

'What's in Aroundu?' she asked.

He looked at her as a patronizing teacher to an ignorant child. He gestured at the bus, at the congestion on the highway. 'We are all going to Aroundu,' he said simply. 'You will see.'

He stretched again, exhausted by the conversation, and was soon asleep, leaning on her shoulder. The Nodder had, similarly, returned to his typing exercises.

She rubbed the control nub in her ear to restart her French lessons, muttering – not for the first time – that she wished the sods would finish their words so she could have any chance of figuring out what they were saying.

The lack of context was also deeply concerning. Why exactly is the man's wife alone? Why are the children giving a butterfly? And under what circumstances will it ever be appropriate to say, 'I am amongst you'?

She was lapsing into a heat-fuddled haze, thinking about boulangeries and gateaux, when the landscape changed as the houses got closer together. She swiped on her rims to bring up a map overlay and could see they were arriving in Tambacounda. She would have thirty minutes at the bus station as they changed batteries and everyone had a chance to get something to eat.

Already there was shouting and movement as people collected their belongings and attempted to shove them back into various bags. Tuft mewled.

'I'll let you out in few minutes, youngster,' she said.

As the bus found an open berth, the girl emerged from beneath her blanket and turned the key. The bus settled, and the doors opened.

The Nodder and Leaner helped her carry Tuft's cage outside and stood stoically as the cat stretched and leaped up on to Shakiso for a hug. The two men decided that the foreign woman was clearly a naïf and needed care.

'Come,' said the Leaner. 'We go there. They have good thiébo.'

Shakiso fiddled through the language app. Somewhere there was a toggle that would get it to do simultaneous translation. She was soon sitting in a loud restaurant stuffed with plastic furniture. The two men washed their hands, and she guiltily followed.

Thiébo turned out to be grilled fish on a bed of broken rice cooked in tomato and tamarind. Shakiso lost herself in the pungent flavours with a happy sigh, wiped the last few grains off the bowl with a finger. Tuft was licking the floor around her bowl.

They heard the klaxons sound and raced back to the bus. Tuft turned into a spitting, furious ball of teeth when they tried to get her back in her cage. Eventually, all crammed in, the bus left.

Shakiso tried staying awake, but the heat and confinement settled on her, and soon she joined the Nodder and Leaner in slumber.

She was woken in Goudiry, where they changed batteries again and grabbed an early dinner. More thiébo, this time with lamb. Tuft sulked.

As they left Goudiry, she noticed large groups of people camped around cooking fires under trees along the highway. There were young children playing football or wrestling, goats weaving their way through the people, and men and women packing goods into wagons or on to donkeys and cows. There was well-ordered chaos and an underlying tension.

'They are the seekers,' said the Nodder, Shakiso's embeds simultaneously translating and surprising her. His voice was treacle-dark, rich and deep. Like a continent.

'So many?' she asked. She said the words softly, and the translation was spoken via small speakers embedded in her rims.

'Yes. They seek freedom. They will make their crossing into the Maghreb soon.'

Seekers. People of no nation: the millions fleeing violence and persecution and famine in the vast conflict zones of central and eastern Africa. The millions she had been tasked with stopping before their journey took them across the Mediterranean to the fearful lands beyond.

Shakiso could see that they were preparing to move and assumed they travelled at night when it was cooler.

77

'Where do these seekers go now?'

'Some will settle along the river. Some to Nouadhibou in Mauritania. They will wait until after the flooding recedes, and cross the Senegal River at Rosso, there to walk along the waters.'

'How do they cross the desert?'

He smiled knowingly. 'They must buy safe passage from Ansar Dine, and hope that they are not betrayed. If they are blessed, perhaps the shayāṭīn will even provide water for their journey.'

'Ansar Dine controls the desert?'

'And all who cross.'

He rubbed a small leather pouch strapped to his wrist. Its surface was shiny and the stitching tight around the edges.

'What is that?' she asked.

'It is my gris-gris. To ask the genii to keep me safe as I travel.' He untied the string holding it in place and took her wrist.

She pulled away. 'No, no. That is yours. I don't—'

He grinned and lifted his T-shirt, revealing a wrestler's muscular stomach and five different long and whip-like gris-gris knotted around his waist. 'I have many. Please. It is my gift.'

Grinning, she held out her left wrist and he deftly knotted it.

'Merci beaucoup,' she said, experimenting with the French words.

'It is my privilege,' he said, touching his heart with his hand.

The baboon lowers his hand, releasing the naked man who collapses to the floor, weeping. The past is revealed, and all the journeys of interconnecting lives have converged on this point. His curiosity is not yet sated, but this man can reveal no more.

Oktar Samboa cringes.

Light and the scrape of boot on stone.

The guards are coming.

12

Samboa is dragged screaming and fighting along the corridor. The walls and floor are smooth underfoot, almost as if polished, and the ceiling is jagged with spikes.

One of the men doing the dragging tires of the struggle and smashes down with the blunt end of his steel flashlight. The corridor is momentarily a criss-crossing light-show of yellow beams through the speleothems hanging above them.

Samboa thinks he sees the baboon following behind, his eyes offering no solace for his torment.

A cell door rattles open, the clang of metal on stone crashing and rebounding down the corridor.

Samboa is flung inside and the door smashed shut.

He groans as he lies on the floor in the corrosive darkness.

'You're wasting energy,' says a voice. 'We may get a chance to fight. Save it till then.'

'Who's that?'

'And be careful when you stand. Some of these stalactites are uncomfortable.'

'Who is that?' he spits again.

'You could try asking nicely, Oktar.'

'Adaro? You bastard! This is your fault.'

Samboa scrambles to his feet, charging at the voice, and clouts his forehead on a thick corded stalactite. He collapses to the floor, panting.

'Rest. They don't feed us enough to waste energy on anger.'

'Where are we? What's going on? No one will talk to me.'

'They're not interested in you. You have nothing they want.'

'The planes?'

'Yes.'

Samboa slows his breathing.

'Is there water here?'

'Head back to the cage door. On the left is the soil bucket, on the right is the water. Don't get those confused.'

Samboa feels his way back towards the metal bars on the door. The baboon is sitting before it, holding his two-headed metal stave in his lap. Samboa whimpers.

'It's to the right,' says Simon.

'Can't you see it?' Samboa's voice in agony.

'What?' asks Simon.

'The beast,' the word ending in a shuddering hiss.

Curiosity from the man at the back of the cave. 'What beast?'

'Like a baboon. Can't you see it?'

'No, I see nothing.'

Samboa sobs.

'Have some water and rest,' says Simon gently.

Samboa crawls past the baboon, feeling above his head for any further obstacles. The bucket is half full, and he drinks greedily.

'What's the baboon doing?' asks Simon.

'Nothing. He's watching me. Messing inside my head. I saw fragments of things. You. The plane crash. And . . .' his voice trailing as he deliberately refuses to mention her. 'What is it?'

'You hope to save this country and you know so little about it?'

'Tell me,' urgency and despair.

'You know about the genii?'

'That superstitious nonsense?'

'I wouldn't mock them. You're the one seeing one of their emissaries.'

'What?'

'The baboon. I think it's Gaw Goŋ. He's supposed to be the greatest of genii storytellers.'

'What does he want with me?'

'Stories. He collects stories for the genii.'

'Why me? Why doesn't he help?'

'It's a possession cult. He needs a pliable mind. You probably caught his attention with all your screaming. And he won't help. He'll be interested in seeing what we do, not in arranging a particular end. His stories need endings. They don't have to be happy ones.'

Samboa regards the baboon sitting quietly. He closes his eyes, his mind grappling with the strangeness, and decides that what cannot be explained must be ignored.

Ragged breathing. Eventually, 'Where are we?'

'We're in a karst cave, probably about two or three hundred metres below ground. There'll be a larger underground city down here somewhere too.'

'For what?'

'Ansar Dine. We're in one of their fortresses.'

Samboa starts sobbing, all his fight draining away. 'We're going to die then,' he says.

'That isn't the plan,' says Simon. 'Cheer up, son. We're not dead yet. At the very least, Gaw Goŋ expects us to have an interesting future or he wouldn't be here.'

'Why did they take us? What did you do to those seekers?'

Troubled silence. 'You shouldn't have followed me.'

'You had them killed,' his voice an accusation.

'Yes,' he pauses, his voice soft. 'I spent months setting this up. What price the life of a single child against destroying Ansar Dine?'

'You're not trying to destroy them; you're trying to bribe them,' says Samboa.

Silence once more, as if a response is being weighed and set aside.

'Why don't you tell them where the planes are? Then we can get out of here.'

'You think it will be that simple?' A sigh. 'They haven't asked yet. Which is why there is no point in wasting energy.'

'Why not? What're they waiting for?'

'Abdallah Ag Ghaly.'

Samboa retches, his flesh clammy and cold.

Simon continues, pushing at Samboa's rising fear. It is possible his plan can still be salvaged. 'He's a bit paranoid and doesn't want anyone else to speak to me before he is in control. Our splendid accommodation is thanks to that one fact, otherwise we'd probably be with his other prisoners.'

Samboa's voice trembling and weak, 'Does that give us time? Your people will be trying to find you?'

'If Ansar Dine were that easy to find, you don't think it would have happened already? There are satellites permanently pointed at the Sahara and Maghreb. A surface gathering as large as this fortress would be obvious.'

'So they hide out in these karsts?'

'I wouldn't call it hiding. This is where they live. There are ancient aquifers all across the desert. There must be thousands of dry cave systems they can use.'

'And Ag Ghaly is coming here?'

'Yes, but I don't think the karsts are linked, otherwise he'd have been here two weeks ago. It could be days, it could be weeks. I don't know.'

'You've got implants, though? They can find us?' Samboa still hoping there is some way out, some way he can survive.

'There's no connection underground. Anyway, they let you keep yours?'

A sob from across the cave.

'Tore them out of your ears?'

'Yes. So why put us together now?'

'No idea. They're not speaking to me either.'

'How do you know all this, then?'

Silence from the other end.

'Adaro?'

'Yes. I'm thinking.'

A sigh.

'Why did you follow me?'

'I want you out of Senegal and into a jail cell.' Samboa's voice is acid. 'I heard a rumour something had been found in the desert, something that Ansar Dine wanted, and I met these seekers who said they had seen the planes. They turned back when they ran out of water. I heard from one of the Rosneft guys that you were trying to meet Ansar Dine to bribe them with the details, so I followed you. If the jihadis didn't want my information, I was hoping I could get proof of your dealing with terrorists. A picture of you meeting jihadis is all I need.'

'Well, looks like you got your wish.'

Samboa whimpers. 'Not like this.'

'Who else knows about this?'

Samboa does not notice the hint of malice in the query, or the other drawing nearer in the darkness.

'A few other seekers. No one knows what's in the planes.'

'And you? Do you know where they are?'

'No, I didn't need to. Those seekers would have had to show them on a map. What are you doing here, Adaro?'

The other man relaxing, leaning back against the wall. His plan is safe. 'You and Rosneft have been very successful at keeping me out of Morocco and Tunisia. I can no longer go by sea. What's left?'

'Libya.'

'So you see, I have no choice but to negotiate with them. Give them what they want in exchange for getting my line through the desert,' the lie coming easily now that Samboa cannot betray him.

'That's why I have to stop you,' says Samboa.

Laughter from the hidden man. Rich, bright, filling the gloom with light and hope.

'Rosneft I understand. It's their death struggle,' he says. 'What's your deal?'

Samboa is panting, his rage overwhelming him. 'I've seen your type. You come to these countries. You take what you want and you leave. We have to stay. We have to deal with the fallout.'

'No,' says Simon. 'You've seen *a* type, and your own bigotry prevents you from seeing how I'm different. And I didn't make the problem.'

'I know that; I'm not a fool,' he says through grinding teeth. 'But the sooner Rosneft get what they want, both of you will leave and we can do what we always do.'

'Sure, trap people in camps so you can feel like a benevolent hero and continue living like local royalty. That's a lovely estate you have up there on the ridge in Dakar.'

'What! You—' standing and smashing his head into a pillar right above his head.

'Ouch. That one's a killer. Sit down, Oktar, please. You're not the only one who wishes you hadn't involved yourself in this.'

Silence.

Breathing, and then a sad sigh.

'I'm sorry, Oktar,' says the hidden man.

'You're not sorry.'

'They won't have put us together for no reason. Ag Ghaly must have arrived.'

'So? You'll talk to him. Come to some arrangement, and they'll let us go.'

'It's not that simple.'

'They're terrorists, Adaro. I'm sure you two will get on just fine. Kindred spirits.'

'Terror is simply how they keep control.'

'They're genocidal maniacs.'

'Only to keep control. They smuggle drugs and people, and they dominate the whole of the Sahara. Anything that offers them more money is good. Anything that threatens their control is bad. I do both.'

'So, you'll tell them where the planes are and then pay them to cross the desert. They'll let us go.'

'It was never about the planes or the solar farms, Oktar. Not for me. They're a means to . . .' He hesitates, 'I'm sorry, Oktar. Ag Ghaly will want to scare me. I claimed you were a colleague when they captured us. He's going to assume he can control me through hurting you.'

'What?' Samboa panicked and breathing hard.

'If I can, do you want me to pass on any message to anyone? And, please, hurry. I think they will be here soon.'

'What?' confused, his mind a frozen blank.

'Oktar?'

Light beams deep along the corridor leading to the cell.

'I can't . . .' stumbling, his thoughts cascading.

A hand, holding his, pulling him close. He clings tightly, his body numb and cold.

He weeps, holding on to warmth.

'I'm sorry, Oktar,' holding his head, feeling his terror.

A shattering noise as the gate is unlocked, light slashing down on them, wrenching Samboa away and smashing the door closed again.

The baboon watches as the naked man is dragged away. He listens to Samboa's wailing long after the retreating flashlights are no longer visible.

When all he can hear is the even breathing of the blue-eyed man, he draws a line in the air, opening a path back to the deep desert and stepping through towards the bright searing reflection of a tree-lined ouahe.

The tributaries of this story have united; now he will follow their waters where they lead.

13

All along the dusty track south, Shakiso has the feeling of going the wrong way. People are moving any direction but towards the camp.

The taxi owner is asleep, stretched out over the front seats, his kufi skull-cap pulled down to shield his eyes. Shakiso is in the back with Tuft sprawled over her lap, panting in the early-morning heat. Behind her, hanging in the window, are a pair of baby shoes, tied shut and serving as a gris-gris protecting against accidentally knocking over a child.

Shakiso was forced to stay overnight in Bakel at a small hotel near the bus station. It was an unquiet experience, leaving her and Tuft grumpy this morning. None of the taxis were prepared to take her to the Ballou camp. It was either too far, or they were uncomfortable transporting a wildcat as a passenger. She waved her card in the air and counted francs until car doors started opening.

The road is slippery with dust, but they are soon at Ballou and passing through the main gates, alongside ranks of white shipping containers shielded from the sun underneath raised sheets of UN-blue shade-cloth. One of the UNHCR camp guards points her in the direction of the Climate school, and she pays off the taxi.

She has never been to a camp that has been so curiously somnolent.

The prefabricated school buildings extend for half a kilometre, endless classrooms designed to cater for thousands of students. Their spare rooms, sufficient to build three more schools, are collapsed and piled high alongside the main administrative building.

There is a muffled silence, many of the classrooms empty and the presence of lessons betrayed only by the bubbling-chiming warble of children calling out to their teachers.

Shakiso passes through the entrance hall, past the canteen and up to the main office. There is no one around.

Moussa Konte, their camp controller, is half-asleep with his console on his lap and his feet up on the desk as she strolls in, Tuft at her heels.

'Howdy, I'm your new boss,' she says as he scrambles to his feet, knocking his console on to the floor and just catching his mug before it wanders off the table.

'That busy, huh?' she laughs, leaning against the door frame, light from the corridor burnishing her hair to a coppery glow.

'I am so sorry, Ms Collard. I was only expecting you next week,' as he bounces around his office trying to straighten the picture on the wall featuring an unlikely frozen lake, and the small lamp in the corner. There is little else, besides the ceiling fan, to keep him entertained.

'That's fine, Moussa. Please call me Shak. I wanted to get in early and see the operation for myself,' offering her hand and shaking his with a warm smile.

'How did you get here? I could have sent a car,' he asks, recovering his composure.

'I took a bus from Dakar.'

'A bus!' He says the word as if she had told him she had arrived by flying canoe.

'Show me around. I want to see how the world's largest UNHCR mission is managing with hardly any seekers to look after.'

Moussa looks miserably at the floor. 'We do have some seekers,' he tries.

'And most of them appear to be children,' she says. 'Show me around, Moussa.'

He guides her outside, past the long rows of warehouses and out towards the area allocated for living quarters.

The ground is flattened and criss-crossed with pathways where once hundreds of thousands of people walked and gathered. Tangles of thorn-tree brushwood form fences lining the paths. Most are falling apart through lack of daily maintenance, and it is possible to see through to the abandoned and collapsed tents and homesteads within.

A few remaining occupied tents are gathered close to the feeding and medical centres. Pipes for water and sanitation run back and forth into washing booths.

Otherwise, it is silent.

Shakiso stares out at the remnants of the camp, astonished at both its vastness and emptiness.

'What do you all do all day long?' she asks, genuinely intrigued. 'I'd be out of my mind with boredom within a morning. Hell, I'm bored just looking at it.'

Moussa shrugs.

'Where has everyone gone? Give me numbers,' she says.

'There are only a handful of arrivals each day. Usually families with sick children, or someone needing an infection treated. Broken bones. They stay until the patient is well, then they go,' He sighs, fidgeting. 'You guessed correctly. This is a dormitory town. The children are here only to go to school, and they leave on weekends.'

She stares at the tents, gnawing at her top lip.

'I passed maybe five hundred seekers on my way here from

Bakel this morning. There are probably thousands more passing by along the river. Most are only looking for somewhere safe to stay. Very, very few are going to put their lives in the hands of Ansar Dine and try crossing the desert.'

Moussa nods and shrugs.

'A year ago, there were half a million people here. Where is everyone going, Moussa?'

He shrugs morosely.

Tuft spots a mouse moving in the shade near one of the tents and stalks silently across the dust.

'Moussa, I'm not Oktar. You can drop the helpless Haratine act for me,' she says.

He meets her gaze for the first time, his eyes curious and alert.

'If I open those warehouses, what will I see?'

He grins. 'Nothing out of the ordinary, and nothing missing.'

She strides ahead and hauls open one of the immense sliding doors. Inside are bags of coarse-ground maize piled high on pallets. They rise to the ceiling, an impenetrable fortress cut with narrow access routes.

She walks into the nearest tunnel, running her hands on either side along the sacks. Moussa chases along behind her and stumbles into her as she abruptly stops. She slips a knife out of her boot and slashes at one of the bags.

Moussa shouts, and then sighs, as sand pours out on to the ground.

'It gets replaced,' he says. 'We are waiting even now for a shipment from the cooperative in Tambacounda. We do not do it for the money.'

'I guessed that much, Moussa,' she says gently, her eyes filled with compassion and humour.

'How did you know?' he asks.

'I would have done the same thing if I'd been stuck here,' she says. 'You're sending food where it's needed, not where it's supposed to be. Why don't you explain the situation?'

He shrugs and leans back on the sacks. 'They go to Aroundu. About one thousand people a day are arriving in Aroundu. They do not want to be here at Ballou. They know what life in the camps is like, and they have no expectation of ever returning home.'

'And Aroundu can't feed and house all those people, so you help out? Who else is involved here? Climate can't have enough to go round.'

Moussa grins. 'We are a long way from Geneva,' he says. 'Oxfam and Médecins Sans Frontières refuse, but UNHCR and most of the others are involved.'

'Why not just move the camp there? I assume you're giving the stuff away?'

'We sell it to the seekers settling in Aroundu and the other new cities. They have no wish for charity. The other seekers receive a free grain allowance from our barges all along the river. And,' he says, 'you know why we cannot move the camp.'

'Politics,' she sighs, slumping back on the wall of probably-sand. 'So, who's in charge there? Who do I need to speak to?'

'There is no one in charge. There are tribal councils, national groups, but no central organization.'

'Moussa, you're working with someone there. That person will be awfully well connected,' she says, raising her eyebrows.

He grins, nodding. 'There is someone. He works in the city centre.'

'Well, let's go,' she says, replacing the knife in her boot and leading the way outside.

'Ah, Tuft, you had breakfast already,' she says, as the caracal comes barrelling towards her, her whiskers tinged with blood.

Moussa steps back nervously, but the cat jumps up demanding a scratch.

'She's OK, just rub her behind the ears. She loves it.'

Moussa scratches gingerly on top of her head and is rewarded with a dry and abrasive lick.

A long shade-cloth keeps the camp vehicles in some semblance of coolness. They get into Moussa's white Range Rover, and he keys in the route.

'I still don't understand, though. What's so special about Aroundu?'

'You'll see,' he says, and laughs, turning up the music and humming along.

They travel back along the same dirt track, turning off to the right before they reach the highway. After twenty minutes, they bump up on to a new sealed road, merging into the frenetic flow of vehicles and passing, along the embankment, the parallel congestion of people pulling carts or carrying suitcases.

A shaded arch high over the road appears before them, sandbags stacked in walls on both kerb sides, and a cluster of white shipping containers modified as offices between them. UN-blue shade-cloth spans the walls.

'Let me guess. That's from Ballou?' studying the activity intensely as they pass.

Senegalese soldiers stare into the vehicle and let them pass under the arch unimpeded. She cranes her neck and spots a queue of people being scanned. It all looks friendly, though. Almost celebratory.

The land gets greener as they travel. Trees and grasses growing, with small thatched huts or clay-walled houses roofed with branches and plastic. She recognizes Climate tents grouped near a solar water pump and what looks to be a group of new arrivals setting up more tents nearby.

Trucks filled with food are going in and others with ceramics, clothing and furniture are coming out. Along the road, groups of workmen are controlling machines printing cable and raising it up on to concrete posts. From within a cloud of dust, she can see an automated grader laying out a road, with surveyors pointing in different directions and shouting at each other. A massive brick-works is churning out blocks which are being yanked away before they are properly annealed. Houses are being built, and every-where she looks something is being constructed.

Shakiso scratches her head. 'It's like they're trying to win the world championship for city-building?'

'We must leave the car here,' says Moussa, as they pull in to a clearing filled with buses and cars. 'There are too many trucks, and it will be easier.'

All around the car park are stalls selling clothing and food. A queue of people are waiting to board a battered shuttle bus. Moussa taps a transparent plastic card on to a reader as they get on.

They end up between two trucks ferrying sand, shedding a fine mist which soon covers everyone inside.

The bus stops in a wide market square. A line of shipping containers fills up the one end, while shops and restaurants make up the rest. In the middle, hundreds of people are standing before goods piled on wagons or beneath shade-cloth, demanding the attention of the drifting river of people.

The sand trucks are emptying their load directly behind the containers.

'What's going on there? Those containers don't look like offices?'

She ignores Moussa trying to steer her towards a nearby office block. Tuft sticks to her heels, looking nervous amid the noise and activity.

The containers form a half-circle. The sand is being poured on to a conveyer belt which winds up and into a silo. At the bottom of the hopper, more conveyers lead towards the containers which, up close, turn out to be machines.

'This is all Chinese?' she asks.

'Yes. They are printers.'

'How does anyone here afford these? This is cutting-edge stuff.'

A tiny Chinese woman steps out of a nearby office, surrounded by a group of men all shouting in a cavalcade of languages, their translators struggling to keep track. The woman looks Shakiso up and down, decides she is not buying anything and ignores her.

A Chinese boy runs up to her and whispers in her ear. He releases his tightly balled fist and pours sand into her cupped hand. Her eyes harden as she massages it between her fingers.

She turns on one of the men following her, flings the sand in his face and issues a volley of abuse which needs no translation.

Clearly the sand is of an inferior quality. The man, twice her size, flinches away from her.

'Right, I need to understand this,' says Shakiso.

They cross the market again towards a double-storey brick building painted brown and cream. It looks as if it has only recently been constructed, with scaffolding still leaning precipitously over the rear walls. There is a large satellite dish on the roof and a group of people leaning over the upper balcony having a noisy coffee break.

Shakiso stares at the familiar Achenia logo bolted across the front.

A man in an eggshell-blue boubou is walking down the stairs towards them as they go inside, across a tiled floor that already has paths worn in its thin glaze.

'Moussa,' he shouts, smiling. 'And you must be Ms Collard?'

Shakiso raises an eyebrow. 'You let him know we were coming?'

'Of course,' says Moussa. 'This is Tiémoko Diagne.'

'Mr Diagne, you're the man with all the answers?'

Tiémoko sways his head from side to side. 'Perhaps. Come, there is space to talk upstairs. It is cooler, and maybe quieter.'

They climb the stairs and enter his office. The table is covered in a large console showing a multicoloured survey chart, and a large format printer is spooling out more plans behind it. A young woman is sitting at the desk, paper files open and scattered as she makes notes and captures the written scrawl in her console.

'I am sorry, Viviane, could we meet here for a few minutes?' asks Tiémoko.

She smiles shyly, quickly gathers a few things, and slips out.

'I'm afraid these offices are now far too small for us. Not so much anyone's office as everyone's,' he says. 'Please, sit as best you can.'

Shakiso continues to stand, walking over to the window and looking out over the market, the city centre filled with trucks, and the horizon surmounted by scaffolding and cranes.

'I've worked in some of the worst hellholes in the world filled with people escaping places that are even worse,' she says quietly. 'Any roots they put down are shallow. They sure don't do that –' gesturing out the window.

'This is like a gold rush. China almost eighty years ago.'

She stares at the printers, watching as components are gathered and stacked before being carted away.

'Whatever you're doing here is awesome. But, guys, why is this a secret?'

The two men look uncomfortable.

'What we are doing is not supported by any government,' says Tiémoko. 'Certainly not Senegal's. You crossed the border coming in. We are on land between three countries and not administered by any of them. Seekers are welcome to enter the city, but the border guards will not let them return.

'You know your own organization's political difficulties here. We are a private company, but ours are little different. There is no clear guidance for any of us,' he shrugs. 'It is no secret, but the legal vacuum makes us all a little careful.'

Shakiso taps her teeth, considering the complexity.

'What's the trigger? Why here?'

Tiémoko looks bashful. 'Opportunism,' he says. 'This area is too dry to farm. A few nomadic herders cross here during the wet, but the towns are abandoned.'

'And you work for Achenia, huh?' says Shakiso, interrupting. 'What are you guys doing here? I was told your main office is based in Saint-Louis.'

He shakes his head. 'Simon is based in Saint-Louis. He likes it there. Most of us work here.

'I'm usually at the university in Dakar. About eighteen months ago, Simon got hold of me to help him buy land in the desert.'

'How do you know him?'

Tiémoko smiles. 'It is a long story. We were in business many years ago, and before that we were in the same year in school.'

'Wonderful,' she says. 'I really have to meet this guy.'

'Inshallah,' he says, his eyes clouding as he thinks of Simon in the hands of Ansar Dine. 'He flew me out, over the border, in his helicopter. There is no property register for any of the land in Mauritania, but Senegal administers it on behalf of the UN. We did a survey, and he bought ten sections. Five hundred square kilometres. He has continued to buy land since then.'

Tiémoko stands and points at a map on the wall. 'There is nothing there. I do not think anyone has tried to farm there in fifty years. Even the nomads avoid it. I asked him, what will you do? He said, grow desert roses.'

'The solar farms,' says Shakiso. 'You're distributing electricity here? Why?'

'We have no choice. Eight months ago, I went to visit Récolte Rouge, our nearest solar farm to Bakel. The land will make you weep. Nothing lives there. It could be the moon.

'Simon and I met with the engineers to discuss the connection of a transmission system running west to link the farms. We travelled back to Aroundu together before he went on to Saint-Louis. We had coffee in a restaurant across the market from here.

'We were talking, remembering old times. I do not remember what —' he pauses. 'There was an explosion, and the front wall of the restaurant vanished. I was thrown to the back. I could hear nothing. Someone was shooting into the room. I was helpless. Simon dragged me to safety. He was wearing some sort of metal-gel armour and shielded me with his body even as bullets hit him.'

'That seems suicidal of him,' says Shakiso. 'The armour's good, but it won't stop your head being blown off.'

'Fortunately, the shooters decided to retreat before that happened,' smiles Tiémoko. 'Simon called in his personal protection drones. It seems these shooters managed to evade them, which is why we were attacked at all.'

Shakiso whistles. 'I've heard of those. Usually only for presidents. And no ordinary assassins if they can mask themselves.'

'We assume it was Rosneft.' Tiémoko shrugs. 'We heard later that our line printer had been sabotaged at sea, and that Morocco and Tunisia would no longer let us run our lines through.

'I was in hospital in Bakel for a few days with concussion. Simon came to visit me, and we discussed what we could do. We cannot store the electricity for long, and the first of our farms are operating. We cannot officially distribute our electricity to Ballou,' he shrugs. 'Politics. The Senegalese government is not comfortable encouraging the arrival of more seekers, but they recognize that our people are exhausted with absorbing so many, so we decided to build a town over the border. Here.'

Moussa nods. 'At first it was a few water pumps. People were trying to farm again. The difficulty is it is too hot and crops will not grow. This is a border zone, though, and thousands of people move back and forth between Mali, Gambia, Nigeria. Before we knew it, people were setting up shops here. The seekers began to settle. Three months ago, the Chinese woman arrived. She brought one of those sand vitrification printers. She needed cheap electricity and lots of sand. Overnight, thousands of people started arriving and building. The camp began to empty, and you have seen what is left.'

'We became very worried about cholera,' says Tiémoko. 'We could not get food or supplies here fast enough for all the people arriving. I came to an arrangement with the camp. They would supply us with water purifiers, sanitation processors, food and tents, and we could send people to the clinic and school.'

Shakiso leans against the wall, enjoying its relative coolness.

'Does Oktar know of this?' she asks.

Moussa looks genuinely amused. 'Of course not. Too busy chasing donors in Geneva, or trying to convince anyone who will listen that the solar farms are just exploiting us. He hasn't been to Ballou in months.'

'That sounds like Oktar,' she says. 'So, what would help?'

Tiémoko points out the window. 'People arrive so quickly, we must avoid disease. Put your resources into development of the sanitation systems.'

Moussa nods and joins in. 'We must also move the hospital and school here,' he says. 'If we move the school, I am sure we can convince Médecins Sans Frontières to bring the hospital.'

'That's good, yes,' says Shakiso. 'What else?'

Moussa and Tiémoko exchange a glance.

'The farmers have need of heat-resistant seed. Break the embargo,' says Tiémoko.

Shakiso grins. 'You mean piss off our associates at Oxfam and Greenpeace and cause a media brain seizure back home?'

Africa and Europe are the only regions in the world where genetically modified agriculture is severely limited. Europe through their continuing superstition about the technology, and Africa as a result of trade boycotts and pressure from the Europeans who comprise their largest donors and export market. It is an informal embargo, but it holds nevertheless.

'I'm not disagreeing,' says Shakiso, grinning as she imagines the outrage. 'I know nothing else will grow here. But we need to make it impossible to stop. I can't take this risk for one small town, no matter how big it's getting. If we can distribute seed to support millions of farmers, then I think I can unlock some funds. We'll need to range far beyond Senegal, though.'

'The rains will be here in two weeks. They must start planting. How will we buy and distribute so much seed, even if we could find a seller?' asks Moussa.

Shakiso's grin stretches even further. 'I think Tiémoko may have some ideas.'

'Please!' Viviane, the young woman who was in the office earlier, is standing red-faced at the door, her eyes wide and terrified. 'Come quickly. Something is happening.'

She turns and rushes down the stairs into the lobby followed by the others. Her terror is contagious.

Someone has set up a projector, and an image fills the entrance hall.

Eight men, all in black, their faces obscured beneath black turbans, are walking across an erg field. Red-burned sand dunes stretch into memory behind them. They carry black flags bearing a white slogan: أنصار الدين.

Ansar Dine.

There is nothing but the sound of the desert: sand, hissing like steam from a kettle, shifting endlessly. A plainchant choir begins to sing, at once chilling and beautiful.

The camera shifts to where another group of black-clad figures are arriving, dragging a white man. He is naked, and his body is beaten and bleeding. They can see him screaming and sobbing and fighting them, sand shrouding him as he pounds the earth.

A man begins to speak.

14

His ear buzzes, waking him. Hollis drags himself from slumber.

It is three a.m.

He squeezes Adrià's thigh and pulls himself upright. He massages his legs, returning circulation to them, checking his toes for warmth. The chair rolls into position, and he lifts his legs over and slides himself in.

A few moments of tugging and manoeuvring, and he is dressed in a robe and loose-fitting track pants.

Adrià groggily surfaces from beneath the covers, shakes his head and smiles.

'You should have woken me, darling. I would have helped,' he says, his voice crackly with sleep.

Hollis smiles. 'Nonsense. You have surgery later. Stay there. It's Sam. I'll make you tea when I'm done.'

'Not until noon. I'm awake. You go speak to him. I'll bring you tea,' says Adrià.

Shaking his head, Hollis rolls silently to the media room. He keeps the lighting subdued as he answers the call.

Sam materializes standing in the centre of the room. He looks exhausted. His eyes bloodshot.

Hollis prepares himself for the usual frustrations of direct communication with the Martian colony. He pulls up a console so he can take notes during the inevitable delays between each of them saying anything.

'Hi,' says Sam. 'Sorry to wake you. Obviously . . . that poor bastard. What a terrible way to . . .' Sam rubs his eyes. Someone behind him brings in a cup of coffee, and Hollis recognizes Nizena, one of the young agronomists.

'Some good news. Our shuttle reached Earth orbit a few hours ago, and we have the new direct relay in place to boost our bandwidth. With that and the current orbital distance, our delay should be down to about twelve minutes. That's almost real-time for us. I think we were pushing forty-five minutes last time we spoke? Thanks, Nizena,' he says, accepting the mug.

Hollis sighs in relief. The delay in each direction has meant that a simple conversation could take hours to complete.

'General news on our side. We will have a planned five hundred new colonists coming back on the shuttle. Not all of them will make it through training, so we'll see where we are in a year. We're able to absorb them, but it makes us aware of how careful our calculations have to be. Nizena is busy sorting out some problems we had in one of the grow tubes. It's not serious, and we should be on track to feed all our new arrivals once that is in place.

'We're building as fast as we can, but obviously there's a huge waiting list. A lot of those people expect to die on Mars, just not of starvation.' He laughs softly.

'I'm glad to get the telemetry from the solar farms. You're getting tremendous yields there. I'm very pleased, and it looks as if the effective work-life of the roses will be about forty years.'

Sam looks up from his notes. Even across 225 million kilometres, he looks devastated.

'I know Si's reasoning, but . . . was this risk necessary? Are you sure you can get him out? Alive?'

He pauses and stares at where he knows Hollis will be.

'Over.'

Transmission passes to Hollis. Behind him, Adrià sneaks in, kisses him on the shoulder and leaves a mug of tea on the table.

Hollis runs his fingers across his face, pinching his jaw. The images yesterday were distressing.

Ansar Dine are experts at this. Too few people for the satellites to pick up and gone too soon for them to find. As much of a nightmare enigma as before.

'*Thus do we take the lives of all apostates. We are true defenders of the faith, and all should fear the whisper of our blades on the wind.*'

The voice was instantly identified as Abdallah Ag Ghaly, although it is unclear whether he was amongst the group, causing serious people in letter agencies across the world to spill the sour travesty they drink instead of coffee and shout for analysis.

Many of those calls came to Hollis.

Adrià had tried to pull him away, but he felt he owed the man being tortured the recognition of his suffering.

On the video footage, Oktar Samboa was beaten, his arms and legs broken with metal clubs. The cracking and tearing of bone and flesh heard even over his wailing. He was held still as his testicles were hacked off. They raised him up, baring his neck, as someone who may have been Ag Ghaly punched a hole into his throat.

The men holding Oktar's head arched his neck further, opening up his gasping, bubbling trachea. They roughly shoved a glass funnel into the hole.

A brown bottle was handed to Ag Ghaly. He pulled out the glass stopper and poured the contents into Oktar's torn throat.

The acid began to bubble and burn immediately, and Oktar was flung to the ground.

He thrashed in the sand, trying to reach for his chest, gasping and sucking, his broken arms and legs flailing.

He took an interminable time to die.

Only then did the broadcast end.

Hollis takes a deep breath, pushing the memory aside, takes another breath, calming himself.

He nods his head and begins recording.

'Sam, I'm pleased to hear from you,' he says. 'Very pleased about the delivery, and cutting transmission time will make this a lot easier. I'll begin liaising with your team and, all going well, we'll be ready next year to lift everything up the elevator.'

He hesitates before continuing. 'I agree. What happened yesterday was horrific. I have no idea how that poor man got himself involved with this. Simon knew the risk he was taking and he felt it was the only way to . . .'

Hollis scratches his head and takes a sip of his cooling tea.

'I'm sorry. We're as close on this as we can be – Tiémoko is working with the Senegalese military for us – but you understand the difficulties as well as I do. Ansar Dine live by spectacle. They're impossible to find and deadly accordingly. Simon believed this was the only chance we would have.

'I've made the arrangements with Bradley over at Ziggurat. I had to remind him who pays his salary.'

It had been a strained conversation. As editor-in-chief of the connect's most popular news and entertainment feed, Bradley guards his privacy behind expensive pay-walls. Hollis had to pay £1,000 to cover a phone privacy block before Bradley would even answer his call. He had screamed 'editorial interference', but Hollis simply pointed out that it was an important story, surely worth interrupting all their subscribers' feeds to broadcast. Bradley threatened to resign. Hollis encouraged him to do so. 'After all,' he thinks, 'what's the point of being majority shareholder if one can't throw around a little authority every now and then?'

'I have a call with Zhi straight after this,' he continues, 'and we'll complete the arrangements. I should be catching him before he goes on one of those long lunches of his.

'I know Zhi still wants to join you there. As soon as you get a proper bar and dancing girls,' he smiles.

'I've had calls from the Chinese, the French. They're waking up to our efforts to change a situation they've expediently frozen in place for half a century. Ag Ghaly enforces a semblance of order out there, and they're not happy with us. Fortunately, the Chinese are more interested in our printer, and France has spent all their money in the Med.

'We're dependent on Simon, but we should have resolution in the next day or so. Everything comes down to whether Ag Ghaly takes the bait.

'Sam, we're watching over him. You know I love him as much as you do.

'Over.'

He has almost half an hour to wait for Sam to receive his message, respond, and transmit his reply back. Written mail would be easier, but there is solace in being able to see and hear each other.

He checks whether Zhi is still available and rolls back into the bedroom. Adrià has fallen asleep again. Hollis stares at him, smiling, gently strokes his head.

His ear buzzes, and he heads back to the media room.

'Thank you, Hollis. I'm grateful for all you do. I know Si has said he'll come here when he's dead –' smiling '– and you're not too keen either, but, should you change your mind, you know we have space for you and Adrià. Give him a big hug from me. Good luck, and speak to you in a few days.

'Out.'

It is not the most efficient way for either of them to communicate, but Hollis feels better for the contact.

He calls Zhi and a phantom of his office blends into the media desk.

'Hollis,' he says, beaming. He stands, a tall, elegantly suited man beside an enormous desk, and performs a little jig. His way of saying hello.

'*Nǐ zěnme yàng?*' says Hollis.

'Your diction is terrible. Please give up. My Engrish is mush berrer,' he says, laughing and playing up his accent.

'Zhi—'

Zhi nods. 'I'm sorry,' he says. 'We must get Simon home first.'

'I'm . . . forgive me. I know you take this seriously.'

Zhi smiles again. 'Everything is ready. We have a team available on shift, and I have booked time on Tienhe-54 for the processing.'

'Does your government know what you're up to? I don't want you suddenly blocked.'

'The most glorious Standing Committee of the Central Political Bureau of the Communist Party of China is desirous of deepening its most auspicious ties with the Maghreb and Sahel,' he says, his tone mocking. 'They understand the value of the opportunity being opened up, and they're being very supportive. There will be no problem.'

'Thank you. And you? How are you doing?'

Zhi's face hardens. 'I saw those butchers yesterday. I owe Simon a great debt. It will be paid.'

15

'What is this place, Duruji?' asks Khalil, feeling safer if he stays close to the older man.

Duruji is as much a product of Ansar Dine's schools as Khalil. He knows only what he was told when he first saw these ghostly towns during his earliest excursions above ground.

'They were places of the *kuffār* where they dug in the rock for valuable metals.'

Below them, visible in valleys and channels amongst the dunes, are rooftops and buildings, gaps where doors and windows once kept the sand out. What was once a small mining town is now an abandoned collection of abstract walls and buckled machinery protruding from the sand.

'Where did they go, Duruji?'

'Ansar Dine came, and we took back the desert for our people. We must be careful here. There are machines within the sand as well as hidden pits. The land can be unstable.'

They walk down the bank of a dune and over a short stretch of asphalt appearing like an island on the rocky ground, climbing again on the other side.

The men are spread out in a long line with Duruji leading, checking their direction occasionally from a small map at his waist.

As he reaches the summit of a dune, he hears a shouted gasp behind him.

'Boss!'

A shrieking, tearing whine and then a roar as the sand gives way and six men vanish into a sinkhole opening beneath them. He sees Khalil reach out instinctively and grab the man behind him as he teeters on the edge of the pit.

There is a thud as the falling men hit a solid floor.

Silence as each remains still.

Is that the end of it?

Wood splinters somewhere in the shadows below.

A scream which rapidly dwindles.

The sand was obscuring the fragile roof of the headroom covering the machinery over the main elevator shaft down into the mine. They have fallen on to wooden beams left as a short-term and rudimentary means to secure the hole when the mine was evacuated. One cracked and has given way.

Duruji looks quickly across the pit, counting. Six men above, at least five in the pit.

'Do not move,' he shouts to the men in the shadows below him. Then, 'Who has the rope?'

They look for the man who carries it.

Faint whispers, a shout from beneath, 'He fell, Duruji.'

Duruji curses. He gestures for his remaining men to move back carefully from the edge.

'We will go to the town and see if there is anything we may use there. Move away from the hole if you can,' he shouts to the trapped men.

Duruji leads the way back over the dunes and into the sub-merged town.

'Search everywhere,' he says. 'It does not need to be a rope. We can use old clothes, pipes, anything that will hold the weight of the others.'

Each of the men heads in different directions, digging their way through sand-filled doorways.

Khalil follows behind Duruji like a lost pup.

The town looks to have been abandoned forty years ago, when Abdallah Ag Ghaly's father first took the desert for Ansar Dine and made of it his empire. The miners who fled these isolated dormitory villages were not expecting to be gone for long and left most of their belongings behind.

Not all the towns were looted. Duruji is hoping that this one escaped notice.

There are offices, yellowed and blank papers flickering out of drawers in overturned tables. Bedrooms, mattresses but no bedding. A bowling and games hall. Everything buried in drifts of sand.

Khalil looks oddly at peace.

'What is it?' asks Duruji.

'It is quiet here,' says the young man. 'I cannot hear the howling, and I have not seen Gaw Goŋ or the strange painted dog.'

Duruji feels relieved. The youth's mania seems to be subsiding.

He leads them back outside and on to the road between the buildings. One of the men is up ahead, emerging from a long, low building. He waves at them and shouts.

'Boss, I have found something.'

The remaining men gather in what seems to have been the mine canteen. There are metal tables and chairs scattered over a concrete floor. The building is in a pocket between the dunes and has suffered little damage. Some of the glass in the windows is still in place, and there is almost no sand.

'Curtains,' says the man who called them. 'Look, boss.' He is gleaming with pride.

'Good. That is good. Let us hope they are not damaged.'

They pull the curtains roughly from their railings, piling them up in the centre of the room. Two of the men begin yanking on each length, testing its strength against their own weight. Some tear; most hold.

After a few hours' work, they have a long length of thick, corded fabric. The knots are large and unwieldy, but it should hold. The sun is setting red and gold through the open windows of the canteen.

'Quickly,' says Duruji. 'We must get to them while it is still light.'

They retrace their way through the buildings, following their footsteps left in the sand from earlier in the day. These are already fading under the steady wind blowing over the surface.

At the top of the pit, Duruji shouts to the waiting men, 'We are here. Are you all there?'

'Yes, boss,' comes the relieved answering call.

'We are going to throw down a rope. Only one can climb. The next must wait until I call.'

Duruji points and the bulky fabric is slowly pushed over the edge, down the slope and into the drop below. Three of the men loop the remaining length around their waists, dig their legs into the sand behind the edge. Once they are sure of their grip, they nod to Duruji.

'The first may climb,' he shouts.

They hear a gentle scrabble below, and the line goes taut.

A clanking and clambering as the man braces himself against the corrugated-iron walls of the headroom and hauls himself up and out. His head appears over the drop, and he drags himself up the remaining slope. Duruji grabs his hand and embraces him.

'Mohamoud, it is good to see you,' smiling for the first time.

One by one the men lever themselves up out of the pit. The last man moans as he drags himself.

'It is my leg, Duruji. It is hurt.'

'We will stay here tonight,' says Duruji. 'That building where we found the curtains is whole. I hope your leg is easier in the morning.'

It is dark by the time they return to the canteen.

Hidden from random passing drones, Duruji turns on his flash-light as the man with the injured leg rolls up his trousers. He runs his hand over the injury. It is swollen, but the flesh is otherwise unmarked.

'It is not broken. You should be well in the morning.'

A celebratory shout from the kitchen.

'Look, boss, canned peaches. And this one looks like beef,' says a man carrying several catering-sized cans in his arms.

They right various tables and pile up the cans.

Then they stare at them for a bit.

'Do you think they will be safe to eat, boss?' asks one of the men, looking nervous.

Duruji shrugs and puts out his hand for the can opener that Khalil is holding like a shield. He opens a can of corned beef and sniffs it.

'You will try it,' handing it to Khalil.

All the men stare at him, their eyes glittering in the torchlight. Khalil looks at them apprehensively, then shoves one of his enormous fingers into the can and gingerly scoops a chunk into his mouth.

They watch as he chews.

'How is it?' asks one.

'It is the best food I have tasted in weeks,' he says, hurriedly scooping the rest into his mouth.

With a roar, the men set upon the remaining cans, and a feast of vegetables, beef and fruit is rapidly consumed. A night without having to eat their food bars is a treasure, and they have no intention of wasting it.

Afterwards, bloated and drowsy, they stretch out on the floor and prepare to sleep. One of the men digs inside his bag and produces a small console.

'Where did you get that?' asks another. The men gather around it in delight.

'The seekers,' he says, waving his hand as if to belittle the effort involved.

The devices do not work in the karst cities, where living beneath tons of rock prevents any link to the connect. They are, in any case, illegal. The only news or entertainment permitted is tightly controlled by Ag Ghaly and the other ruling families of Ansar Dine.

Soldiers, though, are trusted to go to the surface, and many seekers do carry such communications devices. Khalil is soon introduced to the pleasures of self-promotion as the men pose for images. They are careful not to share any real information regarding their activities or location. There are too many legends of fools who posted their position only to end up broadcasting their final moments minutes later as drones turned them to glass.

Having reconfirmed their dominance of a tiny piece of the connect, the men turn to entertainment. A few moments of fiddling and they find a news broadcast. The men stare at the alien images of green forests and dense, glass-clad cities above ground. They are unable to understand the language spoken but are happy to watch the unfamiliar stream of people and places.

For them, Ansar Dine is their world and the Ag Ghaly family have always been their rulers. As hard as their lives as soldiers may be, they are amongst the elite and – back in the karst cities – they enjoy the privileges of their position. They have no reason to want for anything more, and the lives of these apostates are as remote and foreign as watching Saturday-morning children's cartoons, and no more threatening.

Duruji has seen these things before, and they hold little interest for him. He is cleaning his rifle and emptying his boots of sand as he considers his map and the four days before they reach the city where they are to meet Ag Ghaly.

'Boss, boss, come look,' says one of the men in excitement.

On the screen, a flushed-looking news anchor is speaking far too quickly to be understood. The scene cuts to a sandy blur, and then the image of a naked man standing calmly surrounded by black-turbaned jihadis deep within the erg field.

'It is us, boss, it is us!'

16

Light beams at the far end of the corridor, followed by grudging murmurs.

'I am glad this is to be the last of it,' says the man at the rear as he avoids a stalagmite rising from the floor.

A few days ago, they were made to set up a projector and then forced the prisoner to watch as Oktar was tortured. The man said nothing, his blue eyes glowing and inscrutable in the reflected light of the feed.

'He is a shayāṭīn,' the leading man shivering as he twists past a jutting baffle in the rock. 'Our Janab should never have brought him here.'

The blue-eyed man stands at the bars, calmly waiting for them. The two guards wear the same expressions of mild discomfort at his silent strength.

'*Ma d'tolahat*,' says Simon, politely.

One of the men makes a sound as if he is about to reply, but the other thumps him. They motion with the flashlight. Move.

He obliges, walking between them: one in front, one behind.

The corridor winds for half a kilometre. In a few places, they must duck to get under stalactites or squeeze through narrow crevasses. Each of the guards breathes a silent request that this be the final occasion to make this clumsy journey.

The air gradually lightens, becoming less stiflingly humid.

There is a faint blue reflection on the walls. The smell of sweat and ordure, of something rotten, gets worse.

Simon is expecting the cave, when they get there, to be vast. He imagines something the size of a football stadium, or even an aircraft carrier.

This is bigger.

He stops for a moment, absorbing its scale and orientating himself within it. The rear guard shoves him forwards.

There are magnificent caves. Caves filled with startling light reflecting in still crystal pools. Frozen waterfalls, speleothems forming pearls or rimstone dams. Shimmering lakes of water so clear that the blind white fish living there appear to be flying through the air.

This cave, though, is hideous.

Muted luminance comes from strings of low-energy fairy lights bolted to the walls and strung up on free-standing posts forming avenues along the cave floor. Tents huddle between clusters of timber houses, clay walls and thatch roofs. Despite the air rebreathers, like vaulted pillars dispersed throughout the cave, there is an overwhelming smell of cooking and rotting waste.

Shadows cast grotesque forms between the speleothems, creating a disjointed pattern that jars distance and induces vertigo and disorientation. The ragged cave ceiling, so far above, is thick with soot and cooking grease; everything else is covered in pasty brownish-white dust.

Simon follows as his guards continue down through the shanty town. His nakedness is ignored. Just another slave amongst the many. There are women and children equally naked, their bodies covered in welts and scars, busy cleaning or carrying. They do not look up, staring rigidly at the ground.

Men in their black djellabas and turbans sit chattering loudly in groups around piles of stacked green leaves. Their laughter and conversation have the manic edge of the qat addict. It travels poorly, and they must be growing it somewhere down here.

There are weapons everywhere. Each man has at least an AK-47, and there are grenade launchers and a scattering of Igla-AD14s.

A group of men are playing pétanque in a rough sandy oblong alongside a wide trench, steel bars bolted across the serrated edges of the pit forming a cage. The men occasionally glance down into the trench as they play. A man standing on the metal bars, urinating through them, shouts as the guards walk past.

'What is it?' asks the leading guard.

'Let the toubab choose for us,' says the man, completing his ablutions and spitting down through the bars on to the prisoners hiding beneath the edges of the pit below. A thick rope is looped over one of the bars, and a man hangs loosely from it in the middle of the makeshift prison. His wrists and ankles are tied together behind his back and then knotted so that his chest and stomach rest lightly upon the floor, his arms and legs arched above him. He is drenched in urine and excrement. Simon cannot tell if he is still alive.

'Our Janab wants him. We have no time to wait,' says the guard.

'He will be dead soon enough. Let him choose for us,' says the man.

The other guard shrugs and prods Simon forwards to the pétanque terrain. With much shouting, all the men wanting to play come forward and each contributes a single item to create a pile of small, random objects: a bottle cap, a piece of wood, a bit of wire, a torn piece of paper.

One of the players, a man wearing a sweaty T-shirt improbably bearing the statement 'Daddy's girl', holds up three fingers and jabs Simon in the shoulder. 'Choose three,' he says.

Simon picks three things: a bent metal fork, a key and a bottle cap. He continues, creating sets, each a randomly selected three-man team to compete in their never-ending league. Shouts and excitement as the men form up, until all are chosen.

One of the men, wearing a neatly pressed djellaba, picks up the orange jack and flings it towards the far end of the terrain. Each of the players collects two metal boules lying near the edge of the arena, and the game begins.

'They are,' thinks Simon, 'extremely good.'

The shooters fling their boules with devastating accuracy, knocking others out of the terrain. One old man, his djellaba hanging like the remnants of a fire and his eyes straying in different directions, fingers the prayer beads of his *misbaḥah* before each shot and waves them above his head after every success.

With the camaraderie and cheers of support, the careful measurement of distance between the jack and boules using an ancient tape measure, it is almost as if the trench does not exist. Except Simon can still smell it, and imagines he can hear sobbing from below.

One of the guards pushes him, and they continue through the village and into a narrower tunnel at the far end. There is little movement of people until they reach a junction. Tunnels run off in different directions, some going up, others down. A sinkhole to their left is contained within a bracket of steel bars. Two men are waiting there, in front of a caged elevator.

The guards hand him over and wander back the way they came.

'*Ma d'tolahat,*' says Simon, politely.

The two new guards scowl and prod him into the elevator.

One presses and holds the up button. The elevator moves slowly.

They pass two levels, each filled with people incuriously going about their day.

A small delegation are waiting at the third.

It is difficult to tell, given the near-identical black garb, but these guards' djellabas appear more opulent, of finer cloth. The air up here is cleaner, almost fresh. The lighting is brighter and more discreet. Effort has been made to grade the tunnels.

'Ma d'tolahat,' says Simon as he is handed on once more. Still ignored.

This section is a quiet residential area. The karst is a network of tunnels and cavities. Smaller chambers are sealed with elaborate doors. Larger ones have been subdivided into different homes.

They reach a door guarded by two immense figures. Simon looks up at them admiringly. Ancient societies would simply have made them gods. Here they serve as door ornaments.

One of them knocks on the carved wooden door.

It is opened by a small, naked boy. His eyes are flat, dead, and a fresh red hand-shaped weal crosses his face. He walks stiffly past them and on down the passage, a thin trickle of blood trailing down the backs of his legs.

A thin, tall, greying man is standing behind a desk, adjusting his white djellaba. Abdallah Ag Ghaly ignores Simon and his two enormous guards. He starts speaking, as if continuing a conversation he was already having in his head.

'The great failure of your crusader culture is that it does not recognize the power of faith. We have brought a billion people into the *ummah*, and have conquered territory greater than any empire in the last four thousand years. All you are left with is your apostasy, your brutality and your decadence.'

'While you live a life of grandeur in a hole in the ground, selling drugs, raping children and living in your own effluent? I must say, I do like what you've done with the place. Quite gothic. Originally I thought the grotesques were excellent, but then I realized that's just your head—'

As Simon is speaking, Ag Ghaly walks calmly around his desk and strikes him across the face.

Simon does not move, continuing to smile, his eyes bright and alert.

'This act may impress the guards on the lower levels, but they are superstitious peasants. I know better. I can smell your fear,' says Ag Ghaly.

'Really?' says Simon, looking around. 'Are you sure it isn't you guys? Between us, you all smell a little rank. The lack of water—'

Ag Ghaly strikes him again, splitting his lower lip.

Simon's smile becomes even more beatific.

'You know, when you're this close, I can't tell which is worse, your face or your breath. You—'

Ag Ghaly screams in fury and slaps. First his right hand, then his left, back and forth, even as Simon ducks slightly so that most of the blows land painlessly on the top of his head.

The two giants stand impassively on either side throughout Ag Ghaly's wholly ineffective flailing. Simon gets the feeling they must be deaf and mute.

'You will fear me. Before you die. You will fear me,' says Ag Ghaly, panting. 'Your friend learned this, even if he knew nothing else.' His face has turned slightly grey. 'You will fear me.' Sweat gleams on his dark, custard-like skin. He longs to torture this man, to hear him scream, to watch his flesh boil.

'No,' says Simon. 'I will not. That performance of yours with Oktar. Whatever I do, you think to repeat that with me. The outcome is already decided.'

Ag Ghaly grins. His teeth are stained chestnut-dark. 'Yes, you will tell me where the planes are. Then you will meet the same fate as your friend.'

'Why don't you ask your friends in the State Department?

Everyone knows. The French, the Chinese, even the Israelis. Oh, wait, that's right, you don't have any friends. Only slaves and lackeys—'

Screaming and slapping at him again. And then, the moment Simon has been anticipating, pushing for, the reason for the risk he has taken.

'Outside! Outside!' shouting and waving at the guards.

This time Simon is dragged until they get back to the elevator. A guard change, and the elevator is filled with people. The two mute giants remain behind.

'Obviously,' thinks Simon, 'they're impressive, but a deaf guard is useless for any actual defence.'

It becomes unpleasantly hot as they rise. The elevator stops in a shallow chamber filled with the machinery that runs the elevator. It looks as if it has been adapted from an old mine shaft. Here the heat imposes as a throbbing pulse.

A ramp runs up to a trapdoor.

Simon is surrounded by armed men wrapped in invisibility cloaks over their black djellabas and pushed up the ramp. Two of the men unhitch the door and raise it up and out. The light is bleach, the sand scorching.

Simon squeezes his eyes shut, seeing the red of his eyelids and gradually opening them. It takes almost a minute for the colours to resolve, and he notes that the others seem to be recovering more slowly than he. Many of the guards tremble, seeing demons in the shapes and blur as their eyes adapt.

He could, in the few seconds of liberty this presents, try to run.

The erg stretches off in all directions. There is no sound but sand shifting with the wind.

There is nowhere to go.

The guards adjust their turbans tightly across their mouths, ensure their cloaks cover them from any aerial observation, then walk Simon forward into a depression in the sand lower down from the trapdoor. Looking back, even this close, it is almost impossible to spot. Just another clump of shrubs. Unremarkable in the never-ending desert.

They continue onwards, to the top of a high dune and over the other side. Blindfolded and left, you would not know how to return even to the entrance.

Simon scans the faces of each of his guards where he can see them shaded beneath their cloaks. Looking man to man. Judging them. Searching their eyes.

They are young and afraid to be out in the open. If Ag Ghaly has a permanent guard, these are not them.

One of the men is carrying a broadcast camera which he sets up in the sand. The men nervously drop their cloaks and are directed by the cameraman until they are in place.

'That camera is not yet on,' says Ag Ghaly. 'Whether we have need of it depends on your answer.'

'What answer?'

Ag Ghaly slaps him.

'You know that which I seek.'

'Sure, but aren't I a little old for you? You seem to have your choice of little boys,' says Simon.

Several of the guards start beating him, Ag Ghaly screaming and slapping. There is little method to their attack, and the unrelenting heat soon leaves them sweating and exhausted.

'Very well,' says Ag Ghaly, as the men back away, their eyes betraying their fear, Simon standing much as he was before, a cut on one cheek and an expanding bruise across his left eye and forehead. 'We lost a convoy of planes in the desert. They carry $75 billion worth of heroin, and weaponry to equip my army. I want to know where they are. Tell me.'

121

Something clicks inside, and Simon stands up straight. His smile is of the benevolent and the blessed.

He stares straight at Ag Ghaly. His eyes glow, and they carry judgement.

'*Nit ku amul jom, amul dara*,' he says. 'The person who lacks honour, lacks everything.

'*You* may not be broadcasting, Abdallah, but that doesn't mean I'm not.'

On the crest of every dune surrounding them, people begin to appear. There are men and women and children. Each is wearing a small broadcast band on their heads. Each stares silently down at the men.

'I am Simon Adaro, and I brought you here,' he says.

The men look around nervously. One or two half raise their rifles, unsure how to react.

'I brought you, Abdelkrim Surkati, and you, Khalil Ibrahim,' turning and staring at each of the guards. One by one, he names them: Abdullahi Janaqow, Nouri al-Somali, Abdelhakim Tsouli, Mohamoud Hilal, Abdirahman Motii, Ahmad Jama, Musa Benotman, Younes Abusahmain, Noman Belhadj, Saleh Afrah.

The tableau of an unclothed man stripping away the protection of men hiding behind turbans and djellabas against the endless flesh of the erg. He stares at each, his strange blue eyes laying each man naked before the world.

'And I brought you, Abdallah Ag Ghaly,' holding his gaze where he stands in glowering silence.

'I brought you here to ask you: how would you wish to be remembered?

'You can no longer hide. You are known. You are seen.'

One of the youngest, Noman Belhadj, cries out. He throws aside his rifle and runs up the dune, pushing his way through the people standing there. The others hesitate, afraid to look at each other, afraid not to.

Each drops his gun and runs away, over the dune and back towards the entrance to their city.

Only Ag Ghaly remains.

He pulls a pistol from within his djellaba and points it at Simon, advancing on him.

'I don't know what you have done here,' he says. 'I am not like them. I am not a coward. I know how I wish to be remembered.'

Simon puts up his arm, as if to block the bullet.

Ag Ghaly simply rests his arm on it, the muzzle of the pistol against Simon's temple.

'My men will call for help. We will kill these peasants, and you will be dead,' tensing his finger.

Simon smiles.

'No.'

He thrusts his arm upwards, shifting his weight and slamming Ag Ghaly to the ground. The bullet is lost to the sky.

Sand flies up on the slopes as special forces troops cast aside their invisibility cloaks and rush down to Ag Ghaly.

The last thing he sees, before a hood passes over his head, is the glowing blue eyes weighing him in judgement.

II

OUR MEMORY LIKE DUST

Our ideals of liberty, equality and fraternity are being sacrificed to our prejudices and fears. All that will be left is a mess of weak and squabbling states that can only be the playthings of stronger nations. I beg of you, let us not allow Europe to be torn asunder.

Thérèse Fillon, European Union President, October 2022, speech broadcast two days before a French referendum on EU membership

This is a victory for the Conservative Party and a victory for the British people. Generations from now, our descendants will look back and wonder how anyone thought this European Union was ever a good idea. Today, we put a final nail in the coffin of that mistake.

Andrew Seymour, British Prime Minister, April 2030, statement outside Downing Street following the Berlin Minute formally dissolving the European Union

They are old and divided, and we are too generous with our power. My grandfather cautioned patience, but now is the time to put right the greatest disaster of the twentieth century. We will reverse the loss of the Soviet Union and of our authority over tens of millions of people. Put your prices up by a quarter and you will see. They can do nothing.

Leaked Rosneft correspondence, December 2045, allegedly from Oleg Shkrebnev, President of United Russian Federation

17

Even the dry dust sings when the rains return.

As temperatures rise, clouds mass over the ocean and Atlantic winds push them into the coast, where water falls in great big drenching clods. The earth drinks hungrily and quickly, like one permitted but a single annual feast, for the hivernage will last only briefly.

Sloughs and marigots fill, rivers rise, and water stampedes for the shore. Villages all along these ancient desert watercourses trap the fleeing waters in reservoirs and dykes, there to store what they need to use themselves, for their beasts and their crops. Lac de Guiers, upon which most of northern Senegal depends, fills and – for a time – the conflict between the sugar plantations, subsistence farmers, nomadic herders and cities subsides.

For water is scarce, the dry is long, and all struggle under the burning heat.

With the rains, migratory birds come sweeping in along the coast. Great clouds of pelicans and flamingos, garganey, shoveler and ruff. Many have crossed the deserts of the Mediterranean and the Sahara. They settle in the Djoudj wetland where they may rest: some to stay, some to travel again further south.

Their flight takes them over the surging banks of the Senegal River where small overloaded pirogues and boats cross back and forth, ferrying trade goods and people between the villages and farms on either side of what was once the border between Senegal and Mauritania.

One of these pirogues is travelling rapidly downriver, cutting across ferries and passing slower barges distributing food and medical supplies to thousands of seekers camped along the banks. It began its journey four days ago at the river confluence near Ballou, where the waters of the Falémé join those of the Senegal, and will reach the port city of Saint-Louis tomorrow.

Shakiso, leaning out from the bow, looks up to watch the scudding flocks overhead, exhilarated as the wind clutches at her hair and warm rain pools in the folds of her poncho. Tuft is curled in sleep beneath her waterproof, escaping spurts sloshing through tears in the awning over the boat as it rocks in the current.

'Mademoiselle,' says Mustapha, her guide and boat pilot, sitting miserably in a puddle alongside the motor. 'Where do you wish to stop? It is growing late.'

He had assumed their voyage would be leisurely. He would do a little fishing, meet with friends in villages along the way, perhaps do some trading. Instead they have hurtled along as if all the genii are upon them: on the river before dawn each morning and only stopping to rest upon the bank well after dark. And her curiosity? She asks questions of everyone. How long have they lived here? What do they farm? How much do they produce? If they are seekers, she asks even more questions. Where have they come from? What was their journey like? Where will they go next?

'That family we met said there's a big seeker gathering at Bakao. I think we can get there in two hours,' she says without looking back, grinning as she senses him shaking his head and crouching further within his sodden djellaba.

'Look to the seekers,' Moussa had said to her cryptically, seeing her off from Ballou. 'They may have a solution for our distribution problem.' There is plenty of grain available to buy and distribute, but Climate has too few boats and too many people to serve.

On the first morning, they had neared one of the Climate barges stopped along the river distributing propstock for farmers and grain for the seekers.

Dozens of boats had tied up alongside it, forming an impromptu market selling luxuries and reminders of all the distant places the seekers had fled: packets of *egusi* and *ogbona* spices, Malta Guinness from Liberia, bottles of fermented sesame seeds, and bags filled with everything from black beans to powdered yellow maize and pounded yam.

Each transaction was punctuated by the tapping of transparent cards: the same as those Shakiso saw used in Aroundu. She called Moussa immediately.

'Those are the Achenian payment cards?' she said.

'Yes. I thought you would find it interesting,' said Moussa.

'What's driving adoption? Everyone is using them.'

'A banking system for people no one will invest in, backed by a distributed international currency?'

Shakiso laughed. 'Fair enough.'

'People understand that Achenia only issues the card and that no one controls the currency. Their money is safe from any government and no one can take it from them.'

'And, let me guess, you think we can send them cash instead of distributing grain?'

Moussa was silent, and she could feel his tension hoping she will agree.

'We'll be accused of helping the seekers get to Europe,' musing on the risks.

'They sell the grain anyway, and the money we give is little. Our savings mean we can ensure more people are fed,' answered

Moussa. 'You know how difficult it is just to manage our work in the new cities. This way we won't have to spend so much of our time and resources managing distribution as well.'

She could see the chaos and frustration for herself. Seekers struggling to convince traders, their overwhelmed boats already sinking low in the water, to exchange their allowances of grain for goods. All anyone wants is cash.

'You have three months. Test what works and come back with a plan on how we implement this,' she had said.

Flecks of grey and gold dapple the river, its forested flanks growing darker as the sun sets. Through the trees and over the water comes the sound of drumming and singing and, as they round a bend, they near a seeker camp sprawled along the shore.

Mustapha drifts into the beach, nudging their craft between two other boats. He eases himself upright, drops over the side into knee-deep water, drags a muddy rope up on to the bank and anchors it to the shore.

'Mademoiselle,' he says, returning to the boat where Shakiso is collecting her backpack and preparing to carry Tuft. 'Same time tomorrow?' asked with a hint of despair that it will be far too early.

'Yes, same time,' hopping off the bow into the water. She deposits Tuft on the relatively dry sand above the beach and heads towards the loudest of the competing groups of singers. Tuft stretches and yawns, glares at the boat, and follows.

This camp is a strange hybrid of transience and permanence. Sandy paths are wide and hardened by countless passing feet. Tents abut thick-walled clay houses and improvised rooms of corrugated iron and plastic sheeting. Goats and children run and play in the narrow alleyways between the houses. An open muddy square tucked in amongst the houses and alive with the hoots and calls of young men and women playing football is surrounded by food stalls.

She queues at a tiny restaurant, squeezing in beneath their plastic awning to avoid the worst of the rain, and takes a seat on the bench before the cooks. The man and woman running the stand are soaked in sweat, spices and cooking oil. Shakiso receives no more than a querying glance, and she simply gestures that she will have whatever is available.

'Fish or goat?' asked even as a bowl piled high with broken rice is set before her.

'Fish,' she answers. 'And for the cat,' nodding to where Tuft has set her paws on the bench. A dollop of fish is added to her rice and another bowl with the same plonked alongside it.

She is about to pay with her card and, smiling, swaps to the Achenian card Tiémoko had presented to her as a parting gift. No one finds it in the least remarkable.

Dinner is filling, if not tasty, and she soon makes way for the next person waiting patiently behind her for a space. It is too early for sleep and, with the rain easing into a cool evening, she finds herself ambling randomly through the camp, savouring the polyglot of language and culture merging and mingling. There may be someone able to put her up for the night and, if not, there is always the damp discomfort of the boat.

Red and orange flames flicker, bright and welcoming, and she follows along with groups of people heading for the fireside. Hundreds have gathered here: families sharing their evening meal, teenagers laughing and whispering secrets, young lovers exchanging lingering glances. Before them, alongside the heat of the flame, stands a bone-thin man dressed in a greyed and careworn boubou, his eyes pearled with age and his hair an olive-coloured burst about his head. He leans on a long two-headed metal stave surrounded by people who seem awed merely to be close to him.

'That is Gaw Goŋ, of the genii, come to tell us a story,' says a mother to her children, who look as if they do not know whether to be thrilled or terrified.

An elderly woman waves emphatically at Shakiso. 'You will be our guest,' she says, inviting her and making space amongst the blankets, pots and plates.

Shakiso is engulfed into the bosom of quite a large extended family. They are from Bamako and have been in the camp for almost a year, awaiting their chance to cross the desert.

'With that shayāṭīn gone, we hope it will be safe to cross,' says the old woman, handing Shakiso an enormous enamel mug of overly sweetened tea.

Gaw Goŋ raises his stave above his head and the drumming rises, stopping instantly as he slams its foot deep into the earth at his sandals.

Shakiso feels as if the ground trembles and, for a moment, he stares directly at her, knowing her, recognition in his nod and smile.

She blinks and his eyes are flickering flame as he takes up a handful of dust, makes a fist of it and casts it into the fire even as he begins to speak.

'Painted-dog's child, running through the desert . . .'

Tales from Gaw Goŋ: Casamance, l'homme qui mourut deux fois

Painted-dog's child, running through the desert, always hopeful, always hungry. Hunting the endless dusty ochre of the hamada, her paws bouncing lightly on the scalding stones, and her tongue hanging loose in a way her mother considers unbecoming for a future matriarch.

She pauses, scratching at her ribs with a hind paw, sniffing the air. Her curious yellow eyes stare towards a bracket of trees alongside an ouahe, the water searing white against the dark of the land. Rising above the green line of shrubs she can see an idle waft of smoke and smell a taunting hint of lamb stew.

Her stomach grumbles, for it is hours to lunch and some time since her breakfast.

Always hungry, always hopeful, Painted-dog's child sets her nose towards the ouahe. Her white-patch tail blazing, her over-sized paws tangled beneath her, she runs in her hopping, loping way, yipping cheerfully as she goes.

Closer, and within the shade of a tangle of tamarisk bushes clustered around the base of overhanging date palms, she pauses and remembers her manners. She licks at her fur, trying to stop it sticking out and clean off the remnants of breakfast from around her face. She pulls at her huge, black, bowl-like ears.

Ready, or as best she can given the salivating distraction of the nearby cooking pot, she paces forward amongst the dense bourgou along the waterline and peers out through the long grass stalks.

On the other side of the shallow waters are two black-metal round-bellied pots – one large and one small – their looped handles each held up by individual scalded branches. Flames and coals spit and hiss beneath them, neatly surrounded by a stone hearth. A koubour, the three-stringed guitar of the griots, leans against a shaded boulder. Seated with his back towards the young pup is an olive-dark figure, tapping at the larger pot with the long two-headed pointed sombé he holds in one hand.

Painted-dog's child hesitates, for – while she does not know him – she and her brothers and sisters have certainly heard his tales. The fearsome magics and the undescribed punishments that Gaw Goŋ reserves especially for pups who refuse to do as their exasperated mother says.

The figure's back begins to tremble, shaking gently. He turns his head, his burst of fur grey about his long snout and his canines curved and hugely terrifying for the young dog. Baboon's eyes are brown, warm and filled with mirth.

'Aha, aha. Come out, Painted pup,' he says, staring directly at her where she is attempting to hide behind her ears. 'Your belly rumbles so loudly, it will wake the genii of this pool. And then where will we be, for his dinner is not yet ready.'

He chuckles and pats at the earth to his side, puffs of dust pluming at each strike.

Painted-dog's child sorts out her paws, which have become nervously entangled, and skips over to the fireside.

'Forgive me, Great Gaw,' she says, bowing her head and remembering to keep her tongue inside her mouth, 'I did not wish to disturb you.'

Baboon smiles warmly and scratches the pup behind her ears. No one has ever done so before, and the pup finds herself involuntarily slapping at the dust with one paw as she goes cross-eyed. Her tongue flops out of her mouth in a happy grin, and she slumps to the ground, leaning on her elbows.

'You are hungry?'

'Oh, yes, grandfather,' says the pup, her stomach joining in with a plaintive gurgle.

'Aha, aha,' he says, skewering the lid handle with his sombé and lifting it. An overwhelming explosion of spices and gravy causes the pup's ears to tremble, and she feels as if she will lose consciousness.

'Aha, aha,' sighs Baboon. 'You are about to learn a valuable lesson in patience.' He looks down to where Painted-dog's child is attempting to cover her ears with her paws. 'It is not yet ready.'

Baboon replaces the lid, shutting away the fragrance, and adds a thick branch on to the coals. Flames creep quickly up the mottled wood and escape into the sky.

'Tell you what, my child, would you like to hear a story?'

Painted-dog's child raises one paw and eases a tentative eye open. 'Will it be one of those stories where I learn what I have done wrong, grandfather?' she whines nervously, for such tales are common, and she has been doing her best to be good.

'Aha, aha,' laughs Baboon. 'No, my child, I do not tell such tales. Those are best left to the mothers of painted pups,' scratching her behind the ears again and causing her eyes to cross once more.

'The story I will reveal to you takes place far from here, in the world of Men.'

'Will it be a long story, grandfather?' she whimpers, her belly twisting, and drops her chin on to her forepaws.

He laughs. 'Patience, pup, for this is a sacred place and – before we may eat – we owe much to Baana, the genii of this ouahe. My story is as much an offering to him as it is a gift to you.' Smiling kindly, 'Be gentle, child, for you shall not go hungry.'

Baboon scoops at the dust with his left hand, brings it up to his mouth and whispers to it. Painted-dog's child trembles as her heart pounds in her chest, for she can feel the magics draining in to this place.

It is Baboon who holds the dust, but it is Gaw Goŋ who blows it into the flames, the red-brown mist glowing in his eyes. A swirling green-grey pool opens above the flames, shot through with flecks of red and black.

Gaw Goŋ motions at the portal, pulling it wider until it fills the space before them. He whispers again, and the pool clears.

They are looking into a dark place, claustrophobic and filled with rubble. They hear frightened breathing and the rattle of a chest battling to clear.

Movement, and a frayed, brown-skinned figure squeezes his way between shattered concrete beams. A dusty point of light glows on the grimy and bloodied face of a small boy. He is thirsty and hungry, although both sensations have long since faded into a dazed and bewildered exhaustion.

'Father,' he calls out, his voice the dryness of bones.

He rests his head in the light, feeling its caress against his cheek. The first gentle touch in days. His hands and feet tingle, and he weeps without tears.

Eyes darting beneath sunken lids, remembering.

Over the radio, resting against his father on the small sofa in their apartment in Kibuye, he had heard that the *Kabaka* had fled his palace, only across the ring road from their neighbourhood. Distant sounds, as of thunder, and the play of light on the horizon, indicated the advance of the war.

'*Ekyoto ggombolola* is no more,' said a weeping man on the radio. '*Omuliro gwe Buganda guzikide*. The king's fire has gone out. *Agye moukono mu ngabo*. The kingdom is undefended.' Abruptly, the broadcast ended.

His father, exhausted and drained, 'We cannot stay, my son. The soldiers will want to take the palace. Kibuye is too close. Rest as best you can tonight, and we shall leave before sunrise.'

There was no light or water, for both failed weeks ago, and small solar-charged candle-lights turned the room to twilight. His father had earned nothing again that day. There was little need for a builder when so many had fled their homes. He poured the last of the water from the plastic barrel against the wall into a chipped plastic cup. They shared it along with a small bowl of maize-meal he had been able to buy in the market.

His father unfolded a scratched printed image of his mother, looking sad and lost as he did so. Her body had been returned to them a week before, after she had been missing for two days. Everyone knew it was the Kabaka's men, taking their revenge against those they saw as betraying them.

They had buried her, finding a small patch of earth in the over-whelmed graveyard, marking her resting place with an old chair leg, her name scratched on to the post. He had wept for her, bewildered at her sudden absence, praying that this all be a mistake.

By then they and most of the city were trapped within the for-tifications surrounding Kampala.

The radio had been clear, though: the soldiers had fled, leaving the city stranded between the two fronts.

All through their building, and in the apartments alongside, shadows and sounds of people as they prepared to become seekers. Few of the people he knew remained, most having either paid to escape or been killed trying to break through the cordon of soldiers camped around the city.

Morning did not come.

He was asleep when the drones struck, eviscerating his home. He awoke deep within a shifting, terrifying jumble of concrete, pipes, furniture and clothes.

Crawling from beneath a sofa, in the dwindling candlelight he discovered Mrs Kiwuuwa, the old lady who lived on the ground floor and always gave him sweets as a reward for going to school. Her body was cold.

He shouted until his throat felt bloody and raw. He heard no answer.

The batteries faded, and the light was extinguished.

Complete darkness. Silence except for occasional subsidence followed by howling and tearing as the rubble settled once more.

He felt carefully ahead, his fingers creeping into open spaces, probing. He found sharp edges, sheered rebar, strange textures, torn fabric, splintered wood.

There were bodies. A leg, or an arm, soft and liquid and rancid. He could not see them. The sensation was alien and terrifying.

He could smell damp in the air, feel it in the concrete, but there was none sufficient to drink.

After an age of twisting and pulling and crawling, he sleeps in the caress of light threading through the rubble.

He feels his body lifted, held, his brow stroked, 'My son, I have found you. Rest with me, and I will carry you to safety.' Relief and warmth in his father's voice.

He wakes again, alone, in a vast space, light shafting down and across. 'Did I fall asleep in church?' he wonders, thinking of the time his mother and father took him to Rubaga Cathedral, and the way the light in the basilica turned the brick to gold.

In the act of reaching between twisted rebar, spotlit high on the tangled mess of rubble he sees his father. His clothes are torn, but his flesh is unmarked, glowing in the light.

The boy wants to cry out, but he is too tired to move.

He watches as his father crosses to a concrete pillar, bent rebar protruding from it like the exposed bones of an elbow where it connects again deep into the broken mass around them. His father crawling until he reaches the end, which begins to bow lower towards where the boy is resting.

His father rocks up and down on the end until, squealing and almost gracefully, it shifts and drops, with him hanging on painfully all the way down. He leaps off as it hits the bottom, and his eyes fill with delight as he scoops up the boy in his arms.

The boy can feel the warmth and softness of his father's skin, the steady rhythm of his heartbeat.

'My father, I thought you were gone,' he says, softly.

'I have been searching for you for two days,' weeps his father. 'Rest with me, and I will carry you to safety.'

Holding the boy carefully against him, he walks slowly up the ramp he worked so hard to build, and pulls himself and the boy through the opening at the top. They are near the surface now, and the way is easier to see.

His father can see the sky and hear voices calling out, seeking survivors.

He shouts, his voice joyful, and is answered.

Hands lift away the covering debris, revealing him and the boy lying asleep in his arms.

'You are reborn from the earth, child,' raising him from the clawing rubble. A friendly face, unfamiliar accented Swahili. 'What is your name, my son?'

'Isaiah,' losing consciousness once more, but not before calling out, 'Father!'

*

A crackle of fire, and orange flames flickering against the trees on a hill outside the city. Joshua returns from collecting firewood, quietly piling branches, trying not to wake any of the sleeping figures clustered about its warmth.

He looks up towards Esther as she slips in behind him, putting her arms around his waist and resting her head on his shoulder. He turns and kisses her on each eye.

'How is the boy?' he asks.

'Asleep, with Rachel and Hannah on each side. The girls are very protective of him.'

'They take after you,' he smiles.

'I have put another drip up for him tonight. That should be the last he needs for now. We will still need to carry him tomorrow.'

Even as the city was pulverized, seekers arrived from the south, and Red Cross carrier craft flew over from the west. The red and white drones have become as much a symbol of the conflict as have the explosions and destruction.

Each drone drops a package of food or medicine. Their supplies are small, but each party of seekers has sufficient to address basic emergencies.

Esther was a nurse at the mining site in Kigoma where they used to live, and now she cares for their small band.

'How many are with us?' she asks, nodding at those sprawled under the trees and around their fire.

'Perhaps fifty more have joined us since we left Kampala. There are maybe three hundred of us.'

'Too many or too few?' she asks. Too many to travel quickly, or too few to be safe from attack.

'We will be moving more slowly,' he says, 'but we should still be well.'

It may not have been the red and white drones' intention, but the seekers are following their homeward path. Somewhere there is a safe place where these vehicles are based, and that is the direction in which they will go.

Their group arrived soon after dawn at the outskirts of Kampala. Joshua's strategy was that they follow a few days behind in the wake of bombing runs. That way they knew where the various warring factions were likely to be, and they were able to track the Red Cross drones which also followed the battle-front.

They had travelled around Lake Victoria from Tanzania, hundreds of thousands of people escaping the collapse, keeping close to water. From Kampala, they would head west to Lake Albert and then into the jungles of the Congo. There were millions of other seekers scattered through the area. At night, you could see their cooking fires all across the horizon.

'We will give it until dusk,' Joshua had said as they walked through the broken city. Time enough to see if any amongst the rubble may be rescued, not so long as to be trapped there overnight.

There had been many others similarly helping through the day. Too few had been found alive. And always the risk of finding one so injured that there would be little to do to help.

Close to dusk, with the waters of the bay turning grey and gold behind them, they had heard a man cry out. 'We are here, please, help us!'

'I heard him. You heard him. I do not understand,' says Joshua.

The boy, Isaiah, was gathered into the body of a man, arms wrapped protectively about him. At first Joshua had thought them both dead. The man appeared to have succumbed almost instantly to his wounds: his neck broken, his chest collapsed. The boy so small and sunken.

Then the boy coughed, and they delivered him from the earth.

'He was long-since passed. Perhaps when the building first fell. And, yet, he spoke.'

Esther leads Joshua to a blanket near the girls. The boy is breathing easily, sheltered between them.

She sits, pulling Joshua down to her, holding him close and speaking quietly.

'Do you know the story of Casamance, the twice-dead man?'

He shakes his head.

She looks into his eyes, loving him, holding him.

'There was a story my grandmother told me, about a man called Casamance. There was a flood which swept through his village. Many died, leaving the survivors without shelter, stranded on an island far from the reach of help. Many were certain they had seen him drown, trapped beneath a falling tree. Yet, here he was, alive, his flesh warm and unmarked. His children played with him, his wife knew him and, unfailingly, he caught fish for the survivors and kept them safe.

'It was many days before rescue came and, on that day, they found Casamance trapped amongst wood and waste. His body was bloated as if he had been long dead in the waters.

'My grandmother told me that some people who die are sent back by the genii to serve a duty or to protect those they love until they are safe. They know not that they are already dead; have no memory of dying. They are alive and well, but once their responsibility is served they will die, though no new injury befalls them.

'They are all like Casamance: twice-dead.'

Joshua breathes out in a long sigh. 'That is a terrible thing for the living to bear, knowing that one so loved is already with their ancestors.'

Esther's eyes glow in the firelight. 'Perhaps,' she says, 'but there is also the gratitude of having time beyond death to share in love and warmth.'

'Do you think the boy knew? Before?'

Esther nods. 'Yes, I think he knew. He is still confused, but I believe he is grateful for knowing how much his father cared.'

Joshua sighs again. 'It is well. I am glad for him. I am grateful for the twice-dead man.'

18

'I am Gaïndé-le-lion,' says a small boy, roaring and raising his hands as if paws.

'We will be the hunters,' shouts a little girl.

'Who will play lion-child?' asks another.

In delight, they snatch up Tuft and carry her to where they are acting out the story they have just heard, returning to their favourite moments of heroism.

As they run and tumble, Tuft adding to the chasing mayhem, Shakiso smiles in wonder at how children seem only ever to hear the parts of stories that reflect their own naïvety and enthusiasm for life, for Gaw Goŋ's tale is steeped in sadness.

Gaïndé-le-lion is killed by hunters, leaving his family defenceless and they are soon slaughtered. His only son survives by hiding in a cave where he is buried alive in a rockfall. Gaïndé is returned to life by merciful genii so he may rescue his cub, and the two endure much hardship as they travel through a conflict-ridden plain. Each morning, they awake to birds bringing them food. Each day, they travel towards where the birds have come from. Gaïndé takes leave of his child on the edge of foreign pride-lands as the genii reclaim his second life, leaving the cub to join a new family.

Shakiso turns to the old woman, holding her mug of tea as if drawing warmth there. The woman's eyes bear the faraway gaze of one who has experienced more pain than any person should ever endure.

In their reflection, Shakiso sees fragments of a different story. Of a man and his son. Of war and destruction. Of a child born from rubble cradled in the arms of his dead father.

'What?' she asks, bewildered. The truth in the old woman's eyes stills the questions she would ask before she can speak. She looks to see whether the storyteller, this Gaw Goŋ, may have answers, but he has disappeared.

'Did I hear a different story?' she wonders, and shivers.

'In time,' says the old woman, noticing her struggle. 'When you are ready, my child,' and she will say no more, leaving Shakiso watching as the children play.

19

Pazanov crouches as he climbs out of the helicopter, its coaxial rotors slowing above him. One of Uberti's personal protection guards runs to meet him, putting an arm over his shoulder and shouting his greetings above the whine of the electric motor.

'It's not good, Pazanov,' he says. 'I have never seen him this angry.'

Pazanov can only nod, his stomach clenched in fear and rage.

They walk across the landing pad towards the grey columns of the main house at Novo-Ogaryovo, its great doors still chained and locked. Even thirty years after his death, few have the confidence to claim Vladimir Putin's mantle. Like Kuntsevo, Joseph Stalin's old dacha, it remains shrouded in secrets and paranoia, visited only by the occasional caretaker.

The estate belongs to Rosneft: a gift from the president, both to indicate the favour in which the state regards the company, and also to permanently remind them from where that favour comes.

A small motorized cart takes them under the smothering trees to the house Uberti prefers. They park alongside a group of nervous-looking men in white overalls standing beside two trucks. The doors are open, and furniture and fittings wrapped in plastic are neatly packed inside.

'You'll understand,' says the guard. Pazanov feels little curiosity.

The interior guards move quietly, whispering. The house is in silence.

Pazanov walks through the hall and to the office at the back of the house. The door hangs on one hinge. He knocks anyway and waits until he hears an answering grunt.

Inside, the office has been torn to shreds.

An axe is buried in the only section of desk still upright. The rest is splintered shrapnel across the floor. Curtains have been torn from their railings and smoulder in the fireplace. Paintings have been slashed or ripped off the walls. Glass, broken ceramics and potting soil from trampled office plants cover the ruined carpets.

A portrait of Putin remains untouched.

Uberti is sitting calmly in one of the heavy ornamental chairs watching a news broadcast projected into clear space in the far corner. A bottle of vodka, almost empty, rests against the chair leg at his left hand.

He gestures at one of the overturned mahogany chairs without looking up.

Pazanov selects one of the lighter-looking ones and heaves it upright, dragging it alongside Uberti.

A pink fleshy hand motions at the chair and then at the news.

Pazanov sits and watches. Uberti hands him the bottle.

'– for the almost five hundred colonists expecting to travel back with the Mars colony transporter, Dribble 7. We can see freight being unloaded –'

Vast indistinct shipping containers being pushed out of the transporter. A wide pan of the ship against the sunburned rim of the Earth with the newly completed space elevator disappearing to a point below.

Uberti shrugs and changes the news stream.

'– has released footage taken by their special forces troops during last night's surprise raids –'

The grey-haired newsreader is replaced by confusing and disjointed flashes, interspersed with dark figures running, narrow tunnels, and the withering sound of gunfire and explosions. Long lines of turbaned and hooded figures, their hands raised, climbing out of holes in the desert and being herded behind high spools of razor wire. Tents and walls, laughing blue-helmeted UN soldiers standing in garishly furnished rooms. Cowering women and children, naked and coated in grime and bruises, being given blankets to cover themselves. Aerial footage of helicopters flying above the barely distinguishable entrance to one of the cities. A map showing where the eleven cave systems were simultaneously attacked. The UN Security Council meeting, with the stern-faced Russian foreign minister surprising everyone by voting with the majority to selectively suspend the no-fly zone and launch the surprise attacks.

Not that it helped, thinks Pazanov. The Chinese would not let our troops anywhere near the caves. The raids had begun before the Security Council even met.

'– captured the entire senior Ansar Dine leadership. We are waiting to cross to the UN in Beijing, but we expect that a special court will be set up in The Hague to try many of these captives. The Senegalese government has insisted that Abdallah Ag Ghaly will remain in their custody and be tried at the African Court of Justice in Dakar –'

There follow images of journalists running towards a man in a white djellaba walking down the stairs outside an austere brown building. A man in an embroidered ochre-brown boubou and matching kufi skull-cap is briefly seen in the background. It cuts to blurred and censored footage of Oktar Samboa being murdered, jumps to a high three-quarter view of Simon Adaro naked, Ag Ghaly pointing his gun at him as his men flee, pushing their way out through the filming crowd.

'– but the defining image of the last five days has to be this one. English-born businessman, Simon Adaro –'

Uberti, quietly, ends the transmission.

Pazanov waits patiently. He will not end the silence.

A grunt. 'He outmanoeuvred us.'

Taking the bottle, drinking from the neck.

'We thought we were trapping him; instead we were helping him catch Ag Ghaly. We underestimated him,' he shrugs. He turns to Pazanov, looks at him for the first time. 'Are you going to tell me I should have listened?'

Pazanov shakes his head.

'No?' He leans forward, towards Pazanov, his fleshy face close, smelling of sour damp.

'What has changed? For him? For us?' he asks.

Pazanov shifts his arms from the chair and braces his fingers in his lap.

'It is mixed,' he says. 'Ansar Dine is damaged. Their control of the desert crossing, the drugs trade. That may not recover. But they still control Bamako, most of the cities of Niger, Sudan, Chad, the southern parts of Algeria. They're in no danger of going anywhere.'

He thinks of the image of Adaro, the meanness of the cave cities.

'I think their mystery is destroyed. There are uprisings in Khartoum, N'Djamena. For us, it means areas we haven't had to worry about in decades could produce gas and oil. And Adaro now has a clear line through Niger and Libya into the Mediterranean.'

'What about your idea of bombing his farms?' asks Uberti.

'It won't work any more,' says Pazanov. 'The drones might have crossed undetected before, but now there is so much military activity. And his farms are well established. He has twenty of them. They're fifty square kilometres each. How do we bomb that without attracting attention?'

'Kill him?'

'Sure, we'll keep trying. But the plants are running. I'm not sure it would have any effect.'

Uberti throws the empty vodka bottle half-heartedly into the fire grate. It thumps on to the smouldering curtains.

He drags himself upright, limps over to a heavy cupboard in the corner, still in one piece. It lights up as he opens it, packed with hand-labelled bottles of vodka. He opens another and flings the cap on to the floor.

'I still don't understand how they could attack all these places and the obezyany didn't see them coming?'

Pazanov laughs. 'A lesson for all of us. Hiding underground is wonderful if you want to prevent drones from finding you. Not so good if you want to get a warning once you have been found.'

Uberti giggles, a curiously childlike high-pitched chortle. Infectious but peculiar.

'And now we know what had their pants in knots.' He whistles. '$75 billion. That would get me out of bed too. Do we know where it is?'

'No,' says Pazanov. 'Or, if anyone does, no one is saying. I set some trusted people to investigate. Quietly. I'm not sure if the Cheka want it for themselves.'

'You still think there was a shipment of weapons on those planes?'

'Yes. We know there were more than one of them. That's too much cargo space only for drugs. We're trying to trace a man called Filippo Argenti. He's been dealing with Ag Ghaly for a decade.'

'That shyster?' more of Uberti's high-pitched giggling. 'Are you sure? Ag Ghaly must be even more gullible than we thought. No wonder they couldn't fight back. Nothing he sells works,' wiping tears from his eyes.

Pazanov shrugs. 'I don't know him, but our people tell me he may have arranged that last shipment.'

'I knew him years ago. Always looking for one big deal so he could retire. If he got in the middle of $75 billion? Look in Crimea. He probably retired.'

'We'll do that.'

'Good,' says Uberti, resting one heavy hand on Pazanov's shoulder and passing him the bottle.

'Shall we walk?' he asks.

Pazanov, bottle in hand, nods and stands. 'Sure. It'll give them time to refurnish.'

Uberti blinks, looking around the room as if seeing the devastation for the first time. A ripple stirs across his reddened cheeks as he grunts. He gestures vaguely, stomps past the door, bending it further out from the tortured bottom hinge as he passes.

His guards form silently around them as they step outside, cross the gravel and into the darkness of the trees. Behind them, workmen rush indoors to begin clearing.

They walk towards the river, through a gap in the old wall that used to enclose the estate, and then along the bank of the Moskva.

A faint grey blur and Pazanov thinks he sees an ape-like creature walking in parallel to them through the woods, a two-headed stave in one hand. He stares, but the illusion fades when he realizes it is merely a dull gathering of leaves against a pile of brushwood.

'How do you think he did it?' asks Uberti, opening a thin platinum case and lighting hand-rolled cigarettes for each of them.

'Which part?' laughs Pazanov.

'They missed an implant, that much is obvious,' says Uberti.

'So they knew where he was up till he went underground.'

'And they could have rescued him anytime,' continues Pazanov. 'Except they wanted to make a big display of catching Ag Ghaly. That image of Adaro taking him on by himself is triggering uprisings all across Ansar Dine's territory.'

'That's what I want to understand. Why did Ag Ghaly allow himself to be caught like that? And how did Adaro know the names of all those people? Without that, his plan isn't so dramatic,' says Uberti.

They walk on, soggy leaves sticking to their shoes. Their guards walking far ahead and behind, watching and listening to reports from the drones overhead.

'Liao Zhi,' says Pazanov, flinging the remnants of his cigarette into the river.

'Zhi? He's that *kitayoza* who runs Sina?'

'Those jihadis love taking pictures of themselves. Adaro took a risk that whoever took him up would be on the connect. I'm guessing they booked time on one of the Chinese supercomputers to track them down and fed the names back to him as he was looking at them. Putting the feed on everyone's channel was straightforward after that. It made good viewing. Everyone wanted to see it.'

Uberti whistles.

'And those Senegalese Special Forces?'

'They have a unit dedicated to high-value Ansar Dine targets. Present them with such an opportunity?' says Pazanov.

'That still leaves the problem of getting Ag Ghaly to break cover?'

Pazanov shrugs.

'I don't know. Make him angry enough to want to torture Adaro personally?'

Uberti shoves his hands into his pockets and stares across the river.

'I want that mudak dead, but I do admire his balls,' he says. 'So, what can we do?'

'Our problem is that the chaos works for him. Ansar Dine is going to spend the next year fighting itself and anyone else who thinks they can take advantage. Adaro can expand his farms without worrying about them.'

'He must need something? Somewhere he has a base. We can't get any submersibles into the Med. There are already so many drones and boats watching for refugees, I don't think there's a fish that goes unseen. Once he gets his line there, we're finished.'

'Abdallah Ag Ghaly,' says Pazanov.

Uberti sticks out his bottom lip and shakes his head, what?

'If Ag Ghaly escapes, he'll get back to his people and seek revenge.'

Uberti looks sceptical. 'So what? Their base in the Sahara is broken. His remaining people are far to the east.'

'Not if we give him Senegal.'

'How do you plan to do that?'

'The opposition are expected to do well in the local elections in a few months, and it looks as if they're going to win the presidency next year, and they don't have the support of the army.'

Pazanov is speaking quickly, trying to get his plan out before Uberti loses interest or cuts him off again.

'We can smuggle in some of Ag Ghaly's men, support them with some of ours. After the election, but before the new president is inaugurated, we free Ag Ghaly and stage a coup. That will attract every last supporter of his to attack Senegal. The army won't know what to do: defend the borders or try to reinstate an opposition government we decapitated.

'And we win,' he says with sudden intensity.

Uberti shakes his head. 'You're forgetting the Chinese. They won't stand by while we turn another of their markets into a wasteland. We cannot risk it.'

'Whether they take Adaro's technology now or develop their own in ten years, we lose their business anyway, but we can still keep Europe. If we let Adaro win, we will lose both. We have to take this risk, China or not.'

Uberti slaps him on the back, laughing his high-pitched giggle.

'That *arkhipizdrit* sure pissed you off,' he says. 'Good, make it happen.' Serious again. 'But, Pazanov, if this goes wrong, or we are seen to have been involved . . .'

Pazanov is used to the threats that go with fixing problems for Uberti, but he can see that his boss is sweating uncomfortably.

'Germany, France, Spain and Poland are refusing to sign renewals with us unless we cut our fees. I asked why, and they sent us Adaro's pricing. We cannot match him. Over the next two years, *all* the renewals will be due.'

Uberti's eyes are bloodshot and his face clammy.

'Shkrebnev called. I don't need to tell you what he said. Enough to say that Russia's economy will implode if our pricing drops that far.'

Pazanov feels his stomach clenching again.

'Threats don't really matter. If we don't solve this, Shkrebnev will be unforgiving. None of us will have anywhere to hide.'

20

Mud splashes over Shakiso's legs and feet as the passing taxi jolts into one of Saint-Louis' interminable potholes. Tuft, following at her heels, scrambles for shelter behind an old cannon buried improbably upright by the side of the road.

'Mademoiselle,' shouts the driver, hoping to elicit a fare, sullenly continuing when she smiles and waves him away.

She is in no hurry and enjoying walking amongst the crumbling colonial architecture of the old city with its houses and shops built up against and over each other, shuttered against the heat. Time and weather have turned many buildings into surreal rubble sculptures and walls into red-brick filigree.

'You think you could make that jump?' she queries Tuft while estimating the gap between two buildings, imagining running the length of the island and considering the dangers waiting in the rotten masonry. The military base at the northern end creates a no-go area, and there are odd sections – like the fallen abstract water towers in the middle of the city, the cathedral, or the old fort – that offer potential entertainment.

The horizon across the river to the mainland part of the city is crowded with cranes and scaffolding, and the rumble and roar of trucks and the hammering and shouts of construction from across the river are an almost-present static under the sound of rain.

Shakiso passes the hospital on her left, a few patients sitting on the arched balcony outside their rooms watching the ocean, and reaches the southern tip of the island. She climbs up on to the levee holding back the water, revelling in the coolness of the Atlantic breeze and the damson call of birds flying overhead.

Tuft inspects a litter of upturned crates, finding nothing of interest, and joins her on the wall. They watch an Achenian freight drone, a pallet stacked with the last delivery of genetically modified propstock pellets hanging beneath, heading over the city to the Climate distribution centres in the east.

She is just wondering about coffee when a whispered 'Breakfast' from her implant interrupts.

'Come on, youngster,' she says. 'Time for our appointment,' dropping down from the wall and walking up Rue Blaise Dumont until she finds the side street for the hotel and knocks on its carved wooden door.

'Madame,' says the concierge, welcoming her inside and directing her up the stairs towards their restaurant. 'Please, a towel for you,' smiling away her thanks.

She stands at the base of the stairs drying her face and hair. As she finishes, a grey man in a grey suit brushes past her, looking sullen. 'What's he doing here?' she wonders, crouching to rub a resisting Tuft with her towel, observing as the grey man steps into the limousine meeting him outside.

She continues up the stairs, emerging on to a rooftop terrace sheltered from the rain by a stretched canvas awning, looking vaguely for the man she has come to join, and meeting his curious gaze amongst the early-morning diners.

'Mr Adaro, I presume,' warmth in her eyes as he stands to greet her.

'Ms Collard,' he says, taking her hand and smiling. 'I regret nothing but that we haven't met sooner.'

'That might even work on me,' she laughs, the sound of wild places and the easy joy of young children, flopping loosely into the remaining chair. 'What's that?' pouring herself a cup of coffee from his jug and prodding at the bowl of beans amongst his newly arrived breakfast.

'I admit,' he says, 'its looks are against it. But here,' tearing open a croissant and spooning a healthy portion into it, 'taste this.'

She looks sceptical, holding his hand over the croissant as she takes a bite.

'Oh!' she says, her mouth full. 'That's fantastic. What is it?' taking the rest, licking a few errant beans that escaped into her palm.

'*Ndambé*. Slow-cooked beans in tomato. It makes a wonderful breakfast.'

Tuft ambles up the stairs and joins them, winding herself between Shakiso's legs.

'I wanted to thank you and Hollis for the propstock,' she says.

He shrugs. 'I should be thanking you for the contract. GeneWorx has the capacity, and we're happy to help.'

'Sure,' she says, 'but you guys are risking serious legal hassles.'

He looks north, towards the desert. Troop transport helicopters are flying back and forth from the military base at the edge of the city and UN-flagged Chinese naval vessels anchored along the shore, ferrying relief troops to the ongoing operations in the karst cities.

'Did you see the news this morning?'

She nods.

During the military clean-up, following last week's raids on Ansar Dine's cave fortresses, four mass graves were uncovered. Tens of thousands of bodies, dried to hardened leather, emerging from the erg. Forensic experts are being flown in, but early analysis is that the terrorists sometimes chose – for whatever reason – to lead groups of seekers across the desert to these sites and there massacre them.

There is an over-abundance of male bodies, and many think that the women and children were taken to serve as slaves. The scale of the abuse, and the desperate bravery of those challenging the journey to escape war and famine, is causing consternation and embarrassment in Europe.

'I don't think anyone is going to want to stop us, or you. A good harvest will give people a reason to stay,' he says.

'Maybe,' she says. 'You know,' leaning back, a croissant in hand, her knees over the armrest, one foot absently twirling, 'I'm still trying to figure you guys out.'

He laughs, pouring another cup of coffee. 'How did you describe me to Hollis? "Just your average evil capitalist out to make a quick buck off the suffering of the multitudes."'

'Dude,' she says, her eyes narrowing, 'if you have to be captured by terrorists to do that, you're doing it all wrong.'

Tuft leans up and tugs at Simon's knee. He scratches her head and puts the bowl of beans down for her to eat.

'Too simple anyway,' Shakiso says, pushing her hair out of her eyes. 'Tuft and I took a pirogue down from Ballou. I think I had to pay enough to buy the damn thing. We stopped over in Aroundu, Sori Malé and Rosso. They're each near farms of yours, and each of them is growing like nothing I've ever seen. There are over a million people in Rosso. I'm told that last year there were only a few thousand.'

'With so many seekers following the river west, looking for a way up, it's hardly surprising. It's the last line of towns before the desert,' testing her, seeing where she takes this.

She gestures with half a croissant. 'Sure, everything looks like an accident when you don't look too closely. Except those payment cards they're using. That's yours.'

'A successful evil capitalist then?'

'I've seen your ass, my friend, and that is too gorgeous an ass to belong to an evil man.'

Surprised, he throws back his head and laughs.

'Exactly. So, why not trust me?' wiping the bowl of ndambé clean with her finger. 'This is a surprisingly magnificent breakfast.'

'Order your own,' he says, snatching the last croissant before she can grab it. 'And get some *ditakh* juice while you're at it,' grinning at her, his eyes dancing.

She pouts at him. 'What's your business with the grey men?' waving at a hovering waiter.

'The inimitable group known as the Chinese Ambassador? Yuanxing was here to express his gratitude to me for helping the Chinese economy while also pressing me to sell the solar printer designs.'

'He looked miserable. I take it you weren't helpful?' she asks.

'It could be fun if Rosneft lost their other big market when the Chinese cover the Gobi in panels.' He shakes his head and refills his cup. 'But it may cause more chaos than I think is strictly necessary. And I don't do business with tyrants.'

Shakiso stares at him, gauging him. 'What's this all for?'

'Because even doing the honourable thing can be immensely entertaining,' and he smiles, his eyes the bright blue of an endless childhood.

'That's not an answer,' she laughs. 'Ansar Dine, Rosneft – you seem a bit cavalier about getting yourself killed.'

'Not everything worked out the way it was supposed to,' he says quietly.

'What happened there? In the desert?'

He smiles, gathering himself. 'Oktar called me evil because he didn't understand the difference between creation and destruction. Us creatives can be chaotic, but only because we want stuff that doesn't exist yet and you never know where that is likely to take us. Evil people always want things that already exist,' he says. 'Either to have for themselves or to destroy. That makes their movements very predictable.'

'And Ag Ghaly wanted his cargo?'

He nods. 'He also always broadcasts the torture of his European captives. He thinks it humiliates his enemies.'

'Instead you knew it meant they had to take you above ground?'

'Yes, so when Rosneft started spreading the rumour that only I knew where that cargo was, I realized I had an opportunity to tease Ag Ghaly out of hiding and open the Sahara up for my farms. We approached the Senegalese anti-terrorism unit here in Saint-Louis and worked out a plan. They kept track of me through a transponder, and once I was below ground, they surrounded my last known location and waited for me to pop up again and identify Ag Ghaly.'

'How did you know he'd be there?'

'Evil man, very predictable,' laughs Simon. 'You could launch a sizeable rebellion with that cargo, and he wouldn't have trusted anyone with the knowledge of its location. Evil men always fear being overthrown. I knew he'd come to me.'

'And Oktar? How did he fit into that plan?'

He flinches, surprised despite knowing the question needed to be asked, seeing again the confused look on the faces of the seekers.

'You don't have to answer,' she says gently, mistaking his anguish.

He stares rigidly at the table, hiding his turmoil. 'I couldn't pass any message to anyone until I was above ground, and the troops were only to move the moment I identified Ag Ghaly or, failing that, to save my life. The plan was perfect, except for Oktar. He shouldn't have been there.'

'So Oktar couldn't be rescued because no one knew if Ag Ghaly was there yet?'

'People died,' he says, looking up. 'I think capturing Ag Ghaly was more important, but those deaths –' rubbing at his hands '– I am sorry.'

He studies her face before continuing, searching her eyes. 'I was only with Oktar for a short time. I still don't understand what he thought he would achieve. I know what he told me; I just don't understand how he convinced himself it would work.'

'Did he say anything? I mean, anything that would . . .' asks Shakiso, thinking about that day at Orly Airport, his smug look of triumph, wondering what she hoped he might have said.

'No,' says Simon. 'He was too frightened. I'm sorry.'

'Don't be. He didn't deserve that, but he was a bastard anyway.'

'What happened between you?' he asks. 'I was told you worked together.'

She closes her eyes and tries to breathe out her frustration.

'He was my boss just over a year ago when I was based in Benghazi. I was the local Climate depot chief, same role that Moussa has here. I wanted to put some of my ideas into practice. Oktar wasn't interested. He was a sufficiently unpleasant manager that I would have left anyway. One of Climate's main funders sounded me out. They wanted to know if I would take over when Oktar's term ended.

'Then Ansar Dine took things out of my hands and invaded. The Egyptians raided from behind and the next thing our camp was in the middle of a rather nasty war.'

A basket of croissants arrives along with more coffee, a glass of deep-green ditakh juice and a bowl of ndambé. She tries the juice, smiling and raising it to him in thanks, tears open a croissant and chews thoughtfully.

'I was on the last flight out. We were forced to abandon most of the people in the camp, but anyone who had even remote family connections to our staff, I got on those drones.'

'I see I'm not the only one who takes unreasonable risks,' he says.

'It wasn't meant to be,' she says. 'Originally it was a safe post, and then suddenly Ansar Dine was everywhere.'

'What happened once you escaped?' he asks, dragging a chair from next to them and straightening his legs, his feet bare and covered in sand sticking out from beneath his jeans, the hems torn at the heel.

'The drone was packed, people so close we couldn't raise our arms. It almost didn't take off. Out of all those faces I keep remembering Michèle and her family. All of them worked in the camp as teachers. She was a French national, but her husband and father-in-law were both Libyan.'

She smiles, the flint in her eyes softening at the memory, 'She was this tiny woman who somehow produced quadruplets. You'd see her and her husband dashing around the camp, ferrying these kids along with them in this huge pram.

'Only thing is, what I did was illegal. She was supposed to apply and then wait for the French government to decide if they'd let her husband and father-in-law in. We didn't have time for that.

'Oktar was keen to win some fame from the evacuation, so he brought a bunch of officials along to the airport when we arrived in Paris, and they brought gendarmes. They were waiting for us on the tarmac. They checked everyone's visas and pushed anyone they were suspicious of back on the drone and sent it back to Libya. Oktar stood there with this smug look on his face while the rest of us begged and fought for the drones not to take off.'

'That's harsh.' Simon breathes out sharply. 'What happened to them?'

'Ansar Dine,' she says simply. 'They were murdered in Benghazi a few weeks after.'

'And Michèle?'

She shakes her head. 'I don't know. I tried to find her. To find some way to say sorry. I went to see her brother in Paris before I came here,' her eyes distant. 'He hasn't seen her in months. She spent almost a year near catatonic. She gradually came out of it but was suicidal. She kept taking the children and vanishing for days. They didn't know where she went. Her brother said she had become obsessively paranoid before she disappeared. Their family is frantic. I can only hope they find her before she hurts herself or the children.'

'And you?' asks Simon.

'Climate decided I would be disciplined. I was told to be patient. The donors would work things out with the board, but I quit instead.

'I spent the last year running in the Wet and putting all this behind me. I never expected to be back in it.' Shrugging and shaking her head, 'It was Oktar's fault. All he had to do was stay quiet and they would have been through the border. We got them out. They were safe, and he betrayed them.'

'This was just over a year ago?'

'Yes,' she says. 'Why?'

'I had my own run-in with Ansar Dine in Tanzania about then.'

'What were you doing there?'

'That was where we originally intended testing out the identity systems you like so much.'

'Wait, wait,' says Shakiso, interrupting. 'Those are payment cards.'

'You're very impatient,' says Simon, laughing. 'Anyone can issue a payment card. What's the value of an identity?'

'It's mighty early for you to be asking me to think.' She savours her coffee for a while before replying.

'It's about trust, isn't it? I can work anywhere because I can prove who I am. I can open a bank account anywhere, move money anywhere, because I have proof of myself. Here, anyone who is forced from their homes loses more than their stuff. They lose the community who vouch for their ownership of their stuff. If they're ever able to return, they have no way to prove that their homes or farms are theirs.

'My identity is guaranteed by a government that, whatever its merits, is trusted enough to make that guarantee. Around here, even in the best of times, most governments aren't and can't be bothered to provide meaningful identities anyway. People exist only in their own communities.

'These seekers haven't only lost their homes; they've lost the communities who can prove they own their homes. They've lost the people who can vouch for them.'

'Precisely,' says Simon. 'We wanted to see if we could find a way round the problem, but without needing any government to support us.'

'So you invented an identity system?'

He nods. 'Our problem was that people won't use such a thing unless they're already in trouble, or if they're compelled in some way, and we were trying to do this without a government.'

'Right, and without threatening those same erratic governments while doing it,' says Shakiso, 'but this isn't a system you're testing. It turned up fully developed.'

'Which is why you're impatient,' he says. 'I went to Kigoma. Thirty years ago, that area had really productive copper mines, but those industries are dying, and the towns around the mines are a bit like your camps: people don't really have anywhere else to go. Entire economies, thousands of people, depending on the salaries of the miners.

'I hoped that, if I bought the mines, I could introduce our identity systems to pay those salaries and see what happens.

'We had this fantastic mine foreman. Joshua Ossai. Engineering degree from Dar es Salaam, trusted by the miners. I was on my own, and he was first in the community to have me round for dinner. I knew he was vetting me, but we became close friends. He bought into it, convinced the miners that it meant they'd get paid faster and – at worst – was no different from any of the other money systems they use.'

'And? Did it work?' she asks, slipping her feet, equally bare and covered in sand, alongside his on the edge of the spare chair.

'I never found out. Rosneft lost the Zafarani gas fields to Shell. Within about twelve months, they financed a civil war, and I escaped with only the clothes I was wearing.'

'Rosneft did that?'

'Rosneft's executives do what Russian politics demands. I think the war spread further than they expected, and Ansar Dine used the mayhem to expand. Which is probably when they attacked your camp.'

Simon's face darkens. 'I headed for Dar, trying to get my helicopter, but was attacked just outside the airport. One of the Rosneft fixers was there, and a child was killed. I realized too late that the airport would only be safe until he left. By the time I got there, the place was overrun.'

'How did you get out?'

He smiles, his strange eyes glowing. 'I waited till dark, then – how shall I put this – repossessed one of the helicopters the terrorists were using and got the hell out.'

'Hardcore,' she says. 'What happened to Joshua?' She feels she recognizes that name but cannot place it. Another name from another story.

'He was going to take his family and head for the border. Ismael met me at Heathrow to let me know they escaped. I was hoping to see him again but,' pausing, his voice soft, 'Ismael says they're in the hands of the genii now.'

'Who's Ismael?'

'He's a sort of wondering griot. If you're lucky, you might get to meet him.'

'And the genii? There was this storyteller at one of the river camps I stopped at, Gaogong, I think—'

'Gaw Goŋ?' surprise on Simon's face.

'Yes,' says Shakiso, her eyes wide. 'You've heard of him?'

'Yes, although he's supposed to be a baboon.'

'Definitely a man,' she says, looking curious. 'He told a story about a baboon. At least, I think it was . . .' uncertain about her memory again.

Simon smiles. 'If it's the same Gaw Goŋ, then I'm not surprised you're not sure. I'm told each person who hears one of his stories hears something different.'

'And the genii?'

'I've not seen any, but it helps to be pragmatic. Ismael says it doesn't matter if I believe or not, as long as I'm entertaining,' he laughs.

Shakiso stares at the sand on her toes. She rubs them against his feet, chafing them clean.

'Are you flirting with me?' he asks, smiling.

'Yes. You have sexy feet. Shift, I want some room.'

He laughs again, moving his legs over.

'Do you always get what you want?'

'No, but I always ask,' she says, pushing her legs further on to the chair.

'So, you got back to London and looked for a way to hurt Rosneft?'

'Not immediately, no, but – do you know Heathrow Terminal 6?'

'The Tyrants' Terminal? Sure,' she says. All the private planes belonging to the world's least desirable travellers take advantage of the discretion afforded by Terminal 6 when passing through London.

'I like to arrive there and take their rides into the city. I have a ShitList feed in my implant so I can figure out which of the chauffeurs is waiting on one of them.'

His eyes darken. 'When I got back from Tanzania, Rosneft's boss, Farinata Uberti, was due at the same time, so I pretended to be him.'

'What?' she asks, laughing. 'How do you get away with that?'

'That's their weak spot. They're trade in so many lies, they have no idea how to tell what's true any more,' smiling.

'On the way in, while I was enjoying Uberti's very fine taste in vodka, I came up with a plan. My brother is an engineer at the Mars colony. He figured out a scalable way to generate electricity using the one thing they have plenty of—'

'Sand.'

'—sand. For a surprisingly small investment, I could start one of the world's largest energy companies and, along the way, cause Rosneft some pain. The only problem being that the solar farms would be situated in the middle of a major war zone.'

'And when you couldn't get the electricity through, and all these seekers are sitting right there . . .'

'Lots of people with no identity in land that sits outside of any country and who nobody wants. I dusted off our system and gave away a free electricity allowance with each identity. It's a fairly perfect place to try, and our market has been growing exponentially ever since.'

'I like it. It's simple, and I'm not surprised Yuanxing is so grateful to you. Every printing shop seems to be run by a different Chinese family.'

She continues staring at him, enjoying his calmness and strength. 'What's your endgame? Destroy the Russian economy?'

'That won't happen,' he laughs. 'Like here, they will simply adapt. You understand they've imprisoned themselves as well? Making an entire nation so dependent on one replaceable commodity was never going to be a good idea. No, I learned the hard way not to force myself on the world. You always pay a higher price than you can afford.'

'So, what then?' she asks, rubbing her toes against his jeans, dislodging sand on to the chair.

'I'm hoping to live my life with as much fun and excitement as I am able in the time left to me. To create something worth remembering, and give not even a grain of sand to evil men.

'And you?' he asks. 'Why are you here?'

Her eyes harden: the colour of the sea before a storm.

'Depends who's asking,' she says. 'For the funders, my pitch goes like this: everyone has agency. I want us to stop treating seekers as if we can package them neatly into little boxes and manage them like so much excess chattel. Each of them has their own ideas about what they want. All we can do is support the best of what is already here and let them build their own lives.'

'It's a good ambition,' he says, pausing carefully, 'for an organization. What's your real reason?'

'For Michele,' she says. 'For all the people who need somewhere safe, because I can't tear down that wall, and because I couldn't help the last time.'

21

'Where now, Duruji?'

It is near noon, and they are hiding inside an abandoned home-stead on the edge of the hamada. A single tree, dead and partially burned, leans over the roof, and blackened stumps of a hedge surround the periphery of the property. There is an old dirt road wandering through the stones outside leading who knows where.

The group have been travelling south for weeks, trying to find safety and others of Ansar Dine. They are not sure if anyone escaped the fortress cities.

That night in the canteen, they watched as the naked man captured Abdallah Ag Ghaly, saw their leader dragged away like a slave. Their sense of invulnerability and authority has been shattered. Khalil alternates between periods of wild lucidity and moments of tortured delusion where he screams that Gaw Goŋ is chasing him. His ears are chafed raw from where he rubs them incessantly, trying to keep the mad howling out of his head.

Duruji copes by ignoring any doubt. Ag Ghaly will return, and he and his team of elite soldiers must be ready to serve him when he comes.

'We keep going south, to the river. We will find a town, and we will hide there until our Janab returns.'

The men have heard him say this many times. They keep asking, for the reassurance that someone knows what to do.

They have not seen anything or anyone. Their radio calls have gone unanswered. No replies to their messages. No instructions. They assume that their radio station has been taken.

Their rations have almost run out. There is little water. They have been surviving by killing birds and rodents, wastefully shooting at anything that moves, and they have almost no ammunition left between them.

'Duruji, look!'

The man is pointing out the window towards a column of dust rising up along the road.

Rattling along the path is an ancient cream-coloured self-drive Mercedes Benz diesel piled high with boxes and dragging a vast trailer behind it.

It clatters to a halt in the road outside the homestead. The driver's door screeches open and a portly man, who appears only slightly younger than his century-old vehicle, struggles out, leaning heavily on a two-headed stave, his hair a grey burst about his head. He grins, sets a faded blue peak cap firmly on his head and slaps one of the bales on the roof, sending up a cloud of dust.

'Come, Saafaandu,' he shouts, leaning his two-headed stave against the door and digging in the footwell for a bottle of water and a bowl.

A semi-blind, balding Golden Labrador, as stout as its owner, hobbles out from the back of the car, clomps arthritically to the road and drinks thirstily.

The man sips from the bottle, tears open a bar of chocolate and unfolds a yellowing paper map which he lays out on the wide, rusting bonnet of the car.

'I think we should be there in another three or four hours,' he says to the dog.

Duruji and the men stare in astonishment. Khalil groans in the clutches of his madness on the floor. 'Gaw Goŋ is here,' his throat torn.

'Who's there?' shouts the man. He sounds curious rather than frightened. 'Come out. I won't hurt you. It's only me and Saafaandu.'

Mohamoud shrugs at Duruji. None of the other men can understand what this stranger is saying.

'What does he want?' whispers Duruji.

'He says we should not be scared of him,' says Mohamoud, his eyes wide.

'Come with me,' says Duruji. 'The rest of you, stay here.' He points at the only other man who still has ammunition and cocks his head. That man takes up position in the corner, hidden in the shade and watching the road.

Duruji and Mohamoud walk carefully from the homestead towards the car.

'Hello,' says the old man in delight. 'You're the first folks I've seen out here.' He strides towards them, his hand open and out-stretched in greeting. He scarce comes up to Duruji's shoulder. The dog whuffs at them and drops exhausted in the shade of the vehicle.

'Oh, don't mind her. She doesn't even have any teeth left.'

The man appraises the two jihadis and since his hand has not been accepted lowers it slowly to his side.

'You're Ansar Dine, yes? More of you inside?'

Mohamoud translates rapidly. Duruji nods, uneasy at the man's familiarity, as if he had expected them, recognized them.

The old man chortles, looking pleased. 'I was wondering when I would run into you fellows. You hungry? Want to eat? I have plenty of food. Beats eating rats.'

Duruji looks at him suspiciously.

'What do you want, old man?' asks Mohamoud.

'My mine,' says the old man. 'I've waited forty years for you bastards to get yours, and now I'm going back to my mine. But I don't hold a grudge. Your getting me out of the desert probably saved my marriage. So, come eat, then we can part in peace.'

He turns his back on them and walks to the trailer. The rear gate crashes open, and he drags out a grey battery-powered cooler box from amongst a stack of others. He carries it to the boot of the car and places it on top.

Inside it is tightly packed with vacuum-packed bags of chilled cured meats and dried fruit.

'Saafaandu and I were about to have our lunch, and you're welcome to join us,' he says.

So saying, he opens a bag and squeezes out a thick helping of pastrami into the dog bowl. He pulls out an old clasp knife and finds a bag of French loaves from the back seat which he starts cutting into pieces.

Duruji takes a bag, sniffs it and then devours the contents. The others come rushing out from the homestead. Khalil stumbles through the doorway last, hesitating in confusion as he sees the old man smiling at him. 'Gaw Goŋ . . .' his concentration blurring once more, and he joins the others where they have launched themselves at the cooler and begun to inhale the food.

There is no conversation as the men have their first real meal since the night in the abandoned mining town.

Translating for Duruji, Mohamoud asks, his mouth full, 'Why do you have so much food for one person?'

'Wait, wait,' says the old man. He digs through his cavernous pockets and extracts a spectacle case. He opens it carefully and settles a thick set of rims on to his ears. Its oversized controllers are integrated into the arms, and he fiddles with the side panels.

'There,' he says. 'That should do it.'

There is a faint echo as he speaks and the rims translate a half-beat behind him.

'What did you say?'

'Food,' says Duruji. 'Why do you have so much for one man. And a dog?'

'There will be others who will join me. Others who remember what we were doing there.'

Duruji looks back along the road, but the horizon is empty. 'Who are you, old man?'

'Just an old miner on his way back home,' he says.

He smiles, looking at the sky. 'My wife passed two years ago. We had a good life together. Probably better than if I'd stayed out here. She hated it and thought it was a blessing when your people invaded. But she's gone now. Only Saafaandu and me left, and I've never forgotten my mine. I want to see it working again, before I die.'

His gaze is that of a man certain of his place in the world and unafraid of where that is.

Duruji stares at him, unsure of himself. 'Why are you not scared of us?'

The old man looks at them in surprise. 'Why should I be? Your kind are finished. They are hunting you everywhere. Either you will hand yourselves in or you will die.' He nods towards where Khalil is standing, looking lost and terrified, rubbing his ears. 'The big lad. He knows it. He can hear it coming.'

Duruji looks back at Khalil. 'It is his first time above ground. He should not have been up here so long.'

'If you say so.' The old man returns to his map, leaning on his two-headed stave, studying his route and smiling to himself. Duruji feels unsettled by his confidence.

The men huddle at the trailer.

'We should kill him, take his things,' whispers one of the men. 'He is a demon. He scares me.'

Duruji shakes his head. 'No. We are the enemy now. Few will

show us kindness. We should be grateful for what is freely given. In truth, this man scares me too. We must let him go.'

When they have eaten as much as they are able, the old man packs up. He leaves them one of his cooler boxes, then helps his dog back into the car.

'There's a new city about four days' walk from here,' he says to Duruji. 'Head south from here and, when you get to the river, walk upstream. You won't miss it. You could do the right thing and give yourselves up to the border guards there. If not – well, I don't fancy your chances.'

He stares at where Khalil is rubbing viciously at his ears, keening in terror, and shakes his head. The door scrapes closed, the diesel roars, and the last they see of him is the column of dust dissolving into the dark pressure of the horizon as he heads deeper into the desert.

Eventually, all that remains is a shimmering blur which looks almost as if it could be a baboon striding across the sands, gripping his two-headed stave, a painted dog yipping at his side.

22

Dawn, streaked in blues and reds, slices through the rain showering the city of Dakar. Mottled and muddy smells, singing of birth and new life. Clouds of hawks circling overhead shriek and scatter, black shapes against the sky, startled by the pandemonium of drumming and singing which rattles the earth.

A stream of buses enters the city, pouring forth a gay and excited river of people. A deluge dressed in ochre reds and yellows, greens and whites, boubous and djellabas, umbrellas and charms. Children stamp in puddles, their parents shouting in joyful bedlam, embracing friends.

The stadium swells, and the singing, the drumming, the roars, pounding of feet and howl of horns rise in a swirling, towering inferno.

It will be hours before the laamb starts, but people are here as much for this beating, riotous jubilation as they are for their favourite wrestlers. Already, each wrestler's marabouts and jujumen are out on the field, dancing, drumming, singing: a musical challenge, a cacophony of taunts.

Young men, unassociated with any of the formal heats, spar on the sidelines, cheered and celebrated.

At the summit of the main stadium grandstand are two levels of private luxury seating. Most are still empty, although cooks and waiters are busy setting up.

The largest of these booths is set aside for the Parti Démocratique Sénégalais, where volunteers are preparing boxes of T-shirts, flags and umbrellas. Today is their largest rally before the local government elections and, interspersed with the main wrestling events, their leaders will each have the opportunity to speak. Across the city, the ruling Parti Socialiste du Sénégal is holding a similar festival.

As the grandstands fill, enthusiastic party volunteers distribute flags and banners which take root and sprout amongst the crowds.

A breath, as the chaos in the stadium harmonizes and then is released in a massed woof as if of a single exhalation. The wrestlers have arrived.

The marabouts dance and drum, singing the praises of their champions, for, truly, the gods are amongst us. These giants, their arms and legs thick with gris-gris, anointed with potions and herbs, their skin ebony and gleaming with oil and ointments to protect them from the charms of their opponents.

A thin marabout in a long white gabardine cloak and an enormous purple feathered hat, his ankles heaving with gris-gris, struts before his drummers and dancers. His feet sweep up sheets of sand.

'Shago,' he roars at his wrestler, ripping his knife from its sheath and pointing it at his own heart. 'Know that, if you fall, you will also have to bury your own marabout. Your shame you will carry alone always on your shoulders.'

Shago screams, slamming his feet into the sand, advancing on his opponent. The two great warriors grapple, tearing at the earth.

With an immense heave, Shago finds his mark and flings his adversary to the ground.

The crowd answers his victory cry, erupting like the furnace howl of a volcano.

Through the morning, wrestlers take to the sand, lock arms and attempt to fling each other. The first on to his back is the loser. The chants of the marabouts rise in splendour with the rank of their combatants. Between each bout, a speaker from the Liberals takes to the sand and, to roars of approval, declares their forthcoming electoral victory.

'I think I see him,' says Tiémoko, waving and indicating where he is hanging on to their seats.

Simon, and Shakiso holding on to his hand, squeeze their way up through the grandstand, the crush of people threatening to drag them in different directions or topple them into the laps of those seated alongside the stairway.

Tiémoko and Simon embrace, and he leans across to shake Shakiso's hand.

'You,' says Shakiso warmly as a young woman appears from behind Tiémoko. 'You're a long way from Aroundu?' She has not seen Viviane since that day when Oktar . . .

'Of course, you have met in my office?' says Tiémoko, Viviane embarrassed at the attention.

They settle into their seats, jubilation and cheering around them.

'I see even the grey men are here,' says Shakiso, staring up at one of the windowed boxes where a member of the Gong Yuanxing collective stares out at the stadium.

'I believe they're at both events,' says Tiémoko. 'The great advantage of being able to be at more than one place at the same time. They are studiously neutral.'

The grey man appears to see them and withdraws from view.

'Does our being here mean you support the Liberals?' she asks.

'I'd prefer them to win,' says Simon, 'but if I had the foresight of the grey men, I'd have been at both. No, the announcement will be coordinated. Both party leaders get to tell everyone this afternoon.'

Simon turns to Tiémoko. 'I hear the griot has crossed into the desert?'

He nods. 'I spoke with him of our needs, but he has other reasons to take him there. The region is free of Ansar Dine, and many millions wish to cross the sands. Even without the jihadis, the way is long and there is little water. He knows the desert's secrets.'

'I thought the Moroccans and Algerians had closed their borders?'

'True, but there is another route. There were ancient rivers which ran through the desert to the coast in Libya. I believe he will open the way for them.'

Viviane stares in wonder. 'The griot honours you with his trust,' she says.

'The griot has no secrets, only stories he has not yet told,' says Tiémoko, laughing. 'I think I should find us something to drink,' turning to Viviane. 'Will you come with me?'

They make their way down to the food stands, leaving Simon and Shakiso.

Tiémoko and Viviane queue at one of the many food stands beneath the stadium. The crowd swirls and eddies, like a turbulent river.

'This will take some time,' he says to her. 'Would you wait here while I use the restroom?'

She smiles, and he threads his way around the stadium. When he is out of sight, he heads to the elevators leading up to the private stalls. The door opens, and the grey man emerges.

They say nothing, brushing against each other as if oblivious. Their hands touch as Tiémoko passes him a small transparent plastic card. The private keys for the Achenian printers.

They part without acknowledging each other. The grey man returning to his private rooms at the top of the stadium, Tiémoko to Viviane where she stands in the queue.

The day progresses, shadows crossing the arena, heat giving way to a languid dusk, and soon it is time for the Liberal leader, Sidiki Cissoko, to take his place in the event.

He passes down through the stadium, greeting supporters, and the never-ending grapple of those who wish to be near the man many believe to be their future president.

A volunteer meets him along the way, quickly sticking a microphone behind his ear.

In the basement of the stadium, two immense young men are waiting. They are the main event. The wrestlers Pathé and Birima. They are celebrated throughout the land. Fearless and feared.

They stand gently and in awe, as if before their genii.

Sidiki greets them both, holding their hands.

'It is my honour to meet you,' says Pathé, his voice gravel sliding down cliff-tops.

'My father,' says Birima, his voice, too, deep and vast.

'No,' says Sidiki, 'it is I who am grateful. I thank you for your support.'

There is silence as Sidiki walks out into the arena. A lingering hush of reverence.

He stands before them, looking deeply into each part of the waiting crowd. For a moment, each person feels as if they have been seen. That, alone amongst so many, they have had a fragment of this man's attention and time.

'Our moment is at hand,' he says, his voice amplified and intimate.

Calls from the distant crowds.

'Even so, we are not at peace. For too long we have relied on the sufferance of others. Too many here have mothers, fathers, sons and daughters who live in lands not of their birth. Too many here know the pain of losing loved ones to the seeker's journey, to the long roads that take them far from our ancestors.

'Our homes are burning. An arc of fire across land which should be sacred, which should support life, cherish life, and provide abundance for all our people.

'Too long have we run before that fire. It is time we put out the flames.

'I am not here to promise that genii will miraculously restore us and our lands. Lives that are lost, are lost. Hearts that are wounded, are wounded. Our pain is real, and it must be recognized.'

There are shouts from the crowd, acknowledgement and agreement.

'Over the last few months, we in the Liberal Party have sought common ground with our Socialist Party opponents. We have convinced them that change is needed and that mutual cooperation is necessary. Whoever wins, there must be a united understanding for our nation.

'There are many areas where our parties disagree, but there are two where we have found common purpose. Today, I am able to reveal these to you.'

A hush across the stadium. Many hold hands, for rumours have been circulating, and there is both fear and anticipation.

'Thanks to the bravery of a man many of you have come to know, and with the support of our brave men and women in the special forces, we have captured Abdallah Ag Ghaly.'

A sigh, of both relief and superstitious dread.

'There are many who have suffered. We have Abdallah Ag Ghaly, and he will stand trial before our great African Court of Justice, but we need to offer a way out for all those who served him or they will never put down their arms. There are far too many dead lost to the desert, and parents who wish to bury their children if they but knew where they are.

'Ansar Dine and their kind have dehumanized us, and we have dehumanized them. We must no longer fight this way. We need to offer a path to redemption. A small window through which we recognize their humanity, in exchange for the truth. We do not wish to forget our pain, but we must not be imprisoned by it.

'We have agreed with the Socialists that, on the same day that Ag Ghaly stands before the court, we will begin a Truth Commission.

'Our Truth Commission offers this to those who have committed atrocities against those we have loved, against those who have suffered: we are willing to grant full and unconditional amnesty to all those who have ever been party to Ansar Dine in exchange for a complete disclosure of all the facts of all crimes committed.'

A flutter, a murmur, a roar of confusion.

'We do not do this to forget the past, but to release ourselves from being imprisoned by it. Without forgiveness, we as a people have no future. And we do this now, while the war against Ansar Dine still burns, so that we can offer those who still carry hatred in their hearts an alternative to fighting.

'We do this to remove the corrosive acid of resentment and hatred, and to bring peace and harmony to our land.'

Many in the stadium are weeping, for there is much pain, and much that has remained unsaid. There is uncertainty, but there is recognition that the answer to a lifetime of suffering requires absolution.

'Peace will allow us to build, and it will allow investment. You know of the solar farms in the desert to our north, harvesting light where nothing will ever grow?

'It has taken many months of negotiation, but we have reached an agreement with the owner of those farms. 'That electricity will no longer be sold in Europe. It will be sold *here*. We will soon be investing in new energy infrastructure that will bring electricity from those farms to all. We will no longer struggle to teach our children in darkness, or care for our sick in hospitals that lack life-saving equipment, or pump water from our great aqueducts.

'The laying of cable to every home and every business will take time, but it will start very soon.'

It is true. Jubilation in the crowds.

'We have suffered long, but peace is at hand. No longer to be blinded by pain, we will give you back your eyes. And in the coming of that light, we will bring investment and opportunity to your lives. That we live forever in hope.'

In the stadium, a roar, 'Ci – So – Ko, Ci – So – Ko, Ci – So – Ko.'

A chant to raise the sky, and bring life back to the living.

23

Light from the street lamps reflects on the murmuring of the ocean. Stalls clustered around the bay, cheerful conversation from other late-night diners and the flowing rattle of generators.

Simon and Shakiso followed the crowds leaving the stadium down to the coast, finding dinner amongst the crowded restaurant stands before ending up walking along the water line and holding hands.

'So,' she says, leaning against Simon where they sit barefoot on the beach. She caresses his face, gently stroking around his eyes. 'Who'd you trust enough to stick those in?'

'Hollis's husband is a rather good surgeon. They're fully functional rims,' he says. 'Right now I can see your pulse rate is 71 and rising, and you're highly aroused.'

'Idiot,' and she pushes him over into the sand. They tussle briefly before ending up with her resting against him once more.

'Does all this help?' she asks. 'I mean, are you still angry about Hollis?'

'Once,' he smiles. 'It fades. Became something I can use and manage. I've learned not to personalize it. You know, systems not people, but, yes, sometimes it's stronger.'

He takes her hand, holds it to his mouth and kisses her palm. 'What I was fighting against didn't turn out to be any one thing or any one person. It's a whole collection of small things, and I can only fight it in a whole collection of small ways. Anger helped get me going when I realized the scale of that, but it couldn't be the only thing.

'It's strange. There are so many things I could have done with my life. Instead I got angry, created TheShitList on a whim and became wealthier than I had any right to expect. And then I met you.'

She pulls his arm across her belly, staring out at the darkness of the ocean. 'There was a guy I was with years ago,' she says, enjoying the warmth and intimacy, her fingertips stroking the inside of his arm. 'Asafa. He was a tout outside the Empire in Shepherd's Bush.

'I skived off studying for a night. When I got there, the concert was sold out, but I thought I might be lucky if I hung around. There was this young Jamaican guy my age, thin, obviously poor, but dressed in an outrageous top hat and stripy suit and swaggering around like a celebrity.

'He wandered up and down yelling, "Any tickets, I buy." Twenty minutes later, a couple hopped out of a taxi and started arguing with him.

'He knew I was standing there waiting. Knew I could step in any time, and there he is telling them – at a sold-out concert – there's so little hope of him reselling, they may as well just give them away. I think he got them for a fiver, and before they even left he turned to me and offered them for two hundred.

'I ended up going home with him,' she laughs. 'That wasn't a great idea. Beautiful boy, bit of a substance problem.'

'What makes you think of him?' he asks, kissing the smooth arch of her neck, enjoying the warmth of her, the intoxicating spice of her scent filling his breath.

'Sidiki's speech,' she says, staring intensely at the ocean. 'Being an aid brat gives you a weird impression of the world. We lived in magnificent houses, holidayed all over the world, I went to trendy private schools. And the people in the camps are destitute. I thought the world was like that. This helpless broken part kept alive by a wealthy paradise where everyone else is permanently on vacation.

'All these fragments – one of my earliest memories – my mom crying on a drone out of Nairobi. My parents worked for the UNHCR at this century-old seeker city called Dadaab which the Kenyan government decided to bulldoze. Two million people lost everything they had.

'I felt terrible, but we're not really part of it. We never see the conflicts, and we can do nothing about them anyway.

'And the first time I realized that was meeting Asafa. This guy, with education and opportunity, could probably make a fortune. Instead he's trading extra tickets at concert venues. I thought he needed my help, that I could help him.

'And I was wrong,' she says, her voice filled with an awkward mix of defiance and sadness. 'He was happy. Even the drugs. He didn't want to stop even if I wanted him to. We didn't last more than a few days.'

Looking at him, her eyes the colour of the ocean before a storm.

'Michèle. I don't know what I should have done for her. If there was anything I could have done. Whether helping or not helping made any difference to her? And this country. The seekers. Everyone is trying stuff and – I know this all sounds muddled and confused, but I feel like I'm sliding around the edge of understanding something important. I know we shouldn't force people into the camps. I know the stuff we're doing in the new cities is right, but sometimes I wonder if we're doing too much? That people are so much bigger on the inside, that it's possible to help without helping, but . . .'

She hesitates, searching the calm blue understanding in his eyes.

He says nothing. Taking her hand in his, stroking her palm, touching it to his heart and holding her close.

24

'Is it done, Gregor?' asks Pazanov, a cloud and hiss of steam from the espresso machine obscuring his words. 'I am not comfortable with the way Adaro is staring at us.'

'Yes,' says Valuchkin, sweat stubbling his cropped skull as he delicately re-stoppers the vial and palms it back into his pocket. A wide man, Gregor Valuchkin, his shoulders almost as broad as he is tall, and temperamentally nervous in the work as assistant to an assassination.

They are meeting Simon in La Fleuve, a café in the north of Saint-Louis Island buried in amongst the renovated hotels popular with expatriate contractors here for the building boom.

The two are standing at the bar near the entrance to the café, Pazanov watching Simon, who is sitting towards the back of the room, and ensuring he blocks Simon's view of Valuchkin. Near the door, the young owner is lifted off her feet as she embraces an older man arriving for an early lunch. Pazanov can hear her husky laugh over the oblivious everyday conversations of the other patrons.

With Achenia's announcement that they are giving up the energy route to Europe, Pazanov contacted Simon offering to meet and end their hostilities. His enemy must be weakened and distracted, for why else would he refuse the opportunity of running his cable across a desert he has risked so much to clear?

Observing him in person, he is less certain. The other man

seems unusually alert and confident. Too aware. He wishes Valuchkin did not sweat so, for he can smell him even with the humidity and nearness of the kitchen and the tepid smell of food waste in the alleyway outside.

'Watch everything you say and do nothing to attract attention,' says Pazanov, turning to Valuchkin. 'Assume others are listening and watching.'

'You have told me this already. If he drinks, good; if not, we say nothing and leave. I know.' The man's shirt is damp. 'It is the humidity,' he says, seeing the other's scowl.

Pazanov turns from the bar and leads the way towards Simon's table. Valuchkin is carrying a tray on which are three white coffee cups, a steel pot of filter coffee and a small jug of milk.

'Mr Adaro,' says Pazanov, extending his hand.

Simon stands, beaming, his face the epitome of guileless innocence. 'I'm so glad we could finally meet,' he says.

Valuchkin nonchalantly places the tray on his side of the table, just sufficiently out of Simon's reach, and pours carefully from the pot into each of the cups.

'A peace offering,' says Pazanov, 'but not so expensive as to be taken for a bribe.' His smile at his own joke never reaching his eyes. 'This is Valuchkin, here for our —' choosing his words deliberately '— protection.'

Valuchkin nods and puts his hands around the cup closest to Simon. His entire body communicates that he will shortly pass it across the table.

Simon, seemingly ignorant of him, stretches inelegantly and picks up one of the other cups before collapsing back into his seat. His smile is of childlike sincerity and genuine gratitude.

'I accept this in the spirit intended,' he says, raising his cup.

Pazanov offers a quick, curt glare and recovers. He sits and takes the remaining cup, jostling it in his frustration so that it spills into the saucer. His smile returning, like a forced glacier, to his face.

Valuchkin remains standing, awkwardly holding the cup. He glances behind him and mechanically sits down. He gently places the cup on to the table, seeming only to breathe again once he has released it.

Simon's smile is a continuing picture of naïve contentment. He drinks deeply, sighing happily. 'I do love coffee. Thank you. This café is probably one of the best in Saint-Louis; you're in for a treat.'

Pazanov stares at him, politely picking up his cup but not sipping, not noticing as his hand brushes the slops in his saucer.

'I was surprised you called,' says Simon.

'You have decided not to compete with us,' shrugging. 'We do not serve this market, and we have no interest here,' says Pazanov. 'It is only politeness.'

'You accept, then, that I am not a threat to you?' asks Simon.

Pazanov involuntarily purses his lips, as if holding back an instinctive response.

'Shall we say, for the moment, we accept you are no longer interested in Europe? It is not clear to me as to why you have chosen this moment to change your plans.'

Valuchkin is doing his best to pretend that the cup before him holds no fascination, studying the wood grain on the table as if it is a sacred text. Simon appears unaware of his discomfort.

'You've seen the investment pouring in here?' says Simon, cocking his head at the foreigners at the tables around them. 'It turns out the market on my doorstep is more interesting than the one across the Med.'

'That may be as you say,' says Pazanov. 'But the desert is large, and you could still expand your farms. Our respite would only appear to be temporary.'

'An honest businessman would recognize that his dominant position is threatened and start developing new markets and products,' says Simon. 'That's what I'm doing.'

Pazanov grimaces. 'Rosneft is an energy company. We cannot simply become something else.'

'I don't have a monopoly on buying bits of the Sahara.'

'We do not have your technology,' says Pazanov.

Simon continues, hounding his point.

'Haier makes a vitrification printer that does most of what ours does. I think we must have transported around twenty into the region in the past few months. If you work with them, get some primary research done, I'm sure you'd get there.'

Pazanov shrugs. 'It may be so, but I am not here to discuss our business strategy.'

'Then why are you here? It doesn't look as if you came to enjoy the coffee.'

Valuchkin's eyes widen. He glances open-mouthed at Pazanov, who returns a subtle incline of his head.

Valuchkin gestures as if to call a waiter, muttering, 'I think I need . . .' His hand brushes against his coffee cup, threatening to knock it over.

Simon leans forward, his hand moving faster than they expect, catching and righting the cup. Not a drop is spilled.

'Careful there, Valuchkin. Wouldn't want any of that on you. You might get burned,' he says.

'No. Of course not. Thank you,' says Valuchkin, sweating. 'It is the heat,' by way of unnecessary explanation, rubbing at his sodden shirt.

'What is it you want from me, Pazanov?' asks Simon, sitting back.

Pazanov laces his fingers on the table, staring at the toxic cup. Eventually, he looks up.

'As I said when we spoke, I want to end our hostilities.'

'I've never been your enemy, Pazanov. And it's easy to stop being hostile: stop trying to kill me. You didn't need to come all this way to tell me. Unless . . .'

He gasps, goes pale. Trembling, he points at his cup, his eyes wide.

'You've poisoned me! You bastards! That's why you're not drinking!'

He makes as if to stand, a shout for help forming on his lips.

Pazanov looks horrified, his hands go up as if in surrender.

'Quiet, quiet. No one is poisoning anyone. Sit down, please. Sit. Valuchkin drink your coffee. Look,' drinking his. He glares at Valuchkin, gesturing emphatically.

Valuchkin, his eyes wide, sweat on his brow, drinks the coffee in a single, sweeping glug. His hands remain steady. He stares at Pazanov.

'See, we are all friends here. I'm sorry you don't trust us, Mr Adaro. We have come with honest intent.'

Simon allows himself to be mollified. 'What do you want of me, then?'

Pazanov looks across to Valuchkin, who is turning pale. 'Only to reassure you that we will leave you in peace. I am sorry that our trip was wasted. Now,' he says, his hand on Valuchkin's arm, 'if you will excuse us.'

Almost dragging him, they leave. The back of Valuchkin's neck is white and clammy, and he seems disoriented.

Their limousine meets them outside. As Pazanov helps the trembling Valuchkin into the cabin, he notices a group of orange-suited soldiers entering the back of the restaurant through the alleyway.

He swears.

'Look,' he says to Valuchkin. 'Hazmat. They'll be all over that cup. We need to get out of the country quickly.'

'He knew all along,' says Valuchkin weakly, slumping against the seats. He is in shock, for it is too soon for the poison to be absorbed.

'Yes. I will call ahead. We may be able to neutralize the polonium before it does too much damage.'

Valuchkin, soaking the seats in sweat, closes his eyes and imagines the toxin seeping through his bloodstream.

As the limousine rattles across the Faidherbe Bridge, Pazanov feels burdened by a growing unease. That he has not seen something. That he has been disoriented by personalizing this battle. It is like fighting smoke, and the more he grapples for understanding, the more he seems to turn in upon his own doubts.

'Is it easier to kill one man or many?' Natalya had asked, sitting on their wooden porch at the dacha all those months ago after Simon escaped the jihadis.

'I have never killed one,' he had replied. 'But trying feels different. Killing many is a clerical decision. They are there, and then they are not. They are never real to me. But this man is.'

'Perhaps you fail because you do not wish to kill him,' she had said, not asking, not judging. Fearful for what it meant to casually discuss the murder of another.

And he, his thoughts grinding on themselves, what have I missed?

25

'I'm almost there,' says Shakiso, as the Haval turns right over the bridge.

'Perfect timing,' says Simon.

The vehicle slows outside La Fleuve and opens for him to slip inside. Tuft is curled up asleep on one of the front seats.

She takes his hand, confused at the tension in his body. 'What's wrong?'

'Sorry,' he says, looking withdrawn. 'I think I may have killed someone.'

The car navigates its way out of the city and on to the highway heading east. The road passes close by the river where a group of people are washing goats in the murky water. The remaining goats stand beneath the shade of a large ditakh tree, watching nervously as their compatriots struggle against the water, their hooves in the air.

Shakiso touches his face, her nose almost against his, staring into his eyes.

'Tell me.'

They are beyond the city, the landscape giving way to the barren white and grey salt-rimed platter of the floodplain, when he finishes speaking.

'How long would something like that take to kill you?' she asks.

'It depends,' he says, 'but it would be a few weeks. Slow and fairly agonizing.'

'And this Valuchkin? He will die this way?'

'I don't know. If he was able to vomit, get rid of the stuff before it was absorbed, maybe not. It depends what it is. I'm only guessing at polonium, but they do seem to like the stuff.'

Her eyes widen as she slumps back on the curved rear seat, rotating the empty front seat and putting her feet up. She hangs on to his hands, squeezing them tightly.

'I know, abstractly, that they want to kill you. I just never –' she looks up into his eyes again '– promise me you'll stay safe?'

Their relationship has deepened gently over the last few months, and each has found convenient coincidences to ensure they have work in the same towns at the same time. They have reached that stage of intimacy where they would struggle to recall there was ever a time they were not together.

His face softens, and he brings her hands up to his lips, placing a kiss in each palm.

'Hollis was with me, watching the whole time,' he says, touching the bridge of his nose between his eyes. 'I was quite safe, and I have no intention of dying just yet,' pulling her close.

The car slows, turning left off the highway towards the river crossing at Rosso. They both sit up, astonished again at how much the landscape here has changed after almost two months of rain. The dry has returned. The bounty of the wet will be held for a little while longer.

'This is what I wanted to show you,' she says, glad to talk about something more hopeful. 'These propstock pellets of yours are astonishing. There's so much salt in the ground here, nothing else will grow. We've got agronomists travelling all along the waterways demonstrating some of the new techniques, but they tell me they've never seen – don't look at me like that,' wrestling the smirk off his face.

There is a brief, but entertaining, maelstrom of elbows and knees, livened by yowls and dabs with her paws from Tuft, before she manages to trap him between the seats.

'As I was saying,' she says, flicking her fringe back, Simon's body shaking with laughter. 'It's going really well, but the agronomists are worried about licence fees.'

'There aren't any.'

'Which is what I tell them, but they—' lifting her head and rising off him. 'What's this?'

The Haval has slowed to walking pace. Outside, the car is surrounded by a dense throng of people. The low buildings and massed construction cranes of Rosso around them.

'Something happening? I can hear music?' she asks, melody penetrating even through the dense skin of the vehicle. The music seeming a part of the air and the earth.

'No idea,' says Simon. 'Shall we get out and have a look?'

They squeeze their way between the people, Tuft taking one look at the crush and opting to remain behind. The car shifts over to a side street and parks.

Simon takes her hand as they thread their way through the crowd. Un-hulled rice lies drying in ankle-deep drifts on plastic canvas sheets up and down the side streets, people and animals walking through and churning it with their feet.

'What's happening?' he asks of anyone who happens to speak French.

'It is the griot,' says a child with a broad grin. 'He has returned from the desert.'

Simon grips Shakiso's hand tightly, a look of delight on his face. He leads her along a wall, pulling her up to join others sitting on top. Not too far ahead, across a swaying canopy of heads, a man is seated on a low chair playing a koubour. He is wearing a delicately embroidered ochre-brown boubou and matching kufi skull-cap. His feet are in handmade leather sandals. His face is joy and grace.

His song captures the earth and sky, the gentle push of growing things against the soil, the sound of returning birds, and the love which a person of good heart may have for all living things. He sings of the desert, of harshness and intimacy, and of the waters which flow in abundance.

Rosso has become an immense city, sprawling along the river. In this moment, though, it has come to rest, listening quietly as the griot reminds them of their place in the world, of one to another.

Shakiso leans her head on Simon's shoulder, feeling the warmth of his arm across her back, the regular pulse of blood against her cheek. Her breathing harmonizes with his, and with the music filling the world.

Gently, his song comes to an end. Silence. And then the roar of thousands of people celebrating their pleasure.

Simon caresses her body until his hands reach her face, drinking in her eyes and kissing her softly on the lips. She hugs him tightly.

'This is the griot?'

The griot smiles. 'I bring a memory of the desert,' he says and begins a story.

'Painted-dog's child lifts her head from her paws . . .'

Tales from Gaw Goŋ: Baana, le génie des eaux indomptables

Painted-dog's child lifts her head from her paws, looking up at Baboon as he raises the lid of the great black pot, sending out plumes of gravy-laden steam. He unfastens a leather pouch at his waist and scatters black wakando seeds into the stew.

'Aha, aha,' he says, stirring gently. 'It will be ready soon, pup.'

Painted-dog's child whimpers as the lid is sealed once more, her stomach in almost unsustainable anguish.

Baboon smiles kindly. 'Patience, pup. What do you think of my story?'

She stifles thoughts of fragrant feasts and concentrates on the question. 'It is a good story, grandfather. The power of the genii is indeed great.' She lowers her nose, nervous to speak a troubling thought, 'Yet, I do not understand why he would pick one man to return when he permits so many more to die so wastefully?'

'Aha, you are a wise pup. You would see those hurt made whole?'

'Yes, grandfather, for my uncles tell me that we do not hunt for sport, and we may not kill for pleasure, but only to serve the needs of our family. Without the herd, we would not survive. Would this not also be true for the genii, for all living things are of the genii?'

'That is true, Painted pup, but the genii are not hunters as we. Their ways are not our ways. Neither do they serve Men. Their lives are as one with the earth, dry and unending, and they lack our capacity to imagine the world as other than it is.

'So that they may unburden the sameness of the turning of the sun, they act upon the world. Changing things so that we are forced to change too. It is why the seasons are not always the same, that the waters may rise or vanish.

'We are as vessels to create the stories they cannot write for themselves.'

Light and understanding in her eyes. 'I understand, grandfather. Do the genii then guide the great migration of Men you showed me?'

'Yes, my child. They follow Baana's rivers through the hazards of war, remaining safe and nourished by the shores of his waters.'

Painted-dog's child looks north, beyond the plenty of this shady ouahe, into the searing sharp edges of the hamada, the stony desolation of the reg, and the vast sand ocean of the erg.

'Grandfather?' she asks, her voice filled with plaintive dread.

'Aha, aha,' he smiles. 'You see this sacred place, how small it is, and you wonder how Baana will protect these wandering Men once they are beyond the reach of his waters?'

Painted-dog's child nods, her eyes wide and frightened.

Baboon chuckles, the sound the delight of small pebbles being tumbled in a fast-flowing stream. 'We speak of Baana: one of his feet is above, one is below. The genii of one hundred pairs of wings. He is of our time and of all times.

'Once, Sahara, Al-Kubra, the grandfather and most impassable of all deserts, was filled with the rivers of the genii. The greatest of these were the Irharhar, Sahabi and Kufrah. So wide that even a swift-footed pup would travel days to cross them.

'They linger in memory and, for the genii, they run still.'

Painted-dog's child yips in excitement. 'Does that mean we may visit these rivers?'

'Aha, aha,' he laughs. 'Only the most powerful of gaw may call on the genii to reveal these hidden waters. It is a great one indeed who could open a way so large for so many.'

'Do you have such power, my grandfather?' she asks, her tongue hanging loose.

Baboon waves with his sombé at the waters of the ouahe as answer, and scratches behind her ears. Painted-dog's child slaps wildly at the dust with her hind paw, going cross-eyed in delight.

'Come, Painted pup, we will resume our story where the great migration of Men rest on the shores of the hamada, waiting to cross.'

He takes again a handful of dust, whispers to it, and it is Gaw Goŋ who blows it into the flames, the red-brown mist glowing in his eyes. A swirling green-grey pool opens above the flames, shot through with flecks of red and black.

Gaw Goŋ motions at the portal, pulling it wider until it fills the space before them. He whispers again, and the pool clears.

At first they can see nothing but darkness, then points of light which flicker and dance. A constellation of millions of fires all along the banks of the last river bordering the desert ocean.

They fly in towards a single hearth on a rise above the reflected facets of the waters.

It is the familiar face of Joshua, laughing and playing with a group of children, Rachel, Hannah, and Isaiah, the child reborn from the rubble of Kampala, among them. The children are thin but strong, running and chasing each other in the firelight.

Esther sits with a group of women, keeping the fire and tending to their meal. The people seem jubilant, as if preparing for a celebration.

Waiting all along the river bank are the silent *bomboutou*: water drums made from half a calabash floating in a pool of water within another, larger, calabash.

It was Joshua who travelled all along the riverside, speaking with the other bands of seekers, telling them of the genii. Of the opening of the way and of the path which lies after. The seekers will need a tremendous *batou*, the ceremony to call the gaw to intercede with the genii. Only then will the way through the desert be opened for them.

He showed them how to prepare the calabash so that it floats, how to play the water drum so that the sound it makes seems to come up out from the earth. His teaching taken by others to the millions all along the shore.

When the fragrant stew is ready, small bowls are prepared and carried to the water. The children chosen to make the offering to the genii walk out till they are up to their waists in the flowing river.

All along the waters, the children tip their bowls, submerge and wash them clean, saying, 'Great genii, please enjoy this offering of *thiere neverdaye*, even as we join you in celebrating your feast.'

The words spoken, the children return to the bank, flinging themselves into heartfelt embraces.

Each person receives a portion of stew, prepared with the last of their meagre reserves. No one knows how this night was chosen, why it is the most auspicious, but all join in the ceremony.

The millions of seekers have been waiting for this moment, making ready for the crossing. And all celebrate this night.

Joshua and Esther eat together, sharing a bowl. She rests on his shoulder, and they watch where Rachel, Hannah and Isaiah eat with the other children.

There is laughter, a murmur of shared conversation, of memories of the journey so far.

'Thank you, my husband,' she says.

'My wife,' he says, stroking her head. 'I truly believe that the worst is done. The journey ahead will be long and strenuous, but we shall be well.'

She smiles and kisses him, her lips warm and soft on his cheek.

They have camped weeks here at the riverside, waiting for the wet season to arrive and reach its peak. The war zone is behind them, trapped for the moment within the forests to the south. The journey through the swamps and jungles was filled with evil and dread. Many times they thought that they had stumbled into the midst of the conflict, but always the waters led them by.

The great migrating wave of seekers flowed past the refuges set up to deliver the drone packages they have relied on. They are grateful for the aid but do not wish to be dependent on the benevolence of others.

Not all have come this far, though. Even as many seekers now rest along the river, many in the tens of millions more have stayed to start new lives in the new cities growing in the unclaimed land between the border crossings.

Those who continue feel the presence of the genii, a song sung in their breasts, calling them ever onward.

'You should stay,' said Tayib, an immense Sudanese man who joined their group as they crossed over the drying remains of the Aoukalé River into Tchad. They had thought they lost the path there, but Joshua was unfailing, leading them on.

'The toubab do not want us. Why be a peasant in their cities? Stay where you are welcome. We are educated people, and there are many opportunities here for seekers. Your children can go to school. The desert is unsafe, why travel further?'

The border city of Aroundu grew daily, expanding outwards

and absorbing all those arriving. Overhead, drones flew by bringing in building materials and machinery for new factories. Around them the steady arrival of seekers from all across Africa. This was the first safe space many seekers had known, and their energy and optimism were quickly rewarded.

The road into the city was lined with market stalls selling fresh fruit and vegetables, electronic goods, bright fabrics and glittering clothes, and bubbling with the call of people recruiting new workers for the factories and farms which formed the engine of this new place. There was an exciting energy of hope as seekers set aside the fear and horror of their escape and took on the opportunity before them.

Joshua smiled, holding Esther's hand. 'It is well, my friend, but there are few guarantees, even here. We are called north, and we will trust in the genii to take us through.'

Tayib sighed, nodded, and then seized Joshua's hand firmly, embraced Esther, before he turned and led his family into the city.

Joshua and Esther watched him go, then continued, following the river along the border lands, going ever northwards.

They travelled another week along the river, through banks thick with bourgou grasses and kabou shrubs. It was peaceful there, and their journey was untroubled.

Eventually, under a sprawling baobab tree on a ridge looking across the hamada into the deep desert, Joshua halted and set out their camp. There to wait for the appropriate moment to make their crossing.

As days passed, others – similarly drawn to the river – gathered and set up their own camps. Word passed along the waters and soon, in the manner of such things, it was made known that on the sighting of the new moon they would make their batou.

*

It is time. The offering of the genii's favourite food, thiere never-daye, has been made and shared by those gathered along the shore. Their hunger is sated. They have made ready their belong-ings, dressed in clean clothes and prepared for their journey.

Joshua grasps Esther to his chest, and she feels his heartbeat and the warmth and love and light of him. He embraces each of his children, their eyes radiant by the fireside: Rachel, Hannah and Isaiah.

He walks to the shore, standing before his bomboutou, his back straight and his body strong. All along the bank, thousands upon thousands more, lining the water before their drums.

He raises his hands to the bomboutou, hard and strong, pauses and breathes.

It is Joshua who releases the first beat, birthing the rhythm taken up by the other drummers along the shore.

A drumming from the bones of the hamada, as if the heart of the earth itself is beating. The water drums send out their call, the booming so vast it can be heard days to the south in Aroundu and the other border cities. Setting pulses aflame and stirring restless passion in the waiting seekers.

Esther begins to clap and sing, the children following her lead.

All along the southern shore of the softly flowing waters: clapping, drumming, dancing and singing; the crashing of falling mountains, the dancing of continents, the rhythm of the deep.

Each person feels at once both subsumed within the collective soul of all seekers and alone in the complete clarity of knowing their own hearts. The stomping, charging drumming takes possession of them, within their muscles and marrow, driving on their song.

When it feels as if the beating can go on no longer, from in the darkest part of the hamada they see a trail of light bursting along the surface. Phosphorous sparks pounded from the soil in answer to one who stomps and leaps in the darkness. Tiny stars splashing in the liquid dust.

Closer, and the obsidian form of the griot emerges. He spins and leaps, his boubou spread between his outstretched arms like great black wings.

As he dances, he sings, his voice flowing with the warmth and compassion of waters bringing life to even the most parched places.

He dances before the seeking millions, flying in the night, pounded by their rhythm.

He slams his arms together and the earth shakes, heaving back with all his strength. The drummers answer with even greater intensity, the rhythm rising to even more frenetic height, giving strength to the one who will open the way.

The griot resumes his dance, gathering energy from the drumming, slamming his arms together, tearing, wrenching at the way.

An arc, as of the light of ancient kingdoms, shears across the night sky.

The griot sings in triumph, taken up by the drummers all along the shore. They take now their *djembe*, holding the leather-bound drums under one arm, as they join the dance and continue their rhythm.

Joshua steps first into the waters, the light of the way laughing in his eyes, and his djembe singing in his arms.

The millions begin to move, leaping, pounding, dancing, singing, into the way.

Before them, the vast ancient Irharhar river system opens. Clear waters, trees bowed low with fruit, the sighing of a gentle breeze through the grasslands.

For time out of time, they walk amongst the abundance of the genii, wrapped close in their embrace.

Some believe they see Baana, high in the sky. Others see Moussa, and still more Awa. The great genii of legend, granting this moment of peace, showing them the way.

For days they walk, singing, dancing, drumming as the griot leads them by the waters of the secret way.

Joshua with Esther, Hannah, Rachel and Isaiah, laughing, holding hands and drinking deep of the blessings of their journey.

And, with the laughing gurgle of the ancient waters of the genii all around them, the millions, flowing with the dancing pulse of the river, vanish from this earth.

The way is open.

26

'They're still alive,' says Simon, so quietly that Shakiso is not sure she heard, but he looks lighter than she has seen him, as if unburdened. And she has that same strange feeling that the story she heard was not the one which was told.

'Simon, what did you—' she starts but, as his story ends, the crowd begins to break apart, and the cheerful, chaotic industry of the city recommences. Hundreds remain to touch the griot, to be close to him, however briefly, and then – as mysteriously as departing fog – they are alone.

Simon hops off the wall, Shakiso landing lightly alongside him.

'Ismael,' he grins.

The griot takes his hand, pulling him into the billows of his boubou in a welcoming embrace.

'Simon, it is well,' he says, his voice a melody.

His eyes find Shakiso and he takes her hand, surprising her with his strength and the vast compassion with which he folds himself around her.

'This is Shakiso,' says Simon. 'We're heading up to the farm and then back to Saint-Louis, if we can offer you a ride?'

'That would be well,' he says, and they walk back to the Haval, the griot carrying his koubour beneath one arm. Tuft offers a welcoming lick as he takes the remaining front seat.

'I'm relieved,' says Simon.

The griot takes his hand. 'There are still many dangers, but the way is open,' he says.

'Your story,' says Shakiso as the car glides back out on to the road. 'I heard a fable about animals lost in a desert and how genii magically opened a path to a river valley, but –' looking at Simon '– that isn't what . . .'

The griot smiles, his tawny eyes calm, 'These are stories of Gaw Goŋ. They come from the ways of the genii. Each will hear only that which they can bear.'

'What was it really about, though?' she asks, feeling as a child must, struggling to grasp the experience of adults even as her memory of it fades like the remnants of dreams.

'Many things, my child. There are those who seek a way through the desert. I have helped them in their journey.'

'The seekers? They're heading for the Med?'

He nods. Understood, without the words for it, that what drives those who risk the journey is an unquenchable hope for more than what is available in these settler towns; that the risk of their journey is less than that from remaining in place.

'How many?' she asks, instantly responding to the unspoken comment in the griot's smile. 'I'm not sure the Europeans are ready for so many people arriving at once.'

'We were not ready either,' he says, warm good humour in his voice. 'They will manage, as did we.'

She thinks of the millions of seekers all along Senegal's borders, of the cities coping with the arriving deluge, the millions more skirting the southern flank of the desert.

She laughs. 'You're right. I only hope they realize it in time.'

The Haval pitches off the highway at a tiny village and on to a dirt track.

'Whoa,' she says. 'It's ginormous!'

The flat, rocky, dusty vastness of the hamada is clinically cut by the endless almost-uniformly black and absorptive surface of Sable de Lumière.

'I've never seen anything like it.'

The car stops outside the small engineering block. The massive thirty-metre-long bulk printer is beyond it, surrounded by activity. Security drones circle high overhead.

'We're producing the first of the line printers. They'll start from here and head down to Dakar, then link up the rest of the country,' says Simon.

'You will follow the river as well?' asks the griot.

'Yes, we'll go as far east as we can. I don't want to take too many risks, but we should get as close as we can to the fighting.' Touching Shakiso's hand, 'I don't think anyone expects this to bring peace on its own, but it might give people a reason to put down roots again.'

The engineers seem more excited to see the griot than they do Simon. The workers on the nearby farm make their way over as well.

Later, as they're walking amongst the solar roses, Shakiso turns to Ismael, 'What are the griots? Are there many of you?'

He takes her arm, smiling, as they walk. 'We are the memory of the past and future. We remind you of what you already know.'

Shakiso laughs. 'Ismael, that's completely inscrutable.'

'I will tell you a story about the coming of the griots,' he says.

'Only if you promise I can hear it properly,' she says.

Nodding as he holds her hand, 'Here, on the outer edge of the hamada, you will still find trees and farms. Beyond those guelbs and *kedias* is the reg, where there are only stones to eat. And beyond that is the great flowing erg, where sand confuses the unwary. When you travel across the desert, you are closer to yourself and to the earth than you can be anywhere alive. Many make the crossing.

'Before there were buses or off-road vehicles like that Haval, we would walk, leading our beasts beside us. With the coming of Ansar Dine, even if they now flee, the roads are destroyed, and there are few who would risk a vehicle to drive across. We have returned to the ways of our ancestors, walking across the grandfather of all deserts.

'The strong may reach the distant shore in two months, but many will take three. And, always, they must travel from ouahe to ouahe in search of water.

'Once there were two brothers who set off from the village of what is now Djenné, to make their crossing in search of the fabled libraries of Bayt al-Hikma in ancient Baghdad. They were strong young men and were soon deep in the reg. For many weeks, they followed the camel trains along the trade routes. During one of the great harmattans that sweep across the erg, gathering up sand and dust, they became separated from their guides and were soon lost to the desert.

'After two weeks, always heading north, they were without food and low on water. The younger brother was the weaker, and he was suffering.

'Seeing his struggle, the elder said, "Look, my brother, I still have my spear and my blade. I shall hunt for us and bring you meat that you may survive this journey." He ran off over a dune, and soon there was the sound of a fight, and dust rose over the sands.

'The elder soon returned, but he would not show his brother the meat he had found. He prepared it himself and fed it, piece by piece, to his brother. Overjoyed, and with his strength renewed, the two brothers continued.

'After another two days, they reached the fringes of the hamada and knew that, soon, they would reach safety. But the elder brother began to flag, clutching at his side.

'In helping him, the younger brother realized the truth. There had never been any animal to hunt. His brother had cut from his own flesh so that he might live.

'Instead of being horrified, the younger was overwhelmed by this demonstration of fraternal love.

'When they reached their destination, the younger resolved that he would commit his life to singing of his brother's courage and nobility. And so was the younger brother the first griot.'

As he finishes, the solar roses vibrate. A subtle oscillation across their surfaces, like the tremble on the wing of a butterfly, as they shed dust from the persistent northern winds. The harmony, a clean, clear note, travels in waves across the farm.

'There is another, darker, story,' says the griot. 'One which is far older.

'The two brothers travelled, as before, but they quarrelled and, accidentally, the elder murdered the younger.

'Overcome with despair at his crime, he carried the body of his brother to the home of their parents.

'"You are not welcome here," said his family. "Go away with the body of your brother, for we do not know what should be done with it."

'Distraught, the brother went out into their land and sat beneath a tree some way from the house. At mealtimes, he shouted, and he was brought food. However, when the wind blew, then his voice was not loud enough and they did not hear him.

'He found two sticks which he would beat against each other so that they might hear him. Overnight, termites ate into one of the sticks and hollowed it out. When he struck it, he discovered that it produced a louder, harmonious sound. Using this discovery, he obtained a bigger hollow log and struck it with two sticks to create melody. And so he created the first drum.

'On another day, two crows flew above his head and fought. The one killed the other. He watched as the living crow scratched in the earth and buried the corpse of the other in the hole. The brother-killer imitated this act, burying the younger. And so he invented our funerary rights.

'The brother took his hollow log and his sticks and returned to the family home. Many came to listen to his drumming and his stories, and his crime was forgotten, replaced by the love for his music.

'There are many stories of our origins,' says the griot, 'but always there is blood, and the transgression that places us outside society, but also as its reflection and strength.

'My family have been griots for generations, and I am but one of many,' he says.

'But they call you "the" griot,' says Shakiso.

He smiles at her, his eyes the depth of the erg. 'They do me great honour,' he says.

A figure in the distance, on the edge of the farm around the jagged guelb, waves and cries out in greeting.

'Come,' says the griot, 'for I see Amadou calling to us, and we have yet to taste his milk.'

27

'Child!' shouts Moussa, reaching for the boy, who jumps away and sprints across the market.

'You won't catch him,' laughs Tiémoko. 'He is too fast for you.'

'It is maddening,' says Moussa, staring at his wake as he disappears amidst the stalls and bustle. Shaking his head, 'All the other orphans take homes, but this child prefers to live on the streets. We have been trying to reach him for months.'

'I have seen this boy. He calls himself "Donald". One wonders where he found such a strange name?'

They are standing outside the Achenia office in Aroundu. Dust and noise from trucks carrying sand to the vitrifiers are as overwhelming as always.

'Come,' says Tiémoko, 'let us see how we connect these schools.'

The building is crowded with engineers collecting tools and equipment, many hanging out between trips into the city or desert. Project engineers in the age of industrial printers seem to spend half their time sitting around, and the rest rushing to some remote bit of nowhere to rescue a line printer that has inexplicably decided to commit suicide by driving into a gorge.

A group of men and women dressed in heavy boots and helmets push past. '– and some birds were nesting in the fuse box. One of the chicks pecked through the breaker,' shaking their heads and laughing as they head outside.

Tiémoko and Moussa climb the stairs and hunt for an empty office where they can talk.

Infrastructure development is finally keeping pace with the rapidly growing border cities. Even so, Moussa sometimes feels overwhelmed by the pressure. Shakiso has changed the entire organization's focus. Besides collaborating on civil infrastructure development, his role is to recruit teachers, build and extend schools and then hand them over to local communities as quickly as he can. There is no time to actually run them.

'How are you coping?' asks Tiémoko as he pulls up a map from his console and expands the image out and over the entire surface of the white workbench.

Moussa rubs his ear. 'You will see. We have the usual problems of securing building materials quickly enough, and not all our parents agree with our syllabus—'

'Too much science?'

'No, not enough,' he laughs. 'Every parent imagines their child as an engineer.'

'We certainly need them,' says Tiémoko. 'Show me where you have decided.'

Moussa takes a card from his pocket and waves it over the map, transferring the plans. Two enormous red skeletal structures for their new schools show up equidistant from their existing site, forming a triangle.

Tiémoko glances up at Moussa in surprise and back at the plans.

If you drew a network linking each of the people in the city and laid it over the map, you would notice how they cluster into dense aggregations. Not only separated by nationality, but also by tribe, language and peculiar historical entanglements obscure even to members of each group. There are few links between each cluster.

Harare has been growing rapidly as new migrants from Zimbabwe finally complete their long journey. Jurassic Park has been shrinking after a charismatic preacher led his followers further along the river to settle in Rosso. The space remained empty for only a few days before being taken over by arrivals from Bangui.

The relationships between the people in the city are like some mythic creature, growing, changing, adapting. Arrivals are absorbed into groups sharing their common history, or form new communities if they find none who share their values.

There is turmoil and tension, for even as countries collapse, old enmities are carried in hearts still scarred by violence. Sporadic fighting erupts as old scores are renewed.

Historical feuds sit uncomfortably beside parents obsessed with opportunities for their children, constrained further by economic ties in the complex economy.

'I thought you were hoping to break the groups up?' asks Tiémoko. 'It is dangerous to have so many children from so many backgrounds in one place.'

'I said you would see,' says Moussa.

'Shakiso does not share your concern?'

Moussa shakes his head. 'She believes that getting the children to mix will create a "melting pot".'

'Well, I share your fears,' says Tiémoko. 'Anything that goes wrong at such a place —' stabbing his finger into the map '— will set each of these groups against each other. It is too volatile here. Does she not realize?'

Moussa puts up his hands, his jaw set.

'Very well,' says Tiémoko, his voice curt. 'We will need to lay cable there in Versailles, and here in Bang Bang Town.

'Let me see Rosso,' zooming out to a wider regional view and then panning in on Rosso.

'It is the same?'

Moussa nods. 'Would you do me a favour?' he asks.

'My friend,' says Tiémoko, putting his hand on Moussa's arm.

'Would you prepare infrastructure anyway, at these other places?' He transfers a new set of plans, and smaller structures appear scattered across the map. 'Something will happen, and we must be ready to break up these schools, put them where parents most wish them to be. If we do not, other schools will open and we run the risk of them having a more –' he hesitates '– selective approach to the syllabus.'

'What we teach is more important than where we teach it?' smiles Tiémoko. 'It shall be ready for you.'

Tiémoko turns to study the requirements for electrifying the new schools. Moussa watches for a few moments and then goes out on to the balcony overlooking the market. He spots the boy, Donald, creeping behind a stall offering fruit and vegetables. The boy looks better fed than he would expect.

The owner of the stand glares at him and the boy shrugs, turning and walking away as if he had nothing particular on his mind. He continues around behind the vitrification printers.

The Chinese lady – Moussa struggles to remember her name – stomps out of her office. She always carries an air of unsuppressed fury. She shouts at the boy, who grins and runs over to her.

She puts her hand on his shoulder and almost seems to smile. They speak, and then the woman makes a gesture as if to say, wait here. She disappears into her office and returns with a bag of dumplings and a bottle of water.

The boy hugs her tightly and runs off, the food safely tucked under his dusty T-shirt.

Moussa drums his hands on the balcony wall. 'It is good,' he says to himself.

'What is that?' asks Tiémoko from inside.

Returning to the office, 'I must go speak to that Chinese lady.'

'To Mrs Chen? Is everything well?' asks Tiémoko, looking concerned.

'Yes,' smiles Moussa. 'You know her?'

'Her son. Their printer gives them trouble, and I help him with its repair.'

'You can tell me more later,' says Moussa. 'I think that boy trusts her. I will be back in a few minutes.'

Tiémoko watches him leave and shrugs. He returns to the map, scheduling line printers and managing demand on their grid. They have sufficient printers, but he – as does everyone else – struggles to employ enough engineers to keep the printers in order.

'They do so like ditches,' he says to himself.

His ear vibrates. 'Gong Yuanxing.'

He frowns. 'Yes,' he says.

'We accept your terms,' says the voice of one of the grey men. 'When can we have our printer?'

Tiémoko picks up his console and quickly verifies that he has received payment.

'It is all there,' says the grey man.

'Yes,' says Tiémoko. 'I said it would take time, but Simon is heading back to Europe in a few days. He will finally leave the printer in my charge, and I will have the opportunity to manage its security. Give me a few months, and I will contact you again.'

'We will grant you no more than twelve months. Be sure to understand that we will reclaim what is owed should you not deliver.'

The voice is cold, and Tiémoko is sure that he would rather not discover what they intend to reclaim.

'You will have it. Before the end of next year,' he says.

The connection ends.

Tiémoko finds that his hands are trembling and sweaty. He closes his eyes, breathing deeply, resting against the wall.

University life has its own form of intrigue, but he is not certain he is prepared for this type of thing. His heart is pounding. He will be grateful when it is over.

28

'Explain again why we're not eating here?' asks Shakiso, staring wistfully at a couple nibbling their hors d'œuvres.

'Because fifty-degree temperatures, no refrigeration, local standards of hygiene and French cuisine do not always go well together,' says Simon as he guides her to an empty table near the stage.

'But they're eating,' she says plaintively. 'And them, and them, and them.'

'What do you notice about them?' pulling out a white, canvas-covered chair for her and dropping into the one alongside. Tuft has been left in their hotel, where a nervous concierge is attempting to placate her with endless cans of sardines.

'They're all toubab?'

'Indeed. And what do we know about toubab?'

'They are,' she says, shaking her head sadly, 'misguided fools.'

Simon nods, looking apologetic. 'Which is why we ate earlier. Here we stick to the drinks.'

The dry has taken hold across the region, but the larges of the wet may still be enjoyed. As a benefit, Shakiso is experiencing a lull in demand on her time and suggested a vacation. Tomorrow, they will leave from Dakar.

Despite being near midnight, it is still early at Just4Utoo. Except for a few tourists struggling to stay awake as they realize how late entertainment in Dakar starts, the tables are only now beginning to fill.

The floor is roughly sealed concrete, and the open space between the two office blocks to either side is roofed with multiple spans of rubberized canvas, leaving wide gaps open to the stars. On the stage, a technician is fiddling with a green laser light, clicking his fingers in front of it and testing that the shapes it generates are sufficiently random. Another is tightening bolts on the last of the stage lights. The band are straggling in: the drummer hammering at the stays on one of his djembe with a mallet, the bassist sitting and sorting through a box of strings.

Dakar's most popular music venue feels strangely transient, as if a group of musicians have randomly assembled in the hope of an audience.

A young man leaps on to the stage and shakes the hands of the drummer and bassist. He is joined by a guitarist and a young white woman carrying a saxophone almost as large as herself. Without any preamble, he begins to sing, the others following his lead. A string snaps, and the bassist goes back to his repairs. The others continue.

'Is this the part of the project where you get bored?' asks Shakiso, sneaking her bare feet into Simon's lap, tapping along with her toes.

'No,' he smiles, 'not yet. Hollis prefers it at least be making money before I throw it over the fence to him. And it's not as if I'm willing to trust Pazanov and his friends.'

An elderly man, tiny within his faded black suit, leans discreetly over their table and offers them the cocktail menu.

'Which one's the rum and baobab mix?' asks Shakiso. Simon holds up his hand to request the same.

'What will they do?' she asks.

Simon shakes his head. 'Knowing them? Start a revolution.'

'Nothing's changed, then?' she says, snuggling down further into her seat as Simon caresses her feet.

'Oh, I don't know,' he says, smiling.

'I mean besides your posterior now having personal fan service,' she laughs.

Their drinks arrive and she studies him, condensation from the glass dripping over her fingers. She takes his hands, cool wetness trickling between them.

'What made you so strong?'

He grins at her, his eyes crinkling at the corners. 'I'm not sure how to take that.'

'I mean,' she says, 'you seem OK with stuff I feel like I'm still struggling with.'

He caresses her hand with his thumb, studying the soft lines of her face and eyes. Her youth.

All your experiences print themselves upon you. The scars on the surface are the easiest to see and have the least impact. The ones that mount are those on your soul and spirit: when you have cared unconditionally and experienced loss. When you have been placed in situations where, whatever your choice, you will cause hurt and you must make that decision anyway. Life has ambiguity that resolves in ways that linger. Sweet sorrows for all the missing and forever gone. Stories untold, moments unshared.

He can feel the weight of his, and the lightness of hers.

'Do you know the word *saudade*?' he asks.

She shakes her head.

'It's Galician, one of those words that doesn't translate very well. It's the feeling of the love that is left after someone is gone. All the places, sounds, flavours, sensations that tie you to them and them to you. Lost moments of innocence.'

She looks up at the ceiling, her eyes clouding. 'I think I have some of those,' she says, a memory of Michèle, her eyes tense and afraid in the stifling heat of the freight drone on the last flight from Benghazi, the smell of the baby in her arms.

He squeezes her hands, takes them to his lips, kisses them softly and slowly, and holds them there. His breath is warm through her fingers.

'As you put yourself at risk, you gather saudade until there are always reminders of those you have loved and are no longer with you. Moments where you caused pain you would take back if there had been another way, but there was not.

'If you are unafraid, you learn to treasure those moments, make them a part of who you are.'

'So what's your earliest memory of saudade?' she asks.

'You want the sordid details of when I was a spotty teenager?' he laughs.

'Of course; I've told you mine.'

He nods, smiling. 'I was in my first year at Bristol University after the army, and I met a girl,' he says.

'Weird,' she says, interrupting. 'Just realizing how hard it is imagining you as a student.'

'We all have to start somewhere,' smiling.

'So, your first love? Where is she?'

'She wasn't, not for real. I was twenty, on a scholarship, and she was captivating. A skinny blonde with the awful and endearing habit of saying precisely the wrong thing when she didn't mean it. And I loved her.' He shrugs. 'She didn't feel the same way.'

'I cannot believe that is possible. Did you not show her your ass?'

'I'm afraid I was too young to realize its quantitative and acquisitional potential,' he says. 'I don't think it was physical. She was always looking to belong, and I couldn't understand what that meant.'

'I've met people like that,' says Shakiso, looping a frond of hair around a finger. 'They always bounce off me. I've never really thought about it,' she says curiously. 'What's your excuse?'

'I,' says Simon with a great deal of pride offset with a vast grin, 'don't need one. I was in love with someone who didn't feel the same way. Lots of opportunity for introspection.'

'How does that help you with your teenage suffering?'

'I learned that life isn't always symmetrical. Sometimes there is no right choice, and you have to make the least bad one.

'Loving, no matter how unconditional, isn't enough,' looking into her eyes and resting his nose against hers. 'The other person must also love you,' kissing her on each eye, 'and you have to have the courage to let them love you unconditionally too.'

'Do you miss her?'

'Sometimes. Not her. Saudade. Her smell, the sound of her laughter, how it felt to be with her. All that longing and confusion. I haven't seen her in almost thirty years. I'm not sure I'd recognize her now, or have anything to say. We're not those people any more.'

The metal door at the entrance is nudged aside as a battalion of large men in dark suits and sunglasses push their way through and form a short honour guard. The owner of Just4Utoo, an old man in baggy trousers and a brown fedora, rushes forward to greet Sidiki Cissoko.

He leads him towards a large reserved table alongside the stage. As he walks, people stand to applaud, reaching out to touch him or shake his hand. The few foreigners look bewildered and ask those nearby to identify the man at the centre of attention.

The local elections are only weeks away, and the rival presidential candidates have kept up a continuous schedule of rallies and events. Neither gives the impression of sleeping, and their marabouts sing and hector from atop trucks filled with drummers and singers, travelling through the country. Each candidate claims support from amongst the spectrum of celebrities and musicians. Tonight is part of that hounding after votes.

The growing border cities have caused tension. How, people wonder, do these cities create such wealth where there is nothing? What do our politicians offer when so much can be achieved without them? The various local government candidates have struggled to answer. Whoever wins, a tonal change has come.

As Sidiki passes their table, Simon stands and they embrace each other.

'My friend,' says Sidiki, smiling at him and Shakiso.

At the entrance, looking drained and a little unsteady, a white man in jeans and T-shirt arrives, immediately wrapped in a friendly, relieved embrace by the tiny waiter in the oversized suit.

Sidiki and Simon exchange a glance. 'The prawns,' they say, nodding.

Sidiki puts his arm around the owner of Just4Utoo's scrawny shoulders. 'Tell me, Behzad, that man there,' pointing. 'I'm guessing he ate here last night. One day those prawns of yours are going to kill someone. Why do you still serve them?'

Sidiki and Behzad answer in unison, 'Because they are so cheap,' laughing.

The lights go off, leaving the venue in darkness except for glowing candles and luminance leaking from the kitchen. A man begins to sing, his voice deep and redolent of wild places.

'Dee-da-de de dé, dee-da-de de dé, dee-da-de de dé.'

His rhythm taken up by the bass and saxophone.

The venue in silence.

Lights gradually rise and pick out the singer, with his great head and broad chin, his hair an olive-coloured burst about his head, dressed in a tailored mandarin-collared black suit. A faded portrait of his marabout in a frame hangs from a thick silver chain around his neck. He rests one hand on a two-headed stave as he sings.

'The mama keeps on crying. Where is my child?
The fire keeps on burning. Where is my child?' he sings.

Simon, his eyes lost in distance, *'Where is the child?'*

Shakiso noticing, putting her hand to his cheek and pulling him close, kissing him on the forehead.

The young saxophonist takes the lead, her voice the raw sorrow of the millions fleeing conflict and despair, seeking hope and peace. A man in the audience rises, stands before her, bows low and points.

Simon suddenly rubs at his ear, his body tensing. Nearby, Sidiki's guards are moving swiftly towards the entrance.

'What's happening?' whispers Shakiso.

'Men with guns, outside, trying to get in,' he whispers back.

Over the music, they can hear a series of dull reports, shouts, and a rising hubbub of panic near the entrance.

'Time to go?' asks Shakiso, moving to stand.

He shakes his head. 'No. This is silly. They should know there's no way to get close.'

Outside, stillness.

Simon rises, takes Shakiso's hand and heads for the entrance, squeezing through the bewildered crowd.

Two men, their guns carefully held under the feet of the guards, lie motionless in the road. Another three men lie equally prone across the road alongside an open white van filled with what could be improvised explosives. A massacre halted.

'Dead?' asks Shakiso, mystified at the lack of blood given all the shooting.

Simon points upwards where drones hover quietly above them. They are visible only as a peculiar black void against the brightness of the night sky.

'They're non-lethal. My insistence.'

Sidiki joins them. 'Ag Ghaly's men?' he asks.

Simon shrugs. Probably.

'I must call Djimo. The Socialists are meeting at Mbaye's across town. I am sure I was not the only target.'

A guard hands him an earbed which he inserts. 'Djimo? They were there too? It is well.'

Hearing one side of the conversation, 'I expect there will be more of this. Stay well. I do not wish to win this election by default.'

He turns to Simon. 'The beast is dying, but it can still bite,' he says.

Flashing blue lights as police arrive, leaping out of their vehicles and muscling the unconscious attackers.

On the horizon are the hills of the Deux Mamelles, and upon them squats the familiar ugly bulk of Le Monument de la Renaissance Africaine. It rises into the moonlit sky, its three peculiar not-African, not-Korean figures joined and pointing abstractly, as if drawing a great bow. Less a monument to an African renaissance than its most distinctive testament to its losing battle with corruption.

Sidiki glares at it.

With a muffled crump, it explodes. Heat and flame erupt from beneath it, and the monument stumbles, seems to recover its balance, and then collapses into pieces.

The horizon is clear save for a faint glow where fires are burning.

Stunned silence from those watching, recognition of the symbolism of its destruction.

'You know,' says Sidiki, 'I am torn. I would curse Ansar Dine for their attempt on our lives, except for one thing.'

He puts his hand on Simon's shoulder.

'I always hated that statue.'

29

Dust rattles off the door as it scrapes open. The movement stirring up the smell of ordure and stagnant water lingering in the air.

'They are returning, Duruji,' says a man in a torn and faded black djellaba, a badly healing wound across his forehead. He returns to the ridge overlooking the path to the city.

'Good, I'm hungry,' says Duruji, seated in the shade at the rear of the abandoned goat shed. Light from the gaps in the reed mats making up the roof bands the floor and its sparse furnishings: a broken wooden table, legs taped to hold them from splintering; a scattering of chairs, all different; and small piles of blankets where each man may sleep. Hidden in the darkness against the walls is their collection of AK-47s. Only Duruji still has ammunition.

Khalil whimpers in the corner, his head bandaged so that he will stop rubbing at his ears. His huge form trembling and panting in the furthest part of the shadows. It is rare that he escapes his visions and terror of Gaw Goŋ.

As its power withers, the refugees of Ansar Dine have fled.

Those going north join with the seekers gathering at the Mediterranean. Some pretend at being victims in the hope of abandoning their past. A few may keep, in their secret hearts, the ambition of restoring Ansar Dine and answering a call, should it ever come.

Those going south join with the settlers in the growing independent cities. There they similarly seek new lives or, as with Duruji and his men, hold out for the return of their leader.

Sori Malé, constrained by the Senegal border to the south, is stretching east and west along the Senegal River. A city of four million has emerged without expectation or planning, growing too fast for any authority to impose itself. No centrally recognized courts or police or notaries or property register. It should not function save that all interactions are public.

Each person carries their Achenian biomimetic identity card. All their contracts stored anonymously in a distributed public ledger: the property they own, who they do business with, what they buy and sell. Every single thing in the city has an irrefutable record of ownership, an ever-growing network of visible trust permitting a semblance of order even amongst the distrust of so many.

The inevitable criminality in such a city is tangled by this tangible and tactile web.

The shed door widens, sagging back until it rests against a chair. Three men stumble inside, sweaty and exhausted.

'Where's Mohamoud? And our food? Your packs are empty?' Duruji's voice rising in anger.

They respond by shaking their heads, their breathing in short panting gasps, their throats dry.

'We tried, boss,' says the thinnest of the three, collapsing on to a chair. 'It didn't work.'

'What didn't work?'

'The cards,' he says, taking a handful out from inside his djellaba.

Duruji stands, his blocky body filling the tiny space. The three men cower.

'All you had to do was take the cards to the market and buy what we need. How could it not work?'

'I don't know, boss. Mohamoud went in with one of the cards while we stood watch across the street. He was only gone a few minutes, and then we heard shouting and those private guards were running in. They dragged him out into the street and began beating him.'

'And you ran, like cowards?'

'No, Duruji,' says another of the men. 'We wanted to help, but Mohamoud called to us. He pointed to us, and then everyone was attacking us too. We don't have weapons, so we ran.'

'We stopped at a smaller shop where it was quieter. I tried this card,' holding up one, its clear plastic coruscating with seemingly random patterns and colours. 'The shop owner shook his head. We tried to rob him, but he pointed out the window where the guards were coming. We had no choice but to run.'

'Duruji, we do not understand this place. Please, we must find somewhere else,' says the first.

'We stole those cards only yesterday. All you have to do is touch that reader and it pays. No one looks at the card. How can it not work?'

'We don't—'

The light is blocked at the doorway, and an unconscious body is thrown to the floor.

'Because you are fools,' says a guttural voice in heavily accented French.

There is a moment to realize that the body is that of the man who was supposed to be on watch outside.

Duruji and his men leap for their weapons, and stop.

The white man with the shaven scalp at the door is making a small shaking motion with his head. His strange-looking machine pistol is still. Two other men stand to either side behind him.

Duruji glares at them and takes a careful step, planting himself in the centre of the room in front of his men.

The white man ignores him, picking up one of the cards from the floor. 'They're biomimetic. They can only work with the person they belong to. Easy to replace if lost or –' he sneers at them '– stolen.'

He drops the card to the floor, ambling further into the room, looking with distaste at their living arrangements, pausing as he considers Khalil curled on the floor.

'All the payment terminals are linked to the same network. If you use a card that isn't yours, it can call the guards. You'd be better off taking what you need rather than pilfering these silly things.

'You'd have as much luck with our guns,' flinging his machine pistol at Duruji, who snatches it and immediately tries to fire. A crackle of electrical discharge, the smell of burning skin, and he flings it to the ground.

Duruji grinds his teeth in unconcealed fury. 'What is this to you?' he spits, rubbing at the pain in his hands.

'Us?' asks the white man, calmly retrieving his weapon. 'We offer you a message, and an opportunity.' He nods at one of the men still guarding the door, who clips his gun into a bracket on his chest and steps forward to hand over a small console.

The white man motions at the screen and sets it on the table.

A voice speaks, strident and familiar. The refugees of Ansar Dine are jolted, propelled to see the image shining on the table. Even Khalil drags himself over, his eyes alert.

Abdallah Ag Ghaly is seated at a plain white table, a clean white wall behind him. He is dressed in the yellow overalls of a prisoner. He leans forward, into the screen.

'The crusaders have underestimated our resilience. Your resilience. Join me, my brothers, and we will restore the ummah and retake our lands. Trust these men. Go with them. They will show you the way.'

The screen goes dark.

'What is this?' asks Duruji, looking sceptical.

'We have been sent to fetch you,' says the white man.

'Who sent you? Who are you?'

The white man picks up the console, looks for a moment at the blank face, and slips it into a pocket of his jacket. 'Let us say that our employer shares certain interests with your leader. It would be to each of our benefits if Abdallah Ag Ghaly were returned to power.

'Your men lack organization or coordination. Like those fools in Dakar who thought they could take on drones with obsolete toy pistols,' contemptuous as he stares at their AK-47s.

'Nothing is without price,' says Duruji. 'What is it you want from our Janab?'

'In exchange for supporting your return to power? We want you to destroy the solar farms in the desert.'

Duruji laughs, a visceral, self-aware cackle. 'We know your business. You wish to stop that other toubab from destroying your control with the infidels? What if we take your help and then sell the energy anyway?'

The white man smiles, unsettling and insane. 'It does not matter if you try. You will not cross the ocean, and the Europeans would never buy from you. Even so, the machines will not last more than a few months in the hands of you obezyany. Your control of the fields serves us well enough.'

Duruji considers, his men silent in the shadows waiting for his lead.

'What happens if we agree?'

'We have a truck waiting outside. It will take you to our safe-houses in Dakar. We have food, clothes and weapons. We are collecting as many of you as we can find. If you know of any others we can contact, you will tell us,' he says.

Duruji looks at the guns pointed at him. 'Do we have a choice?'

The white man looks surprised. 'Of course,' he says. 'There is always a choice. We can leave you here and either you starve, or the guards find you and beat you to death.'

The white man turns and walks towards the door, his two men immediately going out ahead of him. As he steps outside he turns, the air shimmering and filled with gargantuan shapes on the horizon behind him, 'Are you coming?'

30

Beneath the clear waters of Ramsey Sound, off the rocky coast of St Davids in Wales, are a set of jagged shards. The changing tide squeezes the ocean through the sound, piling up around Ramsey Island and dropping as much as one and a half metres at the full reach of the tide. Glass-still standing waves form here, across the drop, and then churn as the depth of the bed rises towards the stone spire of Horse Rock.

These are the Bitches, and they are treacherous.

They are also tremendously entertaining.

Shakiso's howl of delight is all but smothered beneath the roar and spray. She spins backwards on her kayak, rolling under the wave, then righting herself. Simon sweeps past her on the peak, flinging himself into the air, somersaulting and pirouetting back into the wave.

'Dammit!' he shouts.

'What?' she screams back.

'I'm still blushing!'

'What?'

'I'm still blushing!'

'Woohoo!' shaking with laughter.

Summer has flown past, and Wales is heading into the long dark of winter. Tourists have abandoned the Pembrokeshire coast, and today Simon and Shakiso have the area to themselves.

They have spent the last week paddling along the shoreline, camping on the beach or sleeping in nearby villages. Tuft is staying with friends in London, sulking under her blanket as they left.

Late yesterday afternoon, they had beached in a beautiful cove near Porthlysgi Bay. According to their map, there was a seasonal campsite where they could avail themselves of much-needed hot showers.

Beneath a row of trees were a short line of three tiny private rooms. Each was really no more than two sides of corrugated iron leaned against each other and sealed with doors and windows. Two of them featured late-season tourists parked outside, but the last was open, and empty.

'It looks so warm,' said Shakiso, shivering. 'And I bet we can make a sex in there.'

'We have a lovely tent.'

'In which we almost froze last night. Go on, we can only ask. I'll make it worth your while,' she grinned.

They eventually dredged up the owner from his house, hidden almost a mile from the beach on the farm road leading to town.

'It be twenty pounds per night for each of you for camping,' he said, in tones that conveyed his utter disgust with the whole enterprise of tourism. 'And be sure to get what you need from town before six. I lock the gate, and there is no way to get in or out after that.'

'It's almost six now,' said Simon. 'I see one of the rooms is still free. Do you think we might have it for the night?'

He glared at them.

'No, it is taken,' he said, with great finality. 'Now, if you will leave me be, it is six, and I must go see to locking the gate.'

They watched, only slightly astounded, as he brushed past

them, walked across his yard and wrapped an elaborate chain and padlock around the gate.

They walked quietly back to the campsite. Shakiso's teeth chattered loudly, and she divided her sidelong glances between Simon and the direction of the vacant room.

'I'm sure he won't notice if we just borrow it for a little while?' she said, plaintively.

'We should pitch anyway,' he said.

'But I'm cold.'

'I know a way to make you much warmer,' he said, pulling her close and kissing her. She laughed and nestled into him.

They pulled their kayaks up the beach and on to a flat stretch of grass. There was a small patch shielded from the wind by an overgrown embankment.

Simon pulled their bags out of the kayak bulkheads. He dug through them until he found the tent, staking down the corners and releasing the self-tensioning mechanism which torqued the aluminium poles into position.

Shakiso quickly threw in blankets and provisions and disappeared inside, returning with a towel and change of clothes.

'That shower better be worth it,' she said, heading back up the hill.

An old stone outhouse had been converted into a cooking area and changing rooms. In the summer, this would be filled with laughter and stories. This close to winter, it seemed lonely and damp.

Shakiso dropped her clothes and cranked open the taps to their hottest point. Steam clogged the mirrors and condensed against the walls.

She was just thawing when the shower door opened.

'I heard someone needed their back washed,' said Simon, wrapping himself around her.

'Aaargh, you're freezing!' she shrieked, to laughter.

Later, after a somewhat disappointing dinner – 'Yeah, I think I might have dropped the tomatoes overboard' – they walked around the inside of the farm, along the fence.

'It's mighty definite, this fence,' she said.

'Indeed. One might almost think he had something precious worth keeping.'

'Or some great enemy to keep out?'

'That is more troubling,' agreed Simon.

'Do you think it may be the souls of all those who froze to death after being denied a lifesaving night in that last cottage?' she asked.

'It's not a cottage, darling. It looks more like he's found a use for some old pig shelters.'

'But they look so warm,' she said, her teeth chattering loudly once more.

'I tell you what,' he said, 'once everyone else is fast asleep, if it is still free, we can go borrow it.'

'Yes,' she said, clenching a fist and waving it at him.

It turned out there was not long to wait. As they drew near the rooms, they could see that the remaining couples had already turned in, and contented snores quavered in the evening air.

'Ah,' said Simon. 'An interesting alternative. Freezing or snoring.'

'You weren't intending on sleeping, were you?' laughed Shakiso.

They left all but the clothes they were wearing in their tent and snuck back up to the room in darkness, like two thieves to the scene of a crime.

The door was unlocked, and Shakiso giggled as she slipped inside.

There was a tiny space in front of the bed, and the bed itself took up the rest of the room.

'I'm not convinced our tent isn't larger,' whispered Simon.

'It's warm,' whispered Shakiso, throwing off her clothes and flinging herself on to the covers. 'Come here. I have something to show you.'

Simon leaned an arm on the ceiling immediately above him, resting his head on it, staring at Shakiso. The moon was bright on the water, casting her skin in a blue and white glow.

'You are the most beautiful creature,' he said.

He found her clitoris with his tongue and she gasped, her fingers tightening against his head, pulling him firmly into her. Warmth rose through her body, reaching her face and hands.

'Aargh,' he said, indistinctly. 'Can't breathe,' pulling back. 'And a hair,' extracting it from his mouth.

'Don't stop,' she begged, giggling. 'That was very nice.'

'Nice, darling? Ice cream is nice—'

She squirmed underneath him, pulling him on top of her.

'Ooh, that's nice.'

Giggling, tumbling amongst the blankets, laughing.

'Ouch, I think that's your elbow.'

'Something's in my hair?'

Becoming more breathless.

She rose on top of him, pushing against him inside her.

He felt sweat on her lower back, behind her knees.

Gasping, her mouth wide, frenetic, then slowing, stopping.

A tiny squeak of delight.

He held her until the wave passed.

Only then did he relax and follow her orgasm with his own.

'My gorgeous,' she said.

'Darling.'

'Thank you.'

GAVIN CHAIT

'And you.'

She collapsed into his shoulder, cuddling up against his chest, both still breathing in deep, shaky gulps.

'What colour?' she asked.

'Blue.'

'Boring,' she giggled. 'Mine was the colour of sunlight reflecting on the ocean. When it's still streaky from sunrise.'

Silence, only their breathing in the confines of the hut.

He leaned on his left elbow, looking down at her, stroked her face.

He nodded, grinning.

'Have I told you?'

'No, you haven't,' she said.

'I love you.'

'I love you more,' she said, laughing.

They held each other, their hearts harmonizing, and drifted into sleep.

At two a.m. – and Simon was quite sure it was two a.m., for he was certain that little about what happened next would not be scarred forever into his memory – a set of headlights shone across the room. A groan from outside as a car door opened and someone struggled to wake.

Simon was out of bed in a moment, scrambling in the debris for his clothes. He found shirt and trousers and was fumbling for the rest.

Shakiso was staring blearily at him.

'What?' Receiving a bundle of her clothes full in the face.

'Run,' he hinted.

As he heard a crunch from a footstep outside the door, Simon flung it open.

'They haven't put you in this room as well, have they?' he asked, his voice confident and filled with warm authority.

238

The young man was barely awake; his arms overflowed with blankets, clothing and equipment. In the light from the car interior, his partner was struggling with an inappropriately over-sized suitcase. She looked unhappy with the journey and with being woken up.

'I shall lodge a firm complaint at once,' said Simon, and strode out of the hut, Shakiso directly behind him.

They walked boldly into the darkness, the couple staring bewildered and confused after them.

As soon as they could no longer be seen, Shakiso and Simon sprinted for their tent.

With first light, before the sun had even dared raise itself to the horizon, they collapsed the tent, packed and were on the water.

A few hours later, they caught the tide dropping over the Bitches.

'I blame you,' he shouts.

'Woohoo,' she shrieks, laughing.

'I lost my favourite red underpants,' he shouts.

'I hated those,' she shouts back.

They drop off the standing waves and paddle up the coast. They are in no hurry, enjoying the ocean and each other. If they can, they will camp in Abereiddy or Porthgain.

As they pass the northern reach of Ramsey Island, Shakiso glances to her left.

'What's that?' she asks, pointing out to the horizon.

Simon taps a sequence on the implant in his left earlobe, zooming in on the horizon.

'It's an old supply tug,' he says.

He can just see a threadbare flag at the forecastle, and paint peeling off its name and registration number. *Prince Oisoyame*. It is listing to its port side, trailing a thin slick behind it.

'Those aren't allowed in these waters,' searching for a match.

Shakiso feels a curious tension in her gut.

'We're inside the Perimeter, aren't we? How come it hasn't been spotted?' referring to the radar system monitoring the whole of mainland England.

'Not until they cross in line with that headland. Got it, it's Nigerian. Left Lagos about a month ago.'

Now he can make out the main deck, behind the bridge.

'It's packed with people?' he says, in disbelief and confusion.

'They're seekers. They found a way round the blockade,' he shouts.

'They'll need help,' says Shakiso, tapping at her ear. 'Can you get a freight drone to our stores in Crawley?'

'Sure.'

'Good. I think Elias is still running our depot there. I'll see if he's able to arrange something.'

'The ship looks as if it's sinking. Looks like there are hundreds on board. I'll see if I can get one of our engineers out as well.'

He switches on the small turbine beneath the kayak and jets towards the ship, skipping over the choppy water.

Shakiso is quickly alongside, each using their paddles as rudders and leaning into the sea.

'Let's not get too close,' says Simon, Shakiso signalling her agreement. They have no wish to cause anyone to jump into the water to reach them. Their kayaks are small, and they would soon be swamped.

Shakiso calls the coastguard, giving them her position. The young woman taking notes sounds shocked.

'Do you know how many people are on board?' she asks.

Shakiso shouts the question through to Simon. He shakes his head. 'Several hundred, I think.'

He is speaking to Hollis.

'I've got a helicopter on the way to the Climate stores. Daphne's on the way in one we can use to lift people ashore. Where do you think they're going to stay? That's hardly the best place to come aground.'

'Think you can find some of the local radio stations? Maybe put out a call on the connect for help?' answers Shakiso.

As they get closer, Simon is able to see a crack running up the mid-section of the ship and down into the water. People are packed tightly on the deck, with only enough room to stand. Gulls are flying overhead, diving down to the ship and back up, their shrieks mournful and terrifying.

An orange and white helicopter flies out from along the cliffs, passing over them. White spray closer to the shore as the rescue boat at St Davids Lifeboat Station slides down its tracks, thunks into the water and charges towards them.

Simon spots the call-sign on the bottom of the helicopter and joins their channel.

'This is Simon Adaro in the kayaks below you. We made the call. Over.'

'We'll take over from here. Over,' says a crackly and impatient voice.

'We can help,' he says. 'We have support helicopters packed with supplies heading here. Where do you intend to beach these people? That crack is no good, and you can't bring the ship any closer to the shore. Over.'

The line goes silent, and Simon can imagine the hurried discussion taking place as the helicopter circles over the ship.

'There's a field near Whitesands. We should be able to get people and supplies in there easily. Over.'

'Thanks. We'll meet you there. Out.'

Simon signals to Shakiso. 'We can meet them on the shore,' leaning over and digging his paddle in the water. His kayak turns in a sweeping arc towards the tumbling surf at Whitesands.

The wind is rising, flinging up white fleece on the waves as they pound and bounce across the water.

They cut power as they reach the shoreline, surfing in on the waves and dragging their kayaks up the beach.

Two helicopters arrive. One bears the Achenia logo. The other is the red and white of His Majesty's Coastguard. Each lands in the field at the north end of the beach, sending up sand and grass.

An agitated-looking man walks urgently towards the Achenian helicopter. Simon and Shakiso join them as a hurried conversation starts.

'– and this is Simon Adaro,' says the young woman who piloted the Achenian helicopter. 'Hello, sir,' she grins.

'Hello, Daphne, good to see you.'

'Mr Adaro,' says the young District Officer. 'We're grateful for your help, but you understand that the Coastguard has overall responsibility.'

'I understand that, but most of your capacity is currently blockading the Mediterranean,' he says.

The man raises his hands and smiles. 'That's politics, sir. My job is to prevent loss of life and to protect the coast. We'll take all the help we can get.'

A huge Achenian freight helicopter swings over the bluff and drops on to the grass. An old man hops out, grinning in recognition when he sees Shakiso, and limps across the field. He sweeps her up in his arms.

'You must be Simon,' he says, turning to him. 'I'm Elias, an old friend of Shak's. We've got water, blankets, food – nothing hot, I'm afraid – where do you want us?'

The rotors slow to the point they can speak normally, and everyone begins to sound much less anxious.

The young District Officer looks momentarily overwhelmed. 'We'll need to get people off the ship and bring it under control. I've got two tugs coming in from Pembroke Dock. I'm not sure they're any better than that wreck, but it's all we have. Once the ship is safe, we can start getting people ashore. We'll need to make sure we keep families together, have a record of who is arriving. But, please, make sure everyone gets a blanket and some water. It's going to be a cold night.'

Shakiso smiles and grips his shoulder. 'You're doing fine,' she says.

Cars start arriving, pulling into the parking lot, concerned men and women gathering nearby, unsure what to do.

'We came when we heard it on the radio,' says one old woman. 'Those poor people.'

Many have brought blankets and warm food.

Media drones from Facebook and the BBC hover over the tugs, rebroadcasting individual feeds from people gathering along the cliffs, watching as the tugs draw near. There is a press of people on the deck all pushing to be closer to the sides to see what is happening. A man falls into the water followed by others.

Shouts of horror on the shore.

Rescue boats circle, picking people out of the choppy ocean. Echoing sounds of amplified instructions.

'Please stay on the ship. Please stay on the ship.'

The wind howls into the shore, pushing the water flat. Someone lights a fire. More are lit.

The first seekers are set down on the beach.

A woman, holding her baby, weeps, splashing her face with seawater. Overcome, a woman rushes from amongst the waiting locals, embracing her and leading her and her child towards the blankets.

Coastguard officials run back and forth trying to ensure they have tallied every arrival.

The seekers gather near the fires. Their eyes are haunted, faces gaunt, overwhelmed with exhaustion.

'We ran out of food a week ago –'

'– we threw the dead overboard –'

'– my son –'

'– please, drink –'

'– let me help with your child –'

'– I am grateful –'

White faces and black faces. Eyes and hands and feet and bodies to hold them with.

'I think there's about eight hundred survivors,' says the District Officer, his jacket stained and wet. 'Where are we going to put them? We don't have anywhere?'

'I think people here might have some ideas,' says Shakiso.

'What? No, we'll lose track of them. They can't just go home with anyone.'

'We're inside the Perimeter, and you have the registration numbers of the cars. You'll know where they are,' says Simon.

'It'll be OK,' says Shakiso.

Cars begin leaving, the parking lot emptying, each with a new family on their way to a new home, for – even in the depths of darkness – there are those who will reach out a hand and bring others in need into the light.

Simon and Shakiso walk to the furthest end of the beach. They climb up on to the bluff and watch the lights of the tugs and helicopters out in the water, the murmur and emotion of the people on the shore.

'Have I told you?' he asks.

'No, you haven't,' she says, her eyes bright and smiling.

'I love you,' he says.

'Thank you.'

'There's something I've been wanting to say. Something—'

She puts a finger on his lips.

'I love you,' she says. 'But if it's another woman, I'll kill both of you.'

He laughs, looking sad.

He shakes his head.

He tells her, his words indistinct and broken in the wind.

Her eyes widen.

She asks.

He explains.

She kisses him gently on the lips.

On the nose.

On each cheek.

She rests her forehead on his.

And the wind wipes away her tears.

31

'Tell her the story of the grey men,' says Tiémoko.

They are seated on the rooftop terrace of a hotel restaurant overlooking the ocean. Shakiso and Simon arrived back in Dakar from Wales early this morning, and they intend travelling to Aroundu with Tiémoko tomorrow.

The sounds of the city echo in the distance. In the corner near the entrance, an informal band has been playing the same song repeatedly for the last half hour. Each time they reach what may be the middle of the song, something seems to disrupt them. First it is the mixing desk, then an amplifier; at the moment they are deep in discussions about the quality of their seating.

'I said, I'm never telling that story,' says Simon, giving him a look of extreme discomfort.

Tiémoko's smile is ruthless. 'Do you, or do you not, trust this woman?'

Shakiso grins. 'Yes, dude, do you not trust me?'

Simon looks from one to the other, exasperated. 'Fine,' he says. 'Remember, though, this makes you an accomplice to some of the most illegal behaviour our government has a name for.'

He looks around, somewhat unhappily. No one is paying them any attention, and the noise of chatter and music prevents casual eavesdropping.

'I abbreviated that story of getting Zhi out of England,' he says.

'Which bit?' she asks.

'The bit where he just leaves,' he says.

Tiémoko is smiling and laughing.

'Wait,' says Shakiso, 'let me see how much I remember,' topping up their glasses from the bottle of rioja before continuing. 'So, while Hollis was still in hospital you hacked into the national surveillance system so you could follow cabinet ministers around. Then, after you got conscripted, you roped Tiémoko and that Chinese friend of yours, Liao Zhi, into helping you?'

Tiémoko nods. 'Simon wasn't sure what to do with it, and I thought up the idea of publishing the locations of a list of people to boycott as a form of civil protest.'

'And who came up with the name?' she asks.

Simon and Tiémoko exchange a knowing glance, laughing. 'Zhi. Only he would call something TheShitList.'

'Right,' says Shakiso. 'And how do you get away with publishing a list of senior politicians' actual whereabouts without getting arrested?'

'We had to disguise the source of our information and created this social network tool so people could let us know if they saw someone on our list. Hardly anyone recognized our targets, and we'd fill in the gaps from the surveillance system,' says Simon.

'I don't see how that makes money?'

'That wasn't the intention. To be honest, it was a terrible idea. People liked it, and quite a few politicians were embarrassed when shops refused to sell them things, but it felt petty.'

'What changed?'

'I finished my national service and had more time to focus on it, and a few months later a war criminal in exile in Bahrain announced he was coming on a shopping trip to London. Few knew what he looked like, and no one knew who would be in his retinue. Bahrain gave him a diplomatic passport, and our government said they were powerless to stop him visiting. There were some serious protests outside parliament.

'I got a call from Harrods. They were worried about reputational damage if they accidentally sold anything to these people. We put together a custom package for them. Their security staff would get a warning when anyone on the list arrived, and everyone else could use their rims to identify anyone in this chap's party.

'After that, we got contracts from a number of retailers all prepared to pay extremely well.'

'Then you guys got raided?'

Simon nods. 'We had four good years before they came knocking, but, yes, we obviously shouldn't have had the information we did. I knew we needed an alternative, and we had built an independent surveillance system by then. I hoped they'd leave us alone when they realized, but our government has their own approach to getting their point across. Tiémoko's father was quietly told to take his son and go back to Senegal. Zhi was arrested as an illegal immigrant.'

He laughs, remembering. 'I hid out in my old van behind the police station where they were holding him. They used to put prisoners in these single-person transit pods and shuttle them around. I followed behind as soon as he was in one and hacked the damn thing. I was simultaneously turning off the street cameras filming me while trying to break into this silly pod.'

'Weren't they going to deport him? Couldn't you wait?' asks Shakiso.

Simon glances at Tiémoko, who shakes his head, 'No, not so simple. Zhi really was illegally in the country, and that's an offence. Worse, England's naturalization laws made their shareholding illegal. Tiémoko, at least, had his father's diplomatic protection, but Zhi was doubly cursed. They were threatening ten years of solitary confinement.'

'This is how you were forced out of the company?' asks Shakiso, staring at Tiémoko curiously. 'Do you resent that?'

His eyes cloud briefly, and he exchanges a troubled glance with Simon. 'I have made my peace with it,' he says, eventually.

'Ah,' says Shakiso, carefully dropping the topic in the face of their discomfort. 'So, what really happened?'

'It's fairly elaborate,' says Simon.

Shakiso tilts the wine bottle, swirling the contents, 'The night is but a pup, and I'm sure they have more of this lovely vintage.'

'Go on,' says Tiémoko, smiling. 'I'll help.'

Near the entrance, the band have stopped again, now agitated over something they are viewing on a console. A bone-thin old man dressed in a greyed and careworn boubou, his hair an olive-coloured burst about his head and leaning on a two-headed stave for support, joins them.

Simon sighs, drums his fingers on the table and nods.

'The old surveillance cameras were fairly easy to fool. After Perimeter was turned on, they could track him no matter where he went. We needed to figure out how to avoid it following us around, get Zhi a false identity to travel, and make sure I didn't end up being arrested afterwards.'

He refills his glass to the brim.

'I had been toying with the idea for AnoniCar, and we had twenty cars driving around London. This was early in their development, and we hadn't destroyed the private keys yet.'

'What does that mean?' asks Shakiso.

'The whole point of these cars is that you get in and, from there, no one knows who you are until you get out and Perimeter eventually figures out where you went. But you do need to be identified before you get in, so we can get paid and check that you're not on TheShitList.

'Anyone who could get into the system by using the private key could find out who was in the car by knowing who had got into it in the first place. I was being watched and, even though the system was being tested, I couldn't take the risk of keeping the keys on me.'

'Who had them?'

'I did,' says Tiémoko. 'I wrote some of the original code for the systems.'

'How does it even work?'

'Three-card Monte,' says Simon.

'What?'

'It's a card trick,' says Tiémoko. 'All the cars driving within a similar area are taken on round-about routes and then enter a single warehouse we own. The warehouse is a Faraday cage and is coated in super-black, the same material on the outside of those drones,' pointing upwards to where the drones are circling. 'Do that a few times but, each time, add extra cars or take cars out of circulation.'

'That can't be enough to prevent detection?'

'It isn't,' says Simon. 'We're not trying for complete invisibility. We only suggest you'll have ninety minutes after you leave the vehicle before Perimeter will figure out who you are.'

Shakiso blinks repeatedly. 'People pay for this?'

'They have their reasons,' says Simon.

'And the grey men? How do they feature?'

'The ambassador isn't one person.'

'I know that, although I don't know why,' says Shakiso.

'Blame Perimeter,' says Simon.

'It was developed by the Americans,' says Tiémoko. 'The US is too big for practical use, so it only covers their largest cities and their border walls. England and Wales are small, and cover is complete.

'You have to acknowledge the deviousness of their plan. The Chinese realized their intelligence agents would be tracked anywhere they went. Overnight, every embassy renamed all their staff. They all became one ambassador with the identity chosen from a previous incumbent.'

'Right,' says Shakiso. 'No matter what, the English ambassador is always Liu Xiaoming.'

'Their identities are entirely legitimate as well,' says Tiémoko. 'None of the staff look alike. They may not have the same gender. They all share a single identity.'

Shakiso sits back in her chair, her eyes wide, grinning in admiration. 'I think I see where this goes.'

There is a moment of silence as she works through the implications of the set-up. Shaking her head, she flags a waiter and orders more wine.

'What next? How do you even get an ambassador to use AnoniCar?' she asks.

'Zhi said at least one of them must be enjoying a little infidelity which they would prefer the embassy not to know about,' says Tiémoko.

'And they'd need a private car to drive them there?'

'We ran advertising targeting the embassy, and pretty soon we had someone. Every evening at exactly twenty past seven, this ambassador would step into the car and travel two hours across the city, get out, stay for an hour and then come back. We'd have about five hours during which time an ambassador would be out of circulation and entirely under our control.'

'You stole his identity,' she says in delight. 'Where was Zhi during all this?'

'We were moving him constantly. In and out of AnoniCars, back and forth across the city. It helped that the government were comfortable that the moment he turned up at a border they'd have him. And they were right too. Except we still had the private keys for AnoniCar.'

'And Zhi was able to use that identity?'

'Not on his own. The whole point of this is that, once you're in the car, there's no information going in or out. He had no access to the system. And I couldn't do it because I needed an alibi,' says Simon.

'Which left me,' says Tiémoko, grinning.

'Where were you?' asks Shakiso, looking at Simon.

'Fortunately, Hollis was celebrating his engagement. I was witnessed by all his guests and never once left during the evening,' grins Simon.

'Did Hollis know?'

'Of course, we arranged the date exactly. The ambassador gets into the AnoniCar and travels into our warehouse. Waiting inside are nine other vehicles, one of which contains Zhi. Ten vehicles leave the warehouse. We know which one contains the ambassador.'

'I began leaking information from Zhi's vehicle,' says Tiémoko. 'Very tiny, difficult to crack, but sufficient to identify it as the one carrying the ambassador. The government is extremely interested in what these ambassadors get up to, and they send agents to follow. We took Zhi to the airport, where there's a seat booked in the ambassador's name going direct to Shanghai. No one blinks at an unfamiliar ambassador. Zhi went straight into his seat and was out of English airspace before the real ambassador had returned to the office.'

'And I spent the entire evening eating canapés,' says Simon, with a flourish.

'Completely mad,' says Shakiso, looking around for their waiter and noticing the old man with his two-headed metal stave. He turns away from the console, stares at her and nods in recognition, then stamps the foot of his stave hard on to the tiled floor of the restaurant.

'Hey, that's Gaw Goŋ—' she starts, and falls silent as he begins to speak, his voice filling the restaurant, magnetic in the moonlight, beginning a story.

'Painted-dog's child sighs in deep satisfaction . . .'

Tales from Gaw Goŋ: Dragon, la brèche dans le mur de la honte

Painted-dog's child sighs in deep satisfaction, rolling over on to her back with her paws in the air so that her swollen belly may rest.

She has licked her calabash of thiere neverdaye until it shone. The lamb so tender, it melted away in her mouth, the millet couscous so light she thought it would carry her off into the sky. Unashamed, she ate three bowls.

'Aha, aha. Was it worth the wait, Painted pup?' asks Baboon, wiping the inside of his calabash with a forefinger and licking it clean.

'Oh, yes, grandfather,' she says. 'That was the best stew I have ever eaten.'

The last moments, when the stew was ready, but before she could eat, were agony.

Baboon had carefully filled a calabash with millet and stew, covering it in spicy *kaani* sauce. Walking to the waterline, he stood his sombé upright in the sand, took the calabash in both hands and went out into the water until he was up to his waist.

'Great Baana, please enjoy this offer of thiere neverdaye even as we join you in celebrating your feast,' tipping the calabash into the pool and washing it clean.

He then stood silently, a wondrous smile on his face – the

moments almost unendurable for the starving pup – nodded as if in answer and returned to the shore.

Each has eaten to satiety, and each now sits in contemplation, stomachs warm and gently burbling.

'I do not feel I could move, grandfather,' says Painted-dog's child.

'Aha, aha,' he smiles. 'It is better so, my child. You should not be in haste after eating. And our story is not yet complete.'

'Grandfather,' she says, lowering her nose as she does when nervous to speak a troubling thought.

'Yes, my child,' says Baboon, placing a branch on the coals and rekindling the flames.

'Grandfather,' nervously, 'are the genii ever wrong?'

'My child?'

Hastily continuing in fright, 'The genii cause change so that we must create new stories. I understand this. But, could it be that the genii sometimes cause a harm they did not intend to one in their favour?'

Baboon smiles, a look as of the depths of the harmattan in his tawny eyes. He strokes her gently between her ears, letting her know that there is no danger from such questions.

'Yes, Painted-dog's child. The genii cause change in the full-ness of knowledge that they cannot know the outcome of their intrusions in our lives. Sometimes this means they reward those who cause evil, or punish those who deserve nothing but honour.

'When such events occur, we of the gaw say that it is as if the genii have misspelled wrath. Their purpose may not have been unjust, but that is where events have led.

'We gaw may attempt to intercede, to request of the genii that they make right the wrong, but it can also be that the genii enjoy this unexpected story. We cannot know, and it is why our intercession with the genii must be performed with care. For we have no power to control the might of the genii.'

Painted-dog's child quivers, her fur shivering as she considers her vulnerability.

'Is that where the Casamance come from, the twice-dead?' she asks. 'When the genii return a person of honour to their people, to allow them time that has been unfairly taken?'

Baboon tousles her ears, nodding, and his eyes are filled with the dust of wild places.

'You are indeed a wise child,' he says. 'You do honour to your family.'

Pride and fear twitch across her fur.

'Do not be afraid, child, for the genii intervene but infrequently, and they are never deliberately cruel. It is far more often that our own weakness betrays us.

'Shall I continue our story?'

She scratches her snout with a thoughtful paw, then looks up brightly. 'Yes, please, grandfather. I would enjoy that.'

Baboon takes up a handful of dust, whispers to it, and it is Gaw Goŋ who blows it into the flames, the red-brown mist glowing in his eyes. A swirling green-grey pool opens above the flames, shot through with flecks of red and black.

Gaw Goŋ motions at the portal, pulling it wider until it fills the space before them. He whispers again, and the pool clears.

A little blond boy with pale white skin stares back at them, a combination of curiosity and apprehension in his blue eyes.

'Why don't you tell our viewers what inspired you,' says a neat, professional voice.

The little boy glances up at his mother, looking at him with pride and affection. He grins. 'OK. We were at the beach in Cornwall during the summer.'

'Before that, sweetie,' says his mother.

'Oh, yes,' he says, brushing back his fringe with his fingers, continuing to stare into the camera. 'We were watching on the news how all the seekers are waiting on the beach, and I asked Mum what they were waiting for. She said that they want to cross the sea, but they have no boats and they cannot swim because it's too far.

'Then we went to the beach, and Mum put me in my floater because,' blushing slightly, 'I can't swim properly yet. I asked Mum why we don't draw a floater for the seekers on the beach.'

'And you're a materials engineer?' asks the news anchor, turning to the boy's mother.

'Yes,' she says, looking embarrassed.

'Mum helped me draw a floater which has a light so you can be seen in the dark, and covers you completely so you don't get cold, and has a small jet to help you swim faster, and a snorkel that keeps the water out your mouth even when the sea gets rough,' says the little boy, in a rush.

'We even added in clips so that mums and dads can keep their children close, and a pouch so they can store something to drink and eat.'

'And then what happened?' asks the news anchor.

'Mum put my drawing in her console and showed me how we could make it. She printed one at work for me, and I tried it on at the beach.'

'Were you confident it would work?' the man asks of the young mother.

She laughs. 'No, not even slightly. His dad went out in the water with him, but it was amazing. He was almost undrownable. We had a few other parents come and ask us about the suit. It's completely impractical. Your kid will stay warm and dry, but they're not going to have fun splashing around in something like this. The only real benefit to it over other floaters is that it's cheap to print and can be done in one machine.'

'Is that when you released the designs?'

'Yes. I thought other parents might find it a fun project to play with. I never thought—' she hesitates.

The news anchor nodding to indicate she should stop, 'We go now to Algeria, where millions of seekers are hoping to cross the Mediterranean.'

A news anchor, a twin of the first, is walking along a beach, the sea flat and grey and the surf tumbling white. Behind him is the short stump of a breakwater.

'Petit Port, here in Algeria, only two hundred kilometres across the Mediterranean from Spain, is one point along a coastline that is now estimated to be the entrepôt for almost thirty million seekers hoping to cross into Europe.

'There's only one thing trapping them here: the wall of steel.'

Out to sea, midway between the two coasts, is a line marked in metal. Every country along the northern shore has gathered every military craft they have – whether it flies, floats or swims beneath the waves – and created an impenetrable fortification spanning the Mediterranean. Nets hang beneath and between the surface vessels, and the coast is endlessly patrolled by both submersible and flying drones.

They have been here since the first sparks of the arc of fire were lit: from the moment the first seekers attempted a crossing.

Relief crews are flown back and forth. The eyes on the wall must never lessen their gaze. Any attempt to cross must be blocked.

Every coastal vessel on the southern shore, no matter how small or unseaworthy, has been destroyed. Any new launch is holed before it is scarcely into the surf. There are even rumours of special forces operating amongst the waiting seekers, destroying boat-building works.

Few seekers attempt to swim across, and those who do are easily captured and returned to the beach.

Still the seekers arrive, piling up along the shore, staring out at the pounding surf, imagining how to cross. Coastal towns are overwhelmed with the millions of new arrivals. Sanitation systems have failed, prices for even the most basic goods nearly unaffordable.

Many of those who have come are not with the seekers but hope to profit from them. The seekers have need of accommodation, clothing and all the necessities of life. Thousands of coastal towns have seen industry surge as new printing machines are flown in, producing clothing and goods influenced by such diversity as the Nuer of the Upper Nile, the Dinka of the southern Sudan, the Luo of western Kenya, or even the Azande of northern Congo.

The music, food and culture of the seekers have become an immense ethnic profusion of Africa: a rich stew in which all find nourishment.

The news anchor turns his gaze to where a Luba family from central Congo are preparing their evening meal.

'We are told you will soon attempt to cross the waters,' he says to the eldest man in the group.

That man turns, acknowledging the cameras, and laughs. 'It is no secret.'

'How do you intend to cross?'

He laughs again. 'That is no secret either. We will dress in the floatation suit we have purchased from the printers. See how each of my family has a suit?'

For months, the printers have produced these suits, but no seeker who acquired one has endeavoured to use them. Despite differences of culture, language and ethnicity, each people has kept to a single plan. *We do not go until all can go.*

There has been no organizing figure, although one has been sought. Military and political leaders on the northern border have been paralyzed as to what will happen or how they should respond.

And, yet, someone had to have been first. Someone had to have found the design thought up by a young English boy, adapted it and brought it to the attention of the printers.

'You seek Joshua,' laughs the Luba man.

'Yes,' says the news anchor.

'Good luck,' he says, gesturing along the beach where thousands of people have gathered, some already wearing their floatation suits and looking apprehensively at the waves.

It is said that this Joshua is an engineer from far to the south. That he arrived with one of the largest groups of seekers who emerged mysteriously from the Sahara. It was he who sought out a solution to breach the steel wall, who challenged the printers to produce it, and who set out the condition of ownership. *None may cross until all may cross.*

His meaning is understood.

It has been months since the first printers took up the task. At first it appeared impossible, then excitement took hold at the potential, until – at last – all are ready.

It is tonight, when the sun touches the horizon.

In the watching ships, thousands of sailors turn their eyes to the sun and to the shore.

Movement amongst the seekers as they prepare their suits, secreting money, valuables and cherished memories of home within, and shuffle uncomfortably along the shoreline.

There are gaps along the coast. Places where seekers have not ventured. Where the fighting is too fierce and where there is no safety even in numbers.

The first place to see the sun kiss the edge of the earth is in

Susah, a small town far to the east. Tens of thousands walk out into the water, wash their faces, pray to their gods and commit themselves to their journey.

An old Shona woman, travelling so far on her own, sobs in terror in the surf, unable to move any further. A young Haussa girl notices her, takes her hand and kisses her on the cheek.

'It is well, my grandmother,' she says. 'It would be my privilege if you would take my hand so that I may cross with you.'

The old woman clasps her tightly, 'Thank you, my daughter, for I am without family and much afraid.'

'You are of my family now,' says the girl, leading her towards her brothers and parents.

And so they paddle out into the water, clipped together.

A wave of seekers following the setting sun, launching themselves into the waters. The millions pushing themselves out into the unknown deep.

The old Shona woman begins to sing, a song of courage to overcome her fears. It is in the language of her people, but it is a song of all peoples. Her new family joins her in their own tongue.

'Inshallah. Inshallah,' the words floating above the waves, carried by a crashing tide. 'What the genii will.'

A wave of song follows with the seekers entering the waters. The millions sing and their voice can be heard on the waiting boats in the wall long before they can be seen.

Their singing gives them strength and permits each to know where they are even as the waves rise above their heads and obscure the horizon, even as the dusk gives way to darkness.

It is a young marine looking out from HMS *Dragon* who is first to see the drift of seekers heading towards the wall.

In the moonlit darkness, he can see a thin line of warm orange lights floating in the water, each indicating a single person. He shouts.

'We have our orders,' says his Captain. 'None shall pass.'

The young marine feels a tightening in his chest. He cannot breathe. He stumbles out on to the open bridge. As he opens the door, all inside the deckhouse can hear the singing coming across the waters. In the sky and in the water, a face buried in a burst of fur watching him, curious in him.

'Close that door,' shouts the Captain, but he cannot, held in place by some power he dare not name.

The rhythm swells, drawing them close to the millions who near.

A young radar operator begins to weep. On her console she can see how many, how vast the hope of the millions, how brave their dream. In their song, she can hear their fear and the trust they place in her and her companions. Offering her their lives.

She flees her station, joining the young marine on the open bridge.

'Do your duty,' shouts the Captain as others break ranks to stand in the moonlight, but there is a crackle of doubt even in his throat.

Out on the open bridge, the radar operator takes the hand of the marine. She looks into his eyes.

'What are we?' she asks.

'We're the good guys,' he says, and smiles.

Their Captain joins them, standing alongside. He looks out at the approaching tide. He weeps.

'How would we be remembered?' he asks.

He nods, and leads them down on to the deck. They cast out rigging to hang down into the ocean.

Sailors on the Italian vessel alongside emerge on to their deck. Their captain looks across, and each captain shares a glance. It is unsaid but each knows: the wall is breached.

Out in the water, submersible drones rise to the surface, inflating pods to their sides.

All along the fortress of steel, men and women tasked with holding the wall look to their souls and ask, 'What would we be?', and they find their answer.

The young marine begins to sing, joining those in the coming tide, holding the hand of the radar operator.

The Captain is first to reach out and raise a seeker from the grasp of the ocean.

It is the old Shona woman, weeping in exhaustion and relief, clasping him tightly to her bosom. It is the Captain who feels as if he has been released.

All along the way, vessels fill with seekers.

The wall is breached.

Inshallah.

The way is open.

263

32

There is no clear space near the Climate school in Aroundu, and they loop around the prefabricated building complex looking for somewhere to land.

The streets are filled with a dancing, stamping mob. There is no joy to the singing. Jubilation, defiance, anger, but no joy.

'I'm going to try setting down there,' says Simon, pointing at a small opening in the crowd near the administration buildings. 'Hopefully they'll get out of the way.'

Shakiso, Tuft at her feet, stares out the windows, her jaw tight. Tiémoko appears unconcerned.

Armed men wearing UN-blue helmets come out from the building and start shouting at the crowd, pushing them back.

Simon makes a small gesture, and the security drones unclip from the helicopter and take up position around them. The helicopter rotors change pitch, and they slowly descend.

The noise, as the doors open, is the screaming, roaring outrage of a mob.

'You sure about this?' asks Simon, searching Shakiso's face.

She nods, her thoughts an anguished torrent, staring fixedly ahead. The warmth and companionship of their evening scattered in the moments following Moussa's call.

A man lunges at Simon as they step on to the ground. There is a crackle, and he drops to the floor writhing from electrical discharge.

The drones emit a howling, nerve-jangling alarm and make short charges at the crowd. Tuft stays close to Shakiso, yowling and baring her teeth and claws. People pull back, and the UN soldiers push their way through, surrounding Simon, Shakiso and Tiémoko, and adding their cries to the din.

'This way,' says one of the men, his voice urgent.

The mob seems not to be targeting anything in particular, merely a gathering to express their grievance. With the strangers now identified as part of the UN, the mob loses interest and turns inwards once more.

The soldiers shepherd their charges into the low administrative building and close the doors behind them. More soldiers are inside the building, chatting and drinking the staff coffee from the small canteen. They are observing the mob through the windows but seem untroubled.

'It is not a good time,' says the soldier.

'What's going on?' demands Shakiso.

He shrugs, gestures with his head towards the staffroom where a clamour of heated conversation can be heard.

Moussa is sitting on a table, his arm in a sling, his other hand open as if to calm those shouting. His smile at seeing Shakiso is one of delight and concern.

'I told you not to come,' he says.

She hugs him tightly, releasing him instantly as he groans. 'Sorry,' she says. 'What . . .'

Simon and Tuft stand in the doorway looking around the room. It is filled with a seemingly random assortment of people. Tiémoko recognizes a few faces and is surrounded, embraced and drawn into the discussion.

'Excuse me,' says Moussa to the others, leading Simon and Shakiso back to the canteen.

'It is late,' he says, pushing a button on the coffee machine and setting it to dispense three cups. One of the soldiers gathers his colleagues, and they make space on the sofas.

Moussa looks exhausted and pale, but his hand is firm where he holds his cup.

'We have a problem,' he starts.

'Not Ansar Dine?' asks Shakiso, her face pale.

'No,' shaking his head. 'There are many different nationalities here. Many have fled civil war at home, or even police states, like in Cameroon and Ethiopia. There are spies and agents from these countries here, and there are others who smuggle goods from here back to these countries.'

'That's been happening since the beginning,' says Shakiso. 'That was the point of having these huge schools, to encourage integration.'

Moussa nods. 'That was your plan, yes, but the dynamic of the city has always been volatile. People have put down permanent roots here. Communities are developing, and they do not want outside interference. They want to keep to their own, and they do not trust each other. Not yet. This afternoon armed men raided this school.'

'Why?'

'They are a group of smugglers supporting resistance fighters in Ethiopia. We think they wanted boys to take back to become soldiers. I called for UN support,' indicating the soldiers. 'Before they arrived, Ethiopian government agents got here, and the two groups began to fight inside the school.'

Shakiso looks stunned.

'There were only five of the smugglers and three of the agents. The teachers organized the children, getting them to safety in the hall at the back of the classrooms. I waited near the fighting with the headmaster and one of the other teachers. We wanted to ensure that the soldiers would know where the fighters were and that we could warn the others if they began to move towards the hall.'

He stops as the noise outside lessens. A soldier stands and looks out the window. 'They are leaving now,' he says, looking relieved.

'You were shot,' says Shakiso.

'Yes. A stray bullet. After the soldiers arrived, the fighters tried to flee. One of them shot me as he was running away.'

'Are you—'

'It is not serious,' says Moussa, quickly. 'Three of the fighters were caught. The others were killed. We did not know what to do with these captives. If they are Ansar Dine, we hand them to the Senegalese army to deal with. If they are petty criminals, each district has its own informal courts to deal with them. They are harsh and unfair, but it is what we have. This was different. Many communities send their children to this school. We have twenty-five thousand children in this complex every day.'

It is Simon's turn to look shocked. 'I never realized it was so big.'

Shakiso has turned pale. She folds back on the sofa.

Moussa looks at her with compassion, but he is unflinching. 'I have always been worried about this. About what would happen when so many people who already conflict in so many ways are drawn into some violence through a threat to their children. Those people outside are parents. Most came only to take their children home. Many remained.'

'What do they want?' asks Shakiso quietly.

'It has already happened,' says Moussa. 'The parents took the three fighters. They burned them outside. Their anger remains. They want to know who will protect them. The Ethiopians in the city are in hiding.'

'Where's UNHCR? Surely—'

'This is not a camp, Shakiso,' says Moussa. 'Our agencies have no role here. There are only a few soldiers to protect agency property, like this school. All we may do is offer guidance.'

Simon nods. 'This is where it leads,' he says thoughtfully. A city of millions without the protective structure of a state.

'You have allowed Climate to adapt, Shakiso,' says Moussa. 'We are grateful, but now we are no different from a civil-engineering firm who builds roads. We are not responsible for how people drive, or what the rules are.'

'What happens now?' asks Shakiso, looking numbed.

Moussa smiles. 'It is happening. Come,' and leading them back to the staffroom.

'I have been working with different community groups for months. That woman,' he says, 'was a constitutional lawyer in Kenya. That man was a judge in Rwanda. She, a human rights lawyer in Sudan. Each of them manages legal disputes in their own communities. They want to bring their communities together for a constitutional convention. They want their own courts, their own security. They will find their own solutions.'

Tiémoko joins them. 'Has our hero told you of his bravery?'

Shakiso nods.

'About the child?' says Tiémoko, indicating a Chinese woman with a small boy held tightly in her arms.

Shakiso recognizes her from the printing works.

'That is Donald, one of the many orphans in the city,' he continues, seeing that Moussa has not told them. 'It seems he has taken to sneaking into the school at lunchtime to get a free meal. He was on his own, and the smugglers captured him as he was climbing through a fence near where they were hiding.

'Our Moussa,' looking at him proudly, 'dragged the boy to safety during the fighting.'

Moussa shrugs and blushes, smiling again at Shakiso. 'I said it was not necessary for you to come.'

'You convinced Mrs Chen to adopt him?' asks Tiémoko.

'Not yet, but I called her and she came immediately. He was terrified and fighting with us until she came.'

Shakiso beams at him, looking both proud and lost.

'Shakiso,' says Moussa, taking her hand and speaking as gently and firmly as he is able. 'It is time for you to let go. I must take over now.'

She seems to shrink, recognizing the wisdom in his words. 'I know,' she says.

She stares long into the room where people are writing on boards in small groups, each apparently tackling different concerns. Many are tapping at their consoles while debating, having looked up other statutes to support their opinions. 'You're right, Moussa. We'll leave you to it.'

She embraces him gently. Simon shakes his free hand as Tuft rubs up against his legs.

They return to the canteen, leaving Moussa to rejoin the whirling discussion.

'What will you do?' asks Simon.

Her eyes are the fog of an ocean dawn. 'There was a time when Oktar was the right person for the job. Times changed, and he had no useful answers. I cursed him for not recognizing it. Moussa is the right person now. He lives here. He is of this city. I'm not. And,' she says, 'there's you.'

The soldiers are packing up and beginning to leave. The streets are quiet outside. The anger is spent.

'Did you know about this?' asks Simon, searching Tiémoko's eyes.

He nods. 'Moussa and I speak often. We have been worried about such an eruption for months.'

Shakiso allows her mind to go blank, calming herself. 'Has it only been a few hours since we were listening to that story?' she asks. 'What happened at the end – to the animals – I missed it when Moussa called.'

'What?' asks Simon, looking confused.

'The animals. There were so many different animals, all trying to cross an ocean to get to a promised land. You remember?' worried once more that she did not hear the story that was actually told.

Tiémoko smiles gently. 'They made it. The Wall of Shame is broken,' touching Simon on the shoulder.

'Joshua and his family,' says Simon, his eyes distant. 'Maybe I will get to—'

Tuft whines as Simon staggers, losing his balance briefly. Shakiso grabs on to his arm, Tiémoko at his back.

'What's happening?'

Simon looks disoriented, his skin clammy. His breath in short gasps. Shakiso crouches and holds him tightly, her face torn with anguish. 'Simon?'

He recovers, clarity returning to his eyes.

'I'm sorry, my darling. It's time.' His voice is exhausted.

'Can you stand?'

'I think so.'

'Let's get you home.'

He leans on them as they walk slowly out to the waiting helicopter.

33

'Do you think he realized?' asks Uberti, his feet up on his desk, swirling his vodka in a glass clenched between chubby fingers.

Pazanov is seated in the middle of the room, his knees drawn together, his vodka against his brow. Cigarette smoke twists and rises from the ashtray between them on the floor. Both are watching a Russia Today journalist standing uncomfortably in front of the reopening ceremony at the European Parliament in Strasbourg.

Archival footage of *La traversée des pèlerins*, of people sobbing on the northern beaches of the Mediterranean, police vehicles overturned and in flames, long queues of people voting in Belgium's referendum on joining the Federation, black flags and skinheads marching, an old man holding up an ancient purple EU passport alongside his orange Dutch card and grinning toothlessly, dark-skinned children playing football in a park joined by a laughing rush of fair-haired friends.

The sound is muted, and the images pulse and flicker in the sombre room, fluttering with the spurt and sparks from the fire in the grate.

'I suppose it was inevitable that the blockade would fail once Ansar Dine fell. Too many people crossed the desert for it to hold. He must have realized that, once it did, there would be so much chaos there we could easily get our submersibles in. His line would never be safe,' says Pazanov.

'He made the best of his situation while he tried to figure out how to get across,' says Uberti. 'He's still out-thinking us.

'Still, this all might be good for business. Millions of new "Europeans" all wanting their new electric apartments and new electric cars.'

Pazanov feels the weight of the console in his suit jacket pocket and wonders whether he should show Uberti what he has seen.

'The difficulty is this new Federation,' he says, choosing to wait.

Uberti makes a dismissive gesture. 'Six countries does not make a Federation, and they only join because they fear being alone. It could be years before they're able to work together. No, we will have retired by then, and it can be someone else's problem.

'He has irritated us, certainly, reminded us of the danger of being complacent, but we have lost nothing irreplaceable.'

'Except Valuchkin,' says Pazanov quietly. 'I sent some roses to his widow.'

'What?' asks Uberti, scarcely paying attention as he rises and heads for the liquor cabinet, waving a hand in dismissal. He has no wish for further details. He pours himself another measure of vodka, returning with the bottle and offering it to Pazanov, who shakes his head.

The pressure has eased, and Uberti no longer has the leaden hunted look that shrouded him over the last year. He may even take a vacation down to Crimea this summer.

'Did you find Argenti?' he asks, remembering.

'Yes,' says Pazanov. 'He is in Yalta, and retired, as you thought.'

'How did he get into drugs?'

'He didn't. He transports the arms to Venezuela, where they're loaded along with regular drug shipments from the Caracas Cartel. These deals are normally small and sent via a drone from a submarine, but the blockade has prevented anything getting through for the last three years. Ag Ghaly was desperate. It seems the drug suppliers and Argenti conspired to sell one huge deal and have it flown there in this convoy. Ag Ghaly paid cash up front. I think they may have known before any of us that Ag Ghaly would fall, even before Adaro helped him down.'

'What did Argenti sell him? Not even on his best day could he put together more than $50 million of weapons. His share wouldn't be enough to retire on.'

'He wouldn't say, but I got the feeling those weapons were duds. Perhaps they deliberately sabotaged the delivery? Do you want me to push him?'

'No. Let him have his retirement.'

'The Senegalese presidential election is in three weeks. Should we still go ahead?' asks Pazanov. 'We have about one hundred of Ag Ghaly's veterans in safe-houses in Dakar, and I should be able to get another twenty of our own forces in there before the inauguration.'

Uberti sticks his bottom lip out until he can just see it. He flicks it with a finger, watching it bobble back and forth.

The refurnished office looks almost exactly as it did last spring. Except for a tendency for one of the doors to stick, it looks as if his eruption had never taken place. The office of a siloviki in complete command of his operations.

'No, let them have their peace. You tell me Adaro has not left London in months. Maybe he has tired of his sport and we can buy those farms from him.'

Pazanov picks at a scratch on the chair arm, grimaces and pulls the console from his pocket.

'I'm still not sure we understand what he's doing.'

'Does it matter? He wanted to hurt us. He hurt us. We will recover.'

Pazanov rises and walks over to the table. He flicks his thumb across the console screen.

'I went to the mountains near Bologna last week to have a look at the receiving station he's building there. I wanted to see what is happening and understand if he still intends delivering on his deal with the Europeans. This is what it looks like,' sliding the console across the table.

Uberti stares at it, shaking his head.

'I don't understand. What is this?'

'We don't know. I asked our engineers down in Kursk what it is, and they have no idea either. All they can say is that only part of it is a receiving station. The rest – it looks like some sort of radio satellite dish.'

Uberti thumbs through different pictures, equally blurry and indistinct, turning the console around.

'You couldn't get any closer?'

'The Spanish security weren't happy even with me this close. What I can say is that there is no path to the sea from there. They haven't secured any of the land they would need.'

'How big is it?'

'That's the thing. It's enormous. They have taken over an old wind-turbine farm. The grounds are about fourteen kilometres square. That array, whatever it is, is about half that. They're also continuing to buy and clear land around the station.'

He retrieves the console and flips into another application.

'This is time-lapse satellite footage of the site.'

Uberti watches the jerky transformation of the dusty landscape. A central bowl scraped out and earth carried away, poured into open hoppers on the outskirts of the site. A strange oblong vehicle creeps out and drives down into the depression.

'We think that's a different type of vitrification printer to the one he's been using in the desert. It seems to have some sort of hopper on top. You'll see drones flying back and forth to it. They replace batteries as well as pouring material into it. From what we can see from the footage, it hasn't stopped operations in fourteen months.'

'What is this thing?'

'We don't know.'

'Is it still operating?'

'No,' says Pazanov, sliding the footage through to near the end, speeding up the vehicle which looks like a spider spinning its web, round and round. 'It finished about three weeks ago.'

The footage shows the vehicle being lifted and vanishing out of shot.

'Were we watching this?' asks Uberti.

Pazanov shrugs. 'We watch everything, we watch nothing.'

'He distracted us?'

Pazanov shrugs again.

'What's happening there now?'

'Nothing. Nothing at all. It's guarded but nothing.'

Pazanov sounds frustrated. Uberti seems rooted to his chair.

'He must have permits for whatever he's doing?'

'I checked. He has permits to receive and distribute electricity. Nothing we don't know. I spoke to López in the Ministry. He doesn't care how the electricity is coming in. He has a contract and when it arrives, he'll take it.'

'Are they still expecting it this summer?'

'He didn't say. He doesn't seem to care.'

'Can we close it down?'

'Close what down? It isn't doing anything. Nobody cares that it's there.'

Pazanov can feel the brooding tension knotting up the room. Something he has felt for months. Something nameless. Something he still cannot put a hand to.

275

'Look,' says Uberti, his voice a hoarse squawk.

On the Russia Today broadcast, Simon Adaro is walking stiffly out of the Achenia offices in London. He is holding firmly on to the hand of a young woman. The image shifts abruptly back to the studio where a newsreader is trying to look as if she knows what she should be doing. Her make-up is not complete, and a wisp of tissue paper sticks out from the back of her collar. She keeps looking over the camera shoulder to frantic gestures behind. Her mouth opens and closes, but she is mute.

Uberti turns up the sound.

A continuous stream of text runs across the footage, 'BREAKING NEWS'.

'– solar satellite will supply five hundred gigawatts to the European grid –'

The image cuts to a view above the Earth, showing a series of strange contraptions unfolding endlessly into space. Light from the sun reflected, concentrated into vast arrays and pouring down through a collector to the Earth below.

'– was launched into orbit and assembly completed two weeks ago –'

Pazanov silently takes his console and slips out of the office, leaving behind the howling fury as Uberti begins to smash his furniture into tiny pieces once more.

Beneath the cracking wood and tearing fabric, he hears Adaro speak.

'– how do you wish to be remembered? –'

He hesitates, touching the wall, closes his eyes, seeing Natalya's face and smile, and walks away from Uberti's outrage.

34

Spring is nudging its way out of the winter darkness, and Shakiso can smell the damp warmth of the forest from across the road in Großer Tiergarten. Tuft is standing at her side staring mournfully out at flocks of pigeons flying past.

She looks tired, with a new weight to her presence, more rooted.

Smiling, her face pale, pushing back her fringe, 'You should go inside, Frieda. It will be here soon, and I'm sure the board will want to get started again.'

'Nonsense, Ms Collard. It is the least I can do,' standing very formal in her long grey coat. Frieda does not touch her, and Shakiso is grateful for the space, worried she will lose the control she is struggling to maintain.

The remaining Climate board members are downstairs outside the meeting room, drinking coffee and eating a selection of peculiarly dry biscuits. Shakiso imagines the occasional cough, and apology, as elegantly dressed men and women spray each other with crumbs.

They were supposed to meet all day, a gathering she has delayed almost beyond the point of good manners. Trying to cram a lifetime of intimacy and shared experience with Simon into only a few months. But Shakiso has completed her part, sharing the results of their work in North Africa and her plans for bringing

Moussa Konte into her executive team, securing his role as her successor.

A dot on the horizon and the Achenian helicopter begins its descent towards them.

'I did what you wanted, Frieda,' she says, her lip trembling. 'You know that's what I do for you. And most of this has been pure luck on my part. Ansar Dine. All those new cities. New technologies. And when it went wrong, Moussa was there to fix my mistakes. All I've done is stand in the right place and hand out prizes.'

'Sometimes,' Frieda says, nodding, 'that is both the right thing and the difficult thing to do,' uncharacteristically taking her arm. 'I understand your pain, your need to be with Mr Adaro, but please consider my offer. We need people with your experience to help us in Europe now. Take as much time as you need. We will be here when you are ready.'

'Simon . . . after . . .' She brushes away tears. 'Thank you, Frieda. You'll always be my favourite international tycoon.'

The helicopter lands, stirring up grit and moss from the roof. With a tight smile and backwards glance to Frieda, Shakiso steers Tuft inside, and the door slides closed behind her. The caracal whines and paces inside the cabin. She pulls her close, feeling her warmth.

She presses the return button, and the helicopter lifts, turning towards Budapester Straße. Below her, Frieda waves and nods, then heads inside.

Shakiso leans back, Tuft sprawled across her lap, as the helicopter sets its course to London. She watches the landscape passing beneath her, imagining the millions of lives oblivious to hers. Each with their own joys and tragedies.

'Oligodendroglioma,' she says to herself. Tiny cancer cells diffused throughout Simon's brain. Growing slowly over nineteen years. Each day tightening their grip.

'Cancer's a flesh wound,' she had said, willing it away, pleading for it to be untrue.

He had shook his head. 'Untreatable.' He had hoped to survive it indefinitely, but he can feel himself slipping. Not for him to die in defiance in some distant battle with the sound of trumpets in his ears, but in silence at home in bed.

'What has this all been for?' she remembers asking.

'You already know the answer to that. You're living it. Because even doing the honourable thing can be immensely entertaining,' his smile, and his eyes the bright blue of an endless childhood.

It is quiet in the helicopter cabin, the newsfeed on the display console mute. She watches the cascade of stories, her mind blurring. Looking through the canopy, she imagines a beast-like face in the sky, its eyes searching hers, and falls into an exhausted doze.

In her dream, she sees the four children, older than she remembers, toddlers now.

It is still cold this early in the spring, and wind and rain flutter at their padded jackets. They are thickly bundled under scarves and fleecy beanies, and their mother looks concerned and harassed as she secures them. Their arms stick out stiffly, and passers-by on the crowded platform offer sympathetic smiles at her managing on her own.

She is on her knees, addressing each child in turn until she is satisfied.

'You wait where I told you until I call,' she says as she stands, readjusting her scarf. 'I will go up to the restaurant and see that all is ready.'

Four little heads nod, their eyes dark and serious. They totter off in different directions, tiny round balls wandering between the legs of the taller figures staring out from the railings. Other equally wrapped toddlers wave, and they wave back.

The mother looks at the ticket in her hand and, with a last worried glance after the children, makes her way over to the elevators.

'Madame,' says the attendant. 'Use the machine over there to frank your ticket.'

As she waits at the doors, she can see one of the children standing within the iron lattice of the north leg, looking up towards the top of the tower. A wedding party celebrates in the background. The bride brave in a thin white dress still clutching her corsage, and the air filled with laughter, the tinkle of champagne glasses and softly falling orange and red confetti.

The elevator arrives, and she squeezes her way in amongst the chatter of other visitors. Appropriate exclamations of awe as the carriage rises and gives everyone a view of the city through its glass walls.

The doors open on the second level, and there is a moment of hesitation. There are gendarmes standing outside the doors wearing flak jackets and looking severe.

'Please, if you could show some identity,' says one at the door. 'A routine precaution.'

Each person shows what they have. A dark-skinned émigré is brusquely taken aside, held between two armed soldiers. He looks flushed and defensive.

'Ah, Madame, you are French,' says the gendarme inspecting the mother's passport.

'Oui, monsieur,' she says. 'I am going to the restaurant.'

'Well, Madame,' he says, smiling at her intently, his hand a little too close to her breast, 'I wish you bon appetit.'

She nods nervously and walks quickly towards the restaurant, its name carved in italics above the door: Bastiat.

'Bonjour, Madame,' says the formally dressed concierge, holding a small console in her hands. 'Do you have a reservation?'

The woman still appears flustered. 'No,' she says. 'I am meeting someone, and I think they are already here.'

'Please, Madame,' says the concierge kindly. 'You are welcome,' and gesturing for her to enter the restaurant.

The woman offers a nervous smile and walks deliberately, as if forcing every step. In the centre of the restaurant crowded with breakfast diners, most of whom are staring out at the view of the city, she stops and looks around her.

Her hand trembles only slightly as she touches her ear to make a call.

'My children,' she says, her throat swollen. 'We go to join our fathers.'

Her scream, when it comes, is shattered with despair and anguish.

'For our fathers!'

Her face wet with tears.

Near the elevators, the gendarmes are already turning to run.

They are too late.

Five simultaneous explosions.

Four small bodies evaporate within the wrought-iron legs.

The iron structure tears apart.

The Eiffel Tower falls.

In the air, the screams of the dying and softly drifting orange and red confetti.

Shakiso wakes to a fading face in the sky, its eyes the depths of sorrow, and silent flames on the console screen. A journalist standing before the carnage, weeping as he attempts to explain, his anguish muted.

She turns up the volume.

'– two thousand people trapped. Behind me you can see – oh, god, no—' The camera shifts to the edge of the first level where a man is climbing over the railings, his clothes on fire. He jumps.

Shakiso mutes the console and, shivering, hugs Tuft to her chest.

As the helicopter crosses into English protected airspace, two jet-powered drones draw near. They circle her until the craft is verified. Shakiso's ear vibrates.

'Hollis,' she says, grateful for human contact.

'Darling Shak,' he says. 'We've just heard the news. Best we keep this from Simon.'

She nods quietly, and he feels the gesture in his ear implant.

'English airspace was closed a few minutes ago,' he continues. 'I managed to get permission for you to come in but expect to have an escort as you get to London.

'Shak,' he says. 'I'm so relieved you can be here. I don't think he has long.'

Two drones settle in on either side of the helicopter as it reaches the London periphery. Glaring reflections as they pass over Wet London, the reclamation works pushing steadily down the Thames, and towards the familiar city skyline.

On the console screen, a familiar haunted face. As if watching someone else do so, she unmutes the sound.

'– Michèle Tillisi, whose husband died in Benghazi over two years ago, is suspected as having –'

Feeling ice settle on her heart, turning off the console, pushing her face into Tuft's fur.

They bank, and the helicopter lands gently on top of Achenia's building. The drones circle and then return to their duties.

She can hear muffled conversation as she walks through Hollis's apartment to the guest room, Tuft silently at her heels.

'– been a fantastic ride, Si –' Adrià and Hollis smiling as she walks in, Simon looking thrilled, Sam – with his back to her – not responding at all as his recorded hologram continues speaking '– promised you a lovely spot with a great view. See you soon, big brother,' his voice ragged with static.

Shakiso walks around Sam and kneels beside Simon. His hand,

blue veins visible through his transparent skin, uncertain and trembling as it seeks hers.

'My darling,' she says, filled with anguish at seeing him so frail.

'My —' stops, breathes in shallow gasps, '— love,' smiling.

The hologram transmission ends, Sam standing sadly, his hands opening and closing, seeking connection. Awareness of how much he wants to be there, how great the distance.

Hollis touches her on the shoulder. 'We're drinking lots of tea,' he says. 'Would you like some?'

'Tea —' says Simon, laboured, '— is good.'

She smiles. 'Thank you, please.'

One of the nursing team comes into the room, quietly replaces one of the fluid-filled pouches and leaves.

Shakiso bites her lip, refusing to see the machines and pipes surrounding him. His blood draining out of his side into a homeostasis perfusor and returning again, his head in a cloth cap covered in sensors.

'How's — the — ass?' he asks.

Nodding, her face pale, 'Still got it,' smiling, willing the moments to last.

He sleeps. Hours pass, too few. The sun begins to settle orange and red over the Thames. The light flowing warm and comforting across his face.

He squeezes her hand.

She leans towards him, her ear against his lips.

'Have — I — told — you?' he asks.

And closes his eyes for the last time.

III

FROM FLAME MORE THAN HEAT

Our journey has been one of extraordinary hardship. In time, that difficulty will change. It will not be long before others come, and they will not wait on our invitation. They will be adventurers, families seeking new lives far from conflict, ordinary people. Remember how today feels – your excitement, your fear and anticipation – and welcome our future arrivals as you would wish to have been welcomed. Let them come in peace, for all our hopes and dreams.

Samara Adaro, Socotra Mars base, March 2056, founding speech to
colonists on the first day after planet fall

Too many people are impatient. We must not be so. Even if it is to take more than my lifetime, eventually we will cross. Your children, or their children, will live in a place of freedom and safety. What else are we to do?

Farai Ramuelo, on a beach near El Haouaria in Tunisia, 2058, comments to
a meeting of elders after the sinking of their boat prior to launch

You should see it, the way the fine red sand flows across the desert. We explored ten days from the base and watched two serpent dust devils cross us on the horizon. That's why I'm here, Dad. To see what has never been seen, to be part of something new, to find out what I can be. It was never about leaving. It was always about going towards.

Edith Teriän, agronomist at Socotra Mars base, July 2061, personal
correspondence to her parents

35

Milk flows from all along the banks of Saint-Louis Island. Women and men up to their waists in the river, their clothing clinging wet to their skin, upended jugs and bottles in their hands, and the white flame spreading out until it spans each bank. It pours past the city and the marshy lands beyond it until it reaches the surf and is there churned into the ocean.

From their throats, a song like weeping.

The wet has returned and rain drifts, like warm gossamer, softening and blurring.

Shakiso leans on her elbows against the riveted metal girders of the Faidherbe Bridge watching the waters flowing beneath her. She has been standing here for hours, midway along the bridge.

Tuft lies curled around her feet, seeking shelter from the rain, her tail tucked in as protection against passing feet.

It is almost like being on a ship, with ripples cast in the wake of each vehicle in the incessant traffic driving past. People walk back and forth across the pedestrian walkway, a noisy rumble of conversation overlaid with the clatter of tyres on the iron girders.

A poster from the presidential elections almost three weeks ago floats along in the current, Sidiki Cissoko's face triumphant on the soggy print.

Life moves on without Simon, without her.

She runs her fingers along the cracking paint of the metal

girder. The Faidherbe Bridge. Not even the original, just a name on something. Who remembers the person? Whether he built the bridge himself? Whether he struggled?

Will that be Simon? A cypher in a legend, his name on a bridge, or a plaque on a building somewhere?

'They do not forget,' says a warm, musical voice, and the griot smiles, nodding towards the women and men along the shore. 'It is the fortieth day, and they honour him.'

He stands alongside her, looking downriver, gently resting a hand upon her shoulder. She buries herself in the folds of his boubou, letting go her sorrow and anguish.

They embrace there on the walkway of the bridge, the tall man in his ochre-brown boubou and the slim woman in his arms, a stream of people walking by and respecting their mourning.

'Do you always turn up at the right time?' she asks, wiping her eyes and smiling.

'I am where I am,' he says.

She looks towards Sidiki's face on the poster floating away from them.

The griot's eyes are the warmth and depth of the harmattan. 'What do you most fear, my sister? That Simon will be forgotten? That he will not be honoured?'

She nods, not daring to speak.

The griot runs his hand along the metal of the bridge, as if stroking a great beast.

'It is our nature to forget. Even the greatest of us become shadows upon which others may cast their own dreams and fears. Our memory like dust,' he says, looking to the waters where the last white traces are diminishing in the river, lost to rain and tide.

'He will have honour and memory and it will fade. It is always so.'

She follows his gaze, watching as the waters return to their tawny muddy flow. 'What will they remember, though? The stories they tell about him. I don't recognize him in them. Where do they come from?'

'From where we draw all stories,' he says. 'To hold on to what has been loved and lost, to explain and teach in ways that seep into memory.

'There is a story I would tell.'

'Will I hear it?' she asks, her voice so soft as to be almost submerged in the waters flowing beneath.

The griot puts his hand on her shoulder. 'Painted-dog's child sits quietly, thinking on the migration of so many . . .'

Tales from Gaw Goŋ: Harmattan, la mémoire comme de la poussière

Painted-dog's child sits quietly, thinking on the migration of so many.

'Where are your thoughts, Painted pup?' asks Baboon, as he rubs dust into the baked food remains inside the two black-bellied pots. The waters of the ouahe are sacred, to be used for drinking or offerings, not for cleaning.

'I am not certain I understand all that you have shown me,' she says, sitting up on her elbows. 'I have never seen Men in such numbers, or the strange things in the sky or which float, or waters so vast but which one cannot drink.'

'Aha, aha. Even so,' says Baboon, 'there is a story that you understand.'

'Yes, grandfather. It is the same as when we follow the herds while they are following the waters,' she says, scratching behind her neck with her hind paw. 'The migrating Men seek a place of refuge, where the waters run clear and there is plenty to eat. There are many obstacles they must overcome, just as my family must journey far and struggle greatly to run down our prey.'

'Aha, aha, my child,' says Baboon, taking up his koubour. He begins to hum softly as he plucks and strums, drumming with his fingertips on the stretched skin of the instrument's body.

'Perhaps I am uncertain because I have never seen so many

Men. When does their migration happen? Is the story you have shown me in the future or the past?'

Baboon continues his gentle melody, deep tones filling the bowl of the ouahe. 'Is it the pattern of your fur that predicts your future, my child?'

'No, grandfather, for each of my brothers and sisters are different, and our fur offers no guide to our future.'

'It is similar with a story. The place and time are like painted colours. They permit us to identify a particular story but not to know where that story will go. And the same story may take place in a different setting yet still be the same.'

'Yes, grandfather, but this story seems so far away. Is this in the memory of the genii?'

'You have seen that before each telling I gather dust and blow it into the flames?' he asks. 'Do you know why?'

'That I do not, grandfather. It is of the magics of the gaw.'

'Even our magics require a seed, my child. The dust of the harmattan is carried far. It sees everything and sticks even where it is not wanted.'

Scratching at her ribs, Painted-dog's child sighs. 'It does, grandfather, even as I try to honour my mother and stay clean.'

'Aha, aha,' he laughs. 'It is so, Painted child. Our memory is like dust. It is carried far, sticks tightly and lingers in the past, present and future. Who is to say from where the dust has come?'

Excitement in Painted-dog's child's eyes. 'And so you blow dust for the genii, to remind them of what they already know?'

'Aha, aha,' he smiles. 'None are forgotten as long as the dust from their passing is still with us in this world. Even the least of us are remembered.'

'I am glad, grandfather, for I fear for Joshua and his people in your story. They travel far from their people, and the lands where they journey do not seem to honour the genii.'

'One may achieve honour even in a place not of one's birth,' says Baboon. 'We are reaching the end of this part of our story. Are you ready?'

Painted-dog's child looks nervously into the flames burning almost invisibly in the brilliance of the afternoon. The erg around the ouahe turning orange and red with the arc of the sun.

She draws in a deep breath and nods. 'Yes, grandfather. I am ready.'

Still playing his koubour with one hand, Baboon takes up a handful of dust, whispers to it and, as Gaw Goŋ, blows it gently into the flames, the red-brown mist glowing in his eyes. A swirling green-grey pool opens above the flames, shot through with flecks of red and black.

Gaw Goŋ motions at the portal, pulling it wider until it fills the space before them. He whispers again, and the pool clears.

If the ocean of the Mediterranean was strange for Painted-dog's child, what she sees now lacks even the familiarity of water upon the earth. Before her is a city where fine powdered water, like the great rivers of sand flowing in the erg, hangs in overlapping rolling hills in the sky above.

The city is grey and dark even though it is still early in the afternoon. There is mist and showers of rain falling on to the ground, cold and muffling sound.

A young man wearing a long coat, his neck and head buried in the upturned collar, walks purposefully along an uneven pavement. His thoughts chase and wrestle, stirring his steps to rising fury so that each foot slams into the ground with determined force.

'It is time the council did something. Think of the children who could be hurt. This is outrageous and something must be done. I can be a bystander no longer.'

He carries a recording band crumpled in one hand, thrust deep into his coat pocket where he fiddles and twists it between his fingers.

Past the low brick houses reinforced against the floods which often come through this area. Over iron grids fixed tightly on top of the wide culverts beneath the pavement, filled with their permanent gargling rush of floodwater being drawn away. Nearing the temple with its carved cows on the roof and the dancing many-armed gods on its blue-tinted walls. Turning left into a street cluttered with pedestrians.

The crowds force him out of his churning thoughts, giving him a new source of anxiety. For now he is amongst the foreigners who have flooded this impoverished and previously almost empty area, changing its character and making him feel alien even in his own home.

The old streets, with their tangle of stalls and shops, sing with a different rhythm and simmer with distant flavours. The millions have washed up all the way to this shore where they struggle with its cold and damp even as they flourish and set down fast-growing roots.

He reaches his destination and the source of his turmoil.

A derelict clock tower topped with a tarnished gilded crown stands forlorn in the middle of a shouting, bargaining, living market. Around the outside border marked in bent and leaning metal seats are stalls selling stews, fish broth, vegetables, clothes and printed goods. Music of different tempos and cultures blends into melody at once ancient and new.

The young man stands bewildered for a moment, for it is different from when he was here only weeks ago. Still the millions arrive, and he wonders where they will all go and how they would be stopped.

Children run laughing and excited through the market.

He remembers his objective for, even if these be the children of seekers, their danger is still his to bear. He pulls from his pocket his crumpled recording band and sets it over his brow. It vibrates, a brief indication that it is active, recording everything before him and streaming the image on to the connect.

He is unworried if no one sees it now. It will serve as a record for when he presents his case to the council.

Walking, careful to maintain a steady flow, he skirts the outside of the stalls around the tower.

'I am in the market around the Lewisham clock tower,' he says, as clearly and as bravely as he can so that his voice can be heard above the cheerful tumbling rumble of the people all around him.

He pushes through and between two stalls until he is in the silent oasis like a moat around the tower. He is on the wrong side and walks around until it comes into view.

'You can see the door or, rather, where the door used to be, that leads down from the tower to the works below.'

And it is true, for where an old heavy wooden door used to guard the inner rooms of the tower, there is a dark, open space. The remains of the door hang loose, broken and torn, to the side.

'We passed children playing here, and you can see how many people walk around this place. It is unacceptable that the city council do not recognize the dangers of leaving this way open and that they do not fix it. The guard rail on the staircase inside is corroded and broken, and a person would fall more than ten metres to the rooms below. Think of what would happen if one of the children fell inside? If it was your child—'

He stops as a man begins to shriek in violent rage.

It all seems to happen so quickly. Afterwards, he will review his recording and realize that he saw everything, but as it happens he catches only fragments.

A man wearing a bulky jacket runs up to the clock tower, shouting. People all around scream in terror. A child brushes against the young man's legs, and he looks down, then up again straight into the face of a tall, straight-backed man.

They see each other, eye to eye.

The straight-backed man is in a thick jacket and trousers that he wears with both unfamiliarity and pride. He looks into the young man's eyes as if to say, 'If not me, then who?'

And then the straight-backed man runs with all his strength at the shouting man. He captures him in his arms, and his strength and momentum carry them through the clock tower doorway.

The young man, still recording, watches in confusion, his mouth open, breathing slow as his heart thumps once in his chest.

He hears the scrape as they miss the guard rail and the soft slump as they smash into the solid floor far below.

A moment of silence.

After, he can only say it felt as if the earth rolled like a boat on water. The explosion is so loud that he is unable to hear it, only a strange dead ringing that continues for days.

He is speechless, even when the young paramedic shines a light into his eyes and persistently asks him his name. In his mind, the eyes of the straight-backed man, his look of knowledge, of comfort, of kindness.

There is panic in the city. 'Didn't we tell you these refugees want only our deaths?' says a woman on the evening news. 'When will the government do something? Send them home. We do not want them.'

The prime minister of all England and Wales calls for calm and declares that the army will be brought on to the streets. Seekers will be searched and are subject to curfew. Fire and stones are thrown into their crowded homes, their shops looted and destroyed.

Late in the night, as fear and flames creep through seeker neighbourhoods, the young man's recording is discovered.

It is not believed.

The young man is sought. He is still deafened. Is questioned.

He watches his recording, weeping as he sees again the shared look of the straight-backed man.

The prime minister herself presents the recording to the people. The soldiers will turn around, now to protect and to welcome.

The man in the bulky jacket is known. The security services are embarrassed, for if anyone would do such a thing, it is this man. But he is not of the seekers. He is a white man and so not subject to the suspicion and invasion of thought-of outsiders. Policy must change.

The seeker who sacrificed himself is not known.

One amongst the millions who sought a new life in a distant land.

The young man visits the rubble-filled pit where the clock tower once was. He carries his recording band as if his story is still incomplete. That he owes this unknown man an honour that he knows not how to give.

Row upon row of flowers are piled before the crater. An ocean of colour, an outpouring of grief. In recognition of a man wrongfully accused.

'You are the boy who told the truth,' says an old Shona woman, taking his hand.

His lip trembles, and she folds him into her bosom.

Word spreads, quietly and gently, 'The boy who told the truth is here.' Many have stories of the man he seeks.

'He saved me in the forests of the Congo,' says an old man.

'He found us food when there was none,' says a young girl.

The flower-filled square filling with memory, one mote joining another until the life revealed is larger than any one person could ever claim.

The young man is recording. Each story broadcast. And the seeking millions tell their stories to the listening tens of millions.

'I am Seydou, and he led my family through the war in Uganda.'

'My name is Gideon, and he rescued my daughter from soldiers who would violate her.'

'We are Faysal and Aysha. We are to be married. He kept us together when we were to be sent to different countries.'

The young man is led, hand to hand, a canvas on which stories may be told.

'I am Isaiah, the reborn child, and Joshua was my father. Please, I will take you to my mother.'

A way is made through the quiet streets, and thousands flow, following the young man and the reborn child.

Esther is waiting in the single tiny room shared now only with Hannah, Rachel and Isaiah.

The young man is pressed inside to sit with her.

She smiles at him, and he recognizes the same warmth of the straight-backed man.

'I am sorry for your loss,' he says, tears wet on his cheek and on his collar.

She takes his hand, shaking her head.

'It is well, my son. Do not weep. The genii have blessed him and us with a longer second life than we could have hoped.'

'I do not understand,' he says.

'My husband was a Casamance. A twice-dead man,' she says, her eyes filled with light and love. 'He first died during our escape from the airport in Dar es Salaam when soldiers took others in our party. A child died there.

'His second life was a gift of the genii, so that he could lead us to safety.

'We shared a lifetime on our journey here.'

The young man feels a future open, as of the hope in the beginning of a great voyage. 'I would be grateful if you would tell me of your journey,' he says.

Esther smiles and nods.

And, drifting through the air, memory like dust spreads and settles. That none may forget.

36

'I remember this,' says Shakiso, her voice as if waking. 'From before. It happened a few days after Simon died – all those stories I heard, they were always about Joshua,' realizing she can recall the journey of the man who was Simon's friend, who became the Casamance of legend.

'Why can I hear it now?' she asks, her mouth fighting against emotion, her eyes a frozen ocean.

The griot places his hands on the flat rail of the bridge. 'There is a story about two brothers,' he begins.

Surprised, she laughs, feeling her tension drain away. 'Ismael,' she says, 'always the two brothers with you. I think it's time you recognize that women get a shot at the lead too.'

The griot grins and gestures at the passing multitude. 'I am not sure my people are yet ready for such transformation.'

Shakiso stands, one hand on her hip, the other on the rail, her shirt and jeans tight against her body. 'Dude,' she says firmly, her eyes with a familiar blue brightness, 'you're *the* griot. You're the one telling the stories.'

He laughs, his turn to be surprised. Nodding, 'You are right, but I am only a griot, and I too am still learning.' He takes her hand, holding it gently between his. 'Thank you, my sister. It is well.'

With a chuckle, he begins again, 'Once there were two sisters.'

'Better,' says Shakiso, standing alongside him and both leaning on their elbows and watching the drifting of the waters.

The cadence of his voice rises and falls with the rumble and clutter of trucks and buses over the bridge so that only she may hear his words. She stands leaning over the rails, at moments probing, calm, or seeming to tear at the metal bridge with her hands.

At last the story is at an end and her questions exhausted.

'I think I understand now,' she says. 'Thank you.'

'You are still not at peace, my sister.'

'Simon . . .' she hesitates. 'They've frozen him. They're sending him to Mars. They think they might be able to revive him in forty years or so, once they have a cure for his cancer. He leaves tomorrow with the settlers. Hollis says, if I want, when I'm ready, I can join him.' She shakes her head. 'Is he dead? Do I mourn?'

'There is a story,' says the griot, smiling as she glares at him fiercely, putting up his hands. 'Mourn his loss, my sister, live your life, for even should such a return be possible, it will still be as if you are both reborn.'

She looks up at the sky and across the river towards the mainland.

'I'm not sure what to do next. Any ideas?'

'You would take that guidance?' he asks.

'I'm only a girl,' she says, 'and I still have much to learn.'

The griot smiles. 'Then you should go to Dakar. Go listen to those who speak truth of Ansar Dine and Abdallah Ag Ghaly. You should bear witness. He must be remembered as well.'

'What will I find there?' she asks.

'That is for you to discover. As for Ag Ghaly, even the stones should weep blood at the anguish of his name.'

37

'They're gaining,' says a man in a green vest, his hands sweating in excitement.

'But what then? Those drones carry no artillery. They cannot shoot them down. And, even so, that would destroy the cargo,' says the white man, Belaya, seated at the other end of the table.

A group of the Russian mercenaries have gathered in the cafeteria of the safe-house, an old office block on the outskirts of Dakar, circling chairs and tables to watch the large view-screen. Their trays and food-dirty plates are scattered across the table, with people leaning amongst the debris, their attention bonded to the newsfeed.

Four vast, blocky quadrotor freight drones are flying over the erg, ripples of ochre sand like a petrified ocean below them. Beneath, and suspended on cables strung between them, is an enormous thirty-metre long container, like a building lying on its side.

The stream comes from the pursuing drones. Every few moments, another drone comes into shot.

Early this morning, an Achenian maintenance hub in southern Mauritania came under assault. The attackers' timing was fortuitous. It seems a glitch during a shift change left the area unsecured for only a few minutes. With no real defence, the engineers on site were forced back from the huge printer completing the last of the line printers for linking the solar farms to the electricity grid.

The attackers are anonymous in light grey-green fatigues. The drones are similarly painted. No one knows who they are.

They attached cables to the bulk of the enormous container and hoisted it into the sky.

Achenian freight and security drones were called in and have been following it for hours.

Whoever stole the container do not appear to have concerned themselves with pursuit. They do not shoot back or, given the weight and complexity of ferrying the cargo hanging below, make any attempt to evade the following drones.

An Achenian manager was interviewed, and he reappears on the feed every few minutes to repeat the potted summary. 'One of our industrial vitrification printers was stolen by unknown forces. We would like to know who they are, and we would like our property returned.'

Within minutes of the start of the feed, a young military enthusiast in Estonia posts her assessment. 'That's a Chinese carrier. It has code XB334. You can see it's been painted out. And that belongs to the Chinese military.'

Verification follows, as does a theory, of sorts.

'It's simple,' says the man in the green vest, attempting to summarize for others straggling in. 'The Chinese have wanted that printer since the first solar farm went live. They depend on Rosneft's energy as much as the Europeans. They want to put a series of farms in the Gobi Desert. They cannot buy it, so they have stolen it.'

'Why don't they give up now that everyone knows they're behind it?' asks a sweaty looking man returning from his training duties outside.

'How do you think they will get their property back from the Chinese? Sue them? Start a war? Nyea, once they get that thing inside Chinese airspace, it will not come out. Their only hope is to stop it while it's still over Africa.'

'I do not trust this,' says Belaya. 'We have been trying to destroy that machine for over a year and could not get near it. How could they capture it so easily?' He stands, walking to the cabinet against the wall where they keep bottles of vodka. 'You will see, those kitayoza have not won.'

There are grumbles amongst the mercenaries. 'Fifty dollars they get away,' says one, his voice defiant. A roar as the men shout odds and agree terms.

'Kuffār!' spits Duruji, quietly so that his words do not carry, where he and a group of jihadis are seated at the rear of the cafeteria observing as the mercenaries throw money on the table and shout encouragement at the drones on the screen. 'They drink and gamble. They are unworthy of associating with the ummah.'

The mercenaries have spent months gathering the dispersed survivors of Ansar Dine, and the building is becoming crowded. They outnumber the Russians, but they are underequipped, still using their AK-47s. Each of the mercenaries is loaded with smart armour and weaponry and, as much as the jihadis wish to slaughter them, they recognize they have not the ability to do so. Not safely, anyway.

'When will the white man let you visit our Janab?' asks one.

'Always tomorrow,' says Duruji. 'They do not trust us.'

'How do we know he will be ready for us?' asks another.

He shrugs, nursing his resentment.

Duruji was raised in the karst caves of the deep desert. A child of privilege within the stifling and prescribed hierarchy of Ansar Dine. His experience in exile has been repugnant.

He, along with many of the men, suffers from a latent agoraphobic anxiety whenever he is out in the open. He struggles with his loss of stature. Women walk wherever they wish, unaccompanied and uncovered, yet they fight and scream when he would take them. Children shout and play without supervision. Markets expect him to wait in line and pay for goods. He will do anything to restore Ansar Dine, but his mind lacks the dexterity required to navigate this world. He needs simple explanations and straightforward orders.

He, and the men, crave reassurance from Ag Ghaly that he is waiting for them. That he approves their sufferance of these kuffār.

'It matters not,' says one, his beard long and streaked with white, his djellaba greying and threadbare. 'Our Janab will know what to do.'

Duruji nods. There is not much more they can hope for. There is no access to Ag Ghaly without the help of the Russians.

A gasp as the lead Achenian drone gets too close to the rearmost Chinese drone. They collide and the two tangle. The Chinese drone instantly disconnects from its cable as they spiral down into the sands below. With the container leaning and a cable trailing in the air, the remaining Chinese drones accelerate clear.

'We've had an announcement from the Chinese ambassador to Senegal, Gong Yuanxing,' says the newsreader.

An interchangeable grey man in a grey suit appears in a block at the corner of the feed.

'The People's Republic of China rejects any accusation of interference in the private property of any organization. We are as much victims in this as anyone. We have discovered that unknown spies have stolen our freight drones for their own purposes and are using them in this matter. We join Achenia in demanding the return of our property.'

Cynical laughter from the mercenaries.

'You still fancy your odds?' asks one of the men of Belaya.

He stares at the console. 'They will not get away.'

*

'He is better today, yes?' asks one of the jihadis, nodding his head towards the great hulk of Khalil where he sits alongside Duruji.

The giant is grinding his teeth, his head twitching as he attempts to dislodge the sounds only he can hear from his bandaged ears. This is an improvement. He is able to engage and follow orders. The daily routine of forced training has given him some stability to grasp.

The men would abandon him, but he is a brave fighter and his size is sufficient to intimidate even some of the mercenaries.

They do not let him go out with them when they visit the surrounding markets. He attracts far too much attention, with many expecting him to be a laamb fighter. He seems, thankfully, not to have any interest in the world outside his mania and is docile when left on his own.

Khalil smiles at them, rubbing at the bandages over his ears. Under his breath he is muttering again about Gaw Goŋ and the howling roar in his head.

Duruji nods, staring at the table, feeling nothing but a burning knot of tension.

A roar from those closest to the screen. The coast has come into view and still the Chinese drones stay in the lead.

Suddenly, the Achenian drones pull up short. The image of the Chinese drones gets further and further away until they are a mere dark splotch on the screen, the huge printer hanging as a pendulum beneath.

Over the ocean, the printer explodes. A tiny spark of orange and red expanding and obliterating the drones, flung up and then falling and vanishing beneath the waters. The horizon shimmers and twists.

A choral sigh.

'Told you,' says Belaya. 'Now pay up.'

38

A crowd of people are gathered before the entrance to the court-room. Ordinary men and women: men in kufi and peaked caps, women wearing scarves and shawls, even children looking frightened amidst the unfamiliar pressure of strangers.

'Salle 7,' reads Shakiso. 'I wonder if that's it?'

Tuft squeezes closer to her legs and pulls her tail in to avoid being stepped on.

A court orderly pushes open the check-patterned wooden door from inside the courtroom. A wave of silence passes from the front to the back of the crowd as they wait for him to speak.

He pulls a small console from his black robes and begins to read out a list of names.

'Ms Collard,' says a gentle voice, shy and hesitant.

'Viviane,' says Shakiso in delight. 'Are you working here?'

'Yes, Ms Collard, I am with the Tribunal. Are you looking for the trial?'

'Yes, is this it? And, please, call me Shak.'

Viviane blushes slightly. 'Thank you, Ms – Shak. The trial is this way, I will show you, but it is not yet open.'

'What's this one, then?' asks Shakiso, as she follows. The Court of Justice is a vast circular building with the courts around the outside and a bright tree-filled courtyard rising up from the centre of the marble hall.

'This is the day court. They are waiting to see who will have their cases heard today.'

'Ah,' says Shakiso. 'That probably wouldn't have been as fun – oh . . .' her voice trailing off as she realizes the inappropriateness of her words, recognizing how nervous she is. 'I'm sorry. I think this whole thing is weirding me out.'

They near the far end of the circular hall. The width of the corridor is barricaded with steel-mesh security fencing and soldiers guard the corridor on either side of the entrance. The trial has been underway for three weeks, seemingly sufficient time for the guards to lose interest in the daily routine. They stand in groups chatting or clustered around consoles watching a football match.

'It is well, Ms Collard. I understand your fears,' says Viviane, shy once more. 'I will be honest. This trial – I do not believe anyone attending is not affected by it.'

A small group of lawyers laugh and chatter near the entrance to a court alongside. They are dressed in black robes with a narrow white bib sprouting from their collars and hanging over their chests.

An old man sits on a plastic chair reading from a console. His large and round wife dressed in a bright purple boubou, her head wrapped in a scarf, is seated on the floor at his side eating an orange.

Otherwise, it is silent. No waiting civilians. Only court orderlies going about their business.

'It is still early, Ms Collard. There is a small restaurant below us. We could perhaps . . .'

Shakiso takes her hand firmly. 'That is a fantastic idea. You can tell me how this works.'

They take seats alongside the glass windows looking out on the courtyard, waiting for their coffee. Light shafts down through the trees, and the contrast makes everything glow green.

Shakiso is grateful for the air conditioning. Tuft curls up at her feet and goes to sleep.

'What do you do here?' asks Shakiso. 'I'm sorry. I keep running into you, but I've no idea. I thought you worked with Tiémoko in Aroundu?'

Viviane blushes. 'I am a legal researcher here at the Tribunal. I have been assembling the evidence for the team that will lead the prosecution. Mister Diagne permitted me to work from his offices when I was interviewing seekers in Aroundu who had fled Ansar Dine.'

'How long have you been doing that? How did you get started?'

'I began ten years ago,' she says, looking away and outside, towards the sky. Her eyes cloud and her voice trembles. 'My brother wanted to cross the erg. Ansar Dine took him from us.'

Shakiso feels as if she has inadvertently stumbled into something far greater than her experience.

'I'm sorry, Viviane. Please, you don't need to tell me.'

'No,' says Viviane, looking at her. Her eyes are liquid, her stare direct and firm. 'It is good to talk. Women in my culture do not often get to speak as freely as you do.'

Shakiso smiles, nods, and her eyes are the blue of the deep.

'We were very poor. My father is late, and my mother worked as a cleaner. My brother thought to travel over the waters, to make money and send it back to us. He travelled to the hamada and there met with a group that would cross the desert. They were promised safe passage by Ansar Dine. We never heard from him again.

'I was a young girl. We went to live with my uncle in Dakar. I studied hard at school. One day there was a competition, and I won a bursary to study law at Cheikh Anta Diop University.

'On weekends, I would go speak with the old women in the

markets. They introduced me to those who survived and escaped. I recorded their stories. Every weekend, every evening. I put together a record.

'When the Tribunal was being set up, I was invited to join. I have spent ten years preparing and hoping that Abdallah Ag Ghaly would be captured and face our court. Now he is kept where the records of those he tortured used to be stored.'

Shakiso has an image of this quiet, shy woman listening; of her patient determination to walk amongst so much violence and suffering and remain as she is.

'How many have you heard?'

Viviane's eyes are red, fierce and her shoulders set back in defiance.

'Many thousands,' she says. 'And I would listen to them all.'

'Viviane, my sister, I should learn from you. I wish for even half your courage.'

Viviane leaves to prepare for the court session. Shakiso finishes her coffee and sits staring into the courtyard until she feels ready. It is a mark of her apprehension that she drinks it at all, for the coffee is quite terrible.

She queues for security clearance, passing within the view loop and submitting to a physical inspection of brusque intimacy but little competence. Tuft follows close on her heels.

The courtroom is a vast, triple-height, wood-lined hall filled with plush red chairs and soft, silencing carpet. Cameras are set up looking towards the attendees, the justices, the witnesses, and to where a figure sits immobile.

Abdallah Ag Ghaly is permitted to dress in his own clothes for court. He sits stifled inside his white grand boubou, his head in a frothy flume of a turban. As improbable as a large meringue found unexpectedly on a theatre seat.

Gone are the tantrums and unconstrained shrieks of the first days of the trial. When he would throw himself to the floor, screaming and mewling, 'Stop! Stop! I am of the divine! You have no authority over me!'

He sits. His eyes behind dark glasses. His right hand, gloved in black, supporting his chin. Not a part of him shows.

A soldier advances on Shakiso, his face radiating stocky order.

'I'm sorry, I don't understand,' says Shakiso, having forgotten to start her translation app.

'There, there,' says the soldier, gesturing down a row of chairs. And then an incomprehensible babble she cannot follow.

She moves along the row and sits. Tuft hides under her chair. Both peer back at the soldier to see if this meets his approval. The soldier glares at them, then stomps off.

She notices now the large military presence in the room.

Two-by-two, patrolling short stretches of the room. At every doorway and every junction.

A row of black-clad, armoured special forces are seated in front of Ag Ghaly. They appear to be resting, their eyes half-closed. Two of their number stand directly before him looking over his head, their guns in their hands. They scan the room.

There are many being named during the trial who have managed to keep their ties to Ansar Dine secret. Many who have acted as intermediaries, profiting from the trade in goods and people in the territories it used to control.

Many who would prefer that the trial never take place. That the suffering of so many be forgotten and lost.

People file into the court, taking their places in silence. A small group of journalists to her right and to the back of the hall. The legal advisors and researchers taking their place directly behind the opposing councils.

Viviane smiles at Shakiso as she emerges from one of the side doors, carrying three consoles and a large binder of yellowing

310

papers. She has changed and wears the black robes of a lawyer.

An old woman hobbles along the row towards Shakiso and sits down with a gentle sigh three seats away. A kindly looking old man sits down next to her on her right and smiles at her. He turns on his console and begins reading.

Soon the row on either side of her is full.

The elderly man to her left speaks to her.

'I'm sorry. I only speak English,' furtively tapping at her earlobe to start translation.

'Ah. I was asking. Are you one of the victims?' the elderly man asks again. He looks tired, but his voice is firm.

'No, I'm simply an observer,' she says, flustered.

'These seats are for the victims,' says the elderly man.

'Oh,' standing. 'I'm so sorry. The soldier—'

A bony hand on her arm holding her in place and the tenderness of warm brown eyes.

'Please,' says the old man on her right, a voice of ineffable kindness. 'Stay. You are welcome here.'

She sits down again, her heart pounding, feeling overwhelmed.

'You have met Clément,' says Viviane, leaning over the chairs. 'I am pleased. He is president of the victims' association.'

Clément stands and takes Viviane's hands. A look passes between them, as of two people who have walked long in darkness and now see light. All the years spent taking evidence, preparing for this trial, hoping that they would one day bring Ag Ghaly to justice, shared in that moment.

'If you could excuse us?' he says, and he joins her amongst her papers.

A door on the dais opens, and an orderly walks over to the microphone.

'All rise,' she says.

Three senior judges, their scarlet robes lined with synthetic ermine, take their seats and adjust the consoles on their desks.

Shakiso struggles to follow the formality and process of the court. They are picking up where they left off in yesterday's session. The elderly woman who seated herself near Shakiso takes her place at the witness stand.

The stand is uncomfortably placed in the centre of the court, before the judges but with the two opposing banks of attorneys directly behind. To listen to questions, the witness must twist and turn.

It seems, to Shakiso, a deliberate way to unsettle those testifying into reliving how their unseen assailants would surprise and torture them.

The woman leans to her left on the podium, her hips clearly causing her pain. She coughs through her replies. Eventually an orderly brings her a glass of water, and she is offered the opportunity to sit when she is not speaking.

'You claim that my client raped you. Yet you came voluntarily to live amongst the people of Ansar Dine?' says the small, calm-looking yellow-skinned lawyer leading Ag Ghaly's official defence team. His tone is that of a mildly surprised librarian attempting to help a visitor find a vaguely remembered book.

The woman is rocked by the question. She stumbles over her words, eventually giving way to tears. 'They kidnapped me from my home,' she says, her voice a whisper.

Ag Ghaly's 'real' lawyers – a group of self-proclaimed defenders who refuse to recognize the authority of the court – begin to shout. '*Salope complètement cinglée!*'

'Completely crazy whore,' the words dry and stripped of intent in the translation in Shakiso's ears.

The judges call for order, and the shouting quietens.

'He raped me. Himself. Every day until I escaped,' pointing at Ag Ghaly, her arm rigid, her voice rising over the jeers.

'*Prostituée nymphomane!*' scream the defenders. 'Nymphomaniac prostitute' in Shakiso's ears.

Her ordeal ends, and the woman is helped out of the court.

The man to Shakiso's left rises and, with great dignity, makes his way to the podium. In his left hand, he clutches a small fabric bag.

The court recognizes him. Zoumana Guengueng, the first witness. The first person to file his case with the court. The first person whose story Viviane recorded.

He has waited twenty-five years.

'Today, I keep my oath. An oath I made to myself while a prisoner of that man,' he says, pointing at Ag Ghaly.

He taps at the console before him and reads his statement. He describes the conditions in the prisons. Confinement. Disease. Abuse. Torture. The smell of those suffering around him. The bodies he was made to sleep amongst. Those whose hands he held as they lay dying, giving comfort even unto death.

His jaw tightening, the muscles clenching in his face, he unwraps his bag. Taking out clumsy looking wooden implements. Revealing them individually, like trophies.

A spoon, knife and fork made from bones and flattened, misshapen pieces of metal. A comb made from bits of wood.

'I made these so that, even there, I may live like a person. Even in the place of the shayāṭīn, I am still a person.'

Shakiso is astonished to see that many of the soldiers are brushing back tears.

He testifies. His voice calm and firm and patient.

When the defence attorney deliberately mispronounces his name, he corrects him. 'I am Zoumana Guengueng. Zoumana Guengueng. That man would take even our names from us. I am a person. Zoumana Guengueng. Do not forget it.'

Shakiso's throat is tight, clotted. She finds she has been gripping the armrests.

'It is the end of the first session. Please rise.'

The judges leave.

Ag Ghaly moves for the first time. He stands. All the special forces soldiers gather tightly around him, their eyes wide and watchful. They walk as a unit towards the side exit.

As he goes, a large group of people rise and cheer, clapping loudly and enthusiastically.

Ag Ghaly raises his arms above his head, clasping his hands together as if in triumph.

39

'Another lawyer.' There is little inflection in Abdallah Ag Ghaly's voice. His dark eyes are indifferent and his body slack in his over-sized yellow prison uniform.

'Janab,' says Duruji, resisting an urge to scratch at the agonizing itch in his groin.

The cheap synthetic fabric of his newly acquired black suit is tight and unfamiliar, and attracts copious static. He is a hairy man, and his skin is on fire. Any movement results in painful shocks, and his one attempt at seeking relief merely increased the charge he generated. Even sitting motionless feels as if his skin is being bitten by millions of ants.

'It was the white man's idea. You are not allowed visitors but—'

'Yes,' says Ag Ghaly, waving one hand dismissively. 'I may have lawyers.'

The white man. Belaya. The name the Russian mercenaries call him. He treats the remnants of the Ansar Dine army with derision. Duruji longs to knock off his head.

'Janab, it is good to see you,' says Duruji, relief and respect in his voice.

They are seated uncomfortably within Ag Ghaly's cell, their chairs each positioned slightly too far from the table.

The room is deep within the basement of the African Court of

Justice, converted from a secure filing room to contain this single prisoner. The front wall has been replaced with bomb-proof sheets of glass bolted between steel retaining bars. The walls themselves are welded steel sheets painted an extremely shiny white. There is a squatting toilet alongside the glass, but there are no lights inside the cell, only a spotlight from outside. Two camera lenses face in from the corridor, a console streaming news hanging on the wall between them. All the furniture is welded to the floor: chairs, desk, bed and bookshelf.

Duruji smells of slowly drying sweat, aftermath of his tortured experience reaching the cell. He presented his fake credentials at the court entrance, hoping they would work, fearful they would not, and trying not to respond to every itch and electric snap along his body. Then the march of thorns through increasing levels of security ever deeper beneath the court.

Ag Ghaly's prison guards ignored him. Bored, underpaid and eager to return to watching a football match around a shared console propped over and obscuring the feeds from the cell.

Duruji feels dampness under his arms and over his back. No matter, for the cell has little ventilation and is already quite acrid.

'The man is dead,' he says.

'Yes, and his body has left the Earth,' says Ag Ghaly, his emotions a quiet void. 'I saw his woman with him on the news. Now she comes daily to watch them torture me with lies. Where will I have my revenge?'

'The Russians would have us destroy his solar farms?'

'That,' says Ag Ghaly, his voice caustic, 'is not the vengeance I would have. I want him to suffer, not break his things. I want to tear his skin from him. Pour acid into his veins. Now he is safe from me. No, it is better for us that we keep the farms. Or sell them to the Chinese. They have also been to visit. More lawyers.'

Duruji is a fighter, accustomed to having a weapon in his hand, not to sitting at a desk negotiating the complexity of rival ambitions. His body itches, and he wishes he could scratch. He struggles to pull his concentration together.

'I do not understand, Janab. Why are we working with these kuffār? They are unclean. It is unworthy of the ummah to consort with these—'

Ag Ghaly stands and slaps him. Duruji cowers, flinching as his movement causes static sparks to flare.

'I am sorry, Janab. It is well. I am sorry.'

'You are the one who is unworthy, Duruji. Where was your security when I needed it? Why am I here?' his voice shrill, his indifference torn by frustration and loathing. He slaps at Duruji again, oblivious of the watching cameras.

Duruji quails beneath the blows, helpless as a child before the wrath of an abusive parent. Ag Ghaly is sweating, his breathing fast and irregular. He tires, sits again. Resumes his sneering ambivalence.

Duruji sits hunched, his eyes lowered. Only the sound of Ag Ghaly's rattling breath and the continual subdued chatter of news from the console through the glass behind him.

'I deal with the Russians and Chinese because I use them,' says Ag Ghaly. 'You are too weak to free me without their help. Your men lack organization. Only I can restore the ummah.

'Yes, they are kuffār, but they are rivals. Rosneft know they have lost the battle in Europe. They hope still to keep their business in China.

'The Chinese see an opportunity to extract themselves from Russian control. They tried to take the machines which print those solar collectors. They failed. They are shamed. Now they hope that if we capture the fields we can sell the technology to them.

317

'Each will help us even as they fear betrayal.'

Gong Yuanxing, or a grey man in a grey suit claiming to be him, had visited Ag Ghaly. Their meetings were brief. Each was quite clear about their requirements and neither pretended to have anything but distaste for the other.

'The Russians give us guns, Janab. They have brought over one hundred and eighty of our men to the city. What will the Chinese do for us? They cannot fight. They are –' he spits the word '– businessmen.'

Ag Ghaly sneers. 'Do the Russians share their nice smart weapons with us? Or are we left with scraps?'

Duruji grinds his teeth, crushing his rage into a burning point at the memory of every slight and jibe which the Russians abrade into him and his men.

'Janab, what does it matter? A man is equally dead no matter the weapon. What is better than even an inferior rifle?'

'This is why you will never be a leader, Duruji. You think no further than the weapon in your hand. The Chinese have shared something far more valuable. Information.'

'What could they know, Janab?' asks Duruji.

'The planes, you fool,' he says. 'The Russians won't tell me where they are. The Chinese give it freely. The grey man was here this morning with the coordinates. He believes he has power over us. He with his, "We are not involved in whatever you do to free yourself or secure the fields",' mocking Gong Yuanxing's metallic accent. 'It is good they are so ignorant. None of them understand the importance of this cargo. They think only I wish to sell drugs.'

Duruji is sullen, trapped within his torturing suit. The itching around his testicles has become a driving pain he feels he will never escape. He remembers the look of mocking resentment when the white man gave him this suit and his credentials.

For weeks, he had demanded that he be permitted to leave the safe-house and meet Ag Ghaly. He was told that it would be impossible. Too dangerous. Instead they worked him harder and treated him worse. He refused to yield.

Each day, the Russians who mind them let them know how much they loathe their assigned task. The clothes they are given to wear are old and do not fit. The food they eat is often rotten. Many of the men suffer from stomach cramps. The Russians stay in nice hotels and sleep between clean sheets.

Each day, the Russians drive the men to a disused sports field and make them run and exercise, even in the middle of the day when the heat would drive a dog mad. The men have never trained like this. They have never been a professional army, and the Russians push them, goading them to break.

The men of Ansar Dine simmer. Their hatred growing. They know they must work with these apostates, that their hope of victory depends on them. Duruji grinds his teeth as he thinks on their debasement before the kuffār.

'Janab, the planes. What are they to us?'

Ag Ghaly stares blankly at the mute surface of the table, tracing random patterns with a single forefinger.

'The man is dead,' he says. 'I am alive.'

Duruji shakes his head, regretting instantly the movement.

Ag Ghaly stands and walks over to the glass, glaring up at the twin lenses of the cameras.

'Our ummah is not like the caliphates of old. All bowed before them. Only peasants bow before us. We have been weak. Hiding in our holes in the ground, a danger only to farmers and herders.

'The kuffār over the waters force us to cower beneath the shade of their weapons. They watch and fly their drones over our lands, and we are unable to stop them. We who fight with stones have more courage than they. Stripped of their power they are soft and cowardly. Even one death by our great *šuhadā* causes them to collapse in terror,' he says, indicating the console showing footage of the burning Eiffel Tower. 'Look at how a single martyrdom in Paris has made the French rush to join that Federation.'

He has had nothing to do but watch the news, distorting what he sees to fit his understanding of the world and his place in it.

He leans his head towards the glass, his breath misting on the surface. He breathes harder, creating a canvas of fine dew.

'One man can draw a line, like so,' running his finger through the precipitation. 'And history is changed. The weak cannot cross.

'The man did it when he came here and built those solar farms. He made the Russians dance for him. They ran this way and that, but they could not stop him. They have learned that they ran on a path of his choosing.'

Duruji adjusts himself carefully on his seat as he twists to listen. 'He did that to us too, Janab.'

Ag Ghaly turns, the line on the foggy glass behind him eroding in the heat of the cell.

'Yes. I have been taught a great lesson. To remember the power of one man with a clear vision for what he wishes to achieve. I thought little of the matters of the world. I had become complacent, forgotten our purpose. You failed to protect me, but it was I who opened the door and brought him inside.

'Great men drive history, Duruji. Men who have the power to force others to their will. Men like me. But even a man of great force sometimes needs a tool to bring fear where it is needed.'

'I still do not understand, Janab. What is on those planes?'

'A weapon, Duruji, such that will make even the most powerful quake before us. We will not hide in the ground. We will own this world.

'The man is dead, Duruji. Now there is only me.'

40

Sidiki Cissoko would love to take off his shoes and feel the soft sand of the Soumbédioune beach against the soles of his feet. He does not, self-consciously aware of his security team forming a phalanx along the road behind him. Above him, almost out of sight, hover his watching drones.

He sighs and tries to put them all out of his mind as he walks alongside the stillness of the ocean towards the jumble of boulders at the far end of the cove.

Growing out of the rock is a tangle of wood, plastic, animal bones and discarded clothing. Driftwood pillars wrapped in garbage, fantastical limbs pawing at the sky, their heads formed from rotting bottles or bleached horned skulls, stand in a circle around a beach hut layered in plastic sheets and old blankets.

Sidiki knocks on a plastic bowl hanging from the arch over the sea-side entrance.

'Gaw Goŋ? Weatherman?' he shouts.

'Aha,' comes an answering call, and a bone-thin man, his eyes grey with age and his hair an olive-coloured burst, bends awkwardly as he stoops under the plastic sheet covering the way out of the hut.

'My president,' he says, smiling warmly and putting out both his hands to clasp at those of Sidiki. 'Are you a big man yet?'

Sidiki laughs uneasily. 'No, and I hope never.'

'The cloak of power has much less allure when you are not yet wearing it, yes?'

'Yes, my father, and I struggle with it daily.'

The old man nods, holding on to Sidiki's hands. 'Aha, my child. It is well that you visit me. Do you have time for coffee? Or –' gesturing towards the waiting guards and fleet of black limousines on the road '– do you have other matters?'

'I have time, my father,' says Sidiki. 'I have arranged for my next meeting to be here. One of those alluring matters which is set to tempt me.'

'Aha, aha,' says Gaw Goŋ, and he leads the way inside his sculpture garden.

He upends a plastic barrel and lays an old sheet over it, indicating that Sidiki should sit.

With many a cry of 'Aha', he busies himself finding a battered pot, filling it with water and then thrusting it into the centre of his always-burning fire. He props the pot carefully against the two-headed metal stave he carries, so that it will not tip.

Sidiki sits in the midst of the wild madness of Gaw Goŋ's home looking at the gentle glittering of the ocean. Out in the distance, the horizon shimmers and flickers as if alive with shadows and light.

'The genii have been close this last year,' says Sidiki quietly, staring at the space between sea and sky. 'What do they see, my father?'

He expects no answer, for that is not the way of the Weatherman.

Gaw Goŋ travels at the whim of the genii, collecting stories, but he has lived here on Plage Soumbédioune, beneath the gaze of the surrounding buildings close to the centre of the city, for as long as anyone can remember. He seems oblivious to the entreaties of the smart glass and steel hotels clustering around his beach for him to go somewhere less obvious.

Each morning, he rises early and plucks at whatever flotsam the ocean leaves behind or at the garbage piled up by the thousands of people living nearby. Returning to his sculptures with this random assortment, adding to a standing figure here, demolishing and recreating another there.

Each day, the sculpture shifts and changes.

In the weeks before an ocean storm, the pillars transform into angry, tearing beasts, and calm again once the weather has passed. Sidiki's father has shown him pictures of the garden during the time when he was a student. The image chilling even across the gap of thirty years. Then the pillar beasts seemed to be attacking each other, leaning and violently ripping at the fabric forming their torsos and limbs, reflecting the street riots between youth and soldiers which erupted later that year.

Gaw Goŋ, the Weatherman, reads the storm, no matter what its source.

Since his victory in the election, Sidiki has taken to walking on this beach and seeking Gaw Goŋ's council.

'Aha, we are ready,' and hands Sidiki a battered mug filled with satiny black coffee.

The beans have been ground finely and mixed with cardamom, after the fashion of the Lebanese traders, and it is unfiltered. It forms a thick, matt syrup.

Sidiki holds the mug carefully on his fingertips, waiting for it to cool and for the grounds to settle.

'It is good, my father,' he says, taking a sip.

Gaw Goŋ stares deeply into the eyes of the younger man. 'My child, who are you meeting that troubles you so?'

'Many people, my father. The owner of the largest transport company wishes me to ban other companies ferrying goods to the border cities. The teachers' union fears that the coming of home electricity will cause children to be exposed to free schooling over the connect. So many special interests. Each promises disaster if I do not bow to them, and personal luxuries if I see things their way.

'Today it is the Chinese ambassador, my father. Gong Yuanxing.'

'Aha, the grey men. What is their temptation, my child?'

Sidiki swirls his coffee, watching as the grounds coat the walls of his mug. 'They wish access to the solar farms so that they may copy the technology. Failing that, they want to carry the collectors across the sea.'

Gaw Goŋ clucks and nods. 'Leaving us with nothing? Yes, that is the way of the grey men.'

'I would be failing to honour my trust with our people, and with the man who committed his life to building those fields, if I were to give them up.'

Gaw Goŋ is sitting on his haunches, prodding at his fire with the metal stave. His feet are leathery and his toes splayed wide, his hair a burst of grey on his head. He chuckles. 'Aha, aha. You feel our people are too weak to stand against the threat of a nation so vast and powerful? We are so dependent on them?'

'Yes, my father. That is what I worry.'

On the road, a sleek grey Chinese limousine draws alongside Sidiki's entourage. It is slightly early, but expected, and the security men make space.

Gaw Goŋ observes as Sidiki tenses and begins to rise. 'I would tell you a story, before you go,' placing his hand on Sidiki's knee. 'Have patience, my child. Sit a while.'

'Is it of Leuk-the-hare?' asks Sidiki, smiling.

'Of course,' says Gaw Goŋ.

'Then there is time,' says Sidiki, sitting back once more.

Gaw Goŋ takes a handful of the sand from the beach, makes a fist of it, and casts it into the flames. The grains pop, crackle and shower into sparks.

'After many years of wandering,' he begins, 'Leuk-the-hare decided he should settle down. He worried, though, that he would soon starve if he did not work.

'"I have no interest in farming," he thought, "but I could work with metal and make tools for those who do farm."

'Bouki-the-hyena, his old foe, had an old blacksmith's anvil outside his home. Leuk approached him and asked if he could borrow it from him.

'Bouki decided that this was an opportunity to avenge himself. "Very well, Leuk," he said, "but you will pay me a quarter of what you make."

'Leuk negotiated his way down to an eighth. Now he only needed some way to keep a constant heat in his forge.

'Sègue-the-leopard approached Leuk with an offer. "It has long been a secret in my family that we are able to produce and work flame. I will build and run your forge in exchange for a share of what you make."

'And like that, without any wealth of his own, Leuk was a blacksmith.

'He worked hard, and many of the other animals came to buy his tools to work their farms. Leuk multiplied the wealth invested in him until, after a time, he had made enough to buy a better anvil from Bouki-the-hyena and ask Sègue-the-leopard to expand his forge.

'One day Bouki came to Leuk and said, "I want the secret of the flame that is entrusted you by Sègue. If you do not give this to me, I will take away your anvil."

'Leuk was much afraid, for without his forge he would be unable to smelt, but without his anvil he would be unable to work his metal.'

Sidiki smiles. 'You explain my position well, my father. What would the wise Leuk do in this situation?'

Gaw Goŋ stares long into the flames of his hearth. 'There are others who have anvils, but only Sègue has the secret of fire.'

Sidiki breathes out in a long sigh. He nods. 'And Sègue has always been a friend to Leuk. Thank you, my father. You are always of the wisest.'

He stands and looks out to the road where the door to the grey limousine is smoothly sliding up and open. He hesitates and turns back to Gaw Goŋ.

'Please, my father. You will tell me? If I begin to lose the path. If I am becoming—'

'A big man? Yes, my son. I will always be here to tell you. And I will always have faith that you will listen.'

'Thank you, my father,' says Sidiki, relief in his eyes and his shoulders unburdened.

Feeling lighter, he ducks his head beneath the archway and walks across the beach towards the approaching Chinese ambassador.

One of the interchangeable grey men in a grey suit who forms the collective known as Gong Yuanxing adjusts his grey sunglasses and steps delicately on to the sand.

Sidiki meets him midway from the ocean and halfway along the beach.

'It is a pleasure to meet you once more, Mr President-elect,' says the grey man in his quiet monotone, placing emphasis on the final 'elect'. *You are not president yet.* His French translation spoken by his implant simultaneously with his clipped Mandarin.

'Mr Ambassador, it is kind of you to meet me here,' says Sidiki, speaking in Wolof.

The grey man speaks neither French nor Wolof, but his implant is unmoved by the abrupt change and shifts languages without hesitation.

'You will need to let me know of your decision, Mr President-elect,' says the grey man. It is a statement. An expectation of obeisance from a state which few dare obstruct.

Sidiki says nothing, turning slowly and ambling towards the water sloshing back and forth on the shore. The ambassador looks surprised and follows alongside.

'What do you believe is the true role of the state, Mr Ambassador?' asks Sidiki.

'I am not here to enter a philosophical discussion. This is a business matter. We do not intervene in your governance and have no interest in such questions.'

'But you do, Mr Ambassador. You would make of us a slave state. Our interests are only ours to manage when they do not conflict with yours. An investment made for the benefit of our people does not belong to me and is not mine to give away.'

'We only ask access to the technology. Only if we are unable to develop this technology ourselves will we take the collectors.'

'Only,' says Sidiki. To the ambassador's astonishment, the older man drops to his haunches, slips off his shoes and socks and rolls up his trousers.

Sidiki stands and walks until his shins are immersed in the warmth of the water. He squeezes the softness of the sand between his toes and breathes in the tang of the air.

He turns to face the ambassador, the vastness of the ocean to his back. The air shimmers, and shapes hover within as if in expectation.

'Every day since the election, people come to me and make their demands. They are from business, or our labour unions, or even from other sovereign states.

'Each presents me with a choice that is no choice at all.

'Either I am to yield and accept in exchange a personal gift, or I am to watch as my country suffers some terrible calamity.

'Not one of these demands comes with a demonstration of the benefits to my people.'

The ambassador continues to stand delicately on the dry sand beyond the water's edge. 'It is not our place to look out for the interests of the Senegalese people,' he says.

'No, but it is *mine*,' says Sidiki.

'We are China,' says the ambassador. 'Your need is greater than ours.'

Sidiki's eyes sparkle. 'I feared that was true, but it occurs to me that only those who are afraid have need to offer threats. You offer violence because you have nothing of benefit to give. There are many who offer anvils, but – here on Earth – there is only one source of fire.'

For the first time, the veneer of delicate indifference sheers, and Sidiki can see the tension of the grey man.

'Your answer is no?'

'That is my answer. The solar farms are not mine to give.'

'Then I cannot help you with what is to come,' says the ambassador, pulling at his earlobe and turning abruptly to head back to his waiting limousine.

41

'What is your government up to?' asks Hollis, his voice carrying both apprehension and amusement.

Zhi bows low, his head disappearing beneath the edge of the viewing area in the media room. 'It never occurred to the most honourable Standing Committee of the Central Political Bureau of the Communist Party of China that you had any further need of your property. They did not consider this expropriation, but rather a helpful sharing of ideas as between caring siblings.'

'In English, twitface,' says Hollis.

'They believed Tiémoko when he told them he had no idea it was geolocked.'

Hollis gives a sigh. 'He's in the clear then?'

Zhi looks tired. 'They have greater concerns. Rosneft have increased the energy price by half, and the Party are frantic that costs not be passed on to the people. They're rounding up executives again. Minhai got dragged out of a board meeting in sodding Singapore. Singapore!'

Hollis shakes his head, rolls himself closer to the hologram.

'How did you guys let it get this far? It's not as if your government ever worried about building new power stations.'

Zhi sighs. 'Cockiness. There was a time we didn't need Rosneft. Then it became easier and easier. It stopped our citizens revolting about having to chew their air forty times before breathing.'

'And they thought stealing our printer would solve this problem?'

'Hollis, that machine created two hundred gigawatts out of nothing but sand inside of eighteen months. Of course they think it will solve the problem.'

'I know, I know. Sorry,' he sighs again. 'This was your idea, remember. You thought it was necessary.'

'It was necessary. Tiémoko stole us a year to get the farms established and the lines in place. If they didn't believe they'd get the printer anyway, they would have launched their own attacks. We would have had to fight Rosneft and them.' His face falls. 'I did not anticipate they would make their capture of the printer so public. I believe they wanted Rosneft to understand this as a negotiating tool. The loss has humiliated them.'

'What should we do? The other one is safely back in London, and we're certainly not going to print any more of them. We're flying the remaining line printers in.'

'They're desperate, Hollis. If this place goes up, it'll make the arc of fire look like a boy-scout marshmallow roast.'

Hollis's face softens. 'How're you doing, Zhi? We can get you out.'

'Me?' looking around him. 'I've been stuck in this building for three months. This place is wound up tighter than the Chairman's arsehole. There's no way out, Hollis.'

'And your family? Singapore doesn't sound safe. Can I at least bring them to London?'

Zhi's face flushes with gratitude. 'Please, Hollis. I'd appreciate that.'

'What will you do?'

'Me?' says Zhi, toying with a small carved jade pig on his desk. Through the enormous sweep of windows behind him and across the brown smear of the Huangpu River is the bizarre glass and steel skyline of Waitan. He walks to the window, looking out.

'I have already done it, Hollis. I've sold Sina to Haier, and my cash is leaving the country. Maybe in a few months, once it becomes obvious I can't single-handedly recreate Sam's printer, they'll let me go. Either way, strong-arming me won't achieve anything. It's not as if any of the other billionaires aren't already utterly terrified.'

'If you can only make it to Hong Kong—'

Zhi shakes his head. 'You know there is nowhere on Earth I can go, Hollis. The Party will find me.' He sighs and shrugs. 'I should have gone to Mars. It probably still would have been safer than this mess.'

'The transfer went fine, Zhi. Having the space elevator in place makes a huge difference. The shuttle left for Mars last month. There's six months till we bring the next acclimation group to the Emulator. Plenty of time to get you out.'

'No, not for me. My family. Mingway and Xiǎobō. Could they go?' His eyes pleading.

'Xiǎobō? He's very young, Zhi. Are you sure?'

'There are already children at the colony. Please, Hollis. Whether I make it out or not.'

There are new lines on Zhi's face.

'I'll speak to Sam. I'm sure it will be fine, Zhi. We'll make a plan.'

'Thank you, my friend,' he says in relief. 'Farewell.'

Hollis sits quietly for a few minutes. On his desk is a piece of rubble resting on a carved wooden stand. He rolls over to it, runs his hand over it, listening.

It is from the old Berlin Wall. An innocuous piece of worn concrete with a slash of red and orange paint flaking from its one flat side.

His father gave it to him on his wedding day. Adrià tall and proud in his black frock coat. Simon acting as best man for both of them. All of them laughing and the grass that perfect green of the English summer.

'Be careful what you build,' he had said as he pressed the rubble into Hollis's hands. 'And who you build it for.'

Almost a century ago. His grandfather had been a student in London. He watched the swelling crowds on television. A group of his friends travelled by train to join the protestors. The first cracks in the wall came before they embarked. Arriving into the midst of a celebration as people traversed the wall, hacking it apart. Meeting his grandmother while sitting on the wall sharing a bottle of wine. Her impishly handing him a piece of concrete as a gift. This piece where he rests his hand.

A story passed down in his family.

'Before they started building walls again,' said his father.

His earlobe vibrates. 'Tiémoko,' from his implant.

'Hollis,' he says, his voice taut and strange. 'Ag Ghaly has escaped.'

'What? When?'

'A few minutes ago. It is worse. He has taken Shakiso.'

42

Dakar is a syncopation of glossy buildings, skyscrapers and grid-locked traffic filled with taxis and luxury sedans, tumbled amongst derelict office blocks heaving with laundry hanging from broken windows and ramshackle settlements gripping the edge of its coastal cliffs.

Shakiso spends her morning ambling through the tangled streets of the suburb of Médina: past the brightly painted wooden fishing boats on the shore, through the clattering streets where market stalls and gleaming mobile services and console shops jostle for space with people carrying baskets of fruit and thickly tied bundles of dried fish.

An old man is peeling an immense pile of garlic into individual shiny white cloves. A child chops onion into a fine paste with a blunt and rusting knife. A young woman calls out at passers-by and waves an earbed in one hand and a console in the other. Every few metres someone is sifting sand baking in pans over charcoal braziers, little glimpses of the peanut pods roasting as the sand falls in a silken mist.

People shout and greet each other and share stories and coffee.

She watches a group of old men playing draughts, struggling to understand their variation of the rules. One gestures at her, inviting her to play.

She loses terribly, trapping herself into giving away half her board after only five moves in her first game.

She shares in their peanuts and laughter.

After a few games, she takes her leave. Walking slowly, Tuft at her side, eking out the time before returning to the court.

'I am glad you came,' says Viviane, blushing back shyness. Always surprised that anyone would spend time with her and grateful accordingly.

'Oh,' she says, 'you are cold?'

'It's the armour,' says Shakiso, pulling up her shirt to reveal the white gel-filled fabric beneath. 'I discovered it has this inbuilt cooling function and thought I'd give it a try. See, even Tuft has her own.'

'What is wrong, my sister?' Viviane asks, looking concerned. 'Why would you have need of such protection?'

'I need to run,' says Shakiso, her eyes vulnerable and damp. 'I'm going down to the old industrial site near the harbour, and the armour is in case I fall.'

Viviane looks both horrified and confused.

'It is a thing I do,' says Shakiso gently. 'Mostly for fun but sometimes to clear my head and make peace with myself.'

'What is it, my sister?'

'I'm struggling today,' she says almost inaudibly.

Understanding softens Viviane's concern. 'It is well,' and leads her down to the café below the court.

They sit at the same table as before, looking out into the sunlit courtyard. A gardener is at work, clipping errant leaves and wandering back and forth with a plastic watering can.

'I've been asked to go back to Europe,' says Shakiso. 'There's a new organization being set up to support the seekers there, doing the sort of thing we did with Climate here.'

'You do not feel ready to return?' asks Viviane.

'No, not yet,' she says. 'I still feel like half of something. Unfinished.

'The day Simon died,' her voice soft and her heart feeling as if it must tear apart, 'there was a terrorist attack in France.'

'I remember it, my sister,' says Viviane, reaching across the table to take Shakiso's hands in her own, offering comfort.

'The woman who did it was someone I knew. Someone I tried to help.' Her voice trembles, tears dripping on to the table surface. 'I helped her and her family escape from Benghazi. Her husband and father-in-law got sent back when we arrived in Paris. They were killed by Ansar Dine. Her brother told me she became depressed and suicidal. A local terrorist cell took her in, groomed her, used her at the Eiffel Tower.'

She looks up, her eyes searching Viviane's. 'Simon once told me that sometimes there is no right choice and you have to make the least bad one. I think I made the worst one. If I'd left her behind, she would have stayed with her husband. She would have died anyway, her children too, but she wouldn't have killed anyone else.'

'And who would that make you?' asks Viviane, her voice urgent, cutting across the silence of the room. She grips Shakiso's hands tightly. 'My sister, would you refuse to help a starving child for fear he would grow up to be a killer?'

'No,' says Shakiso, weeping openly, the grief in her heart breaking, like a fever.

'Each person has their own journey,' says Viviane, her voice gentler. 'We may help should they fall, but we cannot afterwards dictate their destination. That is the lesson of the genii, that we choose for ourselves.'

Shakiso nods, calmer now. 'Thank you.'

'There is a place you should visit,' says Viviane. 'Walk along the coast and you will find it. I go there often when I have need.'

'What is it?'

'A place to hold our memories so that they may hurt us less.'

Their coffee arrives. The young man delivering it to their table deposits it there with a level of bored indifference which goes some way to elevating its flavour of boiled grey ditch water. Shakiso and Viviane take comfort from holding their mugs, but neither of them drink.

'Why do we even come here?' asks Shakiso, her eyes smeared with drying tears.

Viviane grins. 'Because it is cheap.'

Shakiso laughs. 'How's the trial? Do you feel you're getting anywhere?'

'Yes, although it goes slowly. Many of our witnesses are old, and the defence examination is difficult for them. Ag Ghaly . . .' her bottom lip tenses. 'He sits there. He has no interest. The suffering of so many passes him by.'

'Does it matter what he thinks?' asks Shakiso.

Viviane smiles. 'No, it does not. He will face justice even so.'

'And Tiémoko?'

Viviane blushes once more.

Shakiso leans forward, staring into Viviane's eyes and smiling. 'If you love him, don't let your shyness hold you back.' She brushes at the mist in her eyes. 'We have so little time in this world.'

'I know it, my sister,' says Viviane.

A man in legal robes walks into the café looking rushed and scans the room. Relief as he finds Viviane. He gestures towards her.

'I am sorry, my sister. I have a meeting I must attend.'

'That's fine, Viviane. I'll visit you again this afternoon.'

Shakiso sits, looking out at the courtyard. Tuft leans her head on her knee to have her ears scratched, purring deep in her chest.

The air conditioning is frigid and, with the armour adding to the chill against her skin, she takes her leave. 'Come, youngster. I think we'll have that run I promised. Just for us. Afterwards, maybe we'll go find that place Viviane thinks we should visit.'

Tuft yawns, her teeth white and sharp, and follows behind as Shakiso heads up the stairs into the main hall.

The usual throngs of those waiting for their hearings and those merely along for company fill the open space with nervousness and conversation.

Shakiso turns away from the exit. One last look at the Ag Ghaly trial. There must be a belief that justice will find people like him.

The soldiers at the security barricades around the courtroom are scarcely awake and pay little heed to the steady stream of people in and out of the court. Shakiso stands outside the barriers and hesitates.

It can wait.

As she turns, there is a sound. Screams and a muted crackle of gunfire from inside the court.

The doors are flung open and men in black djellabas, turbans obscuring their faces, start shooting into the hall.

Shakiso dives to the ground and tries to roll out of the way.

Behind her she hears a voice, 'That one. Her! Take her!'

Ag Ghaly is surrounded by his men: a white king amongst his pawns.

A huge man advances on her, his rifle pointed at her face. His ears are raw and bloody, and his eyes are wide and manic. For a moment, it is if they are enveloped in a dark cloud shrouding them in place.

Tuft leaps, her teeth clamping on to his shoulder and her claws stretching to bury deep into his arm, side and back. Her prey

337

shrieks in terror, floundering as he fights against the sinew and howling fury of the caracal.

A shattering burst of gunfire and Tuft is flung into the air, sliding across the glossy floor, coming to rest motionless against the far wall.

'Tuft!' Shakiso screams.

'Leave him,' shouts Ag Ghaly, indicating the lifeless Khalil. 'Take her. Take her. Go!'

Shakiso kicks and pulls and bites until they overpower her, punching her in the head until her mind is too dulled to resist.

'Why the woman, Janab? What is she to us?'

'You fool. Do you not recognize her? She is the man's woman.'

'We shall have our vengeance then?'

'Yes. All comes to those who are patient. Look, she is awake.'

Knocking her into submission once more.

'Where are the Russians?'

'Kuffār!'

'They have betrayed us. Where are the trucks they promised?'

'Janab, look, we must take those.'

'Yes. Good, Duruji. See there are no witnesses.'

When she recovers, her head is covered within a stifling hessian bag. She is dragged and dumped into what feels like the back of a boat. As she slips into exhausted unconsciousness, she feels the gentle rocking of the water as the boat leaves the shore.

43

'Where is she?' Hollis's voice fraying with anguish.

'They have lost her,' says Tiémoko. He is shocked and frustrated.

He had been on dusty farmland outside Rosso trying to understand how one of their line printers had ended up driving through a groundnut field when he received the call. Stranded between the farmer demanding compensation and his engineers declaring that it looked as if the machine had been dragged there.

The engineer had been waving his console, pointing out the moment when the printer suddenly veered erratically and reported unusual interference.

Tiémoko had taken the console, noticing a news alert popping up.

He had opened and read, trembling as the world around him blurred and vanished.

Then his ear had vibrated. 'Viviane.'

'Mister Diagne,' she said, her voice shy and frightened.

'Viviane! You are well? Please, you are well?'

'Yes, the soldiers are here. But – they have taken Shakiso.'

Her meeting had been in the administrative wing of the court. She was far from the fighting. As soon as the jihadis had left, she was one of the first to venture out and begin trying to find out what had happened. An old man, cradling his wife's head in his lap as she wept from horror and despair, had told her of Shakiso being taken.

'Viviane, when this is over,' says Tiémoko, his voice catching. 'We—'

'Please,' she says, her tone telling him this is not the time, but he heard the smile in her voice.

He called Hollis.

'Ag Ghaly followed the old sewer canal from the court to a truck depot. His men murdered four mechanics there and stole their trucks. They have left the city.'

Tiémoko can hear the sound of Hollis's chair rolling across the room, his exasperated sigh. 'I thought they understood, Tiémoko. We told them of the risk. How did this happen?'

'Our army – they have put too many of their forces beyond our borders chasing the last of the Ansar Dine fighters. They left only the most ineffective of their troops to guard the courts.'

'There must still have been some security there?'

'It was too focused on Ag Ghaly and not on the building. The only security checks were directly outside the courtroom, and those guards barely paid attention. Ag Ghaly's supporters all arrived at the same time, his soldiers amongst them. The guards pushed everyone into the court to save effort. There were more of Ag Ghaly's men around the building. More than one hundred of them.

'Once they started shooting, it didn't matter how good the soldiers around Ag Ghaly were, there were too many inside the court, they were overwhelmed. It was a massacre. They killed everyone they could find. Women. Children . . .' Tiémoko hesitates, and Hollis can hear as he struggles to compose himself.

'I'm sorry,' says Hollis. 'I should have – how is Viviane?'

Tiémoko breathes out, a stuttering sigh. 'Safe. She was in an office far from the fighting. She is already taking witness statements.'

Hollis runs his hands through his hair, shaking his head. 'She's a remarkable woman.'

'It is her way,' says Tiémoko, smiling even through his tension. 'She says it is chaos in the city. One of the soldiers told her that there are currently no orders to chase after Ag Ghaly. Our military has no way to track those trucks.'

'At least we know where they'll be going,' says Hollis darkly. 'That special forces team? They still available?'

Tiémoko grins. 'I have their number. They will be eager to hear from you.'

Hollis is hesitant to ask. 'I know this is going to be low on your list but – did Viviane know what happened to Shakiso's caracal? Tuft?'

'I am sorry, Hollis. Not yet. The troops are still going room to room checking for any explosive traps left behind. They did find a dead jihadi. He had been torn apart by an animal, so we know she was there.'

Hollis sighs. 'What a mess.'

'Why do you think they took her, Hollis?'

'You know that. Pray we find her in time.'

44

Their convoy of trucks lurches over stones like rubble, seeking a road where there is none, and the wind howls against the canvas tarpaulin, crackling and snapping in outrage. The vehicles are obscured in the driving dust of the harmattan, invisible even to each other.

'This place, it is nowhere, Janab. What is there for us?'

'That is where the planes crashed. We can re-arm. More than that. Once we are there you must search for this, see here on the console.' The voice is that of Ag Ghaly.

'I do not understand, Janab. What is this?'

The second voice is that of Duruji. Shakiso is learning to recognize them. She can hear the scuffling in the back of the truck as the console is passed from man to man. She is immobile, her hands and feet securely bound with lengths of canvas cut from the webbing holding the equipment in place. Her breathing is careful and quiet to minimize the dust seeping through the rough sack over her head and to avoid attracting further attention.

Each time she moves, they beat her until she stops.

'It is strange. These glass rings? What are they for?'

'Look,' says Ag Ghaly, 'the vial is fixed at the centre of the loops. No matter how the glass case is moved, the vial always faces upright. And the shock absorbers on the pins fixing the loops to each other prevent the vial from being jolted.'

'This red liquid. What is this?' asks Duruji once more. There is a gap where Khalil should be. He ignores it.

'Fear and power,' says Ag Ghaly. 'Find me this glass case and the kuffār will fall at our feet.'

The truck lurches as it strikes a large boulder. It swings to the left, hits another boulder and the engine whines and stalls.

A panting, exhausted silence inside the truck as the wind scrambles and tears at the canvas.

'We can go no further, Janab.'

'Good, we walk from here. Cover the trucks and bring all that we need.'

Shakiso is dragged along the floor bed by the webbing tied around her ankles. She rolls on to her chest to ease the cramp and agony in her arms locked behind her back.

One of the men pulls her on to his shoulder, dumping her down on the ground nearby. Outside, the wind is a continuous smothering weight and the dust an overwhelming presence.

Shakiso breathes slowly and as deeply as she dares, trying to calm her fragmented feelings of terror and outrage. She feels bruised and uncomfortable but has, so far, not suffered any crippling injury.

Around her are the sounds of the men scrambling to prepare to leave the trucks behind. They work quickly, covering the vehicles in large camouflaged tarpaulins and hammering stakes into the reg to hold the sheets down. Any satellite observers will have difficulty finding them.

Shakiso's ankles are yanked upwards and the straps abruptly cut. She is jerked to her feet by her shoulder.

'You will walk,' says a hissed voice in her ear. 'And if you do not, you will be dragged.'

She feels a rope being tied around her waist. It links her to the man in front and behind.

Each of the men is linked in this way, for the harmattan is blinding. A person stepping out of the line can be lost to the desert even though they be only metres away.

They begin to walk, Duruji and Ag Ghaly in front, the coordinates blinking on their map.

Shakiso takes two tentative steps and clips a boulder, stumbling and losing her balance. She curls inwards, protecting her head and letting the armour on her back absorb her fall. The rope jerks taut against the two men to her front and rear.

They shout in outrage.

One of them calls to the front. 'Duruji, can we not take the bag from her head? She cannot see, and it will slow us down.'

Duruji makes his way along the line. Shakiso carefully clambers to her feet, trying to orientate herself facing forwards.

The bag is yanked clear. She blinks and is instantly blinded by the searing blast of the harmattan in her eyes. She coughs and tries to bury her mouth and nose in her shirt.

Duruji shakes his head. 'We need a turban for her,' he says.

'There is no extra, Duruji, but I can cut some from mine,' says the man tied in front of Shakiso.

'Quickly. We cannot wait.'

The two men charged with flanking Shakiso cut a length from the turban and crudely wrap it around her head.

'Thank you,' she says.

The two men push her. 'Go, go.'

Duruji knots himself in at the front once more, and the column begins walking.

Looking up the line, Shakiso can see that each man carries an AK-47 and a bag filled with what she assumes to be rations and equipment. Duruji and another man also carry large Igla anti-drone guns along with spare backpacks necessary to power them.

After a few hours, the stones and boulders of the reg give way to the soft drift of the erg. Sand sucks at their boots, slowing their pace.

They walk in silence. The yawling, howling madness of the harmattan prevents conversation, and shouting takes too much energy. Each man carries his own water.

No one thinks to share with Shakiso.

Her face hidden within the turban and shrouded in the churning dust, she pops out a thin tube from the collar of her armour with her chin. The bladder holds two litres, and she sips sparingly.

The cramps and bruising from the earlier beatings have eased, and she would, under other circumstances, enjoy the challenge of pitting herself against the desert and the wind.

Instead she carries a flint-like rage.

They did not search her. She holds on tightly to that.

A shout goes down the line, and the men come to a ragged, stalling stop on the lee side of a steep dune. Hard rations are distributed, and each man chews unhappily at the familiar tough, chalky protein bars.

'Give this to her,' says Duruji. 'She must not fall behind.'

Shakiso is sitting with her knees drawn up to her chin, her hands behind her back, roped in place between her minders.

One tosses a silver-wrapped bar into her lap. He watches morosely as she levers the bar up and between her knees, tears the sachet open with her teeth and takes a bite.

'Thanks,' she says cheerfully, refusing them any sense of weakness, chomping on the unpleasant texture.

She recognizes the dull flavour. When she was a student, she would compete in endurance races on weekends. Starting on a Friday afternoon and running, climbing, swimming, cycling and canoeing until Sunday evening along slippery mountain trails, rivers and the open road. These were the bars that were supplied to the competitors along the route. Nutrient-rich and packed with ampakines, designed to keep you awake and alert.

Duruji clearly intends that no one will be resting until they reach their destination.

The searing heat of the day cools into a reddened, golden dusk. The sun is a murky burning orb through the brown foam of the harmattan.

They stop only once before sundown to share out more of the nutrient bars.

They walk through the night.

Dawn sneaks like a yellow blaze through the dust and, with it, the temperature rises.

Shakiso is beginning to feel fatigued. Sand has finally eased its way into her boots, and she can feel chafing against her skin. She grins as she considers that at least she has not spent the last twenty hours carrying a backpack strung with weapons and ammunition through a sandstorm.

Hours pass and the day begins to fade.

She looks around. Along the line, the men move as if sleep-walking, their heads lolling and eyes partly closed. Visibility is limited, obscured by dust and noise, but she is sure she can see a strange, angular black shadow in the air ahead of them.

A jubilant shout and heads jerk up and out of reveries.

It is the broken outer edge of an aircraft wing.

They slow, walking along the wing, and take up the trail of broken metal polished, pitted and scoured by the harmattan.

These are brutal men, and even they are stilled by the immensity of the carnage. Spread out over two kilometres, the dead hulks of the cargo planes lie broken, blackened and twisted.

They stop behind the shelter of a tailpiece forming a wedged arch against the wind. Sand has piled up on the windward side, and a sheet of sand flies over the top like a wave.

'We must search them. Some of our cargo must have survived,' says Ag Ghaly. 'Split the men up into teams. We will make camp here and wait.'

'And her?' asks Duruji.

'What of her? She waits with me.'

Shakiso is cut loose from her minders and flung into the corner of the arch. The men drop the bulk of their gear, taking only their rifles.

Duruji organizes them into five teams and points them in different directions. He sets a transponder at the wide end of the arch and tests that each group can read it. They must be able to find their way back in the dust.

Ag Ghaly stands alone, watching his men, his hands behind his back.

'They will return in three hours, Janab,' says Duruji. 'We will wait with you,' indicating the ten men standing in a semicircle outside the arch.

'Good. I will rest. Make sure the woman does not escape. My intention is not for the kindness the desert will show her.'

Duruji grins, his teeth orange and irregular. 'She will not escape, Janab.'

Shakiso curls her legs beneath her, watching until Ag Ghaly falls asleep and the men gather too far away to watch her closely.

She eases her fingers into the inside of her boot and feels the comforting handle of her knife. Carefully, she pulls it from its clasp and passes it up between her hands. She turns it until the blade is against the canvas of the straps around her wrists.

Slowly, she cuts.

She freezes each time one of the men looks back towards her, her heart pounding against her ribs, and continues again.

Every few minutes, she tests the bonds. Eventually, satisfied that a quick jerk will free her hands, she shuffles the knife back into her boot.

She stretches as best she can, finds a comfortable position, and allows herself to sleep. She will need to be rested for whatever comes next.

45

'He was speaking truth,' says the jihadi plaintively. 'You saw it. You felt it.'

'There was nothing!' says Duruji, his voice burning.

The men are gathered downwind of the tailpiece, braced against the force of the wind. Duruji is watching Ag Ghaly as he sleeps and can see the woman squeezed as far as she can get into the corner of the tail. She is strangely rigid, staring at him. He does not trust her and would sooner have left her behind.

Dust bunches and drives: great fists smashing into the turbulent wall of the harmattan all around them.

Khalil's death has disturbed the fragile sanity of the men. They feel as if a presence has been unleashed ever since the tawny cat buried its claws and teeth into one of their own. Something once only in Khalil's fractured imagination now pressing in on theirs. Distorted shapes in the murk disorienting their already exhausted minds.

'The genii are playing with us, Duruji,' says another, his head jerking back and forth as he stares into the darkness. 'Khalil heard the coming of that cat. What have we not seen?'

Duruji does not know how to answer. He feels Khalil's loss and is surprised by it. There have been many others, men he has known longer, men he first trained with, who have died violently. Mohamoud was the last of those men, the only one left after the chaos of their attack on that airport in Benghazi two years ago. Such is their life. Yet he does not feel as overwhelmed by fear as these men. He has all the reassurance he needs. His Janab is close, and he has resumed his role protecting the man who represents everything he knows.

There was something he needed to remember, though. Something that keeps slipping from his mind, something about the woman – 'No!' his voice harsh and abrupt, pushing aside the rifle of the man next to him. 'He is with us.'

The figure emerging from the dust waves, three shadows roped in behind him.

'Wait here,' says Duruji to the remaining men. 'And be very careful when you see someone. I do not want to be shot when I return.'

Without looking back, he walks out to meet the arrivals. He feels relieved to have something to do, to be out from within the creeping fears of those behind him.

'What is it?' he asks. 'Did you find anything?'

The man looks uncomfortable. 'Yes, boss, but it is not what we are looking for.'

'So, keep looking. Why waste my time with this?'

The man looks at his feet.

Duruji has a crushing sense that his fears are being confirmed. The planes never had any cargo.

'Show me,' he says.

He ties himself to the end of their rope, and they walk back the way they came, following towards a transponder point the men left behind, the rest of their team grouped around it.

The harmattan is beginning to ease, and soon he can see the gleaming structure of an intact aircraft.

'This way, boss. The cargo doors are open,' leading him around the tail and up a slope where sand has half-filled the entrance.

Each man must bend and contort slightly to squeeze inside. The unending pressure of the wind is abruptly cut.

They remain roped together as each turns on a flashlight.

'See, boss, everything has been burned,' showing him piles of blackened ash that must have been the heroin.

Duruji crumbles some in his hands, feeling it vanish into dust.

'And here,' the words spoken in considerable discomfort.

A twisted assortment of metal, gun barrels, ammunition cases and buckled racks lie in a heap further along the hold. Duruji picks up a broken AK-47, turning it in his hands, trying to see whether there is any hope for repair. The buttstock is charred and split, hanging loosely.

'I said we should never have trusted them,' he says quietly.

'Boss?'

'The arms dealer,' he says. 'He sent this garbage. He stole from us.'

'Maybe, boss, but someone else was here before us,' leading Duruji back outside.

46

'Janab, they found something,' says Duruji.

It is late, the night sky lit up by a profusion of stars visible now that the winds have begun to abate.

Ag Ghaly rises awkwardly, leaning on the wall of the wing as he pulls himself to his feet. 'What is it? The case?'

'No, Janab,' says Duruji, apprehension and doubt. 'You must see. I am not sure this is good.'

'Where is it?'

'Not far. Perhaps thirty minutes.'

Ag Ghaly nods, wrapping his turban around his head. He gestures at Shakiso. 'Bring her.'

Shakiso stands quickly, keeping her hands locked tightly together.

Duruji confers with the leader of this group of men and takes the lead.

The dark hulk of an aeroplane looms ahead. This one appears to have landed more or less in one piece.

They walk along the wide flank of its main wing which rises high above them towards where it joins to the fuselage.

'What is this?' demands Ag Ghaly, his voice curt and abrupt.

They are in the lee of the main wing, on a flat stretch of sand. Six piles of black and red rocks are arranged in a row. Human-scale oblongs of heaped stone.

Silence from the men.

'Answer me,' shouts Ag Ghaly.

'These are the pilots, Janab,' says Duruji. 'Someone has buried them.'

'Who? Where is my cargo?'

'We do not know, boss,' says one of the men. 'We can find no cargo. Someone burned everything inside this aircraft. The weapons are all broken.'

The man cowers as Ag Ghaly advances on him.

'Where's my mercury?' shouting and slapping at the man.

'Janab, what mercury?' asks Duruji, trying to intervene.

'The red mercury? Our salvation,' he screams, his voice a howl of rage and anguish, beating the cowering jihadi with his hands and feet.

'Red mercury? You've been had,' says Shakiso quietly. She winds herself tightly, compressing herself. Preparing.

'It must be here,' shouts Ag Ghaly. 'Look! Look!'

Shakiso explodes, tearing the last strands of the canvas from her wrists and flinging herself towards the perpendicular wall of the aircraft rising like a cliff-face before her.

'Stop her!' shouts Duruji.

'Too slow,' she thinks, the sand sucking at her boots as she sprints.

She leaps at the wall. Right foot, left foot, right hand down, left hand just grabbing the top edge of the wing.

For a moment, she feels as if she will fall. A shattering burst of bullets, two of which strike her in the back.

The armour foaming, absorbing the blow, and the momentum adding sufficient to her own, carrying her up and on to the wing.

She rolls along the wide flat surface, trying to breathe. With a cough, she exhales and gasps, pushing herself upright and sprinting to build up speed.

The surface is slippery with dust, but she finds purchase on notches in the fuselage, running up the wall and on to the long broad roof of the plane. She stands to catch her breath and orientate herself.

Below her she can hear shouting and continued gunfire.

She runs towards the cockpit at the front of the plane.

Her ear vibrates, and her implant whispers, 'Hollis.'

47

Uberti would move the chair, but it is bolted into this exact position. It is comfortable enough, sitting here in the twilight, the bottle of vodka in his lap.

It is almost finished. He would go and get another. There is no time.

They are late.

He is grateful.

In all his years as head of Rosneft, he has not simply sat and enjoyed the pleasure of the estate at Novo-Ogaryovo. This is the first time he has ever watched the sun set through the thickly wooded forest and glow gold where it strikes the river. Autumn is falling to winter, and he can smell the change in the leaves, the crispness of the air. Birds sing and scramble through the branches.

He is not a sentimental man, has never given much thought to anything other than the beast he needs to feed to keep Rosneft safe. That responsibility has been lifted.

Uberti's crime is worse than treason. European energy prices are falling. The hierarchy of influence and power that binds the Russian state and its vassals depends on Rosneft's continuing market control. The new orbital power generator has disrupted that authority, revealing the weakness that lies behind all tyrannies.

There is only one punishment in the Russian state due anyone who so betrays a position of influence and trust. Uberti's will come today.

He waits for a call that only three other leaders of Rosneft have taken.

It is one that all are told to expect when they are appointed. Most have served their term efficiently, if not memorably, and passed on their position grateful to go into peaceful retirement.

Three have suffered to displease their higher authority.

It is an exquisite torture. A symphony of bureaucracy and cruelty.

An old metal telephone is mounted on a table on the wooden porch at the rear of the dacha. It, and the table, is bolted in place. Alongside it is a large wooden easy-chair, also fixed in place. They are weathered and beaten.

The wall behind them is plated in a thick metal sheet.

There are two small dents in it, close together. There should be three.

The second man chose to flee rather than take the call. After what happened to him and his family, the third man did not hesitate. He sat as Uberti does now.

Out in the forest is a hunters' hide. Since no one may hunt in these protected woods, it is there for a single purpose.

Uberti has walked there on many occasions. He has noted that the view it affords of the porch on the dacha is ideal. The position of the seat places the occupant's head in a precisely convenient place. He does not know who does so, but the sight through is always cleared of branches which may obstruct the sniper.

There is a telephone mounted on the inside of the hide. A cousin to the one at his side.

He is certain that someone inside that hide is, similarly, waiting for a call.

Only a few more sips and the bottle will be finished.

The phone rings.

'Thank you,' he says, picking it up gently.

'What?' says a familiar voice.

'Thank you for the sunset. I was not expecting that,' he says, and his emotion is genuine.

The voice is brusque, unsentimental. 'Other matters kept us. That was not for your benefit.'

'I know,' he says. 'But, even so. Thank you. I am grateful, and I am sorry it has worked out as it has.'

'Yes,' the voice is brittle. 'Goodbye, Farinata.'

The connection ends.

Uberti smiles, savouring the lingering red and orange through the trees.

The bottle is empty, a cry of birds in the woods, and it drops from his fingers.

48

'What took you so long?' asks Shakiso.

'I didn't want to disturb you,' says Hollis.

'Seriously?'

'Seriously. We weren't sure if you were conscious or whether Ag Ghaly's men would notice your implant.'

'Something seems to have frightened them. They spend all their time whispering or shouting at each other.' Shakiso has almost reached the flight deck. 'They barely notice me, probably forgot about it. Maybe it's Ag Ghaly? He seems to make everyone around him behave like morons.'

The windows have been smashed, and she slips inside. The floor is ankle-deep in sand rising in a slope to the ceiling and blocking the door. The two pilot's chairs are serviceable. There is little room for anything else, and she drops into one.

Empty chocolate biscuit packets protrude from around the chair. Shakiso digs a little on either side of her seat and finds two still sealed in their glossy wrappers, which she tears open.

'You better be coming to get me,' she says, devouring a biscuit.

'Look up.'

Above her a drone appears, shimmering briefly as it decloaks its invisibility field. Its surface is pure black. A peculiar lightless hole in the sky, hovering over the flight deck.

Shakiso brushes back a muddy tear. 'Thanks, Hollis. I knew you'd be there.'

'We figured they'd come for the planes. I thought you'd probably be able to escape them. I'll stay on the line and let you know if any of them are getting near.'

'Where are they now?'

'Ag Ghaly seems to be beating one of his men to death and shouting like a maniac, and the rest are trying to find a way into the plane. You won't be able to stay there for long.'

'And who's coming to get me?'

'The Senegalese army.'

'Should I be pleased about that?'

'Same chaps who were there for Simon.'

Shakiso nods, trembling as her tightly controlled focus wavers. 'They killed Tuft, Hollis.'

'No, they didn't. We found her.'

Alone in a burned-out flight deck on a wrecked plane in the middle of a small war, Shakiso weeps in relief. It is a small thing, and it is everything.

'Thank you.'

'You're going to have to move. There's a chap on the roof heading straight for you.'

Shakiso grabs the edge of the window and pulls herself out. Looking back along the plane, she can see a faint shape leaning into the wind and trying not to slide.

'How far is the drop?' she whispers.

'You should be OK,' says Hollis.

Duruji appears above her as she leaps.

He shouts in frustration, and spots the drone.

In a single movement, he bends, swings the Igla around his back, and fires. The drone plunges.

Shakiso curls, absorbing the landing along her side, and rolls down the slope of the sand piling up beneath the plane. The drone clouts into the sand behind her and slides until it stops alongside.

'Great. You still know where they are?' she says, pushing it off her.

'Most of them are under our control. It's only the men around Ag Ghaly.'

'And me.'

'Yes.'

Shakiso creeps around the nose of the plane, heading back towards where she left Ag Ghaly. The wind and dust mask her movements. It also hides any of the men looking for her.

She pulls her knife from her boot as she nears the forward edge of the wing.

Ag Ghaly is alone except for a battered form at his feet. He is kicking it, his shouting tremulous and wild.

Duruji drops off the far edge of the wing, his back towards Shakiso. He remains motionless, scanning the howling dust-fogged landscape.

Shakiso is behind him. Her knife is in her hand. The noise of the wind, the stinging rush of sand, would mask her approach.

She tenses.

In the sky and in the earth, a presence, curiosity and anticipation. Something which seems to watch and draw breath even as they draw breath.

Two lives have travelled far and suffered greatly to intersect at this exact moment.

She hesitates.

Crouches low instead.

She is not, after all, the sort of person who can easily choose to take the life of another.

And the presence dissipates.

Duruji sees something in the starlit mist, rushes towards Ag Ghaly.

'We are lost, Janab. The kuffār have found us!' His words torn away by the wind. His rifle in his hands. Running with all his strength towards the advancing shadows. Defending with his last breath the man who is his king.

Ag Ghaly, insane with grief, sees only the rifle and a threatening figure racing towards him. He raises his pistol and fires twice.

Duruji's eyes widen. He gasps. Falls.

'My Janab,' he sighs.

Ag Ghaly looks, recognizes, turns, and sees soldiers emerging from the dust.

He puts the barrel of his gun into his mouth.

As he fires, he is thrown to the ground, the bullet lost to the sky, his gun hurled from him.

'No.'

The last thing he sees, before a hood passes over his head, are glowing blue eyes weighing him in judgement.

49

'Aha, my president, you are here for coffee?'

'Yes, my father,' says Sidiki, ducking under the plastic sheet across the archway into the sculpture garden.

Today, the pillar beasts are in repose. Their features seem warm and comforting. A baboon-like creature even reaches across to another which has hair burning like flame, in what looks to be the beginning of an embrace.

'Are you a big man yet?' asks Gaw Goŋ.

Sidiki laughs easily. 'No, my father,' and his voice is unburdened and without shadows.

'Good, my child. That is good,' says the old man, nodding and clucking.

He clears away a pile of sketches and drawings from a wooden stool, its legs each of different provenance, and gestures for Sidiki to sit.

He disappears behind a rug covering the entrance to his home, and there is the sound of rattling and of heavy objects being moved from side to side.

Sidiki sits and watches the ocean, breathing deeply and smiling as – in this place – he feels all the tension of the last few months flow out and away. He is feeling more comfortable in the role of president. He picks up one of the sketches, of a baboon walking in the desert, his sombé in his hands and a painted dog at his side.

Sidiki smiles and grips the beach sand between his toes.

'Aha,' says Gaw Goŋ, returning. 'See how my president blesses even an old man such as I,' waving a new electric hotplate in one hand.

'I heard they have electrified your neighbourhood,' says Sidiki. 'You keep the fire?' gesturing to where the flames still burn.

'A flame is more than heat,' says the old man. 'It is memory, and place. A connector of worlds.'

He plugs in the small stove and places his battered kettle on top. Sitting back on a blanket, he prods at the fire with his two-headed metal stave.

'You are meeting someone?'

'Yes, my father.'

'Aha, aha. A friend?'

'I am not sure, my father. He has not been a friend in the past. But –' he scratches gently at his head '– this feels as if it is a time of change.'

'You feel that too, my child? That is well.'

Brown froth bubbles from the mouth of the kettle, dripping and hissing down on to the hotplate.

'Aha,' crows the old man. 'It is ready,' and pouring two cups into misshapen mugs.

They sit in silence, savouring the flavour and enjoying the soft motion of the water on to the shore. The horizon is clear, the sky unblemished, the genii at rest.

A car pulls up at the roadside. Sidiki's security are spread out along the beach. They respond, conferring and acknowledging the arrival.

The door swings up and open. A soft-bodied toubab steps out, his body awkward and bent, although he is not yet an old man. He motions at someone waiting inside and walks out on to the beach.

'Your guest has arrived,' says Gaw Goŋ.

'Yes,' says Sidiki. 'Stay well, my father. I shall be back in a few minutes.'

He takes his mug, still mostly full with steaming black coffee, and joins the other man at the water.

The white man stares silently at the horizon. He seems lost in reverie.

'You are Rinier Pazanov?' asks Sidiki.

Pazanov nods and holds out his hand. Sidiki passes his mug to his left hand and shakes.

'I visited Agado in London last week,' says Pazanov, staring sullenly at the coffee mug. 'I sat with him in that café of his. Insulting pictures on the walls. He would not serve me even water.'

'There is a list,' says Sidiki, delicately.

'Yes,' says Pazanov. His voice is tired. 'My wife reminds me of it often.'

'You have met with Agado, and now you meet with me. What is it you seek?'

'I am the new head of Rosneft.'

'Yes. I heard of your predecessor's unfortunate passing. Is this a role you have sought?'

Pazanov kicks at the sand, scattering grains into the thin foam on the ebbing surf.

'Once,' he says. 'But it does not feel like a choice I made of my own will. My company is not known for offering much liberty. Or,' he says bitterly, 'compassion for misfortune.'

Russian official media reported Uberti's death as a heart attack brought on by the stress of the company's losses. Unofficial sources say it was suicide.

'My security advisers tell me that a charter flight full of Russian mercenaries left shortly before Ag Ghaly's escape. Apparently you chose not to support him?' asks Sidiki, feeling the other's weight of sadness. 'What do you wish of me?'

'There was nothing to be won from destroying your country. No advantage. It would be an act of petty vengeance.' He coughs, flings the remnants of his cigarette into the water and spits after it.

'We are being granted a reprieve,' Pazanov continues. 'In exchange for certain guarantees, Rosneft must loosen the terms of its contracts and interfere less in the affairs of others. The Russian state must become less dependent on our revenues. There is much that would change, but the role of its senior executive – my role – is still as it always was.'

'And you do not wish for that role to remain unchanged?'

'No,' spoken firmly but with resignation.

'Gaw Goŋ would say that the story chooses its villains and heroes. They have no agency of their own. They cannot strive for a role of their choosing. There are no big men in history. Merely pawns of the narrative which society chooses.'

'They are not in charge then?' asks Pazanov.

'No. They are the least of the characters who may choose. Their role is precisely defined by the circumstances of the story.'

Pazanov nods, looking sad. 'I am tired of being the villain.'

'What will you do?' asks Sidiki.

'There are debts to pay. I do not imagine it will be easy, but I seek redemption.'

Sidiki stares at him, searching him. He laughs softly. 'Then you are already not *the* villain, merely *a* villain. Your future is your own.'

Pazanov smiles. 'As easy as that?'

Sidiki shakes his head. 'No. Opening the door is easy. The path of redemption is not.'

'And for you? Your predecessors were villains too. Have you escaped that role?'

Sidiki looks back along the beach to the sculpture garden. 'I seek guidance daily. I walk here on this beach and ask counsel. That I not be led astray on to the path of the big men who came before me.

'It is difficult.'

Rinier considers. 'It would help me if we could meet every now and then, to walk on this beach, to talk with you. Perhaps we can each keep the other on the way? I have no one else.'

Sidiki thinks and nods. 'That would be well. I would be neither the hero nor the villain, and that would be my salvation.'

'And I may find my redemption.'

They walk in silence along the beach, and the water ebbs and flows.

50

'We'll bring it to you,' says the barista, taking her order.

Shakiso finds a table in the corner where she can look out and watch people passing by in the street, finding reassurance in the everyday interactions of others.

Her eyes are the depths of the erg, and she stares as if seeing everything for the first time. The animated interactions of two smartly dressed women laughing over their croissants. A group of tourists pointing at the pictures on the walls. The hiss and roar of milk being frothed and coffee beans being ground. Traffic flickering and flashing beyond the glass facade.

A young man in a tight white T-shirt collecting his coffee notices her and visibly straightens his shoulders as he walks as if to introduce himself. She watches him curiously, her eyes the story of her journey, his stride faltering, and he chooses to sit on his own.

The inner door to the Achenia lobby opens, and Hollis is smiling in relief as he reaches her table. His chair rises, and he holds her tightly.

There follow the tentative words as spoken between two who have suffered much and must now gently find their way.

'Oh,' says Shakiso, after a time. 'Ismael wanted me to give you this. "A souvenir from the desert," he said.'

She places a glass cube on the table between them. Inside are

367

three concentric glass rings forming a gimbal. A glass vial filled with red liquid is fixed in its centre.

Hollis adjusts the levers on the outside of the case, locking the rings in place. The lid of the case opens and he reaches inside, releasing the vial. He holds it, tilting it back and forth.

The red liquid flows, viscous and sticky against the glass.

'Funny how Ag Ghaly never thought to question an old trope like red mercury,' he says. 'It takes a special sort of craziness to imagine you can control the world with a little vial of liquid.'

'What is it really?' asks Shakiso.

'Some red dye and metal foam gel from an old set of Simon's armour. See,' shaking it suddenly and explosively. The liquid instantly forms a solid foam, returning to liquid form as his hand comes to rest.

'And a little surprise,' smiling. 'One of those experimental fractal circuits. This one is a location transmitter.

'We were never sure what Ag Ghaly thought it would do, but we heard a rumour he was prepared to pay any money to get some. Simon positioned himself as a scientist from the Martian space programme and met with his regular arms dealer. We made it look as impressive as possible and offered a third of the price we were charging as commission if he could get it to Ag Ghaly directly. We thought we were being extremely clever, but the Caracas Cartel and the arms dealer had their own plans. I don't think the red mercury thing fooled them at all. It was simply a very attractive lure for their own scam. They filled the planes with cheap garbage and lied about the landing dates. Ag Ghaly never received our package.'

'Simon was never meant to risk his life like that?'

'No. This was always supposed to go straight to Ag Ghaly. The transmitter would have given us his exact location, and we had an arrangement with the Senegalese Special Forces to pass on the coordinates,' says Hollis. 'We could have arranged for Ag Ghaly to find the landing site, but the transmitter stopped working.'

'Couldn't you replace it and then pass on the location?'

'We're a small private company,' says Hollis. 'We needed the Senegalese army to track the package and capture Ag Ghaly. After the crash, they worried that the arms might end up in some other faction's hands and we'd never catch him. They would only help if we could guarantee Ag Ghaly. At the time, we didn't know everything on the planes was junk anyway.

'Simon tried to salvage the situation and went out to meet him. Maybe if you had been together before, he never would have, but then you might never have met.'

'I asked him, towards the end, but he said you'd explain everything when it was all over. Is it over now?' She smiles, but her eyes are clouded with sadness.

'Everything? Yes, or as close as it can be,' says Hollis, replacing the vial within its case. 'Zhi is still at risk, but he should be with us in the next few days. We're hoping that the Chinese government's new agreement with Rosneft means they've lost interest in him.'

'And the rest? Can you tell me?'

He nods.

'I told you about Trevor, my first love,' his voice tender. 'He was Tiémoko's older brother. Zhi was Tiémoko's best friend. We came together around my hospital bed. Achenia, the company, has always been all of us.'

'But they're not official?'

'No. When we started, the naturalization policy was still in place. It's only recently that it stopped being illegal for foreigners to own English assets. We always kept our agreement, and it's always been *our* company.

'When Sam developed the solar energy systems for Mars, we

saw an opportunity here on Earth for both the orbiter and the desert farms. The solar orbiter depended on getting a space elevator in place, and we knew that would take a few years. Tiémoko thought the cheaper solar collectors would be perfect for East Africa, and he and Simon decided to start immediately. Tiémoko wanted to link his identity systems to payment, and Simon went to Tanzania to set up a pilot.'

'And then Rosneft—'

'Yes,' he reveals a moment of pain. 'That they would destroy an entire country, support terrorists, all to preserve their monopoly – we realized that we had been naïve. Originally, it was simply a business investment. After Tanzania, we all felt it personally. It was men like Uberti who decided that young boys should be conscripted for war. Men like that who killed Trevor and broke my back,' his voice calm despite the anguish in his words. 'That was when we began to disguise our activities.

'We had to keep the solar orbiter secret in case they decided to attack the space elevator. We hid the components amongst the general traffic for the next flight of Martian settlers going up the elevator. And, to make sure they didn't look too closely at the base station in Bologna, we pretended that the solar-farm output was destined for Europe. That was when we came up with the red mercury scam. We would even have built a line across the desert. Everything we did was to keep Rosneft occupied by letting them chase us around.

'Of course,' he laughs softly, 'then we also had to worry about Chinese interest in the technology as well. Zhi whispered a few words to receptive ears about Tiémoko supposedly resenting Simon, and their ambassador in Senegal approached him for access to our systems.

'Senegal was well chosen. There is only one active ambassador there, even though everyone "knows" there are supposed to be many of them. Tiémoko handed him a card with the private access codes to our main printer. It also had a passive location sensor so we always knew where he was.'

'Why did you need that?'

'We heard that Russian mercenaries were recruiting ex-Ansar Dine fighters. We figured that Rosneft would try to release Ag Ghaly and start a war. What we didn't know was when.

'There is a Chinese family in Aroundu who run one of the larger printing works—'

'Mrs Chen?'

Hollis nods. 'Yes. Her son happens to be a lawyer, and he and Tiémoko have become friends. Tiémoko asked him to help us. Over the past few months, whenever we absolutely knew where the Chinese ambassador was, this young man would dress up in a grey suit and visit Ag Ghaly. He likes to talk, and we learned the plan. In exchange, we gave him the coordinates to the planes.'

'Why didn't you tell the Senegalese?'

'We tried,' he says. 'Once the solar orbiter went live and Rosneft caved in to the Chinese, we assumed their plans would be suspended. We had taken Senegal out of the supply chain to Europe. The generals told us we were being overly paranoid.

'I'm sorry, Shak. I let you down.'

She shakes her head, taking his hands. 'You came for me.'

He nods. 'What will you do now?'

'There's that job in Berlin I told you about. I'll be starting there in a few weeks.'

'You've decided then?'

'Yes. There's a story Ismael told me which I've been thinking about. It's about two sisters. I can tell it, although I don't think I'm as good as he is?'

Hollis smiles and nods his head. 'Please.'

371

'Once, there were two sisters,' she begins, her voice bright and her eyes damp.

'Their village of Tessèm was a small place, too close to the desert and too far from the city. Only through care and hard work was it possible for so many to thrive on such barren land.

'Each day, the two sisters would rise before dawn to milk their goats, and then help their family in the fields. After their work was finished, the sisters would go and play by the river beneath the shade of an old spreading tree.

'In the tree and in the water lived the genii of that place. He loved to listen to the two children playing and would often join them in their games. He would take the form of a painted dog and run with them, or of a baboon, and tell them stories.

'Their parents would ask them where they heard these stories, and they told them of the genii, but no one would believe them, for genii are beings of myth.

'One day, the younger sister died.'

Shakiso hesitates, her hands flat on the table. 'I asked Ismael how she died. People don't just die. Something must have happened.

'He told me, "It is a story. It is not the manner of her going that matters, but the measure of her presence and the impact of her absence. She could have died performing a great sacrifice or by accident. Those who love her may wish she'd died differently, but for those who are party to her story and survive her passing, it is her soul and its loss that has the greater toll."'

She closes her eyes and breathes deeply. Hollis places his hands on hers and lends his strength to hers.

'After her death, there was a terrible famine. The people of Tessèm suffered greatly, but other villages had it worse. Thousands sought refuge along the banks of the river near the village. The different tribes squabbled, and minor differences threatened to lead to awful violence.

'The surviving sister said to her parents, "We must ask the genii to help us."

"'This is not the time for myths," they told her, but no one knew what else to do.

'The young girl was malnourished and very weak, but she gathered her strength and made her way down to the place of the genii. She wept as she told the tree and water of her suffering, and of her fear for all the different people who fight instead of working together.

'The genii appeared before her in the form of her younger sister and took her hand, leading her back to Tessèm.

'When her parents saw her walking with her sister, they fell to their knees, fearful of the ghost.

"'This is not a ghost, my parents," she said. "This is the genii of myth who has become real so that she may help us."

'Word spread, and all the different peoples came together to hear the genii speak.

"'I am not here to show you the way," she said. "This brave daughter of Tessèm will guide you, and I will walk with her."

'And so the young girl led them through the secret ways of the desert, guiding them from waterhole to waterhole.

'Each evening, the genii would tell stories such as they had never heard. Over time they forgot their old stories, forgetting that there ever was a time they were not one people.

'Eventually, they reached a place where there was plentiful water and the soil was fertile and they built a new village. A place where all would live and work in peace.

'On a certain day, when the village was thriving, then the girl and the genii walked out into the desert and were never seen again.

'The people of that village mourned their passing and told their children stories of their deliverance and passed their tales into legend.'

Shakiso smiles at Hollis, his eyes wide.

'I heard all these stories without hearing them,' she says. 'I think I understand now. Every story starts with myth to explain reality and create a common legend. The seekers are us too. That's what we've all been doing, creating a new founding story that might eventually unite us.

'Children will hear the stories of our time from their parents and grandparents. Each generation will tell the next to remember, but the stories will change. The specifics lost, the actual people forgotten. We will become enigmas. Story-shaped holes filled with all the hopes and dreams of those who come after.

'I was fighting that, wanting – I don't know – something that doesn't seem clear any more. I've let all of that go,' her eyes the blue clarity of the desert sky. 'There's a place Viviane told me about, a place I can leave my memories so they won't hurt so much. I'm going there first.'

'Does that mean you're leaving us?' asks Hollis, sadness in his eyes.

'No,' she says smiling. 'Never, but I will live my life. When I'm ready, I'll join you guys on Mars. Ismael said it would be a new beginning, and I look forward to that. For now, I'm going to work on answering the question of what we do while we wait for all our myths to pass into legend.'

51

Glass fragments, like the shattering wave of an explosion frozen in time, lean out from the cliffs near Dakar city centre.

Within each fragment is etched a single name: one who has died and whom others would honour. Far too many have been added during the long war with Ansar Dine. Family, friends and survivors come to this place carrying the names of those who are gone and add them to the Place du Souvenir.

The glass is no longer transparent. Eroded and encrusted with the salt from the ocean lying still and placid, gently washing the rocks below.

Sundiata holds a single fragment between his hands, thinks on the name – Adama Camara – and places it tenderly into position. Each glass piece is a geometric puzzle, adding to the monument, giving it strength and allowing it to grow indefinitely.

He likes to place the names early each morning so that the air still carries the coolness of the night and the sun is still rising. That the names feel the hope of the dawn softening the darkness behind and the ocean glowing before.

He smiles and nods, touches the controls, the long arm of the work platform folding itself up and setting the carriage upon the ground. He steps off, and the vehicle drives itself to the administrative buildings behind the museum. Mentally, he begins organizing his day. Counting the number of new names he will cut into glass, and wondering how many will visit, clutching crumpled pieces of paper carrying the names they wish remembered.

As he walks back to his tiny office, he sees a young white woman standing with the sun at her back and a strange, tawny cat at her knee. Her hair burns like a flame, and she stands as if she would tear at the very earth.

'My child,' he says. 'It is well.'

'My father,' she says.

He stands with her as he does for countless mourners.

'It is beautiful,' she says.

It is early for such a caller, but Sundiata knows that, sometimes, he must guide his visitors through the process of grieving.

'Is there someone you would remember, my child?' he asks.

She nods, saying nothing, her fists clenched.

He waits. In her own time, she relaxes her hands.

A small piece of paper, folded over and over. She offers it to him. Her eyes the colour of the most distant ocean.

He opens it. He reads the name, 'Simon Adaro.'

'There is another,' she says quickly.

He examines the paper and, on the other side, he reads, 'Michèle Tillisi.'

'They will be remembered, my child,' he says.

The young woman smiles, and she and the cat walk away.

Epilogue

There was never a plan, but there was an intention. To create rather than destroy. To counter those who would do otherwise without becoming one of them. To live life with as much fun and excitement as I am able in the time granted me and in a kind of hopeful optimism. And to do so with honour, friendship, love, and laughter. What more dare heroic hearts ask of Fate?

Simon Adaro

52

Amadou stands near the fire, his coffee cup warm between his hands. The dawn is rising before him, over the dust on the solar collectors reflecting orange and red against the guelb.

The hard rocky plateau is softened in the light and takes on a gentle beauty which he takes time to appreciate each morning.

It has been a good season. He has doubled his herd once more, and added two hundred sheep. He looks with gratitude down at the long shed filled with the automated milking machines and further towards the enormous cooled shelter. Opaque grow-tubes run almost all the way to the solar farm, filled with the fast-growing grass he now feeds his animals.

Golden dust shards linger in the air as his men shuttle harvested grass to the shelter, and goats – their udders sagging and full – to the milking sheds.

It will soon be time for the ceremony, and they are working quickly to ensure all is well for their absence. Not all of Senegal yet has access to the grid, but it is seen as auspicious to make a show of switching on the connection now, a year since the last election.

'Grandfather?'

The small boy is visiting. His mother, Amadou's youngest daughter, tells him the boy is interested in farming. It may be that this herd will support further generations of his family.

'Yes, my child?' he says.

'Look, grandfather. Someone is coming,' and pointing along the pathway up to the guelb, where a silhouetted figure in a delicately embroidered ochre-brown boubou and matching kufi skull-cap is walking.

'It is well, my child. The griot is honouring us.'

The small boy's eyes are wide. He has not yet met the griot.

'*Azul, Amadou, ma idjani?*' says the griot. 'And your grandson? Come here, my child,' and shaking his hand formally. 'You are most blessed to have such a wise grandfather.'

'Yes, my father,' says the boy, smiling at the old man.

'Are you enjoying the season?'

'Yes, my father. I have been helping the men and learning to care for the herd. It is good to work here.'

'It is well, my child.'

Amadou masks his pride with a brusque gesture. 'Go, child, our guest will want coffee.'

The boy grins as he rushes to the small kitchen.

The griot stands alongside Amadou, looking across the plateau. Neither says a word, comfortable in the silence.

'My father,' says the boy, carefully handing the griot a mug.

'Thank you, my child,' says the griot, resting his hand on the boy's shoulder.

'Prepare yourself, child, we shall be leaving soon,' says Amadou, and the boy grins once more and leaves them.

'You are at peace, Griot?' asks Amadou.

'I mourn for what is lost, but, yes, I am at peace.'

'It is well.'

There is a gentle resonance, as of the progression of many people, on the road leading to the guelb.

'It is time,' says the griot. 'Shall we go?'

Amadou nods, and they walk down the path to the sheds where

the men are waiting, the boy amongst them. From there they walk to the road and join the procession.

Thousands have come, travelling by coach from Rosso and walking from Mbalal. There are young and old, weak and strong. They walk arm in arm, umbrellas raised to the sun.

Many carry djembe, and their drumming rumbles like distant thunder.

The griot walks out before them, and his voice lifts their rhythm into melody.

His voice is filled with joy and memory, telling a story of conflict and redemption.

The walking thousands take up his refrain.

A helicopter swings overhead, landing near a small stage that has been set up alongside the transmission station. The president has arrived, waving as he steps out of the craft and climbs the stairs up to the podium.

From up ahead a woman emerges from between the solar collectors and walks towards the arriving crowds, a tawny cat at her side. Her eyes are the colour of the most distant ocean and her hair burns like a flame.

Behind her, a ripple on the surface of the solar roses and the sands of light begin to sing.

And somewhere out on the plateau, it is that time of day between breakfast and dinner.

The horizon is a shimmering mirage that unites myth and legend, and Painted-dog's child is running through the desert, always hopeful, always hungry.

She hunts the endless dusty ochre of the hamada, her paws bouncing lightly on the scalding stones, her tongue hanging loose in a way unbecoming of a matriarch.

Her white-patch tail blazing, her oversize paws tangled beneath her, she runs in her hopping, loping way, yipping cheerfully as she goes.

Author's Note

I set out to tell a story of how dramatic social change will re-forge our sense of community and identity, and of how memory and history choose their own heroes. I had no anticipation of how much the steady drumbeat of contemporary events would demand attention.

As I was tracing the threads that would become *Our Memory Like Dust*, others were risking their lives in leaky boats attempting to cross the Mediterranean. In Europe and the United States, those who dared to merely seek refuge from conflict have been vilified by far too many people willing to throw away the lessons of the last world war, opening space for the old politics of division and fear to take hold.

And amidst all this is the strident call of nationalism and the wilful determination of majorities to concentrate power in ever-fewer hands. For the narrative of our time is of how so many permitted so few to have dominion over so much.

I drew on a host of sources during my research, and these will take you deeper into the world I describe:

Genii of the River Niger, Jean-Marie Gibbal (1988);

City of Thorns, Ben Rawlence (2016);

Griots and Griottes, Thomas A. Hale (1998);

La Belle Histoire de Leuk-le-Lièvre, Léopold Senghor & Abdoulaye Sadji (1953);

Sustainable Energy – Without the Hot Air, David MacKay (2008).

Jean-Marie Gibbal's work was a powerful motivator to include the mysticism of the people of the Senegal Valley into the narrative, as was Léopold Senghor's mix of human and animal fairy tales. Ben Rawlence's descriptions of life in one of the world's largest and oldest refugee camps recalled the precariousness of existence in informal settlements where I worked in South Africa.

David MacKay's work is much thumbed, and I recommend it to anyone attempting to work out what we can do regarding alternative energy. For those of you looking to understand whether the solar farms are even theoretically possible, I suggest visiting my website (https://gavinchait.com/our-memory-like-dust/) where you will find links to my calculations. Briefly, though, the solar intensity in the Sahara is about $270W/m^2$, of which – theoretically – we could capture about 60 per cent. The solar farms in the narrative capture $135W/m^2$. Each person in Western Europe consumes about 125kWh per day, which I've reduced to 100kWh per day on the assumption that our devices should become more efficient even as more of what we use requires energy.

That implies each person requires a solar concentrator of $30m^2$ for their total energy consumption.

This calculation comes with a major caveat. In MacKay's work, he used a solar capture efficiency estimate of only $14.5W/m^2$, quite significantly less than my own. To which I answer: hey, science fiction.

David MacKay passed away shortly after I started writing, and I can only offer my thanks and sadness that we have lost his insight and good humour.

Many of the events and locations in the narrative are based on my research in Senegal.

I spent a morning at the Hissène Habré trial in Dakar without expecting to understand anything but wanting to get a sense of the process. I came away with a deep impression of the importance of this trial where an African court tried and sentenced an African dictator for his atrocities against his own people. I thank Reed Brody, then of Human Rights Watch, for his patience in explaining the events of the day and providing needed context.

I would also like to thank Marie-Caroline Camara of Au fil du Fleuve in Saint-Louis, who helped me navigate the complexities of culture and location. She entertained some of my weirder requests and found drivers willing to take me to random spots I thought might work in the story. I won't go into the bewilderment of drivers and locals as I would bumble around some dusty town on the Mauritanian border figuring out where things would happen.

Senegal is a wonderful place, and I deeply recommend including it on your travels.

Any horrible errors either in my calculations or in rabidly mixing up and misappropriating culture and tradition are entirely my own responsibility. My intention was to capture a flavour of this relatively unexamined (to English-speaking European eyes) part of the world, and I can only express my gratitude and appreciation for the people who helped me with my research and tolerated my inquisitiveness.

If you would like to immerse yourself further, here is the music playlist along with the relevant scenes where they belong:

'Da', *Talé* – Salif Keita [Simon and Oktar captured]

'Red & Black Light', *Red & Black Light* – Ibrahim Maalouf [Plane convoy forced landing]

'Pour quelques dinars de plus', *Safar* – Imed Alibi [Duruji and Khalil in the desert];

'Baykat', *Sénégal* – Ismaël Lô [Amadou and the griot];

'Pitcha', *Under the Shade of Violets* – Orange Blossom [Escape from Benghazi];

'Ma Ikit (Not Found)', *Kelmti Horra* – Emel Mathlouthi [Running in the Wet];

'Traveller', *The Traveller* – Baaba Maal [The Ballad of the Nodder and the Leaner];

'Sina mali, sina deni (Free)', *Sambolera* – Khadja Nin [Shakiso travels downriver];

'Un regard étrange', *Séquences* – Wasis Diop [Tales from Gaw Goŋ: Casamance, l'homme qui mourut deux fois];

'Noir et Blanc', *Best Of* – Ismaël Lô, Souad Massi [Simon and Shakiso on the beach];

'Le passeur', *Everything Is Never Quite Enough* – Wasis Diop [Tales from Gaw Goŋ: Baana, le génie des eaux indomptables];

'La Clé / Thiabi bi' – Souleymane Faye ['Where is the child?' in Just4Utoo];

'Incha Allah', *Sénégal* – Ismaël Lô [Tales from Gaw Goŋ: Dragon, la brèche dans le mur de la honte];

'Take My Heart', *Black Rock* – Djivan Gasparyan, Michael Brook [A quiet death by the river];

'Kelmti Horra (My Word is Free)', *Kelmti Horra* – Emel Mathlouthi [Shakiso on the Faidherbe Bridge];

'Wale Watu', *Sambolera* – Khadja Nin [Shakiso and Viviane discuss the trial];

'Soni', *Mariama* – Pape & Cheikh [Sidiki listens to Gaw Goŋ];

'Bounawara', *Safar* – Imed Alibi [Shakiso and Ag Ghaly in the desert];

'Mariama', *Mariama* – Pape & Cheikh [The song of the farms of light].

She was there when I began this tale, and she was patient as I traversed its paths in darkness and light. I am grateful.

@GavinChait
February 2017

ABOUT THE AUTHOR

Born in Cape Town in 1974, Gavin Chait emigrated to the UK nearly ten years ago. He has degrees in Microbiology and Biochemistry, and Electrical Engineering. He is an economic development strategist and data scientist, and has travelled extensively in Africa, Latin America, Europe and Asia and is now based in Oxford. His first novel, *Lament for the Fallen*, was critically acclaimed. Shortlisted for the Nommo Award, *Our Memory Like Dust* is his second novel.

For more information on Gavin Chait and his books, see his website at https://gavinchait.com

LAMENT FOR THE FALLEN
Gavin Chait

A strange craft falls from the stars and crashes into the
jungle near an isolated West African community. Inside,
the locals discover the broken body of a man unlike
any they have seen before – a man who is perhaps
something more than human.

His name is Samara and he speaks with terror of
a place called Tartarus – an orbiting prison
where hope doesn't exist.

As Samara begins to heal, he also transforms the lives
of his rescuers. But in so doing, he attracts the attention of
a warlord whose gunmen now threaten the very existence
of the villagers themselves – and the one slim chance
Samara has of finding his way home.

And all the while, in the darkness above, waits the
simmering fury at the heart of Tartarus . . .

'Refreshingly different . . . Exhilarating . . .
Compulsively readable' *GUARDIAN*

Andrew Bannister
THE SPIN TRILOGY

The Spin – an ancient, artificial cluster of eighty-eight planets and twenty-one suns . . .

CREATION MACHINE
It once created a galaxy.
Now it could destroy one . . .

'Expansive world-building, immersive prose and sharp dialogue . . . conjures up the same gnarly, lurid weirdness that made Iain M. Banks' SF epics so memorable' *SFX*

'Fast-paced, intelligent SF, action-packed and immersive' ADRIAN TCHAIKOVSKY

IRON GODS
A long-dormant intellect awakes.
And what it remembers is terrifying . . .

'Ancient, brooding technologies . . . renegade slaves in a stolen starship . . . in Bannister's hands space opera lives on, gaudy and brutal and glorious'
STEPHEN BAXTER

'Wonderful . . . a worthy successor to the potential realised in *Creation Machine* . . . I <u>really</u> like this series'
SFFWORLD

Coming soon:

STONE CLOCK
His death awaits him across a war-ravaged galaxy.
And so does his future . . .

THE LONG EARTH
Terry Pratchett and Stephen Baxter

1916: the Western Front. Private Percy Blakeney
wakes up. He is lying on fresh spring grass. He
can hear birdsong, and the wind in the leaves in
the trees. Where have the mud, blood and blasted
landscape of No Man's Land gone?

2015: Madison, Wisconsin. Cop Monica Jansson
is exploring the burned-out home of a reclusive –
some said mad, others dangerous – scientist when
she finds a curious gadget: a box containing some
wiring, a three-way switch and a . . . potato. It is
the prototype of an invention that will change the
way Mankind views its world for ever.

And that's an understatement if ever there was one . . .

'An absorbing collaborative effort from two SF
giants . . . a marriage made in fan heaven . . .
a charming, absorbing and somehow spacious
piece of imagineering'
Adam Roberts, *GUARDIAN*

'The idea of parallel Earths is one of the most
enduring that science fiction has given us, but rarely
has it been explored with quite so much gusto
as in this new novel by two of the giants of
British speculative fiction . . . a triumph . . .
accessible, fun and thoughtful'
David Barnett, *INDEPENDENT*

THE SPARROW
Mary Doria Russell

Winner of the Arthur C. Clarke Award

After the first exquisite songs were intercepted by radio
telescope, UN diplomats debated long and hard whether
and why human resources should be expended in an attempt
to reach the world that would become known as Rakhat.
In the Rome offices of the Society of Jesus, the questions
were not whether or why but how soon the mission
could be attempted and whom to send.

The Jesuit scientists went to Rakhat to learn, not to
proselytize. They went so that they might come to know
and love God's other children. They went for the reason
Jesuits have always gone to the farthest frontiers of human
exploration. They went for the greater glory of God.

They meant no harm.

Taking you on an extraordinary journey to a distant
planet and to the very centre of the human soul, Mary
Doria Russell's *The Sparrow* is an astonishing and
haunting novel about the nature of faith and what
it means to be 'human'.

'Compulsive reading and may be the year's
best science fiction novel'
John Clute, *MAIL ON SUNDAY*

'A parable about human life on earth, with all its
imperfections, failings, doubts, wisdom and erudition ...
a startling, engrossing and moral work of fiction'
Colleen McCullough, *NEW YORK TIMES*